The Trapper's Daughter

A Story Of The Rocky Mountains

By

Gustave Aimard

The Trapper's Daughter
A Story Of The Rocky Mountains
by Gustave Aimard

ISBN: 978-93-62207-77-7

Published by

DOUBLE 9 BOOKS

2/13-B, Ansari Road
Daryaganj, New Delhi – 110002
info@double9books.com
www.double9books.com
Tel. 011-40042856

ABOUT THE AUTHOR

Gustave Aimard wrote multiple volumes about Latin America and the American frontier. Oliver Aimard was born in Paris. As he previously stated, he was the offspring of two married individuals, "but not to each other". His father, François Sébastiani de la Porta (1775-1851), was a commander in Napoleon's army and a representative of the Louis Philippe government. Sebastiani was married to the Duchess of Coigny. In 1806, the couple had a daughter, Alatrice-Rosalba Fanny. The mother died shortly after she was born. Fanny was reared by her grandmother, Duchess of Coigny. Aimard was placed as a baby with a family that were paid to raise him. By the age of nine or twelve, he was sent off on a herring boat. Later, about 1838, he served briefly with the French Navy. After one more trip to America (when he claims he was adopted into a Comanche tribe), Aimard returned to Paris in 1847, the same year his half-sister, Duchess de Choiseul-Pralin, was cruelly killed by her noble husband. Reconciliation or acknowledgement by his biological family did not occur. After serving briefly in the Garde Mobil, Aimard returned to the Americas.

CONTENTS

PREFACE

In the present volume another series of Indian adventures is concluded, and the further career of the hero is described in the series beginning with the "Tiger-slayer." It must be understood, however, that the stories are not arbitrarily connected—each is complete in itself; but those who have read one volume will, I hope, be sufficiently interested in the hero to desire to know more of his career. The following, therefore, is the order in which the volumes should be read:—

1. TRAIL HUNTER.
2. PIRATES OF THE PRAIRIES.
3. THE TRAPPER'S DAUGHTER.
4. TIGER SLAYER.
6. GOLD SEEKERS.
7. INDIAN CHIEF.

In all probability, M. Aimard will favour us with other volumes; but, in the mean time, the above can be read collectively or separately, with equal interest.

LASCELLES WRAXALL

CHAPTER I
THE JACAL

About three in the afternoon, a horseman, dressed in the Mexican costume, was galloping along the banks of a stream, an affluent of the Gila, whose capricious windings compelled him to make countless detours. This man, while constantly keeping his hand on his weapons, and watching for every event, urged his horse on by shouts and spur, as if anxious to reach his journey's end.

The wind blew fiercely, the heat was oppressive, the grasshoppers uttered their discordant cries under the herbage that sheltered them; the birds slowly described wide circles in the air, uttering shrill notes at intervals: coppery clouds were incessantly passing athwart the sun, whose pale, sickly beams possessed no strength; in short, all presaged a terrible storm.

The traveller seemed to notice nought of this; bowed over his horse's neck, with his eyes fixed ahead, he increased his speed, without noticing the heavy drops of rain that already fell, and the hoarse rolling of distant thunder which began to be heard.

Still this man, had he wished it, could easily have sheltered himself under the thick shade of the aged trees in the virgin forest which he had been skirting for more than an hour, and thus let the heaviest part of the storm pass; but a weightier interest, doubtless, urged him on, for, while increasing his speed, he did not think of drawing his zarapé over his shoulders to protect him from the rain, but contented himself, as each gust of wind howled past him, with drawing his hat a little tighter on his head, while repeating to his horse, in a sharp tone:

"Forward! Forward!"

In the meanwhile, the stream, whose banks the traveller was following, grew gradually narrower, and at a certain spot the bank was completely obstructed by an undergrowth of shrubs and interlaced creepers, which completely prevented any approach. On reaching this point the traveller stopped; he dismounted, carefully inspected the vicinity, took his horse by the bridle, and led it into a copse, where he concealed it; attaching it with his lasso to the trunk of a large tree, after removing the *bozal* to let it browse at liberty.

"Rest here, Negro," he said, as he softly patted it; "do not neigh, for the enemy is at hand—I shall soon return."

The intelligent animal seemed to comprehend the words its master addressed to it, for it stretched out his head and rubbed it against his chest.

"Good, good, Negro! Wait awhile!"

The stranger then took from his holsters a brace of pistols, which he placed in his girdle, threw his rifle on his shoulder, and started hurriedly in the direction of the river. He buried himself without hesitation in the shrubs that bordered the stream, carefully separating the branches which at each step barred his progress. On reaching the edge of the water he stopped for a moment, bent forward, seemed to be listening, and then drew himself up, muttering:

"There is no one; all is safe."

He then stepped on a mass of intertwined lianas, which extended from one bank to the other, and formed a natural bridge. This bridge, apparently so slight, was firm, and though it oscillated under the traveller's footsteps, he crossed it in a few seconds. He had scarce reached the other bank, when a girl emerged from a clump of trees which concealed her.

"At last!" she said, as she ran up to him: "oh! I was afraid you would not come, Don Pablo."

"Ellen," the young man answered, with his whole soul in his glance, "death alone would keep me away."

The traveller was Don Pablo Zarate; the girl, Ellen, Red Cedar's daughter.[1]

"Come," she said.

The Mexican followed her, and they walked on for some time without exchanging a word. When they had passed the chaparral which bordered the river, they saw a short distance before them a wretched *jacal*, which leant solitary and silent against a rock.

"There is my home," the maiden said, with a sad smile.

Don Pablo sighed, but made no reply, and they continued to walk in the direction of the jacal, which they soon reached.

"Sit down, Don Pablo," the maiden went on, as she offered her comrade a stool, on which he sank. "I am alone; my father and two brothers went off this morning at sunrise."

"Are you not afraid," Don Pablo answered, "of remaining thus alone in the desert, exposed to innumerable dangers, so far from all help?"

"What can I do? Has not this life been ever mine?"

"Does your father go away often?"

"Only during the last few days. I know not what he fears, but he and my brothers seem sad and preoccupied, they go on long journeys, and when they return quite worn out, the words they address to me are harsh and snappish."

"Poor child!" said Don Pablo, "I can tell you the cause of these long journeys."

"Do you fancy I have not guessed it?" she replied; "No, no, the horizon is too gloomy around us for me not to perceive the gathering storm which will soon burst over us; but," she added, with an effort, "let us speak of ourselves, the moments are precious; what have you done?"

"Nothing," the young man said, mournfully; "all my researches have been in vain."

"That is strange," Ellen muttered; "and yet the coffer cannot be lost."

"I am as convinced of that as you are; but into whose hands has it fallen? That is what I cannot say."

The maiden reflected.

"When did you notice its disappearance?" Don Pablo went on a moment after.

"Only a few minutes after Harry's death; frightened by the sounds of the fight and the fearful uproar of the earthquake, I was half mad. Still, I can remember a circumstance which will doubtless put us on the right track."

"Speak, Ellen, speak, and whatever is to be done I will do."

The girl looked at him for a moment with an indefinable expression. She bent over to him, laid her hand on his arm, and said, in a voice soft as a bird's song:

"Don Pablo, a frank and loyal explanation between us is indispensable."

"I do not understand you," the young man stammered, as he let his eyes fall.

"Yes you do," she replied, with a sad smile; "you understand me, Don Pablo; but no matter, as you pretend to be ignorant of what I wish to say to you, I will explain myself in such a way that any further misconception will be impossible."

"Speak! Ellen; though I do not suspect your meaning, I have a foreboding of misfortune."

"Yes," she continued, "you are right; a misfortune is really concealed under what I have to say to you, if you do not consent to grant me the favour I implore of you."

Don Pablo rose.

"Why feign longer? Since I cannot induce you to give up your plan, Ellen, the explanation you ask of me is needless. Do you believe," he went on, as he walked in great agitation up and down the jacal, "that I have not already regarded the strange position in which we find ourselves from every side? Fatality has impelled us toward each other by one of those accidents which human wisdom cannot foresee. I love you, Ellen, I love you with all the strength of my soul, you, the daughter of the enemy of my family, of the man whose hands are still red with my sister's blood, which he shed by assassinating her coldly, in the most infamous manner. I know that, I tremble at thinking of my love, which, in the prejudiced eyes of the world, must seem monstrous. All that you can say to me, I have said repeatedly to myself; but an irresistible force drags me on this fatal incline. Will, reason, resolution, all are broken before the hope of seeing you for a moment and exchanging a few words with you. I love you, Ellen, so as to leave for your sake, relatives, friends, family, aye, the whole universe."

The young man uttered these words with sparkling eye, and in a sharp stern voice, like a man whose resolution is immovable. Ellen let her head droop, and tears slowly ran down her pallid cheeks.

"You weep!" he exclaimed, "Oh Heavens! Can I be mistaken? You do not love me?"

"I love you, Don Pablo!" she replied in a deep voice; "yes, I love you more than myself; but alas! That love will cause our ruin, for an insurmountable barrier separates us."

"Perhaps," he exclaimed impetuously; "no, Ellen, you are mistaken, you are not, you cannot be the daughter of Red Cedar. Oh, that coffer, that accursed coffer, I would give half the time Heaven will still grant me to live, could I recover it. In it, I feel certain, are the proofs I seek."

"Why cheat ourselves with a wild hope, Don Pablo? I believed too lightly in words uttered unmeaningly by the squatter and his wife: my childhood recollections deceived us, that is unhappily too certain. I am now convinced of it: all proves it to me, and I am really that man's daughter."

Don Pablo stamped his foot angrily.

"Never, never," he shouted, "it is impossible, the vulture does not pair with the dove, demons cannot be betrothed to angels. No, that villain is not your father! Listen, Ellen; I have no proof of what I assert—all seems, on the contrary, to prove that I am wrong; appearances are quite against me; but still, mad as it may seem, I am sure that I am right, and that my heart does not deceive me when it tells me that man is a stranger to you."

Ellen sighed.

Don Pablo continued.

"See, Ellen, the hour has arrived for me to leave you. Remaining longer with you would compromise your safety; give me then the information I am awaiting."

"For what good?" she murmured despairingly, "The coffer is lost."

"I am not of your opinion; I believe, on the contrary, that it has fallen into the hands of a man who intends to make use of it, for what purpose I am ignorant, but I shall know it, be assured."

"As you insist on it, listen to me, then, Don Pablo, though what I have told you is extremely vague."

"A gleam, however weak it may be, will suffice to guide me, and perhaps enable me to discover what I seek."

"May Heaven grant it!" she sighed; "This is all I can tell you, and it is quite impossible for me to say certainly whether I am not mistaken, for, at the moment, terror so troubled my senses that I cannot say positively I saw what I fancied I saw."

"Well, go on," the young man said, impatiently.

"When Harry fell, struck by a bullet, and was writhing in the last throes, two were near him, one already wounded, Andrés Garote the ranchero, the other, who stooped over his body, and seemed riffling his clothes—"

"Who was he?"

"Fray Ambrosio. I even fancy I can remember seeing him leave the poor hunter with a badly restrained movement of joy, and hiding in his bosom something which I could not distinguish."

"No doubt but he had seized the coffer."

"That is probable, but I cannot say positively, for I was, I repeat, in a condition which rendered it impossible for me to perceive anything clearly."

"Well," said Don Pablo, pursuing his idea; "what became of Ambrosio?"

"I do not know; after the earthquake, my father and his comrades rushed in different directions, each seeking his safety in flight. My father, more than any other, had an interest in concealing his trail, the monk left us almost immediately, and I have not seen him since."

"Has Red Cedar never spoken about him before you?"

"Never."

"That is strange! No matter. I swear to you, Ellen, that I will find him again, if I have to pursue him to hell; it is that scoundrel who has stolen the coffer."

"Don Pablo," the maiden said as she rose, "the sun is setting, my father and brothers will soon return, we must part."

"You are right, Ellen, I leave you."

"Farewell, Don Pablo, the storm is bursting; who knows if you will reach your friends' bivouac safe and sound?"

"I hope so, Ellen, but if you say to me farewell, I reply that we shall meet again: believe me, dear girl, put your trust in Heaven, for if we have been permitted to love, it is because that love will produce our happiness."

At this moment lightning flashed across the sky, and the thunder burst ominously.

"There is the storm," the maiden exclaimed; "go, go, in Heaven's name!"

"Good bye, my well-beloved, good bye," the young man said, as he rushed from the jacal; "put your trust in Heaven, and in me."

"Oh, Heaven!" Ellen exclaimed, as she fell on her knees, "Grant that my presentiments have not deceived me, or I shall die of despair."

[1] See the Trail Hunter and Pirates of the Prairies.

CHAPTER II
INSIDE THE CABIN

After Don Pablo's departure, the maiden remained for a long time thoughtful, paying no attention to the mournful sounds of the raging tempest, or the hoarse whistling of the wind, every gust of which shook the jacal, and threatened to carry it away. Ellen was reflecting on her conversation with the Mexican; the future appeared to her sad, gloomy, and storm-laden. In spite of all the young man had said to her, hope had not penetrated to her heart; she felt herself dragged involuntarily down the incline of a precipice, into which she must fall: all told her that a catastrophe was imminent, and that the hand of God would soon fall terribly and implacably on the man whose crimes had wearied justice.

Toward midnight, the sound of horses was heard, gradually approaching, and several persons stopped before the jacal. Ellen lit a torch of candlewood and opened the door: three men entered. They were Red Cedar and his two sons, Nathan and Sutter.

For about a month past, an inexplicable change had taken place in the squatter's way of acting and speaking. This brutal man, whose thin lips were constantly curled by an ironical smile, who ever had in his mouth mockery and cruel words, who only dreamed of murder and robbery, and to whom remorse was unknown, had been for some time sad and morose: a secret restlessness seemed to devour him; at times, when he did not fancy himself observed, he gave the girl long glances of inexplicable meaning, and uttered profound sighs while shaking his head in a melancholy way.

Ellen had noticed this change, which she could not account for, and which only augmented her alarm; for it needed very grave reasons thus to alter a nature so energetic and resolute as Red Cedar's.

But what were these reasons? Ellen sought them in vain, but nothing gave an embodiment to her suspicions. The squatter had always been kind to her, so far as his savage training permitted it, treating her with a species of rough affection, and softening, as far as was possible, the harshness of his voice when he addressed her. But since the change which had taken place in him, this affection had become real tenderness. He watched anxiously over the maiden, continually striving to procure her those comforts and trifles which so please women, which it is almost impossible to procure in the desert, and hence possess a double value.

Happy when he saw a faint smile play on the lips of the poor girl, whose sufferings he guessed without divining the cause, he anxiously examined her, when her pallor and red eyes told him of sleepless nights and tears shed during his absence. This man, in whom every tender feeling seemed to be dead, had suddenly felt his heart beat through the vibration of a secret fibre, of whose existence he had ever been ignorant, and he felt himself re-attached to humanity by the most holy of passions, paternal love. There was something at once grand and terrible in the affection of this man of blood for this frail and delicate maiden. There was something of the wild beast even in the caresses he lavished on her; a strange blending of a mother's tenderness with the tiger's jealousy.

Red Cedar only lived for his daughter and through his daughter. With affection shame had returned, that is to say, while continuing his life of brigandage, he feigned, before Ellen, to have completely renounced it, in order to adopt the existence of the wood rangers and hunters. The maiden was only half duped by this falsehood: but how did it concern her? Completely absorbed in her love, all that was beyond it became to her indifferent.

The squatter and his sons were sad, and seemed buried in thought when they entered the jacal; they sat down without uttering a word. Ellen hastened to place on the table the food she had prepared for them during their absence.

"Supper is ready," she said.

The three men silently approached the table.

"Do you not eat with us, child?" Red Cedar asked.

"I am not hungry," she replied.

"Hum!" said Nathan, "Ellen is dainty—she prefers Mexican cookery to ours."

Ellen blushed, but made no reply; Red Cedar smote the table with his fist angrily.

"Silence!" he shouted; "How does it concern you whether your sister eats or not? She is at liberty to do as she likes here, I suppose."

"I don't say the contrary," Nathan growled; "still she seems to affect a dislike to eat with us."

"You are a scoundrel! I repeat to you that your sister is mistress here, and no one has a right to make any remarks to her."

Nathan looked down angrily, and began eating.

"Come here, child," Red Cedar continued, as he gave his rough voice all the gentleness of which it was susceptible, "come here, that I may give you a trifle I have bought you."

The maiden approached and Red Cedar drew from his pocket a gold watch attached to a long chain.

"Look you," he said, as he put it round her neck, "I know that you have desired a watch for a long time, so here is one I bought of some travellers we met on the prairie."

While uttering these words, the squatter felt himself blush involuntarily, for he lied; the watch had been torn from the body of a woman killed by his hands when attacking a caravan. Ellen perceived this blush; she took off the watch and returned it to Red Cedar without saying a word.

"What are you about, girl?" he said, surprised at this refusal, which he was far from expecting; "Why don't you take this toy, which, I repeat to you, I procured expressly for you?"

The maiden looked at him sternly, and replied in a firm voice:

"Because there is blood on that watch, and it is the produce of a robbery—perhaps of a murder."

The squatter turned pale; instinctively he looked at the watch, and there was really a patch of blood on the case. Nathan burst into a coarse and noisy laugh.

"Bravo!" he said; "Well done—the little one guessed the truth at the first look."

Red Cedar, who had let his head droop at his daughter's reproaches, drew himself up as if a viper had stung him.

"I told you to be silent," he exclaimed, furiously; and seizing the stool on which he had been sitting, he hurled it at his son's head.

The latter avoided the blow and drew his knife—a struggle was imminent. Sutter, leaning against the walls of the jacal, with his arms crossed and his pipe in his mouth, prepared, with an ironical smile, to remain spectator of the fight; but Ellen threw herself boldly between the squatter and his son.

"Stay!" she shrieked; "Stay, in Heaven's name! What, Nathan, would you strike your father? And are you not afraid to hurt your first-born son?"

"May the devil twist my father's neck!" Nathan replied; "Does he take me for a child, or does he fancy I am disposed to put up with his insults? By heavens! We are bandits; our only law is force, and we recognise no other. My father will ask my pardon, and I will see whether I forgive him."

"Ask your pardon, dog!" the squatter shouted; and bounding like a tiger with a movement swifter than thought, he seized the young man by the throat and fell heavily on him.

"Ah, ah!" he continued, as he placed his knee on his chest, "The old lion is good yet. Your life is in my hands—what do you say? Will you play with me again?"

Nathan howled as he writhed like a serpent to free himself from the grasp that mastered him. At length he recognised his impotence, and confessed himself conquered.

"It is good," he said; "you are stronger than I—you can kill me."

"No," said Ellen, "that shall not be. Rise, father, and set Nathan free; and you, brother, give me your knife—should such a contest take place between father and son?"

She stooped down and picked up the weapon which the young man had let fall from his hand. Red Cedar rose.

"Let that serve you as a lesson," he said, "and teach you to be more prudent in future."

The young man, angered and ashamed of his downfall, sat down again without a word. The squatter turned to his daughter, and offered her the watch a second time.

"Will you have it?" he asked her.

"No," she replied, resolutely.

"Very good."

Without any apparent passion, he let the watch fall, and, putting his heel on it, reduced it to powder. The rest of the supper passed off without incident; the three men ate greedily, not speaking to each other, and waited on by Ellen. When the pipes were lit, the maiden wished to retire to the compartment which served as her bedroom.

"Stay, my child," Red Cedar said. "I have to speak with you."

Ellen sat down in a corner of the jacal and waited. The three men went on smoking silently for some time, while outside the storm still continued. At length, the young men shook the ashes out of their pipes, and rose.

"Then," said Nathan, "all is arranged."

"It is," replied Red Cedar.

"At what hour will they come to fetch us?" Sutter asked.

"At an hour before sunrise."

"Very good."

The brothers lay down on the ground, rolled themselves in their furs, and soon fell asleep. Red Cedar remained for some time plunged in thought, while Ellen did not stir. At length he raised his head.

"Come hither, child," he said.

She came up and stood before him.

"Sit down by my side."

"For what good, father? Speak, I am listening," she answered.

The squatter was visibly embarrassed; he knew not how to commence the conversation, but, after some moments' hesitation, he said:

"You are ill, Ellen."

The maiden smiled sadly.

"Did you not notice it before today, father?" she replied.

"No, my child; I have noticed your sadness for a long time past. You are not suited for a desert life."

"That is true," was all she said.

"We are about to leave the prairie," Red Cedar went on.

Ellen gave an almost imperceptible start.

"Soon?" she asked.

"This very day; in a few hours we shall be on the road."

The girl looked at him.

"Then," she said, "we will draw nearer to the civilised frontier?"

"Yes," he answered, with considerable emotion.

Ellen smiled mournfully.

"Why deceive me, father?" she asked.

"What do you mean?" he exclaimed; "I do not understand you."

"On the contrary, you understand me thoroughly, and it would be better to explain your thoughts to me frankly than try to deceive me for a purpose I cannot divine. Alas!" she continued, with a sigh, "Am I not your daughter, and must undergo the consequences of the life you have chosen?"

The squatter frowned.

"I believe that your words contain a reproach," he replied. "Life is scarce opening for you; then how do you dare to judge the actions of a man?"

"I judge nothing, father. As you say, life is scarce opening for me; still, however short my existence may have been, it has been one long suffering."

"That is true, poor girl," the squatter said, gently; "pardon me, I should be so glad to see you happy. Alas! Heaven has not blessed my efforts, though all I have done has been for your sake."

"Do not say that, father," she quickly exclaimed; "do not thus make me morally your accomplice, or render me responsible for your crimes, which I execrate, else you would impel me to desire death."

"Ellen, Ellen! you misunderstood what I said to you; I never had the intention," he said, much embarrassed.

"No more of this," she went on; "we are going, you said, I think, father? Our retreat is discovered, we must fly; that is what you wish to tell me?"

"Yes," he said, "it is that, though I cannot imagine how you have learned it."

"No matter, father. And in what direction shall we proceed?"

"Temporarily we shall conceal ourselves in the Sierra de los Comanches."

"In order that our pursuers may lose our trail?"

"Yes, for that reason, and for another," he added, in a low voice.

But, however low he spoke, Ellen heard him.

"What other?"

"It does not concern you, child, but myself alone."

"You are mistaken, father," she said, with considerable resolution; "from the moment that I am your accomplice, I must know all. Perhaps," she added, with a sad smile, "I may be able to give you good advice."

"I will do without it."

"One word more. You have numerous enemies, father."

"Alas! Yes," he said, carelessly.

"Who are those who compel you to fly today?"

"The most implacable of all, Don Miguel Zarate."

"The man whose daughter you assassinated in so cowardly a way."

Red Cedar struck the table passionately.

"Ellen!" he shouted.

"Do you know any other appellation more correct than that?" she asked, coldly.

The bandit looked down.

"Then," she continued, "you are about to fly—fly forever?"

"What is to be done?" he muttered.

Ellen bent over him, laid her white hand on his arm, and regarded him fixedly.

"Who are the men about to join you in a few hours?" she asked.

"Fray Ambrosio, Andrés Garote—our old friends, in short."

"That is just," the girl murmured, with a gesture of disgust, "a common danger brings you together. Well, my father, you and your friends are all cowards."

At this violent insult which his daughter coldly hurled in his teeth, the squatter turned pale, and rose suddenly.

"Silence!" he shouted, furiously.

"The tiger, when attacked in its lair, turns on the hunters," the girl went on, without displaying any emotion; "why do you not follow their example?"

A sinister smile played round the corners of the bandit's mouth.

"I have something better in my pocket," he said, with an accent impossible to describe.

The maiden looked at him for a moment.

"Take care," she at length said to him in a deep voice; "take care! The hand of God is on you, and His vengeance will be terrible."

After uttering these words, she slowly withdrew and entered the room set apart for her. The bandit stood for a moment, crushed by this anathema; but he soon threw up his head, shrugged his shoulders disdainfully, and lay down by the side of his sons, muttering in a hoarse and ironical voice:

"God! Does He exist?"

Soon, no other sound was audible in the jacal saving that produced by the breathing of the three men. Ellen was praying fervently, while the storm redoubled its fury outside.

CHAPTER III
A CONVERSATION

On leaving the cabin, Don Pablo recrossed the river, and found his way back to the thicket where he had tied his horse up. The poor animal, terrified by the lightning and the hoarse rolling of the thunder, uttered a snort of pleasure at seeing its master again. Without loss of a moment, the young man leaped into the saddle and started at a gallop.

The rain fell in torrents, the wind whistled violently, the young man feared at each moment losing his way, and groped through the immense solitude which stretched out before him, and which the darkness prevented him from sounding. Like all well-gifted men habituated to an adventurous life, Don Pablo de Zarate was well fitted for struggling. His will grew in proportion to the difficulties that rose before him, and instead of discouraging him, obstacles only confirmed him in his resolution. So soon as he had chosen an object, he reached it in spite of all.

His love for Ellen, born, as it were, through a thunderclap—as, in fact, most true loves spring into life, where the unexpected always plays the chief part—this love, we say, for which he was in no way prepared, and which surprised him at the moment which he least dreamed of it, had assumed, without his will, gigantic proportions, which all the reasons which should have rendered it impossible, only augmented.

Although he bore the deepest hatred for Red Cedar, and, had the opportunity presented itself, would have killed him without hesitation like a dog, his love for Ellen had become a worship, an adoration about which he no longer reasoned, but which he endured with that intoxication and that delight felt in forbidden things. This girl, who had remained so pure and chaste amid this family of bandits, possessed an irresistible attraction for him. He had said in his conversation with her he was intimately convinced that she could not be Red Cedar's daughter. It would have been impossible for him to give his reasons; but with that tenacity of purpose which only some few men possess he necessarily sought the proofs of this conviction which nothing supported, and, even more, he sought these proofs with the certainty of finding them.

For a month past, he had discovered, by an inexplicable chance, Red Cedar's retreat, which Valentine, the skilful trail-hunter, had been unable to detect. Don Pablo had immediately profited by his good fortune to see again the girl he had believed lost for ever. This unexpected success appeared to him a good omen; and every morning, without saying anything to his friends, he mounted his horse upon the first excuse that offered, and rode thirty miles to speak with her he loved for a few moments.

Every consideration was silent in presence of his love: he allowed his friends to exhaust themselves in vain researches, preciously keeping his secret in order to be happy, at least, for a few days; for he perfectly foresaw that the moment must arrive when Red Cedar would be discovered. But, in the meanwhile, he enjoyed the present. With all those who love in this way, the future is nothing, the present is all in all.

Don Pablo galloped on by the glare of the flashes, feeling neither the rain that inundated him, nor the wind that howled round his head. Absorbed in his love, he thought of the conversation he had held with Ellen, and pleased himself with recalling all the words that had been exchanged during the hour, which slipped away almost too rapidly.

All at once, his horse, to which he paid no attention, neighed, and Don Pablo raised his head intuitively. Ten paces ahead of him, a horseman was standing motionless across his path.

"Ah, ah!" said Don Pablo, as he drew himself up on the saddle, and cocked his pistols; "You are very late on the road, comrade. Let me pass, if you please."

"I am no later than yourself, Don Pablo," was the immediate response, "since I meet you."

"Halloh!" the young man shouted, as he uncocked his pistols, and returned them to his holsters; "What the deuce are you doing here, Don Valentine?"

"As you see, I am waiting."

"Whom can you be waiting for at this advanced hour?"

"For yourself, Don Pablo."

"For me!" the Mexican said in surprise; "That is strange."

"Not so much as you suppose. I desire to have a conversation with you, which no one must overhear; and as that was impossible in camp, I came to wait for you as you passed: that is simple enough, I fancy."

"It is; but what is less so, is the hour and spot you have selected, my friend."

"Why so?"

"Hang it, a terrible storm is let loose over our heads; we have no place here to shelter us; and I repeat, it is nearer morning than night."

"That is true; but time pressed, and I could not select the hour to my fancy."

"You alarm me, my friend; has anything new occurred?"

"Nothing that I know of, up to the present; but ere long we shall see something, you may feel assured."

The young man stifled a sigh, but made no reply. While exchanging these hurried sentences, the Trail-hunter and the Mexican had joined, and now rode side by side. Valentine continued—

"Follow me for a few moments. I will lead you to a spot where we can converse at ease, without fear of being disturbed."

"What you have to say to me must be very important?"

"You shall soon judge of that."

"And are you going to lead me far?"

"Only a few paces; to a grotto which I noticed in the flashes."

"Let us go then."

The two men spurred their horses, and galloped silently side by side; they went on thus for hardly a quarter of an hour in the direction of a thick chaparral which skirted the river.

"We have arrived," said Valentine, as he checked his horse and dismounted. "You had better let me go first, for it may happen that the cave we are about to enter may have an occupier not at all disposed to move for us, and it is as well to act prudently."

"What do you mean? To what occupier do you allude?"

"Hang it, I do not know," the Frenchman replied carelessly; "in any case, it is as well to be on one's guard."

While saying this, Valentine produced from under his zarapé two candlewood torches, which he lighted; he gave one to Don Pablo, and the two men, after hobbling their horses, opened the bushes and advanced boldly toward the cave. After walking a few steps, they suddenly found themselves at the entrance of one of those magnificent natural grottos formed by the volcanic convulsions so frequent in these parts.

"Attention!" Valentine muttered in a low voice to his comrade.

The sudden appearance of the two men startled a cloud of night birds and bats, which flew away heavily in all directions, uttering shrill cries. Valentine went on, not troubling himself about these funereal guests, whose sports he so unexpectedly noticed. All at once, a hoarse and prolonged growl came from a distant corner of the cave.

The two men stopped as if rooted to the ground. They found themselves face to face with a magnificent black bear, whose usual residence this cavern doubtless was, and which, standing on its hind legs with open mouth, showed the troublesome persons who came to trouble it so inopportunely in its lair, a tongue red as blood, and glistening claws of a remarkable length. It balanced itself clumsily, according to the fashion of its congeners, and its round and dazzled eyes were fixed on the adventurers in a manner that would cause reflection. Fortunately, they were not the men to let themselves be intimidated for long.

"Hum!" said Valentine, surveying the animal, "I was sure of it; there is a young fellow who seems inclined to sup with us."

"My rifle, on the contrary, will make us sup with him," Don Pablo said with a laugh.

"For Heaven's sake do not fire," the hunter said quickly, as he checked the young man who had already shouldered his rifle; "a shot fired at this spot will produce a fearful row: we do not know what sort of people may be prowling around us; so we must not compromise ourselves."

"That is true," Don Pablo remarked; "but what is to be done?"

"That is my business," Valentine replied; "take my torch, and hold yourself in readiness to help me."

Then, resting his rifle against the side of the cave, he went out, while the Mexican remained alone, facing the bear, which, dazzled and perplexed by the light, did not venture to stir. In a few minutes Valentine returned; he had been to fetch his lasso, fastened to the saddle bow.

"Now, stick your torches in the ground, to be ready for any accident."

Don Pablo obeyed; the hunter carefully prepared the lasso and whirled it round his head, while whistling in a peculiar way.

At this unexpected appeal the bear moved heavily two or three paces forward, but that was its ruin. The lasso started from the hunter's hands, the slipknot fell on the animal's shoulders, and the two men slipped back, tugging at it with all their strength. The poor quadruped, thus strangled and stretching out a tongue a foot long, tottered and fell, striving in vain to remove with its huge paws the unlucky collar that compressed its throat. But the hunters were not conquered by their enemy's tremendous efforts; they redoubled their strength, and did not loose the lasso till the bear had given its last sigh.

"Now," said Valentine, after he had assured himself that Bruin was really dead, "bring the horses in here, Don Pablo, while I cut off our enemy's paws, to roast them in the ashes while we are talking."

When the young man re-entered the grotto, leading the horses, he found Valentine, who had lighted a large fire, busied in flaying the bear, whose paws were gently roasting in the embers, as he had said. Don Pablo gave the horses their food, and then sat down before the fire near Valentine.

"Well," said the latter with a smile, "do you fancy this a comfortable place for a gossip?"

"Yes, it is," the young man carelessly replied, as he rolled between his; fingers a husk cigarette with the dexterity apparently peculiar to the Spanish race; "we are all right here: I am ready for your explanation, my friend."

"I will give it you," the hunter said, who had finished skinning the bear, and quietly returned his knife to his boot, after carefully wiping the blade; "how long have you known Red Cedar's hiding place?"

At this point-blank question, which he was far from expecting, the young man started; a feverish flush covered his face, and he did not know what to answer.

"Why—?" he stammered.

"About a month, I think?" Valentine continued, not appearing to notice his friend's confusion.

"Yes, about," the other replied, not knowing what he said.

"And for a month," Valentine continued, imperturbably, "you have left your father's side each night to go and make love to the daughter of the man who murdered your sister?"

"My friend," Don Pablo said, painfully.

"Would you assert that it is not true?" the hunter went on hastily, as he bent on him a glance which made him look down: "explain yourself, Pablo—I am waiting for your justification. I am curious to know how you will manage to prove to me that you have acted rightly."

The young man, while his friend was speaking, had time to regain, at any rate, a portion, if not all, of his coolness and presence of mind.

"You are severe," he said; "before accusing me, it would be, perhaps, worthwhile to listen to the reasons I have to offer you."

"Stay, my friend." Valentine said, quickly, "let us not turn from the question, but be frank; do not take the trouble to describe your love to me, for I know it as well as you do—I saw it born and grow; still, permit me to tell you certainly I thought that after the assassination of Doña Clara, this love, which had hitherto resisted everything, would die out. It is impossible to love those we despise. Red Cedar's daughter can only appear to you through a blood-stained cloud."

"Don Valentine," the young man exclaimed, in grief, "would you render that angel responsible for the crimes of a villain?"

"I will not discuss with you the famous theory which lays down that faults and crimes are personal; faults may be so, but in desert life the whole family must be responsible for the crimes of its chief; were it not so, no security would be possible for honest people."

"Oh, how can you speak thus!"

"Very good—let us change the ground, as that is disagreeable to you. You possess the noblest and most honourable nature of any man I know, Don Pablo. I presume you never had a thought of making Ellen your mistress?"

"No!" the young man savagely protested.

"Would you make her your wife, then?" Valentine said, with a cutting accent, as he looked him fixedly in the face.

Don Pablo bowed his head in despair.

"I am accursed!" he exclaimed.

"No," Valentine said, as he seized him sharply by the arm, "you are mad. Like all young men, passion sways and overpowers you—you listen to that alone; you despise the voice of reason, and hence commit faults which may speedily become, in spite of yourself, crimes."

"Do not speak thus, my friend."

"You have only reached faults as yet," Valentine said, imperturbably; "but take care."

"Oh, it is you who are mad, my friend, to say such things to me. Believe me, however great my love for Ellen may be, I shall never forget the duties imposed on me by the strange position in which fate has placed me."

"And yet for a month you have known the hiding place of the most implacable enemy of your family, and have kept it a profound secret, in order to satisfy the claims of a passion which can only have a disgraceful result for you! You see us vainly employing all the means in our power to discover the traces of our enemy, and you betray us coldly, deliberately, for the sake of a few love phrases which you find means to exchange daily with a girl, while making us believe that, like ourselves, you are engaged in fruitless researches. What name will you give to your conduct save that of a traitor?"

"Valentine, you insult me, the friendship you have for me does not authorise you to act thus; take care, for patience has its limits."

The hunter interrupted him by a coarse laugh.

"You see it, boy," he said sternly, "already you threaten me."

The young man rolled on the ground in despair.

"Oh!" he exclaimed, "I have suffered enough."

Valentine looked at him for a moment with tender pity, then bent over him, and touching his shoulder:

"Listen to me, Don Pablo," he said in a gentle voice.

CHAPTER IV
A BACKWARD GLANCE

We will now take up our narrative at the point where we left it at the conclusion of the "Pirates of the Prairies." During the six months which had elapsed since the mournful death of Doña Clara, certain events have taken place, which it is indispensable for the reader to know, in order properly to understand the following story.

He will probably remember that White Gazelle was picked up in a fainting condition by Bloodson, while at the side of the old pirate, Sandoval. He threw the girl across his horse's neck, and started at full speed in the direction of the teocali, which served him as a refuge and fortress. We will follow these two important persons, whom we reproach ourselves with having too long neglected.

Bloodson's mad course was frightful to look on. In the shadow of the night the horse bounded forward, trampling beneath its nervous hoofs everything they met, while its outstretched head cleft the air. Its ears were thrown back, and from its widely opened nostrils issued jets of steam which traced long white furrows in the gloom. It dashed forward, uttering snorts of pain, and biting between its clenched teeth the *bozal* which it covered with foam, while its flanks, torn by the spurs of its impatient rider, dripped with blood and perspiration. But the faster it went, the more did Bloodson torment it, and seek to increase its speed.

The trees and rocks disappeared with marvellous rapidity on either side the road, and White Gazelle was presently restored to life by the violent shocks the movements of the horse gave to her body. Her long hair trailed in the dust, her eyes, raised to Heaven, were bathed in tears of despair, grief, and impotence. At the risking of fracturing her skull against the stones, she made useless efforts to escape from the arms of her ravisher, but the latter fixed on her a glance whose passion revealed a ferocious joy, and did not appear to notice the terror he caused the girl, or rather seemed to derive from it an unspeakable pleasure. His compressed lips remained silent, only allowing passage at intervals to a shrill whistle intended to increase the ardour of his horse, which, exasperated by the pressure of its rider, seemed no longer to touch the ground, and devoured the space like the fantastic steed in the ballad of Lenore.

The girl uttered a cry, but it was lost in the gloomy echoes, drowned in the sound of this mad chase. And the horse still galloped on. Suddenly White Gazelle collected all her strength, and bounded forward with such vivacity, that her feet already touched the ground; but Bloodson was on his guard, and ere she had regained her balance, he stooped down without checking his steed, and seizing the girl by her long tresses, lifted her up, and placed her again before him. A sob burst from the Gazelle's chest, and she fainted once again.

"Ah, you shall not escape me," Bloodson yelled; "no one in the world can tear you from my grasp."

In the meanwhile darkness had been succeeded by day; the sun rose in all its splendour. Myriads of birds saluted the return of light by their joyous strains; nature had awakened gaily, and the sky, of a diaphanous azure, promised one of those lovely days, which the blessed climate of these countries has alone the privilege of offering.

A fertile landscape, exquisitely diversified, stretched out on either side the road, and blended with the distant horizon. The girl's body hung down the side of the horse, following unresistingly all the movements imparted to it; with her face covered with a livid paleness, half opened lips, clenched teeth, uncovered bosom and panting chest, she palpitated under Bloodson's hand, which pressed heavily upon her.

At length, they reached a cavern, where were encamped some forty Indians, armed for war; these were Bloodson's companions. He made them a sign, and a horse was brought to him; it was high time, for the one he rode had scarce stopped ere it fell, pouring forth black blood from its nostrils, mouth, and ears. Bloodson mounted, took the girl before him, and started again.

"To the hacienda Quemada (the burnt farm)," he shouted.

The Indians, who doubtless were only awaiting their chief's arrival, followed his example, and soon the whole band, with the stranger at their head, galloped along, hidden by the dense cloud of dust they raised. After five hours' ride, whose speed surpasses all description, the Indians saw the tall steeples of a town standing out in the azure of the horizon, beneath a mass of smoke and vapour. Bloodson and his band had left the Far West.

The Indians turned slightly to the left, galloping across fields, and trampling under their horses' hoofs, with wicked fury, the rich crops that covered them. At the expiration of about half an hour, they reached the base of a lofty hill, which rose solitary in the plain.

"Wait for me here," said Bloodson, as he checked his horse; "whatever happens, do not stir till my return."

The Indians bowed in obedience, and Bloodson, burying his spurs in his horse's flanks, started again at full speed. But this ride was not long. When Bloodson had disappeared from his comrades' sight, he stopped his horse and dismounted. After removing the bridle, to let the animal browze freely on the thick and tall grass of the plain, the stranger raised in his arms the girl whom he had laid on the ground, where she remained senseless, and began slowly scaling the hillside.

It was the hour when the birds salute with their parting strains the sun, whose disc, already beneath the horizon, shed around only oblique and torpid beams. The shadow was rapidly invading the sky; the wind was rising with momentarily increasing violence, the heat was oppressive, large blackish clouds, fringed with grey and borne by the breeze, chased heavily athwart the sky, drawing nearer and nearer to the earth. In a word, all foreboded one of those hurricanes such as are only seen in these countries, and which make the most intrepid men turn pale with terror.

Bloodson still ascended, bearing the girl in his arms, whose lifeless head hung over his shoulder. Drops of lukewarm rain, large as dollars, had begun to fall at intervals, and spotted the earth, which immediately drank them up; a sharp and penetrating odour exhaled from the ground and impregnated the atmosphere.

But Bloodson still went up with the same firm step, his head drooping and eyebrows contracted. At length he reached the top of the hill, when he stopped and bent a searching glance around. At this moment, a dazzling flash shot athwart the sky, illuminating the landscape with a bluish tint, and the thunder burst forth furiously.

"Oh!" Bloodson muttered with a sinister accent, and as if answering aloud an internal thought, "nature is harmonising with the scene about to take place here; but the storm of the Heavens is not so terrible as the one growling in my heart. Come, come! I only needed this fearful melody. I am the avenger, and am about to accomplish the demoniacal task which I imposed on myself; during a night of delirium."

After uttering these ill-omened words, he continued his progress, proceeding toward a pile of half-calcined stones, whose black points stood out of the tall grass a short distance off. The top of the hill where Bloodson was, offered a scene of inexpressible savageness. Through the tufts of grass might be noticed ruins blackened by fire, pieces of wall, and vaults half broken in. Here and there were fruit trees, dahlias, cedars, and a *noria* or well, whose long pole still bore at one end the remains of the leathern bucket once employed to draw water.

In the centre of the ruins stood a large wooden cross, marking the site of a tomb; at the foot of this cross were piled up, with ghastly symmetry, some twenty grinning skulls, to which the rain, wind, and sun had given the lustre and yellowish tinge of ivory. Round the tomb, snakes and lizards, those guests of sepulchres, silently glided through the grass, watching with their round and startled eyes the stranger who dared to disturb their solitude. Not far from the tomb, a species of shed, made of interlaced reeds, was falling to ruin, but still offered a scanty shelter to travellers surprised by a storm. It was toward this shed that Bloodson proceeded.

In a few minutes he reached it, and was thus sheltered from the rain, which at this moment fell in torrents. The storm had reached the height of its fury—the flashes succeeded each other uninterruptedly; the thunder rolled furiously, and the wind violently lashed the trees. It was, in a word, one of those awful nights on which deeds without a name, which the sun will not illumine with its brilliant beams, are accomplished.

Bloodson laid the girl on a pile of dry leaves in one of the corners of the shed, and after gazing on her attentively for some seconds, he folded his arms on his chest, frowned, and began walking up and down, muttering unconnected sentences. Each time he passed before the maiden, he stopped, bent on her a glance of undefinable meaning, and resumed his walk with a shake of his head.

"Come," he said hoarsely, "I must finish it! What! That girl, so strong and robust, lies there, pale, worn out, half dead. Why is it not Red Cedar that I hold thus beneath my heel?—but patience, his turn will come, and then!"

A sardonic smile played round his lips, and he bent over the girl. He gently raised her head, and was about to make her smell a bottle he had taken from her girdle, when he suddenly let her fall on her bed of leaves, and rushed away, uttering a cry of terror.

"No," he said, "it is not possible: I am mistaken, it is an illusion, a dream."

After a moments' hesitation, he returned to the girl, and bent over her again. But this time his manner had completely changed: though he had been rough and brutal previously, he was now full of attention to her. During the various events to which White Gazelle had been the victim, some of the diamond buttons which fastened her vest had been torn off, and exposed her bosom. Bloodson had noticed a black velvet scapulary, on which two interlaced letters were embroidered in silver, suspended round her neck by a thin gold chain. It was the sight of this mysterious cypher which caused Bloodson the violent emotion from which he was now suffering.

He seized the scapulary with a hand trembling with impatience, broke the chain, and waited till a flash enabled him to see the cypher a second time, and assure himself that he was not deceived. He had not long to wait: within a few seconds a dazzling flash illumined the hill. Bloodson looked, and was convinced: the cypher was really the one he fancied he had seen. He fell to the ground, buried his head in his hands, and reflected profoundly. Half an hour passed ere this man emerged from his statue-like immobility; when he raised his head, tears were coursing down his bronzed cheeks.

"Oh! this doubt is frightful!" he exclaimed; "at all risks I will remove it: I must know what I have to hope."

And drawing himself up haughtily to his full height, he walked with a firm and steady step toward the girl, who still lay motionless. Then, as we saw him once before with Shaw, he employed the same method which had been so successful with the young man, in order to recal White Gazelle to life. But the poor girl had been subjected to such rude trials during the last two days, that she was quite exhausted. In spite of Bloodson's eager care, she still retained her terrible corpse-like rigidity: all remedies were powerless. The stranger was in despair at the unsatisfactory results of his attempts to recall the girl to life.

"Oh!" he exclaimed at each instant, "She cannot be dead: Heaven will not permit it."

And he began again employing the measures whose futility had been proved to him. All at once he smote his forehead violently.

"I must be mad," he exclaimed.

And searching in his pocket, he drew from it a crystal flask, filled with a blood-red liquor; he opened with his dagger the girl's teeth, and let two drops of the fluid fall into her mouth. The effect was instantaneous: White

Gazelle's features relaxed, a pinky hue covered her face; she faintly opened her eyes, and murmured in a weak voice—

"Good Heaven! Where am I?"

"She is saved!" Bloodson exclaimed with a sigh of joy, as he wiped away the perspiration that ran down his forehead. In the meanwhile the storm had attained its utmost fury; the wind furiously shook the wretched shed, the rain fell in torrents, and the thunder burst forth with a terrible din.

"A fine night for a recognition!" Bloodson muttered.

CHAPTER V
THE HACIENDA QUEMADA

It was a strange group formed by this charming creature and this rough wood ranger, at the top of this devastated hill, troubled by the thunder, and illumined by the coruscating lightning.

White Gazelle had fallen back again, pale and inanimate. Bloodson gazed out into the night, and reassured by the silence, bent a second time over the girl. Pallid as an exquisite lily laid prostrate by the tempest, the poor child seemed scarce to breathe. Bloodson raised her in his nervous arms, and bore her to a piece of broken wall, at the foot of which he laid his zarapé, and placed her on this softer couch. The girl's head hung senseless on his shoulder. Then he gazed at her for a long time: grief and pity were painted on Bloodson's face.

He, whose life had hitherto been but one long tragedy, who had no belief in his heart, who was ignorant of softer feelings and sweet sympathies; he, the avenger and slayer of the Indians, was affected, and felt something new stirring within him. Tears ran down his cheeks.

"Oh, my God!" he exclaimed anxiously, "Can she be dead? Yes," he added, "I was cowardly and cruel toward this poor creature, and God punishes me."

The name, which he only used to blaspheme, he now pronounced almost with respect; it was a species of prayer, a cry from his heart. This indomitable man was at length conquered, he believed.

"How to help her?" he asked himself.

The rain that continued to fall in torrents, and inundated the girl, at length recalled her to life; she partly opened her eyes, and muttered softly:

"Where am I? What has happened? Oh, I fancied I was dying."

"She speaks, she lives, she is saved," Bloodson exclaimed.

"Who is that?" she asked, as she raised herself with difficulty.

At the sight of the hunter's bronzed face, she was frightened, closed her eyes again, and fell back. She was beginning to remember.

"Take courage, my child," Bloodson said softening his rough voice, "I am your friend."

"You my friend!" she exclaimed, "what means that word on your lips?"

"Oh, pardon me, I was mad, I knew not what I did."

"Pardon you, why? Am I not born to sorrow?"

"What must she have endured?" Bloodson muttered.

"Oh, yes," she continued, speaking as in a dream. "I have suffered greatly. My life, though I am still very young, has, up to the present, been one long suffering; still, I can remember having been happy once—long, long ago. But the worst pain in this world is the remembrance of happiness in misfortune."

A sigh escaped from her overladen chest, she let her head fall in her hands, and wept. Bloodson listened to and gazed on her; this voice, these features, all he saw and heard augmented the suspicions in his heart, and gradually converted them into certainty.

"Oh, speak—speak again!" he continued, tenderly; "What do you remember of your youthful years?"

The girl looked at him, and a bitter smile curled her lips.

"Why, in misery, think of past joys?" she said, shaking her head mournfully; "Why should I tell you of these things—you, above all, who are my direst enemy? Do you wish to inflict fresh tortures on me?"

"Oh!" he said, with horror, "Can you have such thoughts? Alas! I have been very guilty toward you, I allow it, but pardon me—pardon me, I conjure you! I would lay down my life to spare you any pain."

White Gazelle regarded with amazement, mingled with terror, this rough man, almost prostrate before her, and whose face was bathed in tears. She did not understand his remarks after the way in which he had hitherto acted towards her.

"Alas!" she murmured, "My life is that of all unfortunate beings: there was a time when, like other children, I had the songs of birds to lull me to sleep, and flowers that smiled on me when I awoke; I had, too, a sister who shared in my sports, and a mother, who loved and embraced me. All that has fled forever."

Bloodson put up two poles, on which he suspended skins to shelter the girl from the storm, which was gradually clearing off. She watched him as he did so.

"I do not know," she said, sadly, "why I feel a necessity to tell you all this, when you have done me so much harm; whence comes the feeling which the sight of you produces in me? I ought to hate you."

She did not complete the sentence, but hid her face in her hands, sobbing violently.

"It is Heaven which permits it to be so, poor child," Bloodson replied, as he raised his eyes upward, and fervently made the sign of the cross.

"Perhaps so," she said, softly; "well, listen; whatever may happen, I wish to relieve my heart. One day I was playing on my mother's knees, my father was near us with my sister; all at once a terrible yell was heard at the gate of our hacienda; the Apache Indians were attacking us. My father was a resolute man, he seized his weapons, and rushed to the walls. What happened then? I cannot tell you. I was hardly four years of age at this time, and the terrible scene I witnessed is enveloped within my mind in a blood-stained cloud. I can only remember how my mother, who wept as she embraced us both, suddenly fell upon us, covering us with blood; in vain did I try to recal her to life by my caresses—she was dead."

There was a silence. Bloodson listened eagerly to this story with pallid face, frowning brow, convulsively pressing the barrel of his rifle, and wiping away at intervals the perspiration that poured down his face.

"Go on, child," he muttered.

"I remember nothing further; men resembling demons rushed into the hacienda, seized my sister and myself, and set out at the full speed of their horses. Alas, since that period I have never again seen my mother's sweet face, or my father's kindly smile; henceforth I was alone among the bandits who carried me off."

"But your sister, girl, your sister, what became of her?"

"I do not know; a violent quarrel broke out among our ravishers, and blood was shed. After this quarrel they separated. My sister was taken in one direction, I in another; I never, saw her again."

Bloodson seemed to make an effort over himself, then fixing his tear-laden eyes on her, he exclaimed, fervently—

"Mercedés! Mercedés! it is really you? Do I find, you again after so many years?"

White Gazelle raised her head quickly.

"Mercedés," she repeated, "that is the name my mother gave me."

"It is I, I, Stefano, your uncle! your father's brother!" Bloodson said, as he pressed her, almost mad with joy, to his breast.

"Stefano! My uncle! Yes, yes, I remember—I know."

She fell lifeless in Bloodson's arms.

"Wretch that I am, I have killed her—Mercedés, my beloved child, come to yourself!"

The girl opened her eyes again, and threw herself on Bloodson's neck, weeping with joy.

"Oh, my uncle! My uncle! I have a family at last, then. Thank God!" The hunter's face became grave.

"You are right, child," he said, "thank God, for it is He who has done everything, and who decreed that I should find you again on the tomb of those whom we have both been lamenting for so many years."

"What do you mean, uncle?" she asked, in surprise.

"Follow me, girl," the wood ranger replied; "follow me, and you shall know."

The girl rose with difficulty, leant on his arm, and followed him. By the accent of Don Stefano's voice, Mercedés understood that her uncle had an important revelation to make her. They found some difficulty in walking through the ruins, obstructed with grass and creepers, but at length reached the cross, where Bloodson stopped.

"On your knees, Mercedés," he said in a mournful voice; "on this spot your father and mother were buried by me fifteen years ago, on such a night as this."

The girl fell on her knees without replying, and Don Stefano imitated her. Both prayed for a long time with tears and sobs, and then they rose again. Bloodson made his niece a sign to sit down at the foot of the cross, placed himself by her, an after passing his hand over his forehead as if to collect his thoughts, he spoke in a dull voice, with an accent which, in spite of all his resolution, sorrow caused to tremble.

"Listen to me, child," he said, "for what you are about to hear will perhaps help us to find the murderers of your parents, if they still live."

"Speak, uncle," she said in a firm voice; "yes, you are right: Heaven willed it that our meeting should take place thus. Be assured that the murderers will not be suffered to go much longer unpunished."

"So be it," said Don Stefano; "for fifteen years I have been awaiting the hour of vengeance. Heaven will sustain me, I hope, till the moment when it strikes. Your father and I resided at the spot where we now are. This hill was occupied by a vast hacienda, which we built; the surrounding fields belonging to us, and were cleared by two hundred persons in our pay. Heaven blessed our labour, which prospered; everybody loved and respected us around, for our abode was always open to those whom misfortune struck. But if our countrymen esteemed us and applauded our efforts, the owners of an adjoining hacienda had vowed us an implacable hatred. For what reason? That I never succeeded in discovering. Was it jealousy or base envy? In any case these men hated us. There were three of them, and they did not belong to the Spanish race; they were North Americans, or, at any rate, I can for certainty say one of them, of the name of Wilkes, was so. Still, although the hatred that kept us apart was fierce, it was dull, and nothing led to the supposition that it would ever burst into life. About this time, important business compelled me to take a journey of several days. Your father, poor child, and myself, could not separate, for a secret presentiment seemed to warn us. When I returned, the hacienda was utterly destroyed, and only a few pieces of the walls still smoked. My brother and our whole family, as well as the servants, had been murdered."

Bloodson stopped.

"Terminate this sad story, uncle," the girl said, hastily, "I must know all, in order to take my share of the vengeance."

"That is true," Don Stefano replied; "but I have little more to say, and will be brief; during a whole night I traversed these smoky ruins, seeking the corpses of those I loved; and when, after infinite difficulty, I succeeded in finding them, I interred them piously, and took an oath to avenge them over their tomb. This oath I have religiously kept during fifteen years; unhappily, though I have punished many culprits, up to the present the leaders have escaped me by some extraordinary fatality. Your father, whom I found dying, expired in my arms ere he was able to tell me his assassins; and though I have strong grounds for accusing Wilkes and his companions, no proof has yet corroborated my suspicions, and the names of the villains are unknown to me. It was only the day before yesterday, when the scoundrel Sandoval fell, that I fancied I had discovered one of them at last."

"You were not mistaken, uncle; that man was really one of our ravishers," Mercedés replied, in a firm voice.

"And the others?" Don Stefano quickly asked.

"I know them, uncle."

At this revelation, Don Stefano uttered a cry that resembled the howl of a wild beast.

"At last!" he exclaimed, with such an outburst of fury, that the girl was almost terrified.

"And now, dear uncle," she went on, "permit me to ask you one question, after which I will answer yours, if you have any to ask."

"Speak, child."

"Why did you seize me and bring me here?"

"Because I fancied you the daughter of that Sandoval, and wished to immolate you on the tomb of his victims," Bloodson answered, in a trembling voice.

"Did you not hear, then, what the man said to me?"

"No; seeing you bent over him, I thought you were watching him die. Your fainting fit, which I attributed to sorrow, only augmented my certainty; that is why I rushed on you so soon as I saw you fall."

"But the letter you took from me would have revealed all to you."

"Do you think, then, child, I took the trouble to read it? No, I only recognised you by the scapulary hung round your neck."

"The finger of God is in all this," the girl said, with an accent of conviction; "it was really He who directed it all."

"Now it is your turn, Mercedés tell me who the assassins are."

"Give me the letter first, uncle."

"Here it is," he said, handing it to her.

The girl snatched it and tore it into the minutest fragments. Bloodson saw her do it without understanding her motive; when the last piece of paper was borne away by the breeze, the girl turned to her uncle.

"You wish to know the names of the assassins of my father, you say, uncle?"

"Yes."

"You are determined that the vengeance you have been pursuing so long shall not escape you, now that you are on the point of obtaining it, and you wish to carry out your oath to the end?"

"Yes; but why all these questions?" he asked, impatiently.

"I will tell you, uncle," she replied, as she drew herself up with strange resolution; "I, too, have also taken an oath, and do not wish to break it."

"What is its nature?"

"To avenge my father and mother, but to accomplish it I must be free to act as I think proper, and hence I will not reveal those means to you till the time arrives; today I cannot do it."

Such resolution flashed in the girl's jet-black eye, that Bloodson did not attempt to induce her to do what he desired; he understood that any pressing on his part would be useless.

"Very good," he answered, "be it so; but you swore to me—"

"That you shall know all when the moment arrives," she said, as she stretched out her right hand to the cross.

"Your word is enough; but may I at least know what you intend doing?"

"Up to a certain point you may."

"Go on."

"You have a horse?"

"At the foot of the hill."

"Bring it to me, uncle, and let me start; before all, let no one know the ties that unite us."

"I will be dumb."

"If ever you see or hear anything connected with me, believe nothing, feel surprised at nothing; say to yourself that I am acting on behalf of our common vengeance, for that alone will be true."

Don Stefano shook his head, and said:

"You are very young, child, for so rude a task."

"Heaven will help me, uncle," she replied, with a flashing glance; "the task is just and holy, for I desire to punish my father's assassins."

"Well," he continued, "your will be done: as you have said, it is a holy task, and I have no right to prevent you accomplishing it."

"Thanks, uncle," the girl said, feelingly; "and now, while I pray at my father's tomb, do you fetch me your horse, that I may set out without delay."

Bloodson retired without answering, and the girl fell on her knees at the foot of the cross. Half an hour later, after tenderly embracing Don Stefano, she mounted the horse, and started at a gallop in the direction of the Far West. Bloodson followed her as long as it was possible for him to see her in the darkness, and, when she had disappeared, he fell on the tomb on his knees, muttering in a hollow voice:

"Will she succeed? Who knows?" he added with an accent impossible to describe.

He prayed till day, but with the first beams of the sun he joined his comrades, and returned with them to the Far West.

CHAPTER VI
THE APACHES

At the shot fired by Pedro Sandoval, after the fashion, of a peroration to his too lengthened story, as we have seen, the Apaches, who had hitherto kept out of earshot, ran up at full speed. Red Cedar hurried in pursuit of Bloodson, but uselessly; he could not catch up to him, and was compelled to rejoin his comrades. The latter were already making preparations to bury the old pirate, whose body they could not leave to be devoured by the wild beasts and birds of prey. Sandoval was a great favourite of the Apaches, with whom he had lived a long time, and they had on many occasions, been able to appreciate his courage and marauding talents.

Stanapat had assembled his band, and was at the head of a certain number of resolute warriors, whom he divided into two parties, and then approached Red Cedar.

"Will my brother listen to the words of a friend?" he said.

"My father can speak; although my heart is very sad, my ears are open," the squatter answered.

"Good," the chief continued; "my brother will take a party of my young men, and put himself on the trail of the palefaces, while I pay the white warrior the duties proper for him."

"Can I thus leave a friend, before his body is placed in the ground?"

"My brother knows what he ought to do, but the palefaces are rapidly retiring."

"You are right, chief; I go, but I leave you my warriors—my comrades will be sufficient for me. Where shall I find you again?"

"At Bloodson's teocali."

"Good; will my brother soon be there?"

"In two days."

"The second sun will find me with all my warriors by the side of the sachem."

Stanapat bowed in reply: Red Cedar approached the corpse of Sandoval, bent down, and seized his frigid hand.

"Farewell, brother," he said, "pardon me for not being present at your funeral, but an important duty claims me; I am going to avenge you. Farewell, my old comrade, rest in peace, your enemies will not live many days—farewell!"

After this funeral oration, the squatter gave his comrades a signal, bowed once again to Stanapat, and started at a gallop, followed by the other pirates. When their allies were out of sight, the Apaches began the funeral ceremony, which had been interrupted by the conversation between their chief and the pirate. Stanapat ordered the corpse to be washed, the face painted of various colours, while the other Indians surrounded it, bewailing. Some, whose grief was more powerful or exaggerated, made incisions in their arms, or chopped off a joint of one of the left hand fingers, in sign of morning. When all was ready, the sachem placed himself by the head of the corpse, and addressing the company, said:

"Why do you weep? Why do you lament? See, I do not weep; I, his oldest and most devoted friend. He has gone to the other land, the Wacondah has recalled him; but if we cannot bring him back among us, our duty is to avenge him. The palefaces have lulled him, we will kill as many palefaces as we can, in order that they may accompany him, and wait on him, and that he may enter the presence of the Wacondah as a great warrior should appear. Death to the palefaces!"

"Death to the palefaces!" the Indians shouted, brandishing their weapons.

The chief turned his head away, and a smile of contempt curled his thin lips at this enthusiastic explosion. But this, smile lasted no longer than a lightning flash. Reassuming at once, the Indian stoicism, Stanapat, with all the decorum customary on such occasions, clothed the body in the richest robes to be found, and the handsomest blankets. The corpse was then placed in a sitting posture, in the grave dug for it, whose bottom and sides had been lined with wood; a whip, weapons, and some other articles were added, then the earth was thrown in, and the whole covered with heavy stones so that the coyotes could not pull out the body. This duty accomplished, at a signal from their chief the Apaches remounted their horses, and started at a gallop on the road leading to Bloodson's teocali, thinking no more of the comrade from whom they had separated for ever, than if he had never existed.

The Apaches marched for three days; at the evening of the fourth, after a fatiguing day across the sands, they halted at about a league from the Rio Gila, in a thick wood, where they hid themselves. So soon as the encampment was formed, Stanapat sent off scouts in various directions, to discover whether the other war parties of the allied nations were near, and to try and discover at the same time Red Cedar's trail.

When the sentinels were posted, for several warlike tribes of the Far West guard themselves with great care when on the war trail, Stanapat visited all the posts, and prepared to listen to the reports of the scouts, several of whom had already returned. The three first Indians whom he questioned, announced but little of importance; they had discovered nothing.

"Good," said the chief; "the night is dark, my young men have moles' eyes; tomorrow, at sunrise, they will see more clearly; they can sleep this night. At daybreak, they will start again, and perhaps discover something."

He made a signal with his hand to dismiss the scouts, who bowed respectfully to the chief, and retired in silence. Only one remained impassive and motionless, as if the words had not been addressed to him as well as to the others. Stanapat turned and looked at him for some seconds.

"My son, the Swift Elk, did not hear me doubtless," he said; "he can rejoin his comrades."

"The Elk heard his father," the Indian replied, coolly.

"Then why does he remain?"

"Because he has not told what he saw, and what he saw is important to the chief."

"Wah!" said Stanapat, "And what has my son seen which his brothers did not discover?"

"The warriors were seeking in another direction, that is why they did not perceive the trail."

"And my son has found one?"

Swift Elk bowed his head in affirmation.

"I await my son's explanation," the chief went on.

"The palefaces are two bowshot lengths from my father's camp," the Indian answered laconically.

"Oh! Oh!" the chief said doubtfully; "That seems to me too much."

"Will my father see?"

"I will see," Stanapat said as he rose.

"If my father will follow me, he will soon see."

"Let us go."

The two Indians started. Swift Elk led the sachem through the wood, and on reaching the river bank, he showed him a short distance off a rock, whose black outline rose silent and gloomy over the Gila.

"They are there," he said, stretching out his arm in the direction of the rock.

"My son has seen them."

"I have seen them."

"That is the Rock of Mad Buffalo, if I am not mistaken."

"Yes," the Indian answered.

"The position will be difficult to carry," the sachem muttered, as he carefully examined the rock.

This place was called the rock or hill of Mad Buffalo, which name it indeed still bears, for the following reasons. The Comanches had, some fifty years ago, a famous chief who rendered his tribe the most warlike and redoubtable of all in the Far West. This chief, who was called the Mad Buffalo, was not only a great warrior, but also a great politician. By the aid of sundry poisons, but especially of arsenic, which he purchased of the white traders for furs, he had succeeded, by killing all those who opposed him, in inspiring all his subjects with an unbounded superstitious terror. When he felt that death was at hand, and understood that his last hour had arrived, he indicated the spot he had selected for his sepulchre.

It was a pyramidal column of granite and sand about four hundred and fifty feet in height. This pillar commands for a long distance the course of the river which washes its base and which, after making numberless windings in the plain, comes back close to it again. Mad Buffalo ordered that his tomb should be erected on the top of this hill, where he had been accustomed to go and sit. His last wishes were carried out with that fidelity the Indians display in such matters. His body was placed at the top of the hill, mounted on his finest steed, and over both a mound was formed. A pole stuck in the tomb bore the banner of the chief, and the numerous scalps which he had raised from his enemies in action.

Hence the mountain of Mad Buffalo is an object of veneration for the Indians, and when a redskin is going to follow the war trail for the first time, he strengthens his courage by gazing on the enchanted hill which contains the skeleton of the Indian warrior and his steed.

The chief carefully examined the hill: it was, in truth, a formidable position. The whites had rendered it even stronger, as far as was possible, by cutting down the tallest trees they found, and forming thick palisades lined with pointed stakes and defended by a ditch eighteen feet in width. Thus protected, the hill had been converted into a real impregnable fortress, unless regularly besieged.

Stanapat re-entered the wood, followed by his comrade, and went back to the bivouac.

"Is the chief satisfied with his son?" the Indian tasked ere he retired.

"My son has the eyes of a tapir; nothing escapes him."

Swift Elk smiled proudly as he bowed.

"Does my son," the chief continued, in an insinuating voice, "know the palefaces who are entrenched on the hill of Mad Buffalo?"

"Swift Elk knows them."

"Wah!" said the sachem; "my son is not mistaken; he has recognised the trail?"

"Swift Elk is never mistaken," the Indian answered in a firm voice; "he is a renowned warrior."

"My brother is right; he can speak."

"The pale chief who occupies the Rock of Mad Buffalo is the great white hunter whom the Comanches have adopted, and who is called Koutonepi."

Stanapat could not check a movement of surprise.

"Wah!" he exclaimed; "Can it be possible? My son is positively sure that Koutonepi is entrenched on the top of the hill?"

"Sure," the Indian said without hesitation.

The chief made Swift Elk a sign to retire, and, letting his head fall in his hands, he reflected profoundly.

The Apache had seen correctly; Valentine and his comrades were really on the rock. After the death of Doña Clara, the hunter and his friends started in pursuit of Red Cedar, not waiting, in their thirst for vengeance, till the earthquake was quite ended, and nature had resumed its ordinary course. Valentine, with that experience of the desert which he possessed so thoroughly, had, on the previous evening, discovered an Apache trail; and, not caring to fight them in the open, owing to the numerical weakness of his party, had scaled the hill, resolved to defend himself against any who dared to attack him in his impregnable retreat.

In one of his numerous journeys across the desert, Valentine had noticed this rock, whose position was so strong that it was easy to hold it against an enemy of even considerable force, and he determined to take advantage of ndians by the sun, and for that reason must never be polluted by contact with the ground.

In bivouacs, it is suspended between two cross poles fixed in the earth. The pipe bearer is regarded as heralds were formerly among ourselves: his person is inviolable. He is generally a renowned warrior of the tribe, whom a wound received in action has rendered incapable of further fighting.

The sun rose at the moment when the Apaches completed their entrenchments. The whites, in spite of their bravery, felt a shudder of terror run over their bodies when they found themselves thus invested on all sides. The more so, as by the dim light of breaking day they could see on the distant horizon several bands of warriors advancing from different points.

"Hum!" said Valentine, with a toss of his head, "It will be a sharp fight."

"Do you consider our situation a bad one?" the general asked him.

"Detestable."

"*Canarios!*" said General Ibañez: "We are lost in that case."

"Yes," the hunter answered, "unless a miracle occur."

"*Caspita*, what you say is not at all reassuring, my good fellow. Then, in your opinion, there is no hope?"

"Yes," Valentine answered, "one chance is left us."

"What is it?" the general asked quickly.

"That the man who is being hanged feels—the rope may break."

The general shrugged his shoulders.

"Reassure yourself," the hunter said, still in a sarcastic tone; "it will not break, I warrant you."

"That is the fine consolation you offer me," the general said in a tone, half of joke, half of annoyance.

"Hang it, what would you have? It is all I can offer you at this moment; but," he added, suddenly changing his accent, "all this does not prohibit our breakfasting, I suppose."

"On the contrary," the general answered, "for I declare I have a ferocious appetite, which, I assure you, has not been the case for a long time."

"To table, then," Valentine exclaimed with a laugh; "we have not a moment to lose if we wish to breakfast in peace."

"Are you sure of the fact?"

this spot if circumstances compelled him at any time to seek a formidable shelter.

Without loss of time the hunters fortified themselves. So soon as the entrenchments were completed, Valentine mounted on the top of Mad Buffalo's tomb, and looked attentively out on the plain. It was then about midday: from the elevation where Valentine was, he surveyed an immense extent of country. The prairie and the river were deserted: nothing appeared on the horizon except here and there a few herds of buffaloes, some nibbling the thick grass, others carelessly reclining.

The hunter experienced a feeling of relief and indescribable joy on fancying that his trail was lost by the Apaches, and that he had time to make all preparations for a vigorous defence. He first occupied himself with stocking the camp with provisions, not to be overcome by famine if he were, as he supposed, soon attacked. His comrades and himself, therefore, had a grand buffalo hunt: as they killed them, their flesh was cut in very thin strips, which were stretched on cords to dry in the sun, and make what is called in the pampas *charqué*. The kitchen was placed in a natural grotto, which was in the interior of the entrenchments. It was easy to make a fire there with no fear of discovery, for the smoke disappeared through an infinite number of fissures, which rendered it imperceptible. The hunters spent the night in making water bottles with buffalo hides: they rubbed fat into the seams to prevent them leaking, and they had time to lay in a considerable stock of water. At sunrise Valentine returned to his look-out, and took a long glance over the plain to assure himself that the desert remained calm and silent.

"Why have you made us perch on this rock like squirrels?" General Ibañez suddenly asked him.

Valentine stretched out his arm.

"Look," he said; "what do you see down there?"

"Not much; a little dust, I fancy," the general said cautiously.

"Ah!" Valentine continued, "Very good, my friend. And do you know what causes that dust?"

"I really do not."

"Well, I will tell you; it is the Apaches."

"*Caramba*, you are not mistaken?"

"You will soon see."

"Soon!" the general objected; "Do you think they are coming in this direction?"

"They will be here at sunset."

"Hum! You did well in taking your precautions, well, comrade. *Cuerpo de Cristo!* we shall have our work cut out with all these red demons."

"That is probable," Valentine said with a smile.

And he descended from the top of the tomb where he had hitherto been standing.

As the reader has already learned, Valentine was not mistaken. The Apaches had really arrived on that night at a short distance from the hill, and the scout found the trail of the whites. According to all probability, a terrible collision was imminent between them and the redskins; those two races whom a mortal hatred divides, and who never meet on the prairie without trying to destroy each other. Valentine noticed the Apache scout when he came to reconnoitre the hill; he then went down to the general, and said with that tone of mockery habitual to him—

"Well, my dear friend, do you still fancy I am mistaken?"

"I never said so," the general exclaimed quickly; "Heaven keep me from it! Still, I frankly confess that I should have preferred your being mistaken. As you see, I display no self-esteem; but what would you have? I am like that, I would sooner fight ten of my countrymen than one of these accursed Indians."

"Unfortunately," Valentine said with a smile, "at this moment you have no choice, my friend."

"That is true, but do not be alarmed; however annoyed I may feel, I shall do my duty as a soldier."

"Oh! Who doubts it, my dear general?"

"*Caspita*, nobody, I know: but no matter, you shall see."

"Well, good night; try to get a little rest, for I warn you that we shall be attacked tomorrow at sunrise."

"On my word," said the general with a yawn that threatened to dislocate his jaw, "I ask nothing better than to finish once for all with these bandits."

An hour later, with the exception of Curumilla, who was sentry, the hunters were asleep; the Indians, on their side, were doing the same thing.

CHAPTER VII
THE HILL OF THE MAD BUFFALO

About an hour before sunrise, Stanapat aroused his warriors, an them orders to march. The Apaches seized their weapons, formed in file, and at a signal from their chief, entered the chaparral that sep them from the rock held by the white hunters. Although the distand only two leagues, the march of the Apaches lasted more than an hour; was carried out with so much prudence, that the hunters, despite the they kept up, in no way suspected that their enemies were so near then Apaches halted at the foot of the rock, and Stanapat ordered the camp formed at once.

The Indians, when they like, can draw up their lines very fairly. This as they intended to carry on a regular siege, they neglected no precauti The hill was surrounded by a ditch three yards wide and four deep, earth of which, thrown up, formed a breastwork, behind which the Apac were perfectly sheltered, and could fire without showing themselves. In centre of the camp, two huts or *callis* were erected, one for the chiefs, other intended for the council lodge. Before the entrance of the latter, totem or emblem of the tribe, and the sacred calumet were hung up.

We will explain here what these two emblems are, which several write have mentioned, though not described, but which it is very important know, if a desire is felt to study Indian manners. The totem, or *kukevium*, i the national standard, the distinctive mark of each tribe. It is supposed to represent the patron animal of the tribe; coyote, jaguar, buffalo, etc., each tribe having its own; in this instance it was a white buffalo. The totem is a long staff, decorated with feathers of various colours, which are fastened perpendicularly from top to bottom. This standard is only carried by the principal chief of the tribe.

The calumet is a pipe, whose tube is four, six, even ten feet long; the latter is sometimes round, but more frequently flat. It is adorned with painted animals, hair, porcupine quills, or birds of brilliant colours. The bowl is usually of red or white marble; when the stone is of dark colour, it is painted white before using. The calumet is sacred: it was given to the

"Never mind, what can't be cured must be endured; and so to breakfast with what appetite you may."

The three men then proceeded to a leaf hut built up against Mad Buffalo's tomb, and, as they had said, made a hearty breakfast; perhaps, as the general asserted, it was because the sight of the Apaches had put them in a good temper. In the meanwhile, Stanapat, who had already formed his camp, hastened to send couriers in every direction, to have news of his allies as speedy as possible. The latter soon appeared, accompanied by the players of chichikouis and drummers. These warriors were at least five hundred in number, all handsome and well built, clothed in rich dresses, splendidly armed, and offering to prejudiced eyes the most frightful sight imaginable. The chief who arrived with this large party was Black Cat.

We will explain in a few words the arrival of this chief with his tribe among the Apache brothers—an arrival which may seem extraordinary, after the part he had played in the attack on the squatter's camp. Red Cedar had been surprised by the hunters at midnight, and his camp was at once fired by the assailants. The earthquake had so thoroughly complicated the situation, that none of the gambusinos perceived Black Cat's treachery, who, for his part, so soon as he had pointed out the position of the gambusinos, confined himself to sending his warriors ahead, while himself remaining with the rear guard, so as not to compromise himself, and be able to play the part that suited him best at the right moment. His trick was most perfectly successful; the gambusinos, attacked on all sides simultaneously, had only dreamed of defending themselves as well as they could, having no time to perceive if deserters from their allies were in the ranks of their enemies. Hence Black Cat was heartily welcomed by Stanapat, who was delighted at the help that reached him.

During the course of the day other bands entered the camp in turn, so that at sunset nearly fifteen hundred redskin warriors were collected at the foot of the rock, and the hunters were completely invested. The movements of the Indians soon made them comprehend that they did not intend to retire till they had reduced them.

The Indians are the shortest-sighted men in the world; and at the end of two days, as the state of things must be remedied, a grand buffalo hunt was organised. At daybreak, thirty-five hunters, under the orders of Black Cat, left the camp, crossed the wood, and entered the prairie. After a rapid ride of two hours, they forded the Little Tortoise River, on the banks of which they halted to let their horses breathe. During this halt they lit a *bois de vache* fire, at which they cooked their breakfast, and then set out again. At midday they examined the plain stretching out at their feet, from the top of a hill;

they saw, at a considerable distance, several small herds of buffalo, each consisting of four or six male buffaloes, peaceably grazing.

The hunters cocked their guns, went down into the plain, and made a regular charge against these clumsy animals, which can run, however, very fast. Each soon started in pursuit of the buffalo nearest to him.

The buffaloes at times assume the offensive, and pursue in their turn the hunters for twenty to five-and-twenty yards; but it is easy to avoid them; so soon as they perceive the futility of pursuit, they fly in their turn. The Indians and half-breeds are so accustomed to this chase on horseback, that they rarely require more than one shot to kill a buffalo. When they fire they do not shoulder the piece, but, on the contrary, stretch out both arms to their full extent; so soon as they are about ten paces from the animal, they fire in this position, then reload with incredible speed, for they do not ram the ball home with wadding, but let it fall directly on the powder to which it adheres, as they have previously held it in their mouths, and fire again at once.

Through this uncommon speed, the Indians produced in a short time a perfect massacre among the buffaloes; sixty-eight of these animals were killed in less than two hours, Black Cat having brought down eleven as his share. The buffaloes were cut up and loaded on horses brought for the purpose, then the hunters returned gaily to camp, conversing about all the singular or dramatic incidents of the hunt, with all the Indian vivacity. Thanks to this expedition, the Apaches were provisioned for a long time.

A short distance from the camp, the Indians perceived a rider coming toward them at full speed. Black Cat ordered a halt, and waited; it was evident that the person arriving thus could only be a friend, and any doubts were speedily dispelled. The Apaches recognised White Gazelle. We have said elsewhere that the Indians were much attached to this girl; they received her very graciously, and led her to Black Cat, who remained motionless till she joined him. The chief examined her for a moment attentively.

"My daughter is welcome," he said; "does she ask hospitality of the Apaches?"

"No, chief; I have come to join them against the palefaces, as I have done before," she replied, boldly; "besides, you know it as well as I do," she added.

"Good!" the chief continued; "we thank my daughter; her friends are absent, but we expect to see within a few hours Red Cedar and the Long-knives of the East."

A shade of dissatisfaction covered the girl's forehead; but she at once recovered, and ranged her horse by the side of the chief's, saying carelessly—

"Red Cedar can come when he likes—it does not concern me. Am I not a friend of the Apaches?"

"That is true," the Indian said, with a bow; "will my sister set out?"

"Whenever you please, chief."

The hunters started again at a gallop; an hour later, they entered the camp, where they were received with shouts of joy from the Apache warriors. Black Cat ordered a calli to be prepared for the girl; then, after visiting the sentries, and listening to the reports of the scouts, he sat down near the tree, at the foot of which White Gazelle had thrown herself, to reflect on the new duties imposed on her by the engagements into which she had entered with Bloodson.

"My daughter is sad," the old chief said, as he lit his pipe by the aid of a long wand, adorned with feathers, and painted of different colours; for, with that superstition natural to some Indians, he felt persuaded that if he once touched fire with his hands he would die on the spot.

"Yes," the girl answered, "my heart is gloomy; a cloud has spread over my mind."

"My sister must console herself: he whom she has lost will be avenged."

"The palefaces are strong," she said, looking at him fixedly.

"Yes," the chief replied, "the whites have the strength of a grizzly bear, but the Indians have the craft of the beaver; my sister can feel reassured, her enemies will not escape her."

"Does my father know it?"

"Black Cat is one of the great sachems of his tribe, nothing is hidden from him. At this moment all the pirates of the prairie, joined by the half-breeds, are advancing to surround the rock which serves as a refuge to the great pale warrior; tomorrow, perhaps, six thousand redskin warriors will be here. My sister can, therefore, see that her vengeance is assured; unless the palefaces fly through the air, or plunge into the waters, which cannot happen—they are lost."

The young girl made no reply; not thinking of the chief, whose piercing eye was fixed on her, she rose and began walking up and down in great agitation.

"Oh Heavens!" she said in a low voice, "They are lost! Oh, why am I but a woman, and can do nothing for them? How can they be saved?"

"What does my sister say? Has the Wacondah troubled her mind?" the chief asked her, as he stood before her, and laid a hand on her shoulder.

The Spaniard looked at him for a moment, then let her head fall in her hands, muttering in a choking voice,—

"Oh, Heavens! I am mad."

Black Cat took a searching glance around, and then bent down to the girl's ear.

"My sister must follow me," he said, in a firm and significant voice.

White Gazelle raised her head, and looked at him; the chief laid a finger, on his lip, as if to recommend silence to her, and, turning his back, entered the wood. The girl followed him anxiously, and they walked on thus tor some minutes. At length they reached the top of a mound denuded of trees, where the eye could survey all around. Black Cat stopped and made the girl a sign to approach him.

"Here we can talk; let my sister speak; my ears are open."

"What can I say that my father does not know?" the girl replied, suspiciously.

"My sister wishes to save the palefaces, is it not so?"

"Well, yes," she said, with exaltation; "for reasons I cannot tell you, these men, who, a few days back, were hateful to me, have become dear to me; today I would save them at the peril of my life."

"Yes," the old man said, as if speaking to himself, "women are so; like the leaves the wind carries off, their mind changes its direction with the slightest breath of passion."

"Now you know my secret," she continued boldly, "I do not care about having discovered it to you; act as you think proper, but no longer count on me."

"On the contrary," the Apache replied with his sardonic smile, "I count on you more than ever."

"What do you mean?"

"Well," Black Cat continued, after taking a searching glance around, and letting his voice drop, "I wish to save them too."

"You?"

"I. Did not the pale chief enable me to escape the death that awaited me in the Comanche village? Did he not share with me as a brother the firewater of his gourd, to give me strength to sit my horse, and rejoin the warriors Of my tribe? Black Cat is a great chief. Ingratitude is a white vice; gratitude is a red virtue. Black Cat will save his brother."

"Thanks, chief," said the girl, as she pressed the old man's rough hands in hers; "thanks for your kindness. But, alas, time is slipping away rapidly, dawn will be here in a few hours, and perhaps we shall not succeed."

"Black Cat is prudent," the chief replied, "my sister must listen; but, in the first place, she may be glad to warn her friends that she is watching over them."

White Gazelle smiled in response; the Indian whistled in a peculiar fashion, and Sunbeam made her appearance.

CHAPTER VIII
BLACK CAT AND UNICORN

Black Cat had retained a profound gratitude to Valentine through the generosity with which the latter had saved his life. The chief sought by any means possible to pay the debt after the attack on the gambusino camp, during which he had so vigorously supported the hunter. All the time he was being carried down the swollen Gila in the buffalo hide canoes, Black Cat reflected seriously on the events taking place in his sight.

He knew, like all the Indian chiefs of the Far West, the causes of the hatred that separated the whites; moreover, he had been on several occasions enabled to appreciate the moral difference existing between the American squatter and the French hunter. Besides, the question was now settled in his mind; all his sympathies were attracted to Valentine. Still, it would be as well that his help, to be useful, should be freely accepted by his friends, so as to prevent any misunderstanding.

When the earth had regained its equilibrium, and all had returned to the order laid down at the commencement of the universe, Black Cat gave a signal, and the canoes ran a shore. The chief ordered his men to bivouac where they were, and await him; then noticing a short distance off, a herd of wild horses, he lassoed one, tamed it in a few minutes, leaped on its back, and started at a gallop. At this moment the sun rose splendidly on the horizon.

The Apache chief journeyed the whole day without stopping, except a few moments to let his horse breathe, and at sunset he found himself a bowshot from Unicorn's village. After remaining in thought for a few minutes, the Indian appeared to make up his mind; he urged on his horse, and boldly entered the village, which, however, was deserted. Black Cat traversed it in every direction, finding at every step traces of the fearful fight of which it had been the scene a few days previously; but he did not see a soul, not even a dog.

When an Indian is following a trail, he is never discouraged, but goes on until he finds it. Black Cat left the village at the opposite end, looked about for a minute, and then started unhesitatingly straight ahead. His admirable knowledge of the prairie had not deceived him; four hours later he reached the skirt of the virgin forest, under whose green arches we have seen Unicorn's Comanches disappear. Black Cat also entered the forest by the same road as the village population had followed, and within an hour saw the fires flashing through the trees. The Apache stopped for a moment, looked around him, and then went on.

Though apparently alone Black Cat felt that he was watched; he knew that since his first step in the forest, he was followed by invisible eyes. As he had not come however, in any warlike intention, he did not in any way attempt to conceal his trail. These tactics were comprehended by the Comanche sentries, who let him pass without revealing their presence, but still communicated the arrival of an Apache chief on their territory to each other, so that Black Cat's coming was known at the village, while he was still a long way from it.

The chief entered a large clearing, in the midst of which stood several huts. Several chiefs were silently seated round a fire, burning in front of a calli, which Black Cat recognised as the medicine lodge. Contrary to the custom generally adopted in such cases, no one seemed to notice the approach of the chief, or rose to do him honour, and give him welcome. Black Cat understood that something extraordinary was occurring in the village, and that he was about to witness a strange scene.

He was in no way affected by the cold reception accorded to him; he dismounted, threw his bridle over his horse's neck, and, walking to the fire, sat down opposite Unicorn, between two chiefs, who fell back to make room for him. Then, drawing the calumet from his girdle, he filled and lit it, and began smoking, after bowing to the company. The latter replied by the same gesture, but did not interrupt the silence. At length Unicorn took the calumet from his lips, and turned to Black Cat.

"My brother is a great warrior," he said; "he is welcome, his arrival is a happy omen for my young men, at a moment when a terrible chief is about to leave us, and proceed to the happy hunting grounds."

"The Master of Life protected me, in permitting me to arrive so opportunely; who is the chief about to die?"

"The Panther is weary of life," Unicorn replied, in a mournful voice; "he counts many winters, his tired arm can no longer fell the buffalo or the elk, his clouded eye only distinguishes with difficulty the nearest objects."

"The Panther is no longer useful to his brothers, but has become a burden to them; he must die," Black Cat remarked, sententiously.

"That is what the chief himself thought; he has this day communicated his intentions to the council assembled here round the fire, and I, his son, have undertaken to open for him the gates of another world."

"Panther is a wise chief; what can a man do with life when he grows a burden to others? The Wacondah has been kind to the redskins in giving them the necessary discernment to get rid of the aged and weak, and send them to another world, where they will be born again, and after this short trial, hunt with all the vigor of youth."

"My brother has spoken well," Unicorn answered, with a bow.

At this moment a movement took place in the crowd assembled round the sweating lodge, in which the old chief, was. The door opened, and Panther appeared. He was an old man of majestic height—in opposition to the majority of Indians, who retain for a long time the appearance of youth— his hair and beard, which fell in disorder on his shoulders and chest, were of a dazzling whiteness. On his face, whose features were imprinted with unconquerable energy, could be seen all the marks of a decrepitude which had attained its last limits. He was clothed in his handsomest costume, and painted and armed for war.

So soon as he appeared in the doorway of the hut all the chiefs rose. Unicorn walked up to him and respectfully offered his right arm, on which he leant. The old man, supported by his son, tottered up to the fire, before which he squatted. The other chiefs took their place by his side, and the warriors formed a wide circle round them. The great calumet of peace was brought in by the pipe bearer, who presented it to the old man, and when it had gone round the circle, Panther took the word. His voice was low and faint, but, owing to the deep silence that prevailed, it was heard by all.

"My sons," he said, "I am about to depart for another country; I shall soon be near the Master of Life. I will tell the warriors of our nation whom I meet on the road that the Comanches are still invincible, and their nation is the queen of the prairies."

A murmur of satisfaction, soon suppressed, however, greeted these words; in a moment the old man continued—

"Continue to be brave as your ancestors; be implacable to the palefaces, those devouring wolves, covered with an elk skin; let them ever assume the feet of the antelope, to fly more speedily before you, and may they never see the wolf tails you fasten to your heels. Never taste the firewater, that poison, by the help of which the palefaces enervate us, render us weak as women, and incapable of avenging insults. When you are assembling round the war or hunting fire in your camp, think sometimes of Panther, the chief, whose renown was formerly great, and who, seeing that the Wacondah forgot him on earth, preferred to die sooner than be longer a burthen to his nation. Tell the young warriors who tread the path for the first time, the exploits of your chief, Bounding Panther, who was so long the terror of the foes of the Comanches."

While uttering these words the old chief's eye had become animated, and his voice trembled with emotion. The Indians assembled round him listened to him respectfully.

"But what use is it to speak thus?" he went on, suppressing a sigh; "I know that my memory will not die out among you, for my son Unicorn is here to succeed me, and guide you in his turn on the path where I so long led you. Bring my last meal, so that we may soon strike up 'the song of the Great Remedy.'"

Immediately the Indians brought up pots filled with boiled dog's flesh, and at a sign from Panther, the meal commenced. When it was ended the old man lit his calumet, and smoked, while the warriors danced round him, with Unicorn at their head. Presently the old man made a sign, and the warriors stopped.

"What does my father desire?" Unicorn asked.

"I wish you to sing the song of the Great Remedy."

"Good," Unicorn replied, "my father shall be obeyed."

Then he struck up that strange chant, of which the following is a translation, the Indians joining in chorus and continuing to dance:

"Master of Life, thou givest us courage! It is true that redskins know that thou lovest them. We send thee our father this day. See how old and decrepit he is! The Bounding Panther has been changed into a clumsy bear! Grant that he may find himself young in another world, and able to, hunt as in former times."

And the round danced on, the old man smoking his pipe stoically the while. At length, when the calumet was empty, he shook out the ashes on his thumbnail, laid the pipe before him, and looked up to heaven. At this moment the first signs of twilight tinged the extreme line of the horizon with an opaline hue, the old man drew himself up, his eye became animated, and flashed.

"The hour has come," he said, in a loud and firm voice; "the Wacondah, summons me. Farewell, Comanche warriors; my son, you have to send me to the Master of Life."

Unicorn drew out the tomahawk hanging from his belt, brandished it over his head, and without hesitation, and with a movement swift as thought, cleft the skull of the old man, whose smiling face was turned to him, and who fell without a sigh.

He was dead!

The dance began again more rapid and irregularly, and the warriors shouted in chorus:

"Wacondah! Wacondah! Receive this warrior! See, he did not fear death! He knew there was no such thing, as he was to be born again in thy bosom!

"Wacondah! Wacondah! Receive this warrior. He was just! The blood flowed red and pure in his heart! The words his chest uttered were wise!

"Wacondah! Wacondah! Receive this warrior! He was the greatest and most celebrated of thy Comanche children!

"Wacondah! Wacondah! Receive this warrior. See how many scalps he wears at his girdle.

"Wacondah! Wacondah! Receive this warrior!"

The song and dancing lasted till daybreak, when, at a signal from Unicorn, they ceased.

"Our father has gone," he said; "his soul has left his body, which it inhabited too long, to choose another abode. Let us give him a burial suited to so great a warrior."

The preparations were not lengthy; the body of the Bounding Panther was carefully washed, then interred in a sitting posture, with his war weapons; the last horse he had ridden and his dogs were placed by his side, after having their throats cut; and then a bark hut was erected over the tomb to preserve it from the profanation of wild beasts; on the top of the hut a pole was planted, surmounted by the scalps the old warrior had taken at a period when he, still young and full of strength, led the Comanches in action.

Black Cat witnessed all the affecting incidents of this mournful tragedy respectfully, and with religious devotion. When the funeral rites were ended, Unicorn came up to him.

"I thank my brother," the Comanche said, "for having helped us to pay the last duties to an illustrious warrior. Now I am quite at my brother's service, he can speak without fear; the ears of a friend are open, and his heart will treasure up the words addressed to it."

"Unicorn is the first warrior of his nation," Black Cat replied, with a bow; "justice and honour dwell in him: a cloud has passed over my mind and rendered it sad."

"Let my brother open his heart to me, I know that he is one of the most celebrated chiefs of his nation. Black Cat no longer counts the scalps he has taken from his enemies—what is the reason that renders him sad?"

The Apache chief smiled proudly at Unicorn's remarks.

"The friend of my brother, the great pale hunter, adopted by his tribe," he said sharply, "is running a terrible danger at this moment."

"Wah!" the chief said; "Can that be true? Koutonepi is the flesh of my bones; who touches him wounds me. My brother will explain."

Black Cat then narrated to Unicorn the way in which Valentine had saved his life, the leagues formed by the Apaches and other nations of the Far West against him, and the critical position in which the hunter now was, owing to the influence of Red Cedar with the Indians, and the forces he had at his command at this moment. Unicorn shook his head over the story.

"Koutonepi is wise and intrepid," he said; "loyalty dwells in his heart, but he cannot resist—how to help him? A man, however brave he may be, is not equal to one hundred."

"Valentine is my brother," the Apache answered; "I have sworn to save him. But what can I do alone?"

Suddenly a woman rushed between, the two chiefs: it was Sunbeam.

"If my master permits," she said with a suppliant look at Unicorn, "I will help you: a woman can do many things."

There was a silence, during which the chief regarded the squaw, who stood modest and motionless before them.

"My sister is brave," Black Cat at length said; "but a woman is a weak creature, whose help is of but very slight weight under such grave circumstances."

"Perhaps so," she said boldly.

"Wife," Unicorn said, as he laid his hand on her shoulder, "go whither your heart calls you; save my brother and pay the debt you have contracted with him: my eye will follow you, and at the first signal I will run up."

"Thanks," the young woman said, joyfully, and kneeling before the chief, she affectionately kissed his hand.

Unicorn went on—

"I confide this woman to my brother—I know that his heart is great: I am at my ease; farewell."

And after a parting signal he dismissed his guest; the chief entered his calli without looking back, and let the buffalo hide curtain fall behind him. Sunbeam looked after him; when he had disappeared, she turned to Black Cat.

"Let us go," she said, "to save our friend."

A few hours later, the Apache chief, followed by a young woman, rejoined his tribe on the banks of the Gila, and on the next day but one Black Cat arrived with his entire forces at the hill of Mad Buffalo.

CHAPTER IX
THE MEETING

The preceding explanations given, we will resume our story at the point where we left it at the end of chapter seven. Sunbeam, without speaking, offered the Spanish girl a piece of paper, a species of wooden skewer, and a shell filled with blue paint. The Gazelle gave a start of joy.

"Oh, I understand," she said.

The chief smiled.

"The whites have a great deal of knowledge," he said, "nothing escapes them; my daughter will draw a collar for the pale chief."

"Yes," she murmured, "but will he believe me?"

"My daughter will put her heart in that paper, and the white hunter will recognise it."

The girl heaved a sigh.

"Let us try," she said.

With a feverish movement she took the paper from Sunbeam's hand, hastily wrote a few words, and returned it to the young Indian, who stood motionless and stoical before her. Sunbeam rolled up the paper, and carefully fastened it round an arrow.

"Within an hour it will be delivered," she said, and she disappeared in the wood with the lightness of a startled fawn. This little affair took her less time to perform than we have been employed in describing it. When the Indian girl, taught long before by Black Cat the part she had to play, had gone off to deliver her message, the chief said—

"You see that, though we may not save them all, those who are dear to us will at any rate escape."

"May Heaven grant that you are not mistaken, father," the girl said.

"Wacondah is great—his power is unbounded—he can do everything— my daughter can hope."

After this a long conversation took place between the couple, at the end of which, White Gazelle glided unnoticed, among the trees, and proceeded to a hill a short distance from the post occupied by the whites, called Elk Hill, where she had given Don Pablo the meeting. At the thought of seeing the Mexican again, the girl had been involuntarily attacked by an undefinable emotion; she felt her heart contracted, and all her limbs trembled. The recollection of what had passed between her and him so short a time back still troubled her ideas, and rendered the task she had imposed on herself even more difficult.

At this moment she was no longer the rude amazon we have represented her to our readers, who, hardened since her childhood to the terrible scenes of prairie life, braved the greatest perils. She felt herself a woman; all the manliness in her had disappeared, only leaving a timid, trembling girl, who shuddered to find herself face to face with the man whom she reproached herself with having so cruelly outraged, and who, perhaps, on seeing her, would not condescend to enter into any explanation, but turn his back on her.

All these thoughts and many others whirled about in her brain while she proceeded with a furtive step to the place of meeting. The nearer she drew the more lively her fears became, for her mind retraced with greater force the indignity of her previous conduct. At length she arrived, and found the top of the hill still deserted. A sigh of relief escaped from her oppressed chest, and she returned thanks to Heaven for granting her a few moments' respite to prepare herself for the solemn interview she had craved.

But the first moment passed, another anxiety troubled her; she feared lest Don Pablo would not accept her invitation, but despise the chance of safety offered him. Then, with her head thrust forward, her eyes fixed on space, and striving to sound the depths of the gloom, she waited anxiously, counting the seconds. No one has yet been able to calculate how many centuries each moment is composed of to a person who is waiting. The girl was beginning to doubt Don Pablo's arrival; a gloomy despair seized upon her, and she cursed the material responsibility which nailed her inactively to the spot.

Let us describe in a few words what was happening at this moment on the Hill of Mad Buffalo. Valentine, Curumilla and Don Pablo, seated on the crest of the hill, were silently smoking, each thinking apart of the means to be employed to escape from the painful position in which they were, when a shrill whistle was heard, and a long arrow, passing rapidly between the three men, buried itself deeply in the sods of the grassy mount, at the foot of which they were seated.

"What is that?" Valentine, the first to regain his coolness, exclaimed. "By heavens! Can the redskins be beginning the attack already?"

"Let us wake our friends," said Don Pablo.

"A friend!" grunted Curumilla, who had pulled the arrow out and examined it attentively.

"What do you mean, chief?" the hunter asked.

"Look!" the Indian replied laconically, as he gave him the arrow, and pointed to the paper rolled round it.

"So it is," Valentine said, as he unfastened the paper, while Curumilla picked up a burning log and held it to him as a candle.

"Hum!" Don Pablo muttered, "this mode of corresponding appears to me rather strange."

"We will see what it all means," the hunter answered.

He unfolded the paper, on which a few lines were written in Spanish, and read the following—

> "The palefaces are lost; the Indian tribes, assembled from all parts and helped by the Pirates of the Prairies, surround them. The white men have no help to expect from anybody. Unicorn is too far off, Bloodson too much engaged in defending himself to have time to think of them. Don Pablo de Zarate can, if he likes, escape the death that menaces him, and save those who are dear to him. His fate is in his own hands. So soon as he has received this, let him leave his camp and proceed alone to Elk Hill, where he will meet a person prepared to supply him with the means he must seek in vain elsewhere; this person will await Don Pablo till sunrise. He is implored not to neglect this warning; tomorrow will be too late to save him, for he would infallibly succumb in a mad struggle.
>
> "A FRIEND."

On reading this strange missive, the young man let his head sink on his chest, and remained for a long time plunged in deep thought.

"What is to be done?" he muttered.

"Why go, hang it all!" Valentine answered; "Who knows whether this scrap of paper may not contain the salvation of all of us?"

"But suppose it is treachery?"

"Treachery! Nonsense, my friend, you must be joking. The Indians are thorough rogues and traitors, I grant; but they have a fearful terror of anything written, which they believe emanates from the genius of evil. No, this letter does not come from the Indians. As for the pirates, they can use a rifle very well, but are completely ignorant of a goose quill; and I declare, from here to Monterey on one side and to New York, on the other, you will not find one who knows how to write. This letter, therefore, emanates from a friend; but who that friend is, is more difficult to guess."

"Then your opinion is to grant the meeting?"

"Why not? Taking, of course, all the precautions usual in such a case."

"Must I go alone?"

"*Canarios!* people always go alone to such meetings: that is settled," Valentine said with a grin; "still, they are accompanied, and would be fools were they not."

"Assuming that I am willing to follow your advice, I cannot leave my father alone here."

"Your father is safe for the present; besides, he has with him the general and Curumilla, who, I answer for it, will not let him be surprised in our absence. However, that is your affair; still, I would observe, that under circumstances so critical as ours, all secondary considerations ought to be laid aside. Canarios, friend! Think that the safety of all of us may be the reward of the venture."

"You are right, brother," the young man said boldly; "who knows whether I might not have to reproach myself with your death and my father's if I neglected this hint? I go."

"Good," the hunter said, "do so; for my part, I know what is left me to do. Be at your ease," he added with his ironical smile; "you will go alone to the meeting, but if you need help, I shall not be long in making my appearance."

"Very good; but the chief point is to leave this place and reach Elk Hill unnoticed by the thousand tiger-cat eyes the Apaches are probably fixing on us at this moment."

"Trust to me for that," the hunter answered.

In fact, a few minutes later, Don Pablo, guided by Valentine, was climbing up Elk hill, unnoticed by the Apaches.

In the meanwhile, White Gazelle was still waiting, her body bent forward, and listening for the slightest sound that would reveal the presence of the man she had so earnestly begged to come. Suddenly a rough hand was laid on her shoulder, and a mocking voice muttered in her ear:—

"Hilloh, Niña, what are you doing so far from the camp? Are you afraid lest your enemies should escape?"

The Spaniard turned with an ill-disguised movement of disgust, and saw Nathan, Red Cedar's eldest son.

"Yes, it is I," the bandit went on; "does that astonish you, Niña? We arrived an hour ago with the finest collection of vultures that can be imagined."

"But what are you doing here?" she said, scarce knowing why she asked the question.

"Oh!" he continued, "I have also come to revenge myself; I left my father and the others down there, and, have come to explore the country a little. But," he added, with a sinister laugh, "that is not the question at this moment. What the deuce sets you roaming about at this time of night, at the risk of having an unpleasant encounter?"

"What have I to fear—am I not armed?"

"That is true," the pirate replied with a grin; "but you are pretty, and, devil take me if I don't know fellows who, in my place, would laugh at the playthings you have in your girdle. Yes, you are very pretty, Niña, don't you know it? Hang me, as no one has yet told you so, I feel very much inclined to do so; what's your opinion, eh?"

"The wretch is mad with drink," the girl muttered, as she saw the brigand's flushed face, and his staggering legs.

"Leave me," she said to him, "the hour is badly chosen for jesting, we have, more important matters to arrange."

"Stuff, we are all mortal, and hang me if I care what may happen tomorrow! On the contrary, I find the hour splendidly chosen; we are alone, no one can over hear us; what prevents us, then, from expressing our adoration of one another?"

"No one, were it true," the girl answered resolutely; "but I am not in the humour to listen to your chattering; so be good enough to withdraw. I am awaiting here the war party of the Buffalo Apaches, who will soon arrive and take up their position on this hill; instead of losing precious time, you would do better to join Red Cedar and Stanapat, with whom you must settle all the details of the enemy's attack."

"That is true," the bandit answered, the words having slightly sobered him. "You are right, Niña, I will go; but what is put off is not lost; I hope on some other day to find you not so wild, my dear. Good bye!"

And, carelessly turning, the bandit threw his rifle on his shoulder, and went down the hill in the direction of the Apache camp. The young Spaniard, left alone, congratulated herself on escaping the danger that had momentarily threatened her, for she had trembled lest Don Pablo might arrive while Nathan was with her. Still, the news of Red Cedar's position heightened White Gazelle's apprehensions and redoubled her alarm about those whom she had resolved to save at all hazards. At the moment when she no longer hoped to see the young man, and was looking out for him more to satisfy her conscience than in the chance of seeing him, she saw, a little distance off, a man hurriedly walking towards her, and guessed, more than recognised, that it was Don Pablo.

"At last!" she exclaimed joyfully, as she rushed to meet him.

The young man was soon by her side, but on perceiving who it was, he fell back a pace.

"You," he said; "did you write to ask me here?"

"Yes," she answered, in a trembling voice, "I did."

"What can there be in common between us?" Don Pablo said, contemptuously.

"Oh! Do not crush me; I now can understand how culpable and unworthy my conduct was: pardon a madness which I deplore. Listen to me; in Heaven's name do not despise the advice I am about to give you, for your life and that of those you love are at stake."

"Thank Heaven, madam," the young man replied coldly; "during the few hours we were together, I learnt to know you sufficiently to place no faith in any of your protestations; I have only one regret at this moment, and that is, in having allowed myself to enter the snare you have laid for me."

"I lay a snare for you!" she exclaimed indignantly, "when I would gladly shed the last drop of my blood to save you."

"Save me—nonsense! Ruin me, you mean," Don Pablo continued, with a smile of contempt; "do you fancy me so foolish? Be frank, at least; your project has succeeded, and I am in your hands; produce your accomplices, who are doubtless hidden behind those trees, and I will not do them the honour of disputing my life with them."

"Oh, Heaven!" the girl exclaimed, as she writhed her hands in despair, "Am I not sufficiently punished, Don, Pablo? Listen to me, for mercy's sake! In a few minutes it will be too late; I wish to save you, I say."

"You lie impudently," Valentine exclaimed, as he leaped from a thicket; "only a moment ago, at that very spot, you told Nathan, the worthy son of your accomplice, Red Cedar, of the arrival of an Apache war party; deny it, if you dare."

This revelation was a thunderbolt for the girl; she felt that it would be impossible for her to disabuse the man she loved, and convince him of her innocence, in the face of this apparently so evident proof of her treachery. She fell crushed at the young man's feet.

"Oh," he said with disgust, "this wretched woman is my evil genius."

He made a movement to retire.

"A moment," Valentine exclaimed, as he stopped him; "matters must not end thus: let us destroy this creature, ere she causes us to be massacred."

He coldly placed the muzzle of a pistol on the girl's temple, and she did not flinch to escape the fate that threatened her. But Don Pablo hastily seized his arm.

"Valentine," he said, "what are you about, my friend?"

"It is true," the hunter replied; "when so near death, I will not dishonour myself by killing this wretch."

"Well done, brother," Don Pablo said, as he gave a glance of scorn to the Gazelle, who implored him in vain; men like us do not assassinate women. "Let us leave her and sell our lives dearly."

"Nonsense; death, perhaps, is not so near as you may fancy; for my part, I do not despair about getting out of this wasps nest."

They took an anxious glance into the valley to reconnoitre their position; the darkness was almost dissipated; the sun, though still invisible, tinged the sky with those reddish gleams which precedes its appearance by a few moments. As far as the eye could reach, the plain was covered by powerful Indian detachments.

The two men saw that they had but a very slight chance of regaining their fortress; still, accustomed as they were to attempt impossibilities daily, they were not discouraged in the presence of the imminent danger that menaced them. After silently shaking hands, these two brave men raised their heads proudly, and with calm brow and flashing eye prepared to confront the horrible death that awaited them, if they were discovered.

"Stay, in Heaven's name," the maiden exclaimed, as she dragged herself on her knees to Don Pablo's feet.

"Back, viper," the latter answered, "let us die bravely."

"But I will not have you die," she replied, with a piercing cry; "I repeat that I will save you, if you consent."

"Save us! God alone can do that," the young man said mournfully; "be glad that we will not sully our hands with your perfidious blood, and do not trouble us further."

"Oh! Nothing will convince you then!" she said, with despair.

"Nothing," the Mexican answered coldly.

"Oh!" she exclaimed, her eye beaming with joy, "I have found it. Follow me, and you shall join your friends again."

Don Pablo, who had already gone some yards, turned back with hesitation.

"What do you fear?" she said; "you will still be able to kill me if I deceive you. Oh," she added madly, "what do I care for death, so that I save you!"

"In fact," Valentine remarked, "she is in the right, and then in our position, we must let no chance slip. Perhaps, after all, she speaks the truth."

"Yes, yes," the girl implored; "trust to me."

"Well, we will try it," said Valentine.

"Go on," Don Pablo answered laconically; "go on, we follow."

"Oh, thanks, thanks," she said eagerly, covering the the young man's hand with kisses and tears, which she had seized against his will; "you shall see that I can save you."

"Strange creature," the hunter said, as he wiped his eyes with the back of his rough hand; "she is quite capable of doing what she says."

"Perhaps so," Don Pablo replied, shaking his head gloomily: "but our position is truly desperate, my friend."

"A man can only die once, after all," the hunter remarked philosophically, as he threw his rifle over his shoulder; "I am most curious to know how all this will end."

"Come!" the Spanish girl said.

CHAPTER X
A WAR STRATAGEM

The two men followed her, and the three began crawling through the tall grass and silently descending the hill. This painful march was necessarily slow, owing to the innumerable precautions the fugitives were obliged to take so as not to be seen or tracked by the scouts the Indians had scattered all around to watch the movements of the white men, and of any relief which might come to them.

White Gazelle walked actively in front of the hunters, looking cautiously around, stopping to listen anxiously to the slightest sound in the bushes; and when her fears were calmed, she went on giving the men she guided a smile of encouragement.

"Sold!" Valentine said, with a laugh all at once, as he rested his rifle on the ground; "Come, come, the little wench is cleverer than I fancied."

The two men were surrounded by a numerous party of Apache Indians. Don Pablo did not utter a word; he only looked at the girl, who continued to smile.

"Bah!" the Frenchman muttered philosophically in an aside; "I shall kill my seven or eight of them, and after that, we shall see."

Completely reassured by this consoling reflection, the hunter at once regained all his clearness of mind, and looked curiously around him. They were in the midst of Black Cat's war party, and that chief now walked up to the hunter.

"My brother is welcome among the Buffalo Apaches," he said, nobly.

"Why jest, chief?" Valentine remarked; "I am your prisoner, do with me what you think proper."

"Black Cat does not jest; the great pale hunter is not his prisoner, but his friend; he has but to command and Black Cat will execute his orders."

"What mean these words?" the Frenchman said, with astonishment; "Are you not here, like all the members of your nation, to seize my friends and myself?"

"Such was my intention, I allow, when I left my village some days back, but my heart has changed since my brother saved my life, and he may have perceived it already. If I have come here it is not to fight, but to save him and his friends; my brother can, therefore, place confidence in my words—my tribe will obey him as myself."

Valentine reflected for a moment, then he said, as he looked searchingly at the chief:

"And what does Black Cat ask in return for the help he offers me?"

"Nothing; the pale hunter is my brother; if we succeed he will do as he pleases."

"Come, come, all is for the best," Valentine said, as he turned to the girl; "I was mistaken, so I will ask you to forgive me."

White Gazelle blushed with delight at these words.

"Then," Valentine continued, addressing the Indian chief, "I can entirely dispose of your young men?"

"Entirely.

"They will be devoted to me?"

"I have said so, as to myself."

"Good!" said the hunter, as his face brightened; "how many warriors have you?"

Black Cat held up ten times the fingers of his opened hands.

"One hundred?" Valentine asked.

"Yes," the chief replied, "and eight more."

"But the other tribes are far more numerous than yours?"

"They form a band of warriors twenty-two times and seven times more numerous than mine."

"Hum! That is a tidy lot, without counting the pirates."

"Wah! There are thrice the number of the fingers of my two hands of the Long-knives of the East."

"I fear," Don Pablo observed, "that we shall be crushed by the number of our enemies."

"Perhaps so," Valentine, who was reflecting, answered; "where is Red Cedar?"

"Red Cedar is with his brothers, the prairie half-breeds; he has joined Stanapat's party."

At this moment the Apache war cry burst forth on the plain, a tremendous discharge was heard, and the hill of the Mad Buffalo seemed begirt by a halo of smoke and flashing lightning. The battle had began. The Indians bravely mounted to the assault. They marched toward the hill, continually discharging their muskets, and firing arrows at their invisible enemies.

At the spot where the chain of hills touches the Gila, fresh parties of Apaches could be seen incessantly arriving. They came up at a gallop, by troops of three to twenty men at a time. Their horses were covered with foam, leading to the presumption that they had made a long journey. The Apaches were in their war paint, covered with all sorts of ornaments and arms, with their bow and quiver on their back, and their musket in their hands. Their heads were crowned with feathers, among them being several magnificent black and white eagle plumes, with the large falling crest. Seated on handsome saddlecloths of panther skin, lined with red, all had the lower part of the body naked, with the exception of a long strip of wolf skin passed over the shoulder. Their shields were ornamented with feathers, and party coloured cloth. These men, thus accoutred, had something grand and majestic about them which affected the imagination and inspired terror.

Many of them at once climbed the heights, lashing their wearied horses, so to arrive sooner at the battlefield, while singing and uttering their war cry.

The contest seemed most obstinate in the neighbourhood of the palisades; the two Mexicans and Curumilla, protected behind their entrenchments, replied to the Apaches with a deadly fire, bravely exciting each other to die weapons in hand. Several corpses already lay on the plain; riderless horses galloped in every direction, and the cries of the wounded were mingled with the yells of defiance of the assailants.

What we have described in so many words, Valentine and Don Pablo perceived in a few seconds, with the infallible glance of men long accustomed to prairie life.

"Come, chief," the hunter said, quickly, "we must rejoin our friends; help us; if not, they are lost."

"Good," Black Cat answered; "the pale hunter will place himself, with his friend, in the midst of my detachment; in a few minutes he will be on the hill. Above all, the pale chief must leave me to act."

"Do so; I trust entirely to you."

Black Cat said a few words in a low voice to the warriors who accompanied him; they at once collected round the two hunters, who entirely disappeared in their midst.

"Oh, oh," Don Pablo said, anxiously, "just look at this, my friend."

Valentine smiled as he took his arm.

"I have read the chief's intention," he said, "he is employing the only way possible. Do not be alarmed, all is for the best."

Black Cat placed himself at the head of his detachment, and gave a signal. A fearful yell burst through the air—the Buffalo tribe had sounded its war cry. The Apaches, carrying the two men with them, rushed furiously toward the hill, and ere Valentine and Don Pablo knew what was happening, they had rejoined their friends, and Black Cat's warriors fled in every direction, as if a fearful panic had seized on them.

Still the fight was not over; Stanapat's Indians rushed like tigers on the palisades, and let themselves be killed without recoiling an inch. The fight, if prolonged, must end fatally to the whites, whose strength was becoming exhausted. Stanapat and Red Cedar understood this, and hence redoubled their efforts to crush the enemy.

Suddenly, at the moment when the Apaches rushed furiously against the whites to attempt a final assault; the war cry of the Coras was heard, mingled with the discharge of firearms. The Apaches were surprised, and hesitated; Red Cedar looked around, and uttered a curse; the war cry of the Comanches rose behind the camp.

"Forward! Forward at all risks!" the squatter howled, as, followed by his sons and some of his men, he rushed by toward the hill.

But the scene had changed as if by enchantment. Black Cat, on seeing the help that had arrived for his friends, effected a junction with Unicorn; the united bands attacked the Apaches on the flank, while Moukapec, at the head of two hundred picked warriors of his nation, rushed on their rear.

The flight began, and soon changed into a rout; Red Cedar, and a small party of pirates collected around him, alone offered any resistance. From assailants they had become assailed, and there must be an end to it, or in a few minutes all would be over, as their retreat would be cut off.

"Hurrah!" Red Cedar shouted, as he waved his rifle over his head like a mace; "Down with the dogs! Take their scalps!"

"Take their scalps!" his companions exclaimed, imitating his movements, and massacring all that opposed their passage.

They had managed to clear a bloody way, and were slowly moving toward the river, when a man boldly threw himself before Red Cedar—it was Moukapec.

"I bring you my scalp, dog of the palefaces!" he shouted, as he dealt a blow at him with his tomahawk.

"Thanks," the bandit answered, as he parried the blow.

Eagle-wing bounded forward like a hyena, and before his enemy could prevent it, buried his knife in his thigh. Red Cedar uttered a yell of rage on feeling himself wounded, and drew his knife with one hand, while with the other he seized the Indian by the throat. The latter felt that he was lost; the blade flashed above his head, and was buried to the hilt in his chest.

"Ah! Ah!" Red Cedar grinned, as he let down his enemy who rolled on the ground, "I fancy our accounts are settled this time."

"Not yet," the Coras said, with a triumphant smile, and with a dying effort he fired his rifle at the squatter.

The latter let go his reins, and fell by the side of the Indian.

"I die avenged," Eagle-wing said, as he writhed in a last convulsion.

"Oh, I am not dead yet," Red Cedar replied, as he rose on one knee and cleft the Indian's skull; "I shall escape, never fear."

Red Cedar's shoulder was broken, still, thanks to the help of his comrades, who did not give ground an inch, he was able to get on his horse again, and Sutter and Nathan fastened him to the saddle.

"Back! Back!" he shouted, "Else we are lost! Each man for himself!"

The pirates obeyed him, and began flying in various directions, closely followed by the Comanches and Coras. Still some managed to reach the virgin forest, where they disappeared, others the river, which they swam, Red Cedar being one of the former. Valentine and his friends, as soon as they saw the issue of the fight, hastened to leave the hill of the Mad Buffalo, and went down into the plain with the intention of capturing Red Cedar; unfortunately they only arrived in time to see him disappear in the distance; still, the unexpected result of the fight had done them an immense service, not only by rescuing them from the false position in which they were, but also by breaking up the league of the Indian tribes, who, startled by the immense losses they had suffered, would doubtless retire and leave the white men to settle their disputes without interfering further in the quarrel.

As for Red Cedar, his band was annihilated or, dispersed, while himself, seriously wounded, was no longer to be feared. The capture of this man, forced to wander like a wild beast over the prairie, only became a question of time. Stanapat had also escaped with a few warriors, no one knowing in what direction he had gone.

The three united parties camped on the battlefield, according to their custom. The Indians first occupied themselves with scalping the corpses of their enemies. Singular to say, the victors had made no prisoners; the fight had been so obstinate, that every man had only thought of killing his enemy, instead of seizing him. Moukapec's body was raised respectfully, and interred on the hill of Mad Buffalo, by the side of the terrible chief who had first chosen the sepulchre. The sun set at the moment when the last duties had been paid to the fallen warrior, and the council fires were lighted. When all had taken their seats, and the calumet had gone the round, Valentine rose.

"Chiefs," he said, "my friends and I thank you for your generous efforts in trying to deliver the prairies of the Far West from the bandit who has so long desolated them; we are not merely pursuing an idle vengeance, but a work of humanity; this villain dishonours the name of man, and the race to which he belongs. At the present moment, of the numerous bandits who accompanied him, few are left him. The band of the malefactors, which was the terror of the prairies, no longer exists; and their chief himself, I feel convinced, will soon fall into our power. Be ready, when necessary, to help us, as you have done today; until then, return to your villages, and believe that, far or near, we shall retain the recollection of the services you have rendered us, and that, in case of need, you can count on us as we have ever done on you."

After uttering these words which the Indians applauded, Valentine sat down again. There was a lengthened silence, employed by the Indians in conscientiously smoking their calumets. Black Cat was the first to break the silence.

"Let my brothers listen," he said; "the words I utter are inspired by the Master of Life; the cloud that obscured my mind has passed away since my Coras and Comanche brothers, those two brave nations, have restored me the place, to which I had a right, at their council fires. Unicorn is a wise chief, his friendship is precious to me. I hope that the Wacondah will never allow between him and me, or between my young men and his, during the next thousand and fifty moons, the slightest misunderstanding which may rupture the friendship existing at this moment."

Unicorn removed his pipe from his lips, bowed to Black Cat with a smile, and answered—

"My brother Black Cat has spoken well; my heart quivered with joy on hearing him. Why should we not be friends? Is not the prairie large enough and wide enough for us? Are not the buffaloes sufficiently numerous? Let my brothers listen: I seek around me in vain the war hatchet; it is buried so deeply, that the sons and the grandsons of our children will never succeed in digging it up."

Other speeches were made by several chiefs, and the best intelligence did not cease to reign between the allies. At daybreak, they separated in the most cordial manner, each returning to his village. Valentine and his party remained alone. White Gazelle was leaning pensively against the trunk of a tree a few paces from them.

CHAPTER XI
IN THE FOREST

Red Cedar, carried a long distance from the battlefield by the furious galloping of his steed, which he had no longer the strength to control, went on straight ahead, not knowing what direction he was following. In this man, hitherto so firm, and who possessed so energetic a will, the thoughts were overclouded as if by enchantment: the loss of blood, the repeated jolts his horse gave him, had plunged him into a state of insensibility. Had he not been so securely fastened to his saddle, he would have fallen from it twenty times.

He went on with hanging arms, body bent over his horse's neck, and eyes half closed, hardly conscious of what happened to him, or trying to discover. Shaken to the right, shaken to the left, he watched with unmeaning eye the trees and rocks fly past on either side: no longer thinking, but living in a horrible dream, a prey to the strangest and wildest hallucinations. Night succeeded to day: his horse continued its journey, bounding like a frightened jaguar over the obstacles that opposed it, followed by a pack of howling coyotes, and seeking in vain to get rid of the inert weight that oppressed it.

At length the horse stumbled in the darkness, and fell to the ground, uttering a plaintive neigh. Up to this moment Red Cedar had preserved— we will not say a complete and clear knowledge of the position in which he was—but at any rate a certain consciousness of the life that still dwelt in him. When his exhausted horse fell, the bandit felt a sharp pain in his head, and that was all; he fainted away while stammering an imprecation, the last protest of the villain, who, to the last moment, denied the existence of that God who smote him.

When he re-opened his eyes, under the impression of an indefinable feeling of comfort, the sun was shining through the tufted branches of the forest trees, and the birds, concealed beneath the green foliage, were singing their joyous concerts. Red Cedar gave vent to a sigh of relief, and looked languidly around him; his horse was lying dead a few paces from him. He was seated against the trunk of a tree, while Ellen, kneeling by his side, was anxiously following the progress of his return to life.

"Oh, oh," the bandit muttered hoarsely, "I am still alive then."

"Yes, thanks to God, father," Ellen answered softly.

The bandit looked at her.

"God!" he said, as if speaking to himself; "God!" he added with an ironical smile.

"He it was who saved you, father," the girl said.

"Child!" Red Cedar muttered, as he passed his left hand over his forehead; "God is only a word, never utter it again."

Ellen drooped her head; but with the feeling of life pain returned.

"Oh! How I suffer," he said.

"You are dangerously wounded, father. Alas! I have done what I can to relieve you; but I am only a poor ignorant girl, and perhaps what I have attempted was not the right treatment."

Red Cedar turned to her, and an expression of tenderness flashed in his eyes.

"You love me, then?" he said.

"Is it not my duty to do so, father?"

The bandit made no reply; the smile we know played round his Violet lips.

"Alas! I have been seeking you a long time, father; this night chance enabled me to find you again."

"Yes, you are a good girl, Ellen. I have only you left now. I know not what has become of my sons. Oh," he said with a start of fury, "that wretch Ambrosio is the cause of all; had it not been for him, I should still be at the Paso del Norte, in the forests of which I had made myself master."

"Think no more of that, father; your condition demands the greatest calmness; try and sleep for some hours—that will do you good."

"Sleep," the bandit said, "can I sleep? No," he added with a movement of repulsion, "I would sooner keep awake; when my eyes are closed, I see.... No, no, I must not sleep."

He did not finish his sentence. Ellen gazed on him with pity, mingled with terror. The bandit, weakened by the loss of blood and the fever produced by his wounds, felt something to which he had hitherto been a stranger—it was fear. Perhaps his conscience evoked the gnawing remorse of his crimes.

There was a lengthened silence. Ellen attentively followed the bandit's movements, whom the fever plunged into a species of somnolency, and who at times started with inarticulate cries, and looking around him in terror. Toward evening, he opened his eyes, and seemed to grow stronger: his eyes were less haggard, his words more connected.

"Thanks, child," he said, "you are a good creature; where are we?"

"I do not know, father; this forest is immense. I tell you, again, it was God who guided me to you."

"No, you are mistaken, Ellen," he replied with that sarcastic smile peculiar to him; "it was not God who brought you here, but the demon, who feared the loss of so good a friend as I am."

"Speak not so, father," the girl said sadly; "the night is rapidly setting in darkness will soon surround us; let me on the contrary, pray to Heaven to keep far from us the perils that threaten us during the night."

"Child! Does a night in the woods frighten you so, when your whole life has been spent in the desert? Light a fire of dry wood to keep the wild beasts at bay, and place my pistols near me, these precautions will be better, believe me, than your useless prayers."

"Do not blaspheme," the girl said hurriedly; "you are wounded, almost dying; I am weak, and incapable of helping you effectually. Our life is in the hands of Him whose power you deny in vain. He alone, if He will, can save us."

The bandit burst into a dry and snapping laugh.

"Let Him do so then, in the demon's name, and I will believe in Him."

"Father, in Heaven's name, speak not so," the maiden murmured in sorrow.

"Do what I tell you, you little fool," the squatter interrupted her brutally, "and leave me in peace."

Ellen turned to wipe away the tears this harsh language forced from her, and rose sorrowfully to obey Red Cedar, who looked after her.

"Come, you goose," he said to her again, "I did not intend to hurt your feelings."

The girl then collected all the dry branches she could find, which she made into a pile and kindled. The wood soon began cracking, and a long and bright flame rose to the sky. She then took from his holsters the squatter's still loaded pistols, placed them within reach of his arm, and then seated herself again by his side. Red Cedar smiled his satisfaction.

"There," he said, "now we have nothing more to fear; if the wild beasts pay us a visit, we will receive them; we will pass the night quietly. As for the morrow, well, we shall see."

Ellen, without replying, wrapped him up as well as she could in the blankets and hides that were on the horse, in order to protect him from the cold. So much attention and self-denial affected the bandit.

"And you, Ellen," he asked her; "will you not keep a few of these skins for yourself?"

"Why should I, father? The fire will be enough for me," she said gently.

"But, at any rate, eat something, you must be hungry; for, if I am not mistaken, you have had nothing the whole day."

"That is true, father, but I am not hungry."

"No matter," he said, pressing her, "too long a fast may be injurious to you; I insist on your eating."

"It is useless, father," she said with some hesitation.

"Eat, I say," he went on, "if not for your sake, for mine; eat a mouthful to restore your strength, for we know what awaits us in the next few hours."

"Alas! I would readily obey you," she said, letting her eyes sink; "but it is impossible."

"And why so, pray? When I tell you that I insist."

"Because I have nothing to eat."

These words crushed the bandit like the blow of a club.

"Oh, it is frightful," he muttered; "poor girl, pardon me Ellen, I am a villain, unworthy of such devotion as yours."

"Calm yourself, father, I implore you; I am not hungry, a night is soon passed, and tomorrow, as you said, we shall see; but before then, I am convinced God will come to our aid."

"God!" the squatter exclaimed, gnashing his teeth.

"God, ever God, father," the girl answered, with sparkling eye and trembling lip; "God, ever; for, however unworthy we may be of His pity; He is merciful, and perhaps will not abandon us."

"Build then on him, fool as you are, and you will be dead in two days."

"No," she exclaimed, joyfully, "for He has heard me, and sends us help."

The bandit looked and fell back on the ground, closing his eyes, and muttering in a hollow voice the words which for some time past had constantly risen from his heart to his lips, and involuntarily mastered him.

"God! Can He exist?"

A terrible question which he incessantly asked himself, and to which his obstinate conscience was beginning to respond, for the granite coating of his heart was beginning to crumble away beneath the repeated blows of remorse. But Ellen did not notice Red Cedar's state of prostration, she had risen and rushed forward, with outstretched arms, crying as loudly as her voice permitted her—"Help, help!"

The young girl had fancied she heard, for some minutes past, a peculiar rustling in the foliage. This noise, at first remote and almost unnoticeable, had rapidly approached; soon lights had glistened through the trees, and the footsteps of a numerous party had distinctly smitten her ear. In fact, she had scarce gone a dozen yards, ere she found herself in the presence of a dozen mounted Indians, holding torches, and escorting two persons wrapped in long cloaks.

"Help! Help!" Ellen repeated, as she fell on her knees, with outstretched arms.

The horsemen stopped; one of them dismounted, and ran to the girl, whom he took by the hands, and forced to rise.

"Help for whom, my poor girl?" he asked her in a soft voice.

On hearing the stranger's accent so full of tenderness, she felt hope returning to her heart.

"Oh!" she murmured with joy; "my father is saved."

"Our life is in the hands of God," the stranger said, with emotion; "but lead me to your father, and all a man can do to help him, I will."

"It is God who sends you, bless you, my father!" the maiden said, as she kissed his hand.

In the movement he had made to raise her, the stranger's cloak flew open, and the girl had recognised a priest.

"Let us go," he said.

"Come!"

The girl ran joyously forward, and the little party followed her.

"Father, father," she exclaimed, as she came near the wounded man, "I was certain that Heaven would not abandon us; I bring you succour."

At this moment the strangers entered the clearing where the bandit lay. The Indians and the other travellers remained some paces in the rear, while the priest, quickly approached Red Cedar, over whom he bent. At his daughter's words the bandit opened his eyes, and turned his head with an effort in the direction whence this unexpected help arrived. Suddenly his face, before so pale, was covered with a cadaverous tinge; his eyes were enlarged and became haggard, a convulsive quiver agitated his limbs, and he fell heavily back, muttering with terror—

"Oh! Father Seraphin!"

It was really the missionary; without appearing to remark the squatter's emotion, he seized his arm in order to feel his pulse. Red Cedar had fainted, but Ellen had heard the words he uttered, and though she could not understand their meaning, she guessed that a terrible drama was concealed beneath this revelation.

"My father!" she exclaimed mournfully, as she fell at the priest's knees, "My father, have pity on him, do not desert him!"

The missionary smiled with an expression of ineffable goodness.

"Daughter," he answered gently, "I am a minister of God, and the dress I wear commands me to forget insults. Priests have no enemies, all men are their brothers; reassure yourself, your father has not only his body to be saved, but also, his soul. I will undertake this cure, and God, who permitted me to take this road, will give me the necessary strength to succeed."

"Oh, thanks, thanks, holy father," the girl murmured, as she burst into tears.

"Do not thank me, poor girl; address your thanks to God, for He alone has done all. Now leave me to attend to this unhappy man, who is suffering, and whose miserable state claims all my care."

And gently removing the maiden, Father Seraphin opened his medicine box, which he took from the pommel of his saddle, and prepared to dress his patient's wounds. In the meanwhile the Indians had gradually approached, and seeing the state of affairs, they dismounted to prepare the encampment, for they foresaw that, with Red Cedar in his present condition, the missionary would pass the night at this spot.

The person who accompanied Father Seraphin was a female of very advanced age, but whose features, ennobled by years, had a far from common expression of kindness and grandeur. When she saw that the missionary was preparing to dress the wounds, she went up to him and said in a soft voice—

"Can I not help you in any way, holy father? You know that I am anxious to begin my apprenticeship in nursing."

These words were uttered with an accent of indescribable goodness. The priest looked at her with a sublime expression, and, taking her hand, he made her stoop over the wounded man.

"Heaven has decreed that what now happens should take place," he said to her; "you have hardly landed in this country, and entered the desert to seek your son, when the Omnipotent imposes on you a task which must rejoice your heart by bringing you face to face with this man."

"What do you mean, father?" she said with amazement.

"Mother of Valentine Guillois," he continued, with an accent full of supreme majesty, "look at this man well, so as to be able to recognise him hereafter; it is Red Cedar, the wretch of whom I have so often spoken to you, the implacable foe of your son."

At this terrible revelation the poor woman gave a start of fear; but surmounting with a superhuman effort the feeling of revulsion she had at first experienced, she answered in a calm voice—

"No matter, father, the man suffers, and I will nurse him."

"Good, Madam," the priest said, with emotion; "Heaven will give you credit for this evangelic abnegation."

CHAPTER XII
THE MISSIONARY

We will now briefly explain by what strange concourse of events Father Seraphin, whom we have for so long a period lost out of sight, and Valentine's mother, had arrived so providentially to help Red Cedar.

When the missionary left the Trail-hunter, he proceeded, as he expressed a wish, among the Comanches, with the intention of preaching the gospel to them, a holy duty which he had begun to put in execution long before. Father Seraphin, through his character and piety of manner, had made friends of all these children of nature, and converted numerous proselytes in various tribes, especially in Unicorn's.

The journey was long and fatiguing to the Comanche village, and the means of transport were, in a desert country, only traversed by nomadic hordes, which wander without any settled purpose in these vast solitudes. The missionary, however, did not recoil; too weak to ride on account of the scarce cicatrised wound he had received a short time previously, he had, like the first Fathers of the Church, bravely undertaken this journey on foot, which it is almost impossible to accomplish on horseback.

But human strength has its limits, which it cannot go beyond. Father Seraphin, in spite of his courage, was obliged tacitly to allow that he had undertaken a task which he was too weak to carry out. One night he fell, exhausted by fever and fatigue, on the floor of some Indians, who nursed and brought him round. These Indians, who were half civilised, and had been Christians for a long time, would not allow the priest, in his present state of health, to continue his journey; on the contrary, taking advantage of the fever which kept him down and rendered it impossible for him to see what was done with him, they conveyed him back, by slow stages, to Texas.

When Father Seraphin, thanks to his youth and powerful constitution, had at length conquered the malady which kept him confined to his bed for more than a month between life and death, his surprise was great to find himself at Galveston, in the house of the episcopal head of the Mission. The worthy prelate, employing the spiritual powers given him by his character and his title, had insisted on the missionary going on board of a vessel just starting for Havre, and which was only waiting for a favourable wind.

Father Seraphin obeyed with sorrow the commands of his superior; the Bishop was obliged to prove to him that his health was almost ruined, and that his native air could alone restore it, ere he would resign humbly to obedience, and, as he said bitterly, fly and abandon his post. The missionary started then, but with the firm resolution of returning so soon as it was possible.

The voyage from Galveston to Havre was a pleasant one; two months after leaving Texas, Father Seraphin set foot on his native soil, with an emotion which only those who have wandered for a long time in foreign parts can comprehend. Since accident brought him back to France, the missionary profited by it to visit his family, whom he never expected to see again, and by whom he was received with transports of joy, the greater because his return was so unexpected.

The life of a missionary is very hard; those who have seen them at work in the great American desert can alone appreciate all the holy abnegation and true courage there is in the hearts of these simple and truly good men, who sacrifice their life, without the hope of possible reward; in preaching to the Indians. They nearly all fall in some obscure corner of the prairie, victims to their devotion, or if they resist for five or six years, they return to their country prematurely aged, almost blind, overwhelmed with infirmities, and forced to live a miserable life among men who misunderstand and too often calumniate them.

Father Seraphin's time was counted, every hour he passed away from his beloved Indians he reproached himself with as a robbery he committed on them. He tore himself from his parent's arms, and hastened to Havre, to profit by the first chance that presented itself for returning to Texas.

One evening, while Father Seraphin was seated on the beach, contemplating the sea that separated him from the object of his life, and thinking of the proselytes he had left in America, and whom, deprived of his presence, he trembled to find again, plunged in their old errors— he heard sobs near him. He raised his head, and saw at some paces from him a woman kneeling on the sand and weeping; from time to time broken words escaped from her lips. Father Seraphin was affected by this sorrow; he approached, and heard the words: "My son, my poor son! Oh, Heaven restore me my son!"

This woman's face was bathed in tears, her eyes were raised to Heaven, and an expression of profound despair was imprinted on her countenance. Father Seraphin understood with the instinct of his heart that there was a great misfortune here that required unsolving, and addressed the stranger.

"Poor woman, what do you want here? Why do you weep?

"Alas! Father," she answered, "I have lost all hope of being happy in this world."

"Who knows, madam? Tell me your misfortunes. God is great; perhaps He will give me the power to console you."

"You are right, father; God never deserts the afflicted, and it is above all when hope fails them that He comes to their assistance."

"Speak then with confidence."

The strange woman began in a voice broken by the internal emotion which she suffered.

"For more than ten years," she said, "I have been separated from my son. Alas! Since he went to America, in spite of all the steps I have taken, I have never received news of him, or learned what has become of him, whether he be dead or alive."

"Since the period of which you speak, then, no sign, no information however slight, has reassured you as to the fate of him you mourn?"

"No, my father, since my son, the brave lad, determined to accompany his foster-brother to Chili."

"Well," the priest interrupted, "you might enquire in Chili."

"I did so, father."

"And learned nothing?"

"Pardon me, my son's foster-brother is married, and possesses a large fortune in Chili. I applied to him. My son left him about a year after his departure from France, without telling him the motive that urged him to act thus, and he never heard of him again, in spite of all his efforts to find him; all that he discovered was that he had buried himself in the virgin forests of the Great Chaco, accompanied by two Indian chiefs."

"It is, indeed, strange," the priest muttered thoughtfully.

"My son's foster-brother frequently writes to me; thanks to him, I am rich for a woman of my condition, who is accustomed to live on a little. In each of his letters he begs me to come and end my days with him; but it is my son, my poor child, I wish to see again; in his arms I should like to close my eyes. Alas! That consolation will not be granted me. Oh! Father, you cannot imagine what grief it is for a mother to live alone, far from the only being who gave joy to her latter days. Though I have not seen him for ten years, I picture him to myself as on the day he left me, young and strong, and little suspecting that he was leaving me forever."

While uttering these words, the poor woman could not repress her tears and sobs.

"Courage! life is but one long trial; is you have suffered so greatly, perchance God, whose mercy is infinite, reserves a supreme joy for your last days of life."

"Alas, father, as you know, nothing can console a mother for the absence of her son, for he is her flesh, her heart. Every ship that arrives, I run, I inquire, and ever, ever the same silence! And yet, shall I confess it to you? I have something in me which tells me he is not dead, and I shall see him again; it is a secret presentiment for which I cannot account: I fancy that if my son were dead, something would have snapped in my heart, and I should have ceased to exist long ago. That hope sustains me, in spite of myself; it gives me the strength to live."

"You are a mother in accordance with the gospel; I admire you."

"You are mistaken, father; I am only a poor creature, very simple and very unhappy; I have only one feeling in my heart, but it fills me entirely: love of my son. Oh, could I see him, were it only for a moment, I fancy I should die happy. At long intervals, a banker writes me to come to him, and he pays me money, sometimes small sums, at others large. When I ask him whence the money comes, he says that he does not know himself, and that a strange correspondent has requested him to pay it to me. Well, father, every time I receive money in this way, I fancy that it comes from my son, that he is thinking of me, and I am happy."

"Do not doubt that it is your son who sends you this money."

"Is it not?" she said, with a start of joy. "Well, I feel so persuaded of that, that I keep it; all the sums are at my house, intact, in the order as I received them. Often, when grief crushes me more than usual, when the weight that oppresses my heart seems to me too crushing, I look at them, I let them slip through my fingers, as I talk to them, and I fancy my son answers me; he bids me hope I shall see him again, and I feel hope return. Oh! You must think me very foolish to tell you all this, father: but of what can a mother speak, save of her son? Of what can she think but her son?"

Father Seraphin gazed on her with a tenderness mingled with respect. Such grandeur and simplicity in a woman of so ordinary a rank overcame him, and he felt tears running down his cheeks which he did not attempt to check.

"Oh, holy and noble creature!" he said to her; "Hope, hope; God watches over you."

"You believe so too, father? Oh, thanks for that. You have told me nothing, and yet I feel comforted through having seen you and let my heart overflow in your presence. It is because you are good, you have understood my sorrow, for you, too, have doubtless suffered."

"Alas; madam, each of us has a cross to bear in this world; happy is he whom his burden does not crush."

"Pardon my having troubled you with my sorrows," she said, as she prepared to leave; "I thank you for your kind words."

"I have nothing to pardon you; but permit me to ask you one more question."

"Do so, father."

"I am a missionary. For several years I have been in America, whose immense solitudes I have traversed in every direction. I have seen many things, met many persons during my travels. Who knows? Perhaps, without knowing it, I may have met your son, and may give the information you have been awaiting so long in vain."

The poor mother gave him a glance of indefinable meaning, and placed her hand on her heart to still its hurried beating.

"Madam, God directs all our actions. He decreed our meeting on this beach; the hope you have lost I may perhaps be destined to restore you. What is your son's name?"

At this moment Father Seraphin had a truly inspired air; his voice was commanding, and his eyes shone with a bright and fascinating fire.

"Valentine Guillois!" the poor woman said, as she fell in almost a fainting state on a log of wood left on the beach.

"Oh!" the priest exclaimed; "On your knees and thank Heaven! Console yourself, poor mother! Your son lives!"

She drew herself up as if moved by a spring, and fell on her knees sobbing, and held out her hands to the man who restored her son to her.

But it was too much for her: so strong against grief, could not resist joy: she fainted. Father Seraphin ran up to her and recalled her to life. We will not describe the ensuing scene, but a week later the missionary and the hunter's mother started for America. During the voyage Father Seraphin fully described to his companion what had happened to her son during his long absence, the reasons of his silence, and the sacred remembrance in which he had ever held her. The poor mother listened, radiant with happiness, to those stories, which she begged to hear over and over again, for she was never tired of hearing her son spoken of.

On reaching Galveston, the missionary, justly fearing for her the fatigues of a journey through the desert, wished to induce her to remain in that city till her son came to her, but at that proposition the mother shook her head.

"No," she said, resolutely, "I have not come here to stop in a town: I wish to spend the few days left me to live by his side; I have suffered enough to be avaricious of my happiness, and desire not to lose an atom. Let us go, father. Lead me to my child."

Before a will so firmly expressed, the priest found himself powerless; he did not recognise the right of insisting longer; he merely tried to spare his companion the fatigue of his journey as far as possible.

They, therefore, started for Galveston, proceeding by short stages to the Far West. On reaching the border of civilised countries, Father Seraphin took an escort of devoted Indians to protect his companion. They had been in the desert for six days, when suddenly heaven brought them face to face with Red Cedar, dying without help in the heart of the primeval forest.

CHAPTER XIII
RETURN TO LIFE

Charity is a virtue loudly preached in our age, but unfortunately practised by few. The story of the good Samaritan finds but scanty application in the Old World, and if we would discover charity exercised sacredly and simply, as the gospel teaches, we must obtain our examples from the deserts of the New World.

This is sad to say, even more sad to prove, but mankind is not to blame for it; the age alone must be held responsible for this egotism, which has for some years past been planted in the heart of man, and reigns there supreme. To two causes must be attributed the personalism and egotism which crown the actions of the great human family in Europe; the discovery of gold in California, Australia, and on Frazer River, and, above all, the Stock Exchange.

The Bourse is the scourge of the Old World; so soon as everybody fancied that he was enabled to enrich himself between today and tomorrow, no one thought any longer of his neighbour, who remained poor, save as being incapable of ameliorating his position. The result is, that the men who have the courage to leave the intoxicating maëlstrom that surrounds them, to despise those riches which flash around them, and go under the impulse of Christian Charity, the holiest and least rewarded of all the virtues, to bury themselves among savages, amid hordes most hostile to every good and honourable feeling, in the most deadly countries—such men, we say, who, impelled solely by a divine feeling, abandon all earthly enjoyments, are chosen vessels, and in every respect deserve well of humanity.

Their number is much larger than might be supposed at the first blush, and that is very logical; the passion for devotion must go side by side with the thirst for gold, in order that the eternal balance of good and evil which governs the world should remain in those equal proportions which are conditions of its vitality and prosperity.

Red Cedar's condition was serious; the moral commotion he underwent in recognising the man whom he had once attempted to assassinate, had brought on a frightful attack of delirium. The wretch, a prey to the most gnawing remorse, was tortured by the hideous phantoms of his victim, evoked by his diseased imagination, and which stalked round his bed like a legion of demons. The night he passed was terrible. Father Seraphin, Ellen, and Valentine's mother did not leave him for a second, watching over him anxiously, and frequently compelled to struggle with him in order to prevent him dashing his head against the trees, in the paroxysms of the crisis that tortured him.

Strange coincidence! The bandit had a similar wound in his shoulder to the one he had formerly dealt the missionary, which had compelled the latter to go and seek a cure in Europe, a voyage from which he had only returned a few days, when Providence permitted him to find the man who wished to assassinate him, lying almost dead at the foot of a tree.

Towards day the crisis grew calmer, and the squatter fell into a species of slumber, which deprived him of the faculties of feeling and perception. No one else slept during this long and mournful night, spent in the heart of the forest; and when Father Seraphin saw that Red Cedar was calmer, he ordered the Indians to prepare a litter to receive him. They were much disinclined to the task; they had known the squatter for a lengthened period, and these primitive men could not understand why, instead of killing him when chance threw him into his power, the missionary lavished his assistance on such a villain, who had committed so many crimes, and whose death would have been a blessing to the prairie. It required all the devotion they had vowed to Father Seraphin for them to consent to do, very unwillingly we allow, what he ordered them.

When the litter was, ready, dry leaves and grass were spread over it, and the squatter was laid on this couch in an almost complete state of insensibility. Before leaving the forest the missionary, who knew how necessary it was to rekindle the drooping faith of the redskins, for the sake of the patient, resolved to offer the holy sacrifice of mass. An altar was improvised on a grassy mound, covered with a rag of white cloth, and the mass was read, served by one of the Indians, who offered his services spontaneously.

Assuredly, in the large European cathedrals, beneath the splendid arches of stone, blackened by time, to the imposing murmur of the organ re-echoing through the aisles, the ceremonies of the faith are performed with greater pomp; but I doubt whether they be so with more magnificent simplicity, or are listened to with greater fervour than this mass, said in the heart of a forest, accompanied by the striking melodies of the desert, by the pale-browed priest, whose eyes glistened with a holy enthusiasm, and who prayed for his assassin groaning at his feet.

When mass was over, Father Seraphin gave a signal, four Indians raised the litter on their shoulders, and the party set out, Ellen being mounted on the horse of one of the bearers. The journey was long; the missionary had left Galveston to go in search of Valentine, but a hunter accustomed to traverse great distances, and whose life is made up of incessant excursions, is very difficult to discover in the desert; the missionary, therefore, decided on going to the winter village of the Comanches, where he was certain to obtain precise information about the man he wished to see.

But his meeting with Red Cedar prevented him from carrying out this plan; Unicorn and Valentine were too inveterate against the squatter for the missionary to hope that they would consent to resign their vengeance. The conjuncture was difficult; Red Cedar was a proscript in the fullest sense of the term; one of those outlaws, whose number is fortunately very limited, who have the whole human race as their foe, and to whom every country is hostile.

And yet this man must be saved; and after ripe reflection, Father Seraphin's resolution was formed. He proceeded, followed by his whole party, to the grotto where we have met him before, a grotto which often served as the Trail-hunter's abode, but where, in all probability, he would not be at this moment. Through an extraordinary chance, the missionary passed unseen within a pistol shot of the spot where Valentine and his friends were encamped.

At sunset they prepared for passing the night; Father Seraphin removed the bandage he had placed on Red Cedar's wounds, and dressed them: the latter allowed it to be done, not seeming to notice that any attention was being paid him; his prostration was extreme. The wounds were all healthy; that on the shoulder was the worst, but all foreboded a speedy recovery.

When supper was over, prayers said, and the Indians, wrapped in their blankets, were lying on the grass to rest from the fatigues of the day, the missionary, after assuring himself that Red Cedar was quietly sleeping, made a sign to the two women to come and sit by his side, near the fire lit to keep off wild beasts. Father Seraphin was slightly acquainted with Ellen; he remembered to have frequently met the girl, and even conversed with her in the forest, at the period when her father had so audaciously installed himself on Don Miguel Zarate's estates.

Ellen's character had pleased him; he had found in her such simplicity of heart and innate honour, that he frequently asked himself how so charming a creature could be the daughter of so hardened a villain as Red Cedar: this seemed to him the more incomprehensible, because the girl must have needed a powerful character to resist the influence of the evil examples she constantly had before her. Hence he had taken a lively interest in her, and urged her to persevere in her good sentiments. He had let her see that one day God would reward her by removing her from the perverse medium in which fate had cast her, to restore her to that great human family of which she was ignorant.

When the two women were seated at his side, the missionary gave them, in his gentle, sympathising way, a paternal admonition to support with patience and resignation the tribulations Heaven sent on them; then he begged Ellen to tell him in detail all that had occurred in the prairie since his departure for France. The girl's narrative was long and sad, and frequently interrupted by tears which she could not repress. Valentine's mother shuddered on hearing things so extraordinary to her described; heavy tears ran down her wrinkled cheek, and she crossed herself, muttering compassionately—

"Poor child! What a horrible life."

For, in truth Ellen was describing, her life; she had witnessed and suffered from all these terrors, all these atrocities, whose sinister and bloody images she unrolled before her hearers. When the story was ended she buried her face in her hands and wept silently, crushed by the revival of such poignant sorrows and the re-opening of still bleeding wounds. The missionary gave her a long look, stamped with gentle pity. He took her hand, pressed it, and bending over her, said with an accent of kindness which went straight to her heart—

"Weep, poor girl, for you have suffered terribly; weep, but be strong; God, who tries you, doubtless reserves for you other blows more terrible than those which have fallen on you; do not try to repulse the cup which is brought to your lips; the more you suffer in this life, the more happy and glorified you will be in another. If God chastise you, a poor stainless lamb, it is because He loves you; happy those whom He thus chastises! Derive your strength from prayer, for that elevates the soul, and renders it better; do not yield to despair, for that is a suggestion of the demon who renders man rebellious to the teaching of Providence. Think of your divine Master, remember all He suffered for us; thus you will recognise how little your sorrows are when compared with His, and you will hope; for Providence is not blind; when it weighs heavily on a creature, it is preparing to reward her a hundredfold for past sufferings."

"Alas, father," Ellen replied, sorrowfully, "I am only a miserable child, without strength or courage; the burden laid on me is very heavy; still, if it be the will of the Lord that it should be so, may His holy name be blessed! I will try to stifle the feelings of revolt which are at times a wound in my heart, and struggle without complaining against the fate that overwhelms me."

"Good, my sister, good," the priest said; "the great God, who searches all hearts, will have pity on you."

He then made her rise, and led her a short distance to a spot where a bed of dry leaves had been prepared by his care.

"Try and sleep, my child," he said; "fatigue is crushing you; a few hours' rest is indispensable for you."

"I will strive to obey you, father."

"May the angels watch over your slumbers, my child," the priest replied; "and may the Almighty bless you, as I do."

Then he returned slowly and thoughtfully to Valentine's mother. There was a long silence, during which the missionary reflected deeply; at length he said—

"Madam, you have heard this poor girl's narrative; her father was wounded when fighting with your son. Valentine, I feel assured, is not far from us; still, the man we have saved claims all our care, and we must watch that he does not fall into the hands of his enemies, I therefore ask you to delay awhile in rejoining your son, for Red Cedar must be placed in safety. Above all, I implore you to maintain the deepest silence as to the events of which you have been and will be a witness. Forgive me, but I implore you to delay the time of your meeting."

"Father," she said, spontaneously, "for ten years, without despairing for a day or a moment, I have been patiently awaiting the hour which will rejoin me to my beloved son. Now that I am certain of seeing him again, that no doubt as to his existence dwells in my heart, I can wait a few days longer. I should be ungrateful to God and to you, who have done so much for me, if I insisted on the contrary course. Act as your charity and your devotion impel you to do; fulfil your duty without troubling yourself about me; God has willed it that we should come across this man. The ways of Providence are often incomprehensible; obey it by saving him, however unworthy he may be of pardon."

"I expected your answer: still, I am pleased to see that you confirm me in what I intend to do."

The next morning, at daybreak, they started again, after saying prayers together, according to the custom established by the missionary. Red Cedar was still in the same state of prostration, and the two following days passed without any incident worthy of recording. At the evening of the third day they entered the defile, in the centre of which, on one of the mountain sides facing it; the cavern was. Red Cedar was carried up to it cautiously, and placed in one of the distant compartments, far from all external sounds, and so as to be concealed from the sight of any strangers whom accident might lead to the cavern while he was in it.

It was with a feeling of indescribable joy that Valentine's mother entered the grotto which served as an abode to that son whom she had been so long afraid she should never see again, and her emotion was extreme on finding a few valueless articles used by Valentine. The worthy woman, so truly a mother, shut herself up alone in the compartment which the hunter had made his sleeping room, and there, face to face with her reminiscences; she remained for several hours absorbed in herself.

The missionary pointed to each the room they would occupy; he left his comrades to their repose, and sat down by the side of the wounded man, where Ellen already was installed as nurse.

"Why do you not sleep, my child?" he asked her.

Ellen pointed to the sufferer with a gesture full of nobility.

"Let me watch over him," she said; "he is my father."

The missionary smiled softly and withdrew. At daybreak he returned. Red Cedar, on hearing him come, gave vent to a sigh, and rose with difficulty on his bed.

"How are you, brother?" the missionary asked, in his gentle voice.

A febrile flush covered the bandit's face, a cold perspiration beaded on his temples, his eyes flashed, and he said in a low voice, broken by the extreme emotion that oppressed him —

"Father, I am a wretch unworthy of your pity."

"My son," the priest answered gently, "you are a poor straying creature, on whom I doubt not God will have pity, if your repentance be sincere."

Red Cedar let his eyes sink; a convulsive movement agitated his limbs.

"Father," he muttered, "would you teach me how to make the sign of the cross?"

At this strange request in the mouth of such a man, Father Seraphin clasped his hands fervently, and raised his eyes to Heaven with an expression of sublime gratitude. Was the evil angel defeated? Or was it a farce played by this perverse man to deceive his saviour, and by these means escape the numerous enemies that sought his death?

Alas! Man is so extraordinary a composite of good and evil, that perhaps at this moment, and in spite of himself, Red Cedar was acting in good faith.

CHAPTER XIV
AN OLD ACQUAINTANCE OF THE READER

After the fight, when Black Cat's Apaches had retired on one side, and Unicorn's Comanches on the other, each detachment proceeding in the direction of the village, and the hunters were alone on the prairie, Valentine perceived White Gazelle leaning pensively against a tree, and absently holding the bridle of her horse, which was nibbling the grass. The hunter understood that he and his comrades owed a reparation to this girl, whose incomprehensible devotion had been so useful to them during the moving incidents of the tragedy which had just ended. He therefore went up to her, and bowing courteously, said in a gentle voice—

"Why remain thus aloof? Your place is by our side; hobble your horse with ours, and come to our fireside."

White Gazelle blushed with pleasure at Valentine's words, but after a moment's reflection, she shook her head, and gave him a sorrowful look, as she said:

"Thanks, caballero, for the offer you deign to make me, but I cannot accept it; if you and your friends are generous enough to forget all that there was reprehensible in my conduct towards you, my memory is less complaisant; I must, I will requite by other services more effectual than those I have rendered you today, the faults I have committed."

"Madam," the hunter replied, "the feelings you express do you only more harm in our eyes; hence do not refuse our invitation. As you know, we have no right to be very strict on the prairie; it is rare to meet persons who repair so nobly as you have done any error they may commit."

"Do not press me, caballero, for my resolve is unchangeable," she said with an effort, as she looked in the direction of Don Pablo. "I must depart, leave you at once, so permit me to do so."

Valentine bowed.

"Your wish is to me an order," he said; "you are free; I only desired to express my gratitude to you."

"Alas! We have done nothing as yet, since our most cruel enemy, Red Cedar, has escaped."

"What?" the hunter asked in astonishment; "is Red Cedar your enemy?"

"A mortal one," she said, with an expression of terrible hatred. "Oh! I can understand that you, who have hitherto seen me aid him in his designs, cannot conceive such a change. Listen: at the period when I tried to serve that villain, I only believed him to be one of the bandits so common in the Far West."

"While now?"

"Now," she went on, "I know something I was ignorant of then, and have a terrible account to settle with him."

"Far from me be any wish to pry into your secrets; still, permit me to make one observation."

"Pray do so."

"Red Cedar is no common enemy—one of those men who can be easily overcome. You know that as well as I do, I think?"

"Yes, what then?"

"Would you hope to succeed in what men like myself and my friends, and aided by numerous warriors, could not achieve?"

White Gazelle smiled.

"Perhaps so," she said; "I too have allies, and I will tell you who they are, if you wish to know, caballero."

"Pray tell me, for really your calmness and confidence startle me."

"Thanks, caballero, for the interest you feel for me; the first ally on whom I build is yourself."

"That is true," the hunter said with a bow; "if my feelings toward you did not promote the alliance, my duty and self-interest would command it. And can you tell me the name of the other?"

"Certainly, the more so as you know him: the other is Bloodson."

Valentine gave a start of surprise, which he immediately checked.

"Pardon me," he said politely; "but you really have the privilege of surprising me inordinately."

"How so, caballero?"

"Because I fancied that Bloodson was one of your most bitter enemies."

"He was so," she said, with a smile.

"And now?"

"Now, he is my dearest friend."

"This goes beyond me. And when was this extraordinary change effected?"

"Since the day," the girl cleverly replied, "when Red Cedar, instead of being my friend, suddenly became my enemy."

Valentine let his arms fall, like a man who gives up in despair attempting to solve a riddle.

"I do not understand you," he said.

"You will soon do so," she answered.

She bounded into her saddle, and leaning over to Valentine said—

"Good bye, caballero; I am going to join Bloodson; we shall meet again soon."

She dug her spurs into her horse's flanks, waved her hand once again, and soon disappeared in a cloud of dust.

Valentine thoughtfully rejoined his friends.

"Well?" Don Miguel said.

"Well!" he replied, "that woman is the most extraordinary creature I ever met."

On getting out of sight of the hunters, White Gazelle checked her horse, and let it assume a pace better suited for those precautions every traveller must take on the prairie. The girl was happy at this moment; she had succeeded not only in saving the man she loved from a terrible danger, but had also restored her character in Valentine's sight. Red Cedar, it was true, had escaped; but this time the lesson had been rude, and the bandit, everywhere tracked like a wild beast, must speedily fall into the hands of those who had an interest in killing him.

She rode along carelessly, admiring the calmness of the prairie and the play of the sunshine on the foliage. Never had the desert appeared to her so glorious—never had greater tranquillity reigned in her mind. The sun, now declining, exaggerated the shadow thrown by the tall trees; the birds, hidden beneath the dense verdure, were singing their evening hymn to the Almighty; when she fancied she saw a man half reclining on the slope of one of those numberless ditches dug by the heavy winter rain. This man, by whose side a horse was standing, was apparently absorbed in an occupation which the girl could not understand, but which puzzled her extremely. Although she rode up quickly, the individual did not put himself out of the way, but calmly continued his incomprehensible task.

At length she was opposite him, and could not restrain a cry of astonishment as she stopped to look at him. The man was playing alone at *monte* (the Mexican lansquenet) with a pack of greasy cards. This appeared to her so extraordinary that she burst into a loud laugh, and at the sound the man raised his head.

"Aha!" he said, not appearing at all surprised, "I felt certain someone would arrive; that is infallible in this blessed land."

"Nonsense," the girl said, with a laugh; "do you believe it?"

"*Canarios!* I am sure of it," the other answered; "and you are a proof of it, since here you are."

"Explain yourself, my master, I beg, for I confess that I do not understand you the least in the world."

"I thought so," the stranger said, with a toss of his head, "but for all that, I stick to my assertion."

"Very well; but be good enough to explain yourself more clearly."

"Nothing is easier, señor caballero. I come from Jalapa, a town you must know."

"Yes, through the medicinal productions that owe their name to it."

"Very good," the other said, with a laugh; "but that does not prevent Jalapa being a very nice town."

"On the contrary; but go on."

"I will. You will be aware then that we have a proverb at Jalapa."

"May be so; in fact, there is nothing surprising about the fact."

"True again; but you do not know the proverb, eh?"

"No, I am waiting for you to quote it."

"Here it is; 'If you wish for your company, deal the cards.'"

"I do not understand."

"Why, nothing is easier, as you shall see."

"I wish for nothing better," the girl said, who was extraordinary amused by this conversation.

The stranger rose, placed the cards in his pocket with the respect every professional gambler shews to this operation, and, carelessly leaning on the neck of the girl's horse, he said:

"Owing to reasons too long to narrate, I find myself alone, lost in this immense prairie which I do not know, I an honest inhabitant of towns, not at all conversant with the manners and habits of the desert, and consequently exposed to die of hunger."

"Pardon me for interrupting you; I would merely observe that as we are some three hundred miles from the nearest town, you, the civilised man, must have been wandering about the desert for a considerable length of time."

"That is true: what you say could not be more correct, comrade, but that results from what I mentioned just now, and which would take too long to tell you."

"Very good; go on."

"Well, finding myself lost, I remembered the proverb of my country, and taking the cards from my *alforjas*, though I was alone, I began playing, feeling certain that an adversary would soon arrive, not to take a hand, but to get me out of my trouble."

White Gazelle suddenly reassumed her seriousness, and drew herself up in her saddle.

"You have won the game," she said; "for, as you see, Don Andrés Garote, I have come."

On hearing his name pronounced, the ranchero, for it was really our old acquaintance, suddenly raised his head, and looked the speaker in the face.

"Who are you, then," he said, "who know me so well, and yet I do not remember ever having met you?"

"Come, come," the girl said with a laugh, "your memory is short, master: what, do you not remember White Gazelle?"

At this name the ranchero started back.

"Oh, I am a fool: it is true; but I was so far from supposing—pardon me, señorita."

"How is it," White Gazelle interrupted him, "that you have thus deserted Red Cedar?"

"Caramba!" the ranchero exclaimed; "say that Red Cedar has deserted me; but it is not that which troubles me; I have an old grudge against another of my comrades."

"Ah?"

"Yes, and I should like to avenge myself, the more so, because I believe that I have the means in my hands at this moment."

"And who is that friend?"

"You know him as well as I do, señorita?"

"That is possible; but, unless his name be a secret—"

"Oh, no," the ranchero quickly interrupted her, "the man I mean is Fray Ambrosio."

The girl, at this name, began to take a great interest in the conversation.

"Fray Ambrosio!" she said, "What charge have you to bring against that worthy man?"

The ranchero looked the girl in the face to see if she were speaking seriously; but White Gazelle's face was cold and stern; he tossed his head.

"It is an account between him and me," he said, "which heaven will decide."

"Very good; I ask for no explanation, but, as your affairs interest me very slightly, and I have important matters of my own to attend to, you will permit me to retire."

"Why so?" the ranchero asked quickly; "we are comfortable together, then why should we separate?"

"Because, in all probability, we are not going the same road."

"Who knows, Niña, whether we are not destined to travel in company since I have met you?"

"I am not of that opinion. I am about to join a man whom I fancy you would not at all like to meet face to face."

"I don't know, Niña," the ranchero answered, with considerable animation; "I want to revenge myself on that accursed monk called Fray Ambrosio; I am too weak to do so by myself, or, to speak more correctly, too great a coward."

"Very good," the girl exclaimed, with a smile; "then how will you manage that your vengeance does not slip from you?"

"Oh, very simply; I know a man in the desert who detests him mortally, and would give a great deal to have sufficient proofs against him, for, unfortunately, that man has the failing of being honest."

"Indeed."

"Yes, what would you have? No man is perfect."

"And who is this man?"

"Oh, you never heard of him, Niña."

"How do you know? At any rate you can tell me his name."

"As you please; he is called Bloodson."

"Bloodson?" she exclaimed, with a start of surprise.

"Yes—do you know him?"

"Slightly; but go on."

"That is all; I am looking for this man."

"And you have, you say, in your possession the means of destroying Fray Ambrosio?"

"I believe so."

"What makes you suppose it?"

The ranchero shrugged his shoulders significantly; White Gazelle gave him one of those profound glances which read the heart.

"Listen," she said to him, as she laid her hand on his shoulder; "I can help you to find the man you seek."

"Bloodson?"

"Yes."

"Are you speaking seriously?" the gambusino asked, with a start of surprise.

"I could not be more serious; still, I must be sure that your statement is true."

Andrés Garote looked at her.

"Do you also owe Fray Ambrosio a grudge?" he asked her.

"That does not concern you," she answered; "we are not talking of myself, but of you. Have you these proofs? Yes, or no."

"I have them."

"Truly?"

"On my honour."

"Follow me, then, and within two hours you shall see Bloodson."

The ranchero quivered, and a smile of joy lit up his bronzed countenance as he leaped on his horse.

"Let us be off," he said.

In the meanwhile, day had surrendered to night, the sun had long been set, and an immense number of stars studded the heavenly vault; the travellers rode on silently side by side.

"Shall we soon arrive?" Andrés Garote asked.

White Gazelle stretched out her arm in the direction they were following, and pointed at a light flashing a short distance off through the trees.

"There it is," she said.

CHAPTER XV
CONVALESCENCE

Red Cedar recovered but slowly in spite of the constant attention shown him by Father Seraphin, Ellen, and the hunter's mother. The moral shock the bandit had received on finding himself face to face with the missionary had been too powerful not to have a serious effect on his constitution. Still, the squatter had not relapsed since the day when, on returning to life, he had humbly bowed before the man of God. Whether it was true repentance, or a part he played, he had persevered on this path, to the edification of the missionary and the two women, who never ceased to thank Heaven from their hearts for this change.

So soon as he could rise and take a few steps in the cavern, Father Seraphin, who constantly feared Valentine's arrival, asked him what his intentions were for the future, and what mode of life he proposed adopting.

"Father," the squatter answered, "henceforth I belong to you: whatever you counsel me, I will do; still, I would remind you that I am a species of savage, whose whole life has been spent in the desert. Of what use should I be in a town among people whose habits or characters I should not understand?"

"That is true," the priest said; "and then, without resources as you are, old and ignorant of any other labour than that of a wood ranger, you would only lead a miserable existence."

"That would prove no obstacle, father, were it an expiation for me; but I have too deeply offended ever to return among them; I must live and die in the desert, striving to requite, by an old age exempt from blame, the faults and crimes of a youth which I hold in horror."

"I approve your design, for it is good; grant me a few days for reflection, and I will find you the means to live as you propose."

The conversation broke off here, and a month elapsed ere the missionary made any further allusion to it. The squatter had always shown Ellen a certain coarse and rough friendship, perfectly harmonising with the coarseness and brutality of his character; but since he had been able to appreciate the girl's utter devotion, and the self-denial she had displayed for his sake, a species of revolution had taken place in him; a new feeling was awakened in his heart, and he began loving this charming creature with all the strength of his soul.

This brutal man suddenly grew softer at the sight of the girl; a flash of joy shot from his savage eyes, and his mouth, habituated to curses, opened gladly to utter gentle words. Frequently, when seated on the mounted slope, near the cavern, he talked with her for hours, taking an infinite delight in hearing the melodious sound of that voice whose charms he had hitherto been ignorant of.

Ellen, hiding her sorrows, feigned a delight which was far from her mind, not to sadden the man she regarded as her father, and who seemed so happy at seeing her by his side. Certainly, if anyone at this moment had an ascendency over the old pirate's mind, and could bring him back to the right path, it was Ellen. She knew it, and used the power she had acquired cleverly, to try and convert this man, who had only been a species of evil genius to humanity.

One morning, when Red Cedar, almost entirely cured of his wounds, was taking his accustomed walk, leaning on Ellen's arm, Father Seraphin, who had been absent for two days, stood before him.

"Ah, it is you, father," the squatter said on seeing him; "I was alarmed at your absence, and am glad to see you back."

"How are you?" the missionary asked.

"I should be quite well if I had entirely recovered my strength, but that will soon return."

"All the better; for if my absence was long, you were to some extent the cause of it."

"How so?" the squatter asked, curiously.

"You remember you expressed a desire some time back to live in the prairie?"

"I did."

"It appears to me very prudent on your part, and will enable you to escape the pursuit of your enemies."

"Believe me, father," Red Cedar said, gravely, "that I have no desire to escape those I have offended. If my death could recal the crimes of which I have been guilty, I would not hesitate to sacrifice my life to public justice."

"I am happy, my friend, to find you imbued with these good sentiments; but I believe that God, who in no case desires the death of a sinner, will be more satisfied to see you repair, by an exemplary life, as far as in your power, all the evil you have done."

"I belong to you, father; whatever you advise me will be an order to me, and I will obey it gladly. Since Providence has permitted me to meet you, I have understood the enormity of my crimes. Alas! I am not alone responsible for them: never having had any but evil examples before me, I did not know the difference between good and evil. I believed that all men were wicked, and only acted as I did because I considered I was legitimately defending myself."

"Now that your ear is open to the truth, your mind is beginning to understand the sublime precepts of the gospel. Your road is ready traced; henceforth you will only have to persevere in the path on which you have so freely entered."

"Alas!" the squatter muttered, with a sigh, "I am a creature so unworthy of pardon, that I fear the Almighty will not take pity on me."

"Those words are an insult to Deity," the priest said, severely; "however culpable a sinner may be, he must never despair of the divine clemency; does not the gospel say, there is more joy in heaven over one sinner that repenteth, than over ten just men who have persevered?"

"Forgive me, father."

"Come," the missionary said, changing his tone, "let us return to the matter which brings me to you. I have had built for you, a few leagues from here, in a delicious situation, a jacal, in which you can live, with your daughter."

"How kind you are, father," the squatter said, warmly; "how much gratitude I owe you."

"Do not speak of that; I shall be sufficiently recompensed if I see you persevere in your repentance."

"Oh, father, believe that I detest and hold in horror my past life."

"I trust that it may ever be so. This jacal, to which I will take you so soon as you please, is situated in a position which renders it almost impossible to discover. I have supplied it with the articles requisite for your life; you will find there food to last several days, arms and gunpowder to defend you, if attacked by wild beasts, and to go hunting with; I have added nets, beaver traps—in a word, everything required by a hunter and trapper."

"Oh, how kind you are, father," Ellen said with tears of joy in her eyes.

"Nonsense, say nothing about that," the missionary remarked, gaily; "I have only done my duty. As a further security, and to avoid any possible indiscretion, I have not told the secret of your retreat to any one: the jacal was built by my own hands, without the assistance of a stranger. You can, therefore, feel certain that no one will trouble you in the hermitage."

"And when can I go to it, father?"

"Whenever you please; all is ready."

"Ah, if I did not fear appearing ungrateful, I would say I will go at once."

"Do you think you are strong enough to undertake a journey of fifteen leagues?"

"I feel extraordinarily strong at this moment, father."

"Come, then; for had you not made the proposition, I intended to do so."

"In that case, father, all is for the best; and you are not vexed to see me so anxious to leave you, father."

"Not at all, be assured."

While talking thus, the three persons had descended the mountainside, and reached the ravine, where horses were awaiting them, held by an Indian.

"In the desert," the missionary said, "it is almost impossible to do without horses, owing to the great distance one has to go; you will therefore oblige me by keeping these."

"It is too much, father, you really overwhelm me with kindness."

Father Seraphin shook his head.

"Understand me, Red Cedar," he said; "in all I do for you there is far more calculation than you suppose."

"Oh!" Red Cedar said.

"Calculation in a good action!" Ellen exclaimed, incredulously; "you must be jesting, father."

"No, my child, I speak seriously, and you will understand; I have tried to regulate your father's life so well, place him so thoroughly in a condition to become a brave and honest hunter, that it will be impossible for him to find the slightest pretext for returning to his old errors, and all the fault will attach to him if he does not persevere in the resolution he has formed of amendment."

"That is true," Red Cedar answered; "well, father, I thank you for this calculation, which makes me the happiest of men, and proves to me that you have confidence in me."

"Come, come, to horse!"

They started.

Red Cedar inhaled the air deliciously; he felt born again, he was once more free. The missionary examined him curiously, analysing the feelings which the squatter experienced, and trying to form some opinion of the future from what he saw. Red Cedar understood instinctively that he was watched by his comrade; hence, to deceive him as to his feelings, he burst out into a loud expression of his gratitude, part of which was certainly true, but which was too noisy not to be exaggerated. The missionary pretended to be taken in by this device, and talked pleasantly throughout the ride.

About six hours after leaving the cave, they reached the jacal. It was a pretty little hut of interlaced reeds, divided into several rooms, with a corral behind for the horses. Nothing was wanting; hidden in the bottom of a valley, very difficult to approach, it stood on the bank of a small stream that flowed into the Gila. In a word, the position of this wild abode was delightful, and nothing was more easy than to be perfectly happy in it.

When the travellers had dismounted, and led their horses into this corral, Father Seraphin went over the jacal with his two *protégés*. All was as he had stated; and if there was not much to increase comfort, at any rate everything strictly necessary had been provided. Ellen was delighted, and her father pretended, perhaps, to be more so than he really was. After spending an hour with them Father Seraphin took leave of the squatter and his daughter.

"Will you leave us, already, father?" Ellen said.

"I must, my child; you know that my time is not my own," he answered, as he leaped on his horse, which the squatter brought him.

"But I hope," Red Cedar said, "that your absence will not be long, and that you will remember this jacal, where two persons live who owe their all to you."

"I wish to leave you at liberty. If I visited you too frequently, you might see in that a species of inquisition, and that impression would annoy you; still I will come, do not doubt it."

"You can never come too often, father," they both said, as they kissed his hands.

"Farewell, be happy," the missionary said, tenderly; "you know where to find me, if you have need of consolation or help. Come to me, and I shall be ever ready to help you to the extent of my ability: little though I can do, God, I feel convinced, will bless my efforts. Farewell."

After uttering these words, the missionary set spurs to his horse, and trotted away.

Red Cedar and his daughter looked after him so long as they could see him, and when he disappeared in the chaparral, on the other side of the stream, they gave vent to a sigh, and entered the jacal.

"Worthy and holy man!" the squatter muttered, as he fell into a butaca. "Oh! I will not crush the hopes he has built on my conversion!"

At this moment Red Cedar was not playing a farce.

CHAPTER XVI
AN ACCOMPLICE

Red Cedar accustomed himself more easily than his daughter thought possible, to the life prepared for him. After all, no change had taken place in his existence; with the exception of the mode of procedure, it was still the same labour, that is to say, a desert life in all its splendid liberty; hunting and fishing, while Ellen remained at home to attend to household duties. At night, however, before retiring to rest, the girl read her father a chapter from a Bible Father Seraphin had given her. The squatter, with his elbow on the table, and a pipe in his mouth, listened to her with an attention that surprised himself, and which each day only increased.

It was an exquisite picture presented in this obscure nook of the great American desert, amid this grand scenery, in this wretched hut, which the slightest breath of wind caused to tremble, by this athletic old man, with his energetic and stern features, listening to this palefaced and delicate girl, whose fine features and shadowy outline formed so strong a contrast with those of her hearer.

It was the same life every day; the squatter was happy, or, at least, fancied himself so; like all men whose life has been but one long drama, and who are made for action, recollections held but little place in him; he forgot, and fancied himself forgotten.

Ellen suffered, for she was unhappy; this existence, with no outlet and no future, was full of disenchantment for her, as it condemned her to renounce for ever that supreme blessing of every human creature, hope. Still, through fear of afflicting her father, she carefully shut up in her heart her sorrow, and only displayed a smiling face in his presence. Red Cedar yielded more and more to the charms of a life which was pleasant to him. If, at times, the recollection of his sons troubled the repose in which he lived, he looked at his daughter, and the sight of the angel he possessed, and who had devoted herself to his happiness, drove any other thoughts far away.

In the meanwhile, Father Seraphin visited the tenants of the jacal several times; and if satisfied with the resignation with which the squatter accepted his new position, the dull sorrow that undermined the maiden had not escaped his clear-sighted glance. His experience of the world told him that a girl of Ellen's age could not thus spend her fairest years in solitude, without contact with society. Unfortunately, a remedy was difficult, if not impossible, to find; the good missionary did not deceive himself on this point, and understood that all the consolations he lavished on the maiden, were thrown away, and that nothing could effectually combat the listlessness into which she had fallen.

As always happens in such cases, Red Cedar did not in the slightest degree suspect his daughter's grief; she was gentle, affectionate, attentive to him; he profited by it all, finding himself perfectly happy, and in his egotism, not seeing further. The days slipped away, each resembling the other; in the meanwhile, the winter came on, game became rarer, and Red Cedar's absences from home grew longer. Around the tops of the mountains were collected the grayish clouds, which daily descended lower, and would eventually burst over the prairie in the shape of rain and snow.

Winter is a terrible season in the Far West: all scourges combine to assail the unhappy man whom his evil destiny has cast into these disinherited countries without the means to brave their frightful climate, and, victim to his want of foresight, he presently dies of hunger and misery, after enduring inconceivable tortures. Red Cedar knew the Far West too long and too thoroughly not to perceive the arrival of this season with a species of terror; hence he sought, by all possible means, to procure the necessary provisions and indispensable furs.

Rising at daybreak, he galloped over the prairie, exploring it in every direction, and not returning home till night compelled him to give up the chase. But, as we have said, game was becoming more and more rare, and consequently his journeys longer.

One morning Red Cedar rose earlier than usual, left the jacal noiselessly for fear of waking his daughter, saddled his horse, and started at a gallop. He had found, on the previous evening, the trail of a magnificent black bear, which he had followed to within a short distance of the cave to which it retired, and he intended to attack it in its lair. To do that, he must make haste, for the bear is not like other wild beasts: it seeks its food during the day, and generally leaves its abode at an early hour. The squatter, perfectly acquainted with the animal's habits, had therefore taken up the trail as soon as he could.

The sun had not yet risen; the sky of a dark blue, was only just beginning to assume on the extreme verge of the horizon those opaline tints which presently turn into pink, and are the precursors of sunrise. The day promised to be splendid: a light breeze slightly bowed the leafy summits of the trees, and scarce wrinkled the little stream whose bank the squatter was following. A light fog rose from the ground, impregnated with those sharp odours which expand the chest so gloriously. The birds woke one after the other beneath the leaves, and softly produced the melodious concert they perform each morning to salute the re-awakening of nature. By degrees the darkness was effaced, the sun rose brilliantly on the horizon, and the day broke splendidly.

Red Cedar, on reaching the entrance of a narrow gorge, at the end of which was the bear's den, in the midst of a chaos of rocks, stopped a few minutes to regain breath, and make his final preparations. He dismounted, hobbled his horse, and gave it its forage, then, after assuring himself that his knife played easily in the sheath, and his rifle was in good order, he entered the defile.

The squatter walked in with outstretched neck, and eye and ear on the watch, when suddenly a hand was laid on his shoulder, and a hoarse laugh smote his ear. He turned with surprise, but this surprise was converted into terror at the sight of the man who, standing before him with arms folded on his chest, was regarding him with a look of mockery.

"Fray Ambrosio!" he exclaimed, as he fell back a step.

"Halloh, gossip," the latter said; "on my soul, you must be hard of hearing: I called you a dozen times, and you did not deign to answer me. *Satanas!* I was obliged to touch you before you would see that somebody wanted you."

"What is your business with me?" the squatter asked in an icy tone.

"What I want, gossip? That's a strange question: don't you know it as well as I do?"

"I do not understand you," Red Cedar said, still perfectly calm; "so explain yourself, if you please."

"I will do so, my master," the monk answered, with a mocking smile.

"But make haste, for I warn you that I am in a hurry."

"Can it be possible! Well, I have plenty of time, so you must find some to listen to me."

The squatter gave a passionate start, which he, however, immediately checked.

"Yes, it is so," the monk said coolly; "I have been looking for you a long time."

"Come, a truce to talking! Here I am, explain yourself in two words. I say again, I am in a hurry."

"And I repeat that I do not care if you are. Oh! You may frown, gossip, but you must listen to me."

Red Cedar stamped his foot angrily, taking one step to the monk, he laid his hand on his shoulder, and looked fiercely in his face.

"Why, master," he said in a short, harsh voice, "I fancy, on my side, that we are changing parts, and that you treat me very curtly; take care, I am not patient, as you know, and if you do not mind, my patience might soon fail me."

"That is possible," the monk answered impudently; "but if we have changed our parts, whose fault is it, pray, mine or yours? Your sons are right in saying that you have turned monk, and are no longer fit for anything."

"Villain!" the squatter shouted, and raising his hand—

"That will do! Insults now! Don't be bashful: I like you better that way, at least I recognise you. Hum! what a change! I must confess that those French missionaries are real sorcerers: what a misfortune that since the independence the inquisition no longer exists!"

Red Cedar looked at the monk, who fixed on him his fierce eye with a diabolical expression; the squatter was suffering from one of those bursts of cold passion, which are the more terrible, because they are concentrated. He felt an extraordinary itching to crush the scoundrel who was mocking him, and made impotent efforts to repress the anger which was beginning to get the mastery of him. The monk was not so much at his ease as he pretended to be. He saw the squatter's frown grow deeper, his face become livid; all this foreboded a storm which he was not anxious to see burst to his presence.

"Come," he said, in a softer key, "why should old friends quarrel? *Con mil demonios*—I am only here with a good intent, and to do you a service."

The squatter laughed contemptuously.

"You do not believe me," the monk continued, with an air of beatitude; "that does not surprise me, it is always so. Good intentions are misunderstood, and a man believes his enemies in preference to his friends."

"A truce to your nonsense," the squatter said, impatiently; "I have listened to you too long already; let me pass, and you can go to the devil."

"Thanks for the proposition you make me," the monk said with a laugh; "but if you have no objection, I will not take advantage of it, at least for the present. But, jesting apart, there are two persons close by anxious to see you, and whom I am sure you will be delighted to meet."

"Whom do you mean? I suppose they are rogues of your own sort."

"Probably," the monk said; "however you shall judge for yourself, gossip."

And, not waiting for the squatter's answer, the monk imitated thrice the hiss of the coral snake. At the third time a slight movement took place in the shrubs a short distance off, and two men leaped into the defile. The squatter uttered a cry of surprise, almost of terror, on seeing them: he had recognised his two sons, Nathan and Sutter. The young men walked up quickly to their father, whom they saluted with a respect mingled with irony, which did not escape his notice.

"Ah, there you are, father," Sutter, said, roughly, as he banged the butt of his rifle on the ground, and rested his hands on the muzzle; "a man has a hard run before he can catch you up."

"It seems that since our separation father has turned Quaker; his new religion, probably, orders him not to frequent such bad company as ours."

"Silence, you villains!" the squatter shouted, stamping his foot; "I do what I please, and no one that I know of has a right to interfere."

"You are mistaken, father," Sutter, said drily; "I, for instance, consider your conduct unworthy of a man."

"Not mentioning," the monk supported him, "that you place your confederates in a fix, which is not right."

"That is not the question," Nathan said; "if father likes to turn Puritan, that is his business, and I will not find, fault with him; but there is a time for everything. To my mind, when a man is surrounded by enemies and tracked like a wild beast, he ought not to put on a sheepskin, and pretend to be harmless."

"What do you mean?" the squatter asked impatiently; "Explain yourself, once for all, and let us make an end of this."

"I will do so," Nathan went on; "while you are sleeping in a deceitful security, your enemies are watching and constantly weaving the web in which they have hopes of enfolding you shortly. Do you fancy that we have not known your retreat for a long time? Who can hope to escape discovery in the desert? We did not wish, however, to disturb your repose till the moment arrived for doing so, and that is why you did not see us before today."

"Yes," the monk remarked; "but at present time presses: while you trust to the fine words of the French missionary, who cured you and lulls you to sleep, in order always to keep you under his thumb, your enemies are silently preparing to attack you, and finish with you once for all."

The squatter gave a start of amazement.

"Why, that man saved my life," he said.

The three men burst into a laugh.

"What use is experience?" the monk said, turning to the young men with a significant shrug of his shoulders. "Here is your father, a man whose whole life has been spent in the desert, who forgets at once its most sacred law, eye for eye, tooth for tooth, and will not understand that this man, who, he says, saved his life, merely cured him to torture him at a later date, and have the pleasure of depriving him of that life when he is in rude health, instead of the miserable amount left him when they met."

"Oh, no," the squatter shouted, "you lie! That is impossible!"

"That is impossible!" the monk replied, with pity; "Oh, how blind men are! Come, reflect, gossip; had not this priest an insult to avenge?"

"It is true," Red Cedar muttered with a sigh; "but he forgave me."

"Forgave you! Do you ever forgive anybody? Nonsense, you are mad, gossip! I see there is nothing to be got out of you. Do what you like—we leave you."

"Yes," said the squatter, "leave me; there is nothing I wish more."

The monk and his comrades went away a few paces, but Fray Ambrosio suddenly returned. Red Cedar was still standing at the same spot with hanging head and frowning brow. The monk saw the squatter was shaken, and the moment had arrived to deal the great blow.

"Gossip," he said, "a parting word, or, if you prefer, a last piece of advice."

"What is there now?" Red Cedar said, nervously.

"Watch over Ellen!"

"What!" the squatter yelled, as he bounded like a panther and seized Fray Ambrosio by the arm, "What did you say, monk?"

"I said," the other replied, in a firm and marked voice, "that your enemies wish to punish you through Ellen, and that if that accursed monk has hitherto appeared to protect you, it was because he feared lest the victim he covets might escape him."

At these fearful words, a horrible change took place in Red Cedar; a livid pallor covered his face, his body was agitated by a convulsive quivering.

"Oh!" he shouted with the roar of a tiger, "let them come, then!"

The monk gave, his comrades a triumphant glance; he had succeeded, and held his palpitating prey in his hands.

"Come," Red Cedar continued, "do not desert me; we will crush this herd of vipers. Ah, they fancy they have me," he added, with a nervous laugh; that almost choked him, "but I will show them that the old lion is not conquered yet. I can count on you, my lads, and on you, Fray Ambrosio?"

"We are your only friends," the monk replied, "as you know perfectly well."

"That is true," he went on; "forgive me for having forgotten it for a moment. Ah, you shall see."

Two hours later the three men reached the jacal, and on seeing them enter, Ellen felt a shudder of terror run over her; a secret foreboding warned her of misfortune.

CHAPTER XVII
MOTHER AND SON

So soon as Father Seraphin had installed Red Cedar and Ellen in the jacal, and assured himself that the new life he had procured them was supportable, he thought about keeping his promise to Valentine's mother.

The worthy female, in spite of all her courage and resignation, felt her strength daily growing less; she said nothing, she did not complain; but the certainty of being so near her son and yet unable to see him, to press him in her arms after such a lengthened separation, such cruel alternations of cheated hopes and frightful deceptions plunged her into a gloomy melancholy from which nothing could draw her; she felt herself dying by inches, and had arrived at the terrible point of believing that she would never see her son again, for he was dead, and that the missionary, through fear of dealing her a terrible blow, deceived her with a hope which could never be realised. Maternal love does not reason.

All that Father Seraphin had told her to cause her to be patient had only lulled her grief for a while, till it broke out again in redoubled impatience and anxiety. All she had seen and heard since her landing in America had only increased her anxiety, by showing her how life in this country often only hangs by a thread. Hence, when the missionary informed her that in a week at the latest she should embrace her son, her joy and anxiety were so great that she almost fainted.

At first, she did not believe in such happiness. Through hoping against hope so long, she had reached such a state of distrust that she supposed that the good priest only told her this to make her patient for a while longer, and that he promised this meeting just as hopeless sick people are promised things which can never be realised.

In the meanwhile, Father Seraphin, though certain that Valentine was at this moment on the prairie, did not know where to lay his hand on him. So soon as he reached the grotto he inhabited provisionally, he sent off the Indians in four different directions to obtain information and bring him positive news of the hunter. Valentine's mother was present when the missionary despatched these couriers; she heard the instructions he gave them, saw them start, and then began counting the minutes till their return, calculating in her mind the time they would employ in finding her son and in returning: the incidents that might delay them; in short, making those countless suppositions to which people give way who are impatiently awaiting anything they eagerly desire.

Two days elapsed, and none of the couriers returned; the poor mother, seated on a rock, with her eyes fixed on the plain, awaited them, motionless and indefatigable. At the close of the third day, she perceived, at a great distance, a black point, rapidly approaching the spot where she was; gradually, it became more distinct, and she recognised a horseman galloping at full speed up the valley.

The mother's heart beat as if ready to burst. It was evidently one of the missionary's messengers; but what news did he bring? At length, the Indian dismounted, and began scaling the hill side; the old woman seemed to regain her youthful limbs, so rapidly did she go to meet him, and cleared in a few minutes the space that separated them. But when they were face to face, another obstacle rose before her: the redskin did not understand a word of French; she, for her part, could not speak Indian. But mothers have a species of language, a freemasonry of the heart, which is understood in all countries; the Comanche warrior stopped before her, folded his arms on his chest, and bowed with a gentle smile, merely uttering the word —

"Koutonepi!"

Valentine's mother knew that the Indians were accustomed to call her son thus; and she suddenly felt reassured by the man's smile, and the way in which he had spoken her son's name. She took the warrior by the arm, and dragged him to the grotto, at the entrance of which Father Seraphin was reading his breviary.

"Well!" he asked on seeing her, "What news?"

"This man could tell me nothing," she replied, "for I do not understand his language; but something assures me he brings good news."

"With your leave, I will question him."

"Do so, for I am anxious to know what I have to expect."

The missionary turned to the Indian, who stood motionless a few yards off, and had listened to the few words spoken.

"The brow of my brother, the Spider, is damp," he said; "let him take a place by my side and rest: he has had a long journey."

The Indian smiled gravely, and bowed respectfully to the missionary.

"The Spider is a chief in his tribe," he said in his guttural and yet melodious voice; "he can bound like the jaguar, and crawl like the serpent: nothing fatigues him."

"I know that my brother is a great warrior," the missionary answered: "his exploits are numerous, and the Apaches fly on seeing him. Has my brother met the young men of his tribe?"

"Spider has met them: they are hunting the buffalo on the Gila."

"Was their great chief Unicorn with them?"

"Unicorn was with his warriors."

"Good! My brother has the eye of a tiger-cat: nothing escapes him. Did he meet the great paleface hunter?"

"Spider smoked the calumet with Koutonepi and several warriors, friends of the pale hunter, assembled round his fire."

"Did my brother speak with Koutonepi?" the priest asked.

"Yes, Koutonepi is glad at the return of the father of prayer, whom he did not hope to see again. When the walkon has sung for the second time, Koutonepi will be near my father with his comrades."

"My brother is a wise and skillful warrior: I thank him for the way in which he has carried out the mission with which he was entrusted, a mission which no other warrior would have performed with so much prudence and tact."

At this well-dressed compliment, a smile of joy and pride played round the Indian's lips, who withdrew after respectfully kissing the missionary's hand. Father Seraphin then turned to Madame Guillois, who anxiously awaited the result of this conversation, trying to read in the priest's looks what she had to hope or fear. He took her hand, pressed it gently, and said to her with that sympathetic accent which he possessed in the highest degree—

"Your son is coming, you will soon see him: he will be here this night, within two hours at the most."

"Oh!" she said with an accent impossible to render; "God! Be blessed!"

And, kneeling on the ground, she burst into tears. The missionary watched her anxiously, ready to help her if her extreme emotion caused her to break down. After a few moments she rose smiling through her tears, and took her place again by the priest's side.

"Oh!" she said eagerly, "he is my son, the only being I ever loved; the child I nursed at my breast, and I am going to see him again! Alas! We have been separated for ten years—for ten years the mark of my kisses has been effaced from his forehead. You cannot understand what I feel, father—it cannot be explained; to a mother her child is everything."

"Do not let your emotion overpower you."

"Then, he is coming?" she repeated eagerly.

"In two hours at the most."

"What a long time two hours are!" she said with a sigh.

"Oh! all human creatures are like that," the missionary exclaimed. "You, who waited so many years without complaining, now find two hours too long."

"But I am waiting for my son, my beloved child; I cannot see him soon enough."

"Come, calm yourself, you are quite in a fever."

"Oh! fear nothing, father, joy never kills. The sight of my son will restore my health, I feel sure."

"Poor mother!" the priest could not refrain from saying.

"Am I not?" she said. "Oh, it is a terrible thing, if you but knew it, to live in these continued horrors, to have only a son who is your joy, your delight, and not to know where he is, or what he is doing, whether he is dead or alive. The most cruel torture for a mother is this continual uncertainty of good and evil, of hope and disappointment. You do not understand this, you can never understand it, you men; it is a sense wanting in you, and which we mothers alone possess—love of our children."

There was a short silence, then she went on:

"Good heaven! How slowly time passes. Will not the sun soon set? Which way do you think my son will come, father? I should like to see him arrive, though I have not seen him for a long time. I feel certain that I shall recognise him at once; a mother is not mistaken, look you, for she does not see her child with her eyes, but feels him in her eyes."

The missionary led her to the entrance of the cave, made her sit down, placed himself by her side, and said, as he stretched out his arm in a southwestern direction:

"Look over there, he must come that way."

"Thanks!" she said, eagerly. "Oh, you are as kind as you are virtuous. You are good as a saint, father. God will reward you, but I can only offer you my thanks."

The missionary smiled softly.

"I am happy," he said, simply.

They looked out, the sun was rapidly sinking in the horizon; gloom gradually covered the ground; objects were confused, and it was impossible to distinguish anything, even at a short distance.

"Let us go in," Father Seraphin said; "the night chill might strike you."

"Nonsense," she said, "I feel nothing."

"Besides," he went on, "the gloom is so dense that you cannot see him."

"That is true," she said, fervently, "but I shall hear him."

There was no reply possible to this. Father Seraphin took his seat again by her side.

"Forgive me, father," she said, "but joy renders me mad."

"You have suffered enough, poor mother," he answered, kindly, "to have the right of enjoying unmingled happiness this day. Do what you please, then, and have no fear of causing me pain."

About an hour elapsed ere another word was uttered by them: they were listening; the night was becoming more gloomy, the desert sounds more imposing, the evening breeze had risen, and groaned hoarsely through the *quebradas*, with a melancholy and prolonged sound. Suddenly Madame Guillois sprang up with flashing eye, and seized the missionary's hand.

"Here he is," she said, hoarsely.

Father Seraphin raised his head.

"I hear nothing," he replied.

"Ah!" the mother said, with an accent that came from her heart, "I am not mistaken—it is he! Listen, listen again."

Father Seraphin listened with greater attention, and, in fact, a scarcely perceptible sound could be heard on the prairie, resembling the prolonging roaring of distant thunder. The noise became gradually louder, and it was presently easy to distinguish the gallop of several horses coming up at full speed.

"Well," she exclaimed, "was it fancy? Oh! A mother's heart is never mistaken."

"You are right, madam; in a few minutes he will be by your side."

"Yes," she muttered, in a panting voice.

That was all she could say—joy was stifling her.

"In Heaven's name," the missionary exclaimed, in alarm, "take care! This emotion is too great for you; you are killing yourself."

She shook her head with a careless gesture, full of inexpressible happiness.

"What matter?" she said; "I am happy—oh, very happy at this moment."

The horsemen entered the defile, and the gallop of their horses grew very loud.

"Dismount, gentlemen," a powerful voice shouted, "we have arrived."

"'Tis he! 'Tis he!" she said, with a movement as if going to rush forward; "it was he who spoke—I recognised his voice."

The missionary held her in his arms.

"What are you about?" he exclaimed, "you will kill yourself!"

"Pardon me, father, pardon me! But on hearing him speak, I know not what emotion I felt; I was no longer mistress of myself, but rushed forward."

"A little patience, he is coming up; in five minutes he will be in your arms."

She started back hurriedly.

"No," she said, "not so, not so, the recognition would be too hurried; let me enjoy my happiness without losing a morsel. I wish him to find me out as I did him."

And she hurriedly dragged Father Seraphin into the grotto.

"It is Heaven that inspires you," he said; "yes, this recognition would be too abrupt—it would kill you both."

"I was right, father, was I not? Oh, you will see—you will see. Hide me at some spot where I can see and hear everything unnoticed; make haste, here he is."

The cavern, as we have said, was divided into a number of cells, each communicating with the other; Father Seraphin concealed Madame Guillois in one of these, whose walls were formed of stalactites, that had assumed the strangest forms. After hobbling their horse, the hunters climbed the mountain. While coming up, they could be heard talking together; the sound of their voices distinctly reached the inhabitants of the grotto, who listened greedily to the words they uttered.

"That poor Father Seraphin," Valentine said; "I do not know if you are like myself, caballeros, but I am delighted at seeing him again. I feared lest he had left us forever."

"It is a great consolation for me in my grief," said Don Miguel, "to know him so near us; that man is a true apostle."

"What is the matter, Valentine?" General Ibañez suddenly asked; "Why do you stop?"

"I do not know," the latter replied, in a hesitating voice, "something is taking place in me which I cannot explain. When Spider told me today of the father's arrival, I felt a strange contraction of the heart; now it is affecting me again, though I cannot say for what reason."

"My friend, it is the joy you feel at seeing Father Seraphin again, that is all."

The hunter shook his head.

"No," he said, "it is not that, but something else; what I feel is not natural: my chest is oppressed, I am choking, what can be happening?"

His friends anxiously collected round him.

"Let me go on," he said, resolutely; "if I have bad news to hear, it is better to do so at once."

And, in spite of the exhortations of his friends, who were alarmed at seeing him in this state, he began running up the mountain side. He soon reached the platform, when he stopped to take breath.

"Come on!" he said.

He boldly entered the cavern, followed by his friends, but at the moment he went in, he heard his name called; at the sound of this voice the hunter started; he turned pale and trembled, and a cold perspiration covered his face.

"Oh," he murmured, "who calls me thus?"

"Valentine! Valentine!" the soft voice repeated.

The hunter hesitated and bent his body forward, his face assumed an indescribable look of joy and alarm.

"Again! Again!" he said, in an indistinct voice, as he laid his hand on his heart to check its beating.

"Valentine!" the voice repeated. This time Valentine bounded forward like a lion.

"My mother!" he cried; "My mother, here I am!"

"Ah, I felt certain he would recognise me," she exclaimed, as she rushed into his arms.

The hunter pressed her to his bosom with a sort of frenzy; the poor woman lavished her caresses on him, crying and half mad with joy and terror at seeing him in this state. She repeated the experiment she had made. He kissed her face, with her white locks, unable to utter a word. At length a hoarse groan burst from his chest, he breathed faintly, and he melted into tears, saying, in an accent of indescribable tenderness—

"My mother! Oh, my mother!"

These were the only words he could find. Valentine laughed and wept at once; as he sat on a rock, holding his mother on his knees, he embraced her with delirious joy, and was never wearied of kissing her white hair, her pale cheeks, and her eyes, which had shed so many tears.

The spectators of the scene, affected by this true and simple affection, wept silently round the mother and son. Curumilla, crouched in a corner of the cave, was looking fixedly at the hunter, while two tears slowly glided down his bronzed cheeks.

When the first emotion was slightly calmed, Father Seraphin, who had till then kept aloof, not to trouble the glorious outpourings of this interview, stepped forward, and said in a gently imperious voice, as he held up the simple copper crucifix in his right hand:

"My children, let us return thanks to the Saviour for His infinite goodness."

The backwoodsmen knelt down and prayed.

CHAPTER XVIII
THE CONSULTATION

A man must have lived a long time apart from beings he loves, separated from them by immeasurable distances, without hope of ever seeing them again, in order to understand the sweet and yet painful emotions Valentine experienced on seeing his mother again. We, the greater part of whose life has been spent in the deserts of the New World, amid the savage hordes that occupy them, speaking languages having no affinity with our own, forced into habits not at all agreeing with those of our country—we can remember the tender feelings that assailed us whenever a straying traveller uttered in our presence that sacred name of France so dear to our heart.

Exile is worse than death; it is an ever bleeding wound, which time, in lieu of cicatrising, only increases every hour, every minute, and changes at length into such a craving to breathe one's native air, were it only for a day, that exile contracts that terrible and incurable disease to which physicians give the name of nostalgia. The moment comes when a man, remote from his country, feels an invincible desire to see his country again, and hear his language again; neither fortune nor honours can contend against the feeling.

Valentine, during the many years he had spent in traversing the desert, had always had this memory of his country present to his mind. During his conversations with Father Seraphin he had spoken to him of his mother, that good and holy woman whom he never hoped to see again, for he had given up all thoughts of returning home for a long time past. The feverish existence of the desert had so seduced him, that every other consideration yielded to it, especially after the misfortunes of his early youth and the wounds of his only love. When, therefore, he saw himself reunited to his mother, and understood they would never separate again, an immense joy occupied his mind.

The entire night passed away like an hour, in delicious conversation; the hunters collected round the fire, listened to mother and son describing with that accent that comes from the heart the various incidents of their life during the long conversation. A few minutes before sunrise; Valentine insisted on his mother taking rest; he feared lest, at her advanced age, after the piercing emotions of such a day, such a lengthened absence of sleep might injure her health. After various objections, Madame Guillois at length yielded to her son's wishes, and retired to a remote compartment of the grotto.

When Valentine supposed his mother asleep, he made his friends a sign to sit down near him; the latter, suspecting that he had a serious communication to make to them, silently obeyed. Valentine walked up and down the cavern with his hands behind his back and frowning brow.

"Caballeros," he said, in a stern voice, "day is about to break, it is too late for any of us to think about sleep, so be good enough to aid me with your counsels."

"Speak, my friend," Father Seraphin replied, "you know that we are devoted to you."

"I know it, and you more than anyone else, father—hence I shall be forever grateful to you for the immense service you have rendered me. You know I forget nothing, and when the moment arrives, be assured that I shall pay my debt to you."

"Do not speak about that, friend; I knew the intense desire you had to see your mother again, and the anxiety that tortured you on the subject of that cruel separation; I only acted as anyone else would have done in my place, so dismiss the affair, I beg; I desire no other reward than to see you happy.

"I am so, my friend," the hunter exclaimed, with emotion; "I am more so than I can say, but it is that very happiness which terrifies me. My mother is near me, 'tis true, but, alas! You know the life to which a desert existence, made up of fighting and privation, condemns us; at this moment especially, when following out our implacable revenge, ought I to make my mother, a woman of great age and weak health, share the changes and dangers of that life? Can we, without cruelty, compel her to follow us on the trail of the villain we are pursuing? No, not one of you, I feel convinced, would give me that advice; but what is to be done? My mother cannot remain alone in this cavern abandoned, far from all help, and exposed to numberless privations. We know not whither the duty we have sworn to accomplish may drag us tomorrow. On the other hand, will my mother, so happy at our meeting, consent so promptly to even a temporary separation—a separation which circumstances may indefinitely prolong? I therefore beg you all, my only and true friends, to advise me, for I confess that I know not what resolution to form. Speak, my friends, tell me what I should do."

There was a lengthened silence among the hunters. Each understood Valentine's embarrassment, but the remedy was very difficult to find, as all were in their hearts made rest by the thought of pursuing Red Cedar closely, and not giving him respite until he had been punished for all his crimes. As usual under such circumstances, egotism and private interests took the place of friendship. Father Seraphin, the only disinterested person, saw clearly, hence he was the first to speak.

"My friend," he answered, "all you have said is most just; I undertake to make your mother listen to reason; she will understand, I feel assured, how urgent it is for her to return to civilisation, especially at the present period of the year; still, we must spare her feelings, and lead her back quietly to Mexico, without letting her suspect the separation she fears, and you fear too. During the journey hence to the civilised frontier, we will strive to prepare her for it, so that the blow may not be so rude when the moment for parting arrives. That is the only thing, I believe, you can do under the present circumstances. Come reflect; if you have any plan better than mine, I will be the first to submit."

"That advice is really the best that can be given me," Valentine said, warmly; "hence I eagerly adopt it. You will consent then, father, to accompany us to the frontier?"

"Of course, my friend, and further, were it necessary. Hence, do not let that trouble you; all we have now to decide is our road."

"That is true," said Valentine; "but here lies the difficulty. We must lodge my mother at a clearing near enough for me to see her frequently, and yet sufficiently distant from the desert to guard her against any danger."

"I fancy," Don Miguel remarked, "that my hacienda, at the Paso del Norte, will suit admirably; the more so, as it offers your mother all the guarantees of security and comfort you can require for her."

"In truth," Valentine exclaimed, "she would be most comfortable there, and I thank you cordially for your offer. Unfortunately, I cannot accept it."

"Why not?"

"For a reason you will appreciate as well as I do; it is much too far off."

"Do you think so?" Don Miguel asked.

Valentine could not repress a smile at this question.

"My friend," he said quietly to him, "since you have been in the desert, circumstances have forced you to take so many turns and twists, that you have completely lost all idea of distances, and do not suspect, I feel assured, how many miles we are from the Paso."

"I confess I do not," Don Miguel said in surprise. "Still, I fancy we cannot be very far."

"Make a guess."

"Well, one hundred and fifty miles, at the most."

"My poor friend," Valentine remarked, with a shrug of his shoulders, "you are out of your reckoning; we are more than seven hundred miles from the Paso del Norte, which is the extreme limit of the civilised settlements."

"The deuce!" the hacendero exclaimed, "I did not fancy we had gone so far."

"And," Valentine went on, "from that town to your hacienda is a distance of about fifty miles."

"Yes, about that."

"You see, then, that, to my great regret, it is impossible for me to accept your generous offer."

"What is to be done?" General Ibañez asked.

"It is awkward," Valentine replied, "for time presses."

"And your mother cannot possibly remain here; that is quite decided," Don Miguel objected.

Curumilla had hitherto listened to the talk in his usual way, not saying a word. Seeing that the hunters could not agree, he turned to Valentine.

"A friend would speak," he said.

All looked at him, for the hunters knew that Curumilla never spoke save to give advice, which was generally followed. Valentine gave a nod of assent.

"Our ears are open, chief," he said.

Curumilla rose.

"Koutonepi forgets," he quietly remarked.

"What do I forget?" the hunter asked.

"Koutonepi is the brother of Unicorn, the great Comanche Sachem."

Valentine struck his forehead in his delight.

"That is true," he exclaimed; "what was I thinking about? On my honour, chief, you are our Providence: nothing escapes you."

"Is my brother satisfied?" the chief asked joyously.

Valentine pressed his hand warmly.

"Chief," he exclaimed, "you are the best fellow I know; I thank you from my heart: however, we understand each other, I think, and need say nothing about that."

The Araucano Ulmen warmly returned his friend's pressure, and sat down, merely muttering one word, which contained all his impressions—

"Good."

The other persons, however, had not understood this little scene. Although they had been living for a long time in the company of the Aucas, they had not yet grown accustomed to his silence or learned to translate it; they therefore anxiously waited till Valentine gave them the explanation of the few sentences he had exchanged with his friend.

"The chief," Valentine said quickly, "has found at once what we have been racking our brains in vain to discover."

"How so? Explain," Don Miguel asked.

"What, you do not understand?"

"On my honour I do not."

"Yet it is very simple; I have been for a long time an adopted son of the Comanches; I belong to Unicorn's tribe; that chief will not refuse, I feel sure, to shelter my mother at his village. The redskins love me; Unicorn is devoted to me; my mother will be nursed and kindly treated by the Indians, while, on the other hand, it will be easy for me to see her whenever I have a moment to spare."

"*Canarios!*" General Ibañez exclaimed, "On my honour, chief," he added, as he gaily tapped the Araucanian's shoulder, "I must allow that we are all asses, and that you have more sense in your little finger than we have in our whole body."

This discussion had lasted some time, and the sun had risen for nearly an hour, when it terminated. Madame Guillois, entirely recovered from the emotions of the night, appeared in the grotto and kissed her son. When breakfast was over, the horses were saddled, and they set out.

"Where are you taking me to, my son?" the mother asked the hunter; "you know that henceforth I belong entirely to you, and you alone have the right to watch over me."

"Be at your ease, mother," Valentine answered; "although we are in the desert, I have found you a retreat in which you will not only be protected from every danger, but where it will be possible for me to see you at least once a week."

Valentine, like all men endowed with a firm and resolute character, instead of turning the difficulty, had preferred to attack it in front, persuaded that the harder the blow he dealt was, the shorter time its effect would last, and he should be enabled to lessen its consequences more easily. The old lady stopped her horse instinctively and looked at her son with tear-laden eyes.

"What do you say, Valentine?" she asked in a trembling voice; "Are you going to leave me?"

"You do not quite understand me, mother," he replied; "after so long a separation I could not consent to keep away from you."

"Alas!" she murmured.

"Still, my dear mother," he continued stoically, "you will have to convince yourself of one fact, that desert life is very different from civilised life."

"I know it, already," she said sighing.

"Very good," he continued; "this life has claims which it would take too long to explain to you, and necessitate constant marches and counter marches, going at one moment here, at another there, without apparent reason, living from hand to mouth, and eternally on horseback."

"Come," my boy, "do not make me suffer longer, but tell me at once what you wish to arrive at."

"At this, mother, that this life of unending fatigue and danger may be very agreeable to a young man like myself, endowed with an iron constitution, and long accustomed to its incidents; but that it is materially impossible for you, at your age, weak and sickly as you are: now you are my only comfort and treasure, mother; I have found you again by a miracle, and am determined to keep you as long as possible. For that reason I must not expose you through an improper weakness, to fatigues and privations which would kill you in a week."

"Well, then?" asked the mother timidly, involuntarily conquered by her son's peremptory accent.

"This is what I have resolved," said he insinuatingly, "as I do not wish you to suffer; we must be together as much as we can, if not always."

"Oh, yes," she said; "I only ask to see you ever, my child; what do I care for aught else, provided I am near you, can console you in sorrow, and rejoice in your joy!"

"Mother," the hunter said, "I believe I have arranged matters as well as possible. Father Seraphin will tell you any other plan would be futile."

"Let me hear it," she murmured.

"I am taking you to the village of the Comanches, whose adopted son I am; their chief loves me as a brother; the village is only a few leagues off, and you will be there among friends, who will respect you and pay you the greatest attention."

"But you, my child?"

"I will visit you as often as I can, and, believe me, few days will pass without my seeing you."

"Alas! My poor child, why insist on leading this life of danger and fatigue? If you liked, we could be so happy in a little village at home. Have you forgotten France entirely, Valentine?"

The hunter sighed.

"No, mother," he said, with an effort, "since I have seen you again, all the memories of my youth have revived; I know now the desire I had to see France again some day; the sight of you has made me understand that a man cannot voluntarily resign those home joys, whose charm he can only truly understand when unable to enjoy them. Hence I soon intend to remove you from this country disinherited by Heaven, and return to our native land."

"Alas!" she said, with an accent of soft reproach, "We should be so happy there; why not return at once?"

"Because it cannot be, mother; I have a sacred duty to accomplish here; but I pledge you my word of honour that when I have fulfilled the duty I have imposed on myself and am free, we will not remain an hour longer here. So have patience, mother; perhaps we may start for France within two months."

"May Heaven grant it, my child," the old lady said, sadly; "well, your will be done, I am prepared to wait."

"Thanks, mother; your kindness renders me happier than I can describe to you."

The old lady sighed, but gave no answer, and the little party marched silently in the direction of the Comanche village, the outskirts of which they reached at about three in the afternoon.

"Mother," Valentine said, "you are not yet used to Indian fashions; do not be frightened at anything you may see or hear."

"Am I not near you?" she said "What can I feel afraid of?"

"Oh!" he said, joyfully, "you are a true mother."

"Alas!" she answered, with a stifled sigh, "You are mistaken, child, I am only a poor old woman, who loves her son, that is all."

CHAPTER XIX
BLOODSON

White Gazelle had rejoined Bloodson, who was encamped with his band on the top of a hill, where the prairie could be surveyed for a long distance. It was night, the fires were already lit, and the rangers, assembled around the *braseros*, were supping gaily. Bloodson was delighted at seeing his niece again; both had a long conversation, at the end of which the Avenger, as he called himself, ordered the ranchero to approach.

Despite of all his impudence, it was not without a feeling of terror that worthy Andrés Garote found himself face to face with this man, whose glances seemed trying to read his inmost thoughts. Bloodson's reputation had been so long established on the prairies that the ranchero must feel affected in his presence. Bloodson was seated in front of a fire, smoking an Indian pipe, with White Gazelle by his side; and for a moment the ranchero almost repented the step he had taken. But the feeling did not last an instant; hatred immediately regained the upper hand, and every trace of emotion disappeared from his face.

"Come here, scoundrel," Bloodson said to him. "From what the señora has just said to me, you fancy you have in your hands the means of destroying Red Cedar?"

"Did I say Red Cedar?" the ranchero answered; "I do not think so, excellency."

"Whom did you allude to, then?"

"To Fray Ambrosio."

"What do I care for that scurvy monk?" Bloodson remarked, with a shrug of his shoulders; "his affairs do not concern me, and I will not trouble myself with them; other and more important duties claim my care."

"That is possible, Excellency," the ranchero answered, with more assurance than might have been assumed; "but I have only to deal with Fray Ambrosio."

"In that case you can go to the deuce, for I shall certainly not help you in your plans."

Andrés Garote, thus brutally received, was not discouraged, however; he shrugged his shoulders with a cunning look, and assumed his most insinuating tone.

"There is no knowing, Excellency," he said.

"Hum! That seems to me difficult."

"Less so than you fancy, Excellency."

"How so?"

"You bear a grudge against Red Cedar, I think?"

"How does that concern you, scoundrel?" Bloodson asked, roughly.

"Not at all; the more so as I owe him nothing; still, it is a different affair with you, Excellency."

"How do you know?"

"I presume so, Excellency; hence I intend to offer you a bargain."

"A bargain!" Bloodson repeated, disdainfully.

"Yes, Excellency," the ranchero said, boldly; "and a bargain advantageous to yourself, I venture to say."

"And for you?"

"For me too, naturally."

Bloodson began laughing.

"The man is mad," he said, with a shrug of his shoulders, and, turning to his men, added—"where the deuce was your head when you brought him to me?"

"Nonsense," White Gazelle said, "you had better listen to him; that will do you no harm."

"The señora is right," the ranchero eagerly replied; "listen to me, Excellency, that pledges you to nothing; besides, you will be always able to decline if what I propose does not suit you."

"That is true," Bloodson replied, contemptuously—"Speak then, picaro, and be brief."

"Oh, I am not in the habit of making long speeches."

"Come to the point."

"It is this," the ranchero said, boldly; "you wish, I do not know why, and do not care, to revenge yourself on Red Cedar; for certain reasons, unnecessary for me to tell you, I wish to avenge myself on Ambrosio; that is clear, I fancy?"

"Perfectly so—go on."

"Very well. Now this is what I propose to you—aid me to avenge myself on the monk, and I will help you with the bandit."

"I do not need you for that."

"Perhaps you do, Excellency; and if I did not fear appearing impudent to you, I would even say—"

"What?"

"That I am indispensable to you."

"*Voto a Dios!*" Bloodson said, with an outburst of laughter, "This is beyond a joke; the scoundrel is absolutely making fun of me."

Andrés Garote stood unmoved before the ranger.

"Come, come," the latter continued, "this is far more amusing than I at first fancied; and how are you indispensable to me?"

"Oh, Excellency, that is very simple; you do not know what has become of Red Cedar?"

"That is true; I have been seeking him in vain for a long time."

"I defy you to find him, unless I help you."

"Then you know where he is?" Bloodson exclaimed, suddenly raising his head.

"Ah! That interests you now, Excellency," the ranchero said, with a crafty look.

"Answer, yes or no," the ranger said, roughly; "do you know where he is?"

"If I did not, should I have come to you?"

Bloodson reflected for a moment.

"Tell me where he is."

"Our bargain holds good?"

"It does."

"You swear it?"

"On my honour."

"Good!" the other said joyfully; "now listen to me."

"Go on."

"Of course you are aware that Red Cedar and the Trail-hunter had a fight?"

"I am—go on."

"After the battle, all bolted in different directions; Red Cedar was wounded, hence he did not go far, but soon fell in a fainting fit at the foot of a tree. The Frenchman and his friends sought him on all sides, and I believe they would have made him spend a very unpleasant quarter of an hour if they had laid hands on him. Fortunately for him, his horse had carried him into the middle of the virgin forest, where no one dreamed of pursuing him. Chance, or rather my good fortune, I now believe, led me to the spot where he was; his daughter Ellen was near him, and paying him the most touching attention; it really almost affected me. I cannot tell you how she got there, but there she was. On seeing Red Cedar, I thought for a moment about going to find the French hunter, and telling him of my discovery."

"Hum! And why did you not carry out that idea, scoundrel?"

"For a very simple, though conclusive reason."

"Let us hear it," said Bloodson, who had begun to listen with extreme interest to the ranchero's wandering statement.

"This is it," he went on. "Don Valentine is a rough fellow; I am not in the odour of sanctity with him; besides, he was with a crowd of Apaches and Comanches, each a bigger scamp than the other; in a word, I was frightened for my scalp, and held off, as I might have plucked the chestnuts from the fire for another man's profit."

"Not badly reasoned."

"Was it now, Excellency? hence, while I was reflecting on what I had better do, a band of some ten horsemen came, I know not whence, to the spot where that poor devil of a Red Cedar was lying half dead."

"He was really wounded?"

"Oh, yes, and dangerously, I undertake to say; the leader of the party was a French missionary you must know."

"Father Seraphin?"

"The very man."

"What did he?"

"What I should certainly not have done in his place—he carried Red Cedar away with him."

"In that I recognise him," Bloodson could not refrain from saying. "And where did he take the wounded man?"

"To a cavern, where I will lead you whenever you like."

"You are not lying?"

"Oh, no, Excellency."

"Very good, go and sleep; you can count on my promise, if you are faithful to me."

"Thanks, Excellency; be at your ease, self-interest urges me not to deceive you."

"That is true."

The ranchero withdrew, and an hour later was sleeping as every honest man should do, who feels conscious of having performed his duty. The next morning at daybreak Bloodson's band set out. But in the desert it is often very difficult to find those you seek, owing to the nomadic life everybody is obliged to lead in order to gain his livelihood; and Bloodson, who wished first to consult with Valentine and his friends, lost much time before learning the exact spot where they were. At length, one of the scouts told him that the Frenchman was at Unicorn's winter village, and he proceeded there at once.

In the interim, Bloodson ordered Andrés Garote to watch Red Cedar's movements, as he did not like to take a decisive step till he had acquired a certainty. Nothing would have been easier than to go to Father Seraphin, and demand the surrender of the wounded man; but he felt a repugnance to this. Bloodson shared in the respect the holy missionary inspired all within the Far West; and he would not have dared to summon him to surrender his guest, certain as he was beforehand that the other would peremptorily refuse; at the same time he did not like to employ violence to wrest his prey from a man whose character he admired. He must, therefore, await until Red Cedar, cured of his wounds, quitted his protection; and this Bloodson did, though having his movements watched.

At length Andrés Garote appeared, all joyous, in Bloodson's camp; he was the bearer of excellent news: Father Seraphin, after curing Red Cedar, had installed him in a jacal, where he and his daughter lived like two anchorites. Bloodson uttered a shout of joy at this news. Without even taking time to reflect, he leaped on his horse, leaving the temporary command of the band to his men, and started off at full speed for Unicorn's village.

The distance was not great, and the ranger covered it in less than two hours. Bloodson was beloved by the Comanches, to whom he had frequent opportunities of being useful; hence he was received by them with all the honours and ceremonies employed in such cases. Unicorn, accompanied by some of the principal chiefs of the tribe, came to receive him a short distance from the village, yelling, firing their muskets, and making their horses curvet. Bloodson gladly yielded to the chief's wishes, and galloped along by his side.

The Comanches are excessively discreet; they never take the liberty of asking questions of their guests before the latter authorise them. So soon as Bloodson had taken his seat by the fire of the council lodge, and smoked the great calumet of peace, Unicorn bowed to him gravely, and took the word.

"My paleface brother is welcome among his red friends," he said; "has my brother had a good hunt?"

"The buffaloes are numerous near the mountains," Bloodson answered; "my young men have killed many."

"All the better; my brother will not suffer from famine."

The ranger bowed his thanks.

"Will my brother remain some days with his red friends?" the chief again asked; "they would be happy to have him among them for a season."

"My hours are counted," Bloodson answered. "I merely intended paying a visit to my brothers to ask after their fare, as I passed their village."

At this moment Valentine appeared in the doorway.

"Here is my brother, Koutonepi," Unicorn said.

"He is welcome," the ranger said; "I wished to see him."

"What accident has brought you here?" the hunter asked him.

"To tell you where Red Cedar is hidden at this moment," Bloodson answered, distinctly.

Valentine started; and bent on him a piercing glance.

"Oh, oh," he said, "that is great news you give me."

"I do not give it, but sell it to you."

"What? explain yourself, pray."

"I will be brief. There is not a man on the prairies who has not a terrible account to settle with that vile bandit?"

"That is true."

"The monster has burdened the earth too long—he must disappear."

Bloodson uttered these words with such an accent of hatred, that all present, although they were men endowed with nerves of steel, felt a shudder course through their veins. Valentine looked sternly at the ranger.

"You owe this man a heavy grudge?" he said.

"Greater than I can express."

"Good, go on."

At this moment Father Seraphin entered the lodge, but was not noticed, so greatly was the attention of the audience concentrated on Bloodson. The missionary stood motionless in the darkest corner, and listened.

"This is what I propose," Bloodson went on. "I will reveal to you where the villain is lurking; we will spread so as to envelope him in an impassable circle, and if you or the chiefs here present are luckier than I, and seize him, you will deliver him into my hands."

"What to do with him?"

"To take an exemplary vengeance on him."

"I cannot promise that," Valentine said slowly.

"For what reason?"

"You have just given it: there is not a man on the prairie but has a terrible account to settle with this villain."

"Well?"

"The man he has most outraged is, in my opinion, Don Miguel de Zarate, whose daughter he so basely murdered. Don Miguel alone has the right to deal with him as he thinks proper."

Bloodson gave a start of disappointment.

"Oh, were he here!" he exclaimed.

"Here I am, sir," the hacendero replied as he stepped forward; "I too have vengeance to take on Red Cedar; but I wish it to be great and noble, in the light of the sun, and the presence of all: I do not wish to assassinate, but to punish him."

"Good," Bloodson exclaimed, stifling a cry of joy; "our thoughts are the same, caballero; for what I desire is to deal with Red Cedar, according to Lynch Law, in its entire rigour, on the very spot where he committed his first crime, and in the sight of the population he has horrified. In the Far West, I am not only called the Son of Blood, but also the Avenger and the judge."

After these words, spoken with feverish energy, there was a gloomy silence which lasted some time.

"Vengeance is mine, saith the Lord," a voice said, which made the hearers start.

All turned round; Father Seraphin, with his crucifix in his hand, and head erect, seemed to command them all by the grandeur of his evangelic mission.

"By what right do you make yourselves the instruments of divine justice?" he continued. "If this man was guilty, who tells that repentance has not come at this hour to wash the stains from his soul?"

"Eye for eye, tooth for tooth," Bloodson muttered in a hoarse voice.

These words broke the charm that enchained the audience.

"Eye for eye, tooth for tooth," they exclaimed wrathfully.

Father Seraphin saw he was conquered: he understood that all reasoning would fail with these blood-thirsty men, to whom the life of their fellow men is nothing, and who rank vengeance as a virtue.

"Farewell," he said in mournful voice; "farewell, poor misguided men. I dare not curse you, I can only pity you; but I warn you that I will do all in my power to save the victim you wish to immolate to your odious passions."

And he went out of the lodge.

When the emotion caused by the priest's words had calmed down, Don Miguel walked up to Bloodson, and laid his hand on the one the ranger offered to him.

"I accept Lynch Law," he said.

"Yes," all present shouted, "Lynch Law."

A few hours later, Bloodson regained his camp, and it was after this interview that Valentine had the conversation with Don Pablo, as he returned from Red Cedar's jacal, which we described at the beginning of the volume.

CHAPTER XX
RED CEDAR

Now that we have explained the incidents that took place during the six months that had elapsed between Doña Clara's death and the conversation in the cavern during the storm, we will resume our narrative where we left it at the end of chapter three.

Only a few minutes after the hacendero's son had left, the door of the jacal was roughly opened—four men entered. They were Red Cedar, Fray Ambrosio, Sutter, and Nathan. They appeared sad and gloomy, and the water poured down from their clothes as if they had come out of the river.

"Halloh," the monk said; "what! No fire or light, and nothing in the calli to greet us. You do not care much for us, I fancy."

Red Cedar kissed his daughter on the forehead, and turning to Fray Ambrosio, to whom he gave a passionate glance, he said roughly—

"You are in my house, my master: do not oblige me to remind you of that fact; so begin by being civil to my daughter, if you do not wish me to give you a lesson."

"Hum!" the monk remarked with a growl; "Is this young woman so sacred, that you should fire up at the slightest word addressed to her?"

"I do not fire up," the squatter replied, sharply, as he struck the table with his fist; "but your way of speaking does not please me, I tell you; so do not oblige me to repeat it."

Fray Ambrosio made no answer; he understood that Red Cedar was in a state of mind unfavourable for a discussion; he therefore prudently refrained from any remark that might lead to a quarrel, which he seemed as anxious to avoid as the squatter to pick it. During the exchange of these few sentences, Ellen, helped by her brothers, had lit a torch of candle wood, rekindled the fire, the absence of which was felt, and placed on the table a meal, sufficient, if not luxurious.

"Caballeros," she said in her gentle voice, "you are served."

The four men sat round the table with the eagerness of hungry persons who are desirous of breaking a long fast. Before raising the first morsel to his lips, the squatter, however, turned to his daughter.

"Ellen," he said to her kindly, "will you not sit down with us?"

"Thank you, father, but I am not hungry; it would be really impossible for me to swallow the least morsel."

The squatter sighed, but raising no objection, he began to serve his guests, while Ellen retired into the darkest corner of the shanty. The meal was sad; the four men seemed busy in thought, and ate quickly and silently. When their hunger was appeased, they lit their pipes.

"Father," Nathan suddenly said to Red Cedar, who was sorrowfully watching the smoke ascend in spirals to the roof; "I have found a trail."

"So have I," the monk remarked.

"And I, too," the squatter said; "what of that?"

"What of that?" Fray Ambrosio shouted. "Canarios, gossip, you take things very lightly. A trail in the desert always reveals an enemy."

"What do I care for that?" Red Cedar replied, with a shrug of his shoulders.

"What?" the monk shouted, as he sprang up; "That is very fine, on my word; to hear you, one might fancy you were an entire stranger to the question, and that your life is not at stake like ours."

"Who tells you that I wish to defend it?" the squatter replied, giving him a look which made his eyes fall.

"Hum!" the monk remarked, after a moment's silence; "I can understand that you do not cling to life; you have gone through so much, that you would not regret death; but there is one thing you forget, gossip, not referring to myself, though I have a right to reproach you."

The squatter carelessly shook the ashes out of his pipe, filled it again, and went on smoking as if not paying the slightest attention to the monk's remarks. The latter frowned and clenched his fists, but recovering his temper almost immediately, he continued, with feigned indifference, while playing with his knife—

"Yes, you forget one thing, gossip, which however, is worth remembering."

"What is it?"

"Your children, cospita!"

The squatter gave him an ironical glance.

"Oh, *por Dios santo!*" the monk went on; "I do not refer to your sons, for they are strong and resolute men, who can always get out of a scrape; I do not trouble myself about them at all."

"About whom, then?" the squatter asked, looking at him sharply.

"Why, for your daughter Ellen, canarios! What will become of her, if you die?" the monk said, with that boldness peculiar to timid persons, who wish to know at once if the mine they have fired will crush them. The squatter shook his head sadly.

"That is true," he said, with a glance at his daughter.

The monk smiled—the blow had told, so he went on.

"In destroying yourself, you destroy her," he said; "your obstinacy may cause her death, so take care."

"What is to be done?" the squatter asked.

"Take our precautions, *voto de Dios!* believe me, we are watched; remaining longer here would be the utmost imprudence."

The squatter's sons nodded their assent.

"It is evident," Sutter observed, "that our enemies have discovered our trail."

"And that they will soon be here," Nathan added.

"You hear?" the monk went on.

"Once again I ask, what is to be done?" Red Cedar asked.

"Caspita, be off as speedily as possible."

"Where can we go at this advanced season of the year? The snow will soon cover the ground, and interrupt all communication; if we leave the jacal, we run a risk of dying of hunger."

"Yes, if we remain in the desert," the monk observed, in an insinuating voice.

"Where do you propose going then?" the squatter asked.

"What do I know? There is no lack of towns, I suppose, on the Indian border; we might, if absolutely necessary, return to the Paso del Norte, where we have friends, and are certain of a kind reception."

Red Cedar looked him full in the face, and said ironically—

"Out with your whole thought, señor Padre; you have an object in wishing to return to the Paso, so let me know it."

"Caspita, you are as clever as I am," the monk exclaimed, blushing the while; "what need have we to humbug one another?"

The squatter rose, and kicked back his stool.

"You are right," he said passionately, "let us deal openly with one another. I wish nothing better, and to give you an example, listen to me. You have never lost out of sight the reason that made you enter the desert; you have only one object, one desire, to reach the rich placer, the situation of which you learned by assassinating a man. Neither the fatigue you have endured, nor the peril you have incurred, has made you renounce your scheme; the hope of a rich crop of gold blinds you, and makes you mad. Is it so or not?"

"It is true," the monk coolly replied, "what next?"

"When our band was destroyed, and completely dispersed, this was the reasoning you employed—a reasoning," he added, with a bitter smile, "which does honour to your sagacity and firmness of character; 'Red Cedar all but knows the site of the placer. I must induce him to return with me to the Paso, to form another band, because if I leave him alone in the desert, so soon as my back is turned, he will go in search of the treasures, and carelessly discover it.' Have I not guessed aright, gossip?"

"Nearly so," the monk answered, furious at seeing his plans so clearly read through.

"I thought so," Red Cedar continued; "but, like all bad men, gangrened to the heart, you went beyond your object, by attributing to me the same sordid instincts you possess; and you thought that because I am an assassin, I may be a thief: that is the error in which you fell, gossip. Understand me," he said, stamping his foot violently; "were the coveted treasure at this moment beneath my heel, I would not stoop down to pick up a nugget. Gold is nothing to me, I despise it. When I consented to guide you to the placer you naturally assumed that avarice led me to do so; but you are mistaken; I had a more powerful and nobler motive—revenge. Now, do not trouble me more about your accursed placer, for which I care as little as I do for a nut. And with that, good night, gossip; I am going to sleep, or try to do so, and recommend the same to you."

And, without awaiting the monk's reply, the squatter turned his back and stalked into an inner room. For some time past, Ellen had been asleep, and so the monk remained alone with the squatter's sons. For some minutes they remained in silence.

"Bah," the monk at length said cautiously, "however much he may struggle, it must happen."

Sutter shook his head dubiously.

"No," he said, "you do not know the old one; once he has said no, he sticks to it."

"Hum!" Nathan added, "He has greatly changed lately; of all his old character, he seems only to have kept his obstinacy; I am afraid you will fail, señor Padre."

"Live and learn," the latter said gaily; "tomorrow has to come; in the meanwhile, gentlemen, let us follow his advice, and go to sleep."

Ten minutes later all slept, or seemed to sleep, in the jacal: the storm lasted the night through, howling furiously. At daybreak, the squatter rose, and went out to see what sort of weather it was. The day promised well; the sky was pure, and the sun rose radiantly. Red Cedar, therefore, started for the corral to saddle his horse, and those of his comrades. Before leaving the household, however, he looked around, and suddenly uttered an exclamation of surprise as he started back. He had noticed a horseman coming up at full speed.

"Father Seraphin!" he muttered in astonishment; "What serious reason can bring him here, at such an hour and in such haste?"

At this moment the other entered the keeping room, and the squatter heard the sound of the footsteps behind him. He turned quickly.

"Hide yourselves," he said hoarsely.

"What's the matter?" the monk asked furiously, as he stepped forward.

With one blow of his fist, the squatter hurled him to the middle of the room.

"Did you not hear me?" he said passionately. But, although Red Cedar's blow had been so powerful, he could not prevent the monk recognising Father Seraphin.

"Ah, ah," he said, with an ugly smile, "Father Seraphin! If our friend wished to confess, was not I enough? He need not only have told me, instead of sending for that European magpie."

Red Cedar here turned as if a viper had stung him, and gave the three men such a glance of ferocity, that they involuntarily recoiled.

"Villain," he said, in a hollow voice, and a terrible gesture, "I know not what prevents me killing you, like the dog you are. If one of you dare utter a syllable against this holy man, by Heaven, I will flay him alive. Hide yourselves, I insist."

Subjugated by the squatter's accent, the three men left the room without replying, and ten minutes later Father Seraphin checked his horse, and dismounted in front of the jacal. Red Cedar and his daughter hurried forward to meet the father, who walked into the hut, wiping the perspiration that stood on his forehead. Red Cedar offered him a butaca.

"Sit down, father," he said to him, "you are very hot; will you take some refreshment?"

"Thanks," the missionary answered, "but we have not a moment to lose, so listen to me."

"What has happened, father? Why have you come in such haste?"

"Alas!" he went on, "because you are menaced by a terrible misfortune."

The squatter turned pale. "It is but just," he muttered, with a frown; "the expiation is beginning."

"Courage, my children," the missionary said, affectionately, "your enemies have discovered your retreat, I know not how; they will be here tomorrow—perhaps today—you must fly—fly at once."

"For what good?" the squatter remarked; "the hand of God is in this— no man can escape his destiny; better to wait."

Father Seraphin assumed a serious air, and said in a stern voice—

"God wishes to try you; it would be cowardice, suicide, to surrender yourself to those who desire your death, and Heaven would not pardon you for doing so. Every living creature must defend life when attacked. Fly—I bid you—I order you."

The squatter made no reply.

"Besides," Father Seraphin continued, in a tone he strove to render gay, "the storm may blow over; your enemies, not finding you here, will doubtless abandon the pursuit; in a few days, you will be able to return."

"No," the squatter said disconsolately, "they desire my death. As you order me to fly, father, I will obey you, but, before all, grant me one favour."

"Speak, my son."

"I," the squatter went on, with ill-concealed emotion, "am a man; I can, without succumbing, support the most excessive fatigue, brave the greatest dangers; but—"

"I understand you," the missionary quickly interrupted him; "I intend to keep your daughter with me. Be at your ease, she shall want for nothing."

"Oh, thanks, thanks, father!" he exclaimed, with an accent such a man might have been thought incapable of.

Ellen had hitherto listened to the conversation in silence, but now she stepped forward, and placing herself between the two men, said with sublime dignity:

"I am most grateful to both of you for your intentions with regard to me, but I cannot abandon my father; I will follow him wherever he goes, to console him and aid him in suffering the retributions Heaven sends on him, as a Christian should do."

The two men prepared to interrupt her.

"Stay!" she said, warmly; "hitherto I have suffered through my father's conduct, for it was guilty; but now that repentance fills his soul, I pity and love him. My resolution is unchangeable."

Father Seraphin gazed at her in admiration.

"It is well, my child," he said; "Heaven will remember such pure and noble devotion."

The squatter pressed his daughter to his heart, but had not the strength to utter a word—he had never felt such sweet emotion before. The missionary rose.

"Farewell," he said, "and take courage; put your trust in God, who will not abandon you. I will watch over you at a distance. Farewell, my children, and bless you. Go, go, without delay."

Then, tearing himself by an effort from Red Cedar's arms, Father Seraphin remounted, dug his spurs into his horse's flanks, and started at full speed, after giving his protégés a parting wave of the hand.

"Oh!" Red Cedar muttered, "That could not last, for I was almost happy."

"Courage, father," Ellen said to him softly.

They re-entered the jacal, where the men were awaiting them.

"Go and saddle the horses," the squatter said, "we are going away."

"Ah!" the monk whispered Sutter, "did I not tell you the demon was on our side? Canarios! He would not forget us, as we have done so much for him."

The preparations for quitting the jacal were not long, and an hour later, the five persons started.

"In what direction do we go?" the monk asked.

"Let us go in the mountains," the squatter answered, laconically, as he took a melancholy glance at this wretched hut, in which he had perhaps hoped to end his days, and which fate compelled him to leave forever. The fugitives had scarce disappeared behind a clump of trees, when a cloud of dust rose on the horizon, and five horsemen soon appeared, coming up at full speed. They were Valentine and his friends.

The hunter must have obtained precise information from Bloodson as to the situation of the jacal, for he did not hesitate a moment, but rode straight in. Don Pablo's heart beat, as if to burst his chest, though he apparently remained unmoved.

"Hum!" Valentine said, when about a dozen yards from the jacal, "Everything is very silent here."

"The squatter is no doubt out hunting," Don Miguel observed, "we shall only find his daughter."

Valentine began laughing.

"Do you think so?" he said. "No, no, Don Miguel, remember Father Seraphin's words."

General Ibañez, who was the first to reach the jacal, dismounted and opened the door.

"Nobody!" he said, in surprise.

"By Jove!" Valentine said, "I suspected that the bird had flown; but this time he will be very cunning if he escapes us. Forward, forward! They cannot be far ahead."

They started again. Curumilla remained behind for a second, and threw a lighted torch into the shanty, which was soon burned down.

"The fox is unearthed," the Indian muttered to himself, while rejoining his comrades.

CHAPTER XXI
CURUMILLA

About a month after the events we have just described, in the early part of December, which the Comanches call, in their picturesque language, "the Moon of the roebuck that sheds its horns," and a few minutes after sunrise, a party, consisting of five or six men, whom, by their garb, it was easy to recognise as wood rangers from the Far West, climbed one of the highest peaks of the Sierra de los Comanches, the eastern chain of the Rocky Mountains, running down into Texas, where it terminates in the Guadaloupe mountains.

The weather was cold, and a dense layer of snow covered the sides of the mountains. The slope which these bold adventurers were following, was so scarped that, although accustomed to travel in these regions, they were often compelled to bend their backs and creep along on their hands and knees. But no difficulty baffled them, no obstacle was great enough to make them turn back.

At times, worn out with fatigue, and bathed in perspiration, they stopped to take breath, lay down on the snow, and picked up some handfuls to allay the ardent thirst that devoured them; then, after resting a little while, they courageously set out again, and clambered up the eternal ice, whose gigantic masses became with each moment more abrupt.

Were these men in search of a practicable road in this frightful labyrinth of mountains, whose peaks rose around them, at an immense height, in the icy regions of the sky? Perhaps, however, they wished, for reasons known to themselves alone, to gain a spot whence they could have an extensive prospect.

If such were their hope, it was not deceived. When, after incessant toil they all at last reached the summit of the peak they were scaling, they suddenly had before them a landscape, whose grand appearance amazed and startled them through its sublime immensity. In whatever direction they looked, they were confounded by the majesty of the panorama unfolded at their feet.

In truth, the Rocky Mountains are unique in the world, bearing no resemblance with the Pyrenees, Alps, and Apennines, and those magnificent chains of mountains which here and there stride across the old world, and seem with their barren crest to protest against the pride of creatures, in the name of the Creator.

The hunters were hanging, as it were, over a world. Beneath them was the Sierra de los Comanches, an immense mountain broken up into snowy peaks, displaying all their gloomy caverns, deep and awe-inspiring valleys, their brilliant lakes, their dark defiles and their foaming torrents, which bounded noisily downward; then, far beyond these savage limits, the eye was lost in an unbounded landscape, bathed in a hazy distance, like the surface of the sea in calm weather.

Owing to the purity and transparency of the atmosphere, the adventurers distinguished the smallest objects at a surprising distance. However, in all probability, these men had not undertaken so perilous an ascent through motives of curiosity. The mode in which they examined the country and analysed the immense panorama unrolled before them, proved, on the contrary, that very serious reasons had urged them to brave the almost insurmountable difficulties they had overcome, in order to reach the point where they were.

The group formed by these men with their bronzed faces, energetic features and picturesque garb, as they leant on their rifles, with eyes fixed on space and frowning brow, had something grand about it; at this extraordinary elevation, at the summit of the peak covered with eternal snow, which served them as a pedestal in the midst of the chaos that surrounded them.

For a long time they remained there without speaking, trying to distinguish in the windings of the *quebradas* the slightest break of the ground, deaf to the mournful growling of the torrents that leaped at their feet, and the sinister rolling of the avalanches, which glided down the mountain side, and fell with a crash into the valleys, dragging trees and rocks with them.

At length the man who appeared the leader of the party passed his hand over his brow, damp with exertion, though the cold was intense in these regions, and turned to his companions to say, "My friends, we are now twenty thousand feet above the level of the plain, that is to say, we have reached the spot where the Indian warrior sees for the first time after death the country of souls, and contemplates the happy hunting grounds, the brilliant abode of just, free, and generous warriors. The eagle alone could rise higher than ourselves."

"Yes," one of his comrades replied, with a shake of head; "but, though I keep looking around, I see no possibility of getting out."

"Hilloh, General!" the first speaker interposed, "What is that you are saying? We might fancy, which Heaven forbid, that you were despairing."

"Well," the other, who was General Ibañez, replied, "that supposition would not be without a certain degree of correctness; listen to me, Don Valentine; for ten days we have been lost on these confounded mountains, surrounded by ice, and snow, and with nothing to eat, under the pretext of finding the hiding place of that old villain Red Cedar, and I do not mind confessing to you, that I am beginning, not to despair, but to believe that, unless a miracle happen, it will be impossible for us to get out of this inextricable chaos in which we are enclosed."

Valentine shook his head several times. The five men standing on the peak were really the Trail-hunter and his friends.

"No matter," General Ibañez continued, "you will agree with me that our position, far from improving, is growing with each moment more difficult; for two days we have been completely out of provisions, and I do not see how we shall procure any in these icy regions. Red Cedar has tricked us with that diabolical cunning which never fails him, he has led us into a trap we cannot get out of, and where we shall find death."

There was a mournful silence. The despair of these energetic men, coldly calculating, amid the steep, northerly country that surrounded them, the few hours of existence still left them, had something crushing about it. Scarce able to stand, more like corpses than men, with haggard features and eyes reddened with fever, they stood calm and resigned, gazing on the magnificent plains stretching out at their feet, on which thousands of animals sported and covered everywhere with trees, whose fruit would so quickly have checked their hunger.

But between them and these plains stood an insurmountable barrier, which neither strength nor cunning could carry: all that was humanly possible, these men had done during the last two days to save themselves. All their plans had been foiled by a strange fatality, which made them constantly go round in a circle among these mountains, which are so like each other, and all their attempts had broken down.

"Pardon me, my friends," Don Miguel de Zarate said, with a crushing accent of sorrow, "pardon me, for I alone am the cause of your death."

"Speak not so, Don Miguel," Valentine quickly exclaimed, "all is not lost, yet."

A heart-rending smile played round the hacendero's lips.

"You are ever the same, Don Valentine," he said; "good, and generous, forgetting yourself for your friends. Alas! Had we followed your advice, we should not be dying of famine and misery in these desolate mountains."

"That will do," the hunter said, gruffly; "what is done cannot be undone; perhaps it would have been better had you listened to me some days back, I grant; but of what use is recrimination now? Let us rather seek the means to get out of this."

"It is impossible," Don Miguel continued, disconsolately, and letting his head fall in his hands, he gave way to sad reflections.

"Caray!" the hunter exclaimed, energetically, "Impossible is a word we Frenchmen have erased from our dictionary. Hang it! As long as the heart beats, there is hope. Were Red Cedar more cunning than he is, which would be most difficult, I swear you that we shall find him, and get out of this hobble."

"But how?" Don Pablo eagerly asked.

"I do not know; still I am certain we shall escape."

"Ah, if we were only by the side of those two horsemen," the general said, with a sigh, "we should be saved."

"What horsemen do you allude to, general I where do you see them?" the hunter asked.

"There," he replied, "near the clump of cork trees. Do you see them?"

"Oh," said Valentine, "they are riding quietly, like men who know they are on the right road, and have nothing to fear."

"They are very lucky," the general muttered.

"Bah! Who knows what awaits them on turning from the road they are now following so peacefully?" the hunter remarked, with a smile; "No one can answer for the next minute; they are on the road from Independence to Santa Fe."

"Hum! I should like to be there too," the general growled between his teeth.

Valentine, who first looked carelessly at the horsemen, now followed them with interest, almost with anxiety; but they soon disappeared in a bend of a road. For a long time, however, the hunter remained with his eyes fixed on the spot where he had first seen them; gradually he began frowning, a deep wrinkle was hollowed on his forehead, and he leaned on his rifle, motionless and dumb, but seeming to be suffering from great agitation.

Involuntarily, his comrades followed with growing interest the current of his thoughts, which could be read, as it were, on their companion's brow. He remained for some time thus absorbed, but at length he raised his head, and looked around with a bright and intrepid glance.

"My friends," he said, joyously, as he struck the butt of his rifle on the ground, "regain courage, I believe I have found the way of getting safe and sound out of the wasp nest into which we have thrust our heads."

His comrades gave vent to a sigh of relief, almost of joy. They knew the hunter, they were aware how fertile the mind of this brave and devoted man was in expedients, and how inaccessible to despondency; they put entire faith in him. Valentine told them he believed he could save them; they did not suspect what means he would employ, but that was his business, not theirs. Now they were calm, for they had his word, which he had never been known to break; they had only to wait patiently till the hour for their deliverance arrived.

"Bah!" the general answered, gaily, "I was sure we should get out of this, my friend."

"When shall we start?" Don Pablo asked.

"As soon as it is night," Valentine replied; "but where is Curumilla?"

"On my word I do not know. I saw him about half an hour ago, gliding along the mountain side, as if he had suddenly gone mad; but I have not seen him since."

"Curumilla does nothing without a reason," the hunter said with a shake of the head; "you will soon see him return."

Indeed, the hunter had scarce finished speaking, when the Indian chief shewed his head level with the platform, and with one leap he rejoined his friends. His zarapé, knotted at the four corners, hung behind his back.

"What have you there, chief?" Valentine asked, with a smile: "Can it be food?"

"Cuerpo de Cristo!" the general exclaimed, "it would be welcome, for I have a wolf's appetite."

"Where could provisions be found in this fearful region?" Don Pablo exclaimed, in a hollow voice.

"My brothers will see," the chief simply answered.

And he threw his zarapé on the snow, where Valentine undone the knots. The hunters uttered a cry of joy, for it contained a hare, a young peccary, and several birds. These provisions, arriving so opportunely, when the hunters had been fasting for nearly forty-eight hours, seemed to them the result of magic.

To understand the emotion the four men experienced at the sight of the much-desired food, a man must have himself gone through all the agony of hunger, without any hope of stilling it—it was almost frenzy. When the first impression was slightly calmed, Valentine turned to the chief, and pressed his hand tenderly, as a tear rolled down his cheek.

"My brother is a great sorcerer," he said to him.

The Ulmen smiled softly, and stretched out his arm to an eagle flying a short distance from the spot where the hunters stood.

"We shared," he said.

Valentine could not restrain a cry of admiration, for all was explained to him. The Araucano, whom nothing escaped, had seen the eagle, guessed that it had a brood, and clambered up to its nest to procure a portion of their food, while on the summit of the peak his comrades were all but yielding to their despair.

"Oh!" Valentine said joyfully, "We are saved, since we shall regain that strength we so much need to carry out the plan we have formed. Follow me, we will return to the camp, gaily eat the dinner the eagles have supplied us with, and start this evening."

Comforted by these words, the hunters followed him, and the little party went lightly down the mountain, up which they had clambered in the morning with such difficulty and despair in their hearts.

CHAPTER XXII
EL MAL PASO

The hunters only spent one hour in going down, though it had cost them eight to ascend. Their bivouac was formed at the top of a scarped rock, in an impregnable position.

After their visit to the jacal, they were not long in finding traces of the fugitives, and followed them during four days. As these traces led to the Sierra de los Comanches, the hunters bravely entered the obscure mountain defiles, but all at once the trail disappeared as if by enchantment, and it was impossible to find it again.

The hunters' incessant search had only produced the disastrous result of losing themselves in the sierra, and in spite of all their efforts they could not discover the path leading to the right road. For two days their provisions had been completely exhausted, and they were beginning to feel the icy clutch of hunger.

The position was no longer tenable, and they must escape from it at all risks. Valentine and his companions had, therefore, in spite of their failing strength, climbed up the peak in order to look for a road. But this bold attempt had obtained two results instead of one, for Valentine not only declared he had found what he was seeking, but Curumilla had also procured food. Hence, the five men joyously returned to that camp, which they had quitted with death in their hearts.

No one, who has not been in a similar situation, can imagine the feeling of perfect happiness that seizes on a man when he passes, without any transition, from the extremest despair to the greatest confidence. So soon as they reached the encampment, Valentine rekindled the fire, which they had not lit for two days, as it was useless. Still, as the sight of the smoke would arouse Red Cedar's suspicions, if he were, as was very possible, in the vicinity, the hunters roasted their meat in a cavern opening in the side of the hill on which they encamped. When all was ready, they began eating.

It was only when their first hunger was appeased that they thought of thanking the Indian chief for the abundant meal he had procured them by his skill, and of which they had such pressing need. But then they perceived that the Araucano had not obtained the provisions they were eating without incurring serious danger; in fact, Curumilla had on his face, chest, and shoulders serious wounds, inflicted by the beaks and talons of the eagles, which must have boldly defended their provisions.

With the Indian stoicism which nothing can equal, Curumilla, perfectly calm and silent, was staunching the blood that poured from his wounds, disdaining to complain, but, on the contrary, appearing vexed at the anxiety his comrades evidenced.

When the meal was at an end, Valentine solemnly lit his pipe, the others did the same, and ere long they were almost hidden in a cloud.

"Caballeros," Valentine said presently, "God has come to our assistance, as He always does, when men have a firm faith in His omnipotence. He has deigned to supply us with the means to restore our strength, so we must not feel despondent; by this time tomorrow we shall have escaped from this unlucky trap. When you have finished smoking, lie down on the ground and sleep. I will awaken you when the time comes, for at the hour of departure you must feel ready to undertake a long journey. We have about four hours' daylight left, so profit by them, for I warn you we shall have plenty to do tonight in every way. Now that you are warned, you had better follow my advice."

And, adding example to precept, Valentine shook the ash from his pipe, returned it to his belt, lay down on the ground, and almost immediately slept. His comrades probably found the advice good, for they followed it without hesitation, and in ten minutes all were asleep excepting Curumilla.

How long their sleep had lasted when Valentine awakened them, they could not say, but the night had set in. The sky, studded with an infinity of stars, stretched out over their heads its dark blue vault: the moon appeared to be floating in a sea of mist, and spread over the landscape a melancholy light, which imparted a fantastic appearance to objects.

"Up with you," Valentine said in a low voice, as he tapped his comrades in turn on the shoulder.

"Are we off?" General Ibañez asked, as he checked a yawn, and drew himself up, as if worked by a spasm.

"Yes," was all the hunter answered.

Ere long all were ready to start.

"We must profit by the darkness," Valentine remarked, "our enemies are doubtless watching round us."

"We are at your orders, my friend," Don Miguel answered.

By a sign, the hunter collected his comrades round him.

"Listen to me carefully," he said, "for, before attempting the bold enterprise I have conceived, I wish to have your full consent. Our position is desperate: remaining longer here is death: death by hunger, cold, thirst, and wretchedness, after enduring intolerable sufferings for I know not how many days. You are quite convinced of this, I fancy?"

"Yes," they replied unanimously.

"Good," he continued; "trying longer to find the road we have lost would be a vain attempt, which would have no chance of success."

"Yes," they said again.

The hunter continued—

"Well, then, I am about to make an equally mad attempt at this moment. If it does not succeed, we shall perish; but at any rate we shall do so without suffering—almost instantaneously. If we succeed by a miracle—for it is almost a miracle I expect from the inexhaustible mercy of Heaven—we are saved. Reflect ere replying; my friends, are you firmly resolved to follow me, and obey me in all I order, without hesitation or murmuring? In a word, surrender your own will for a few hours only to follow me? Answer me."

The hunters exchanged a glance.

"Command, my friend," the hacendero said, answering for his comrades; "we swear to follow and obey you, whatever may happen."

There was a moment's silence, which Valentine was the first to break.

"Very good," he said, "I have your promise, and must now accomplish mine."

With a gesture of sublime dignity, the wood ranger took off his hat, and raised his eyes to Heaven.

"Oh Lord," he murmured, "our life is in thy hands: we confide in thy justice and mercy." Then, turning to his comrades, he said in a firm voice—

"Let us go!"

The hunters prepared to leave their camp, and Valentine placed himself at the head of the little band.

"And now," he added sharply, "the greatest silence."

The hunters advanced in Indian file, Valentine leading, Curumilla last. In this dark night it was certainly no easy task to proceed through this inextricable chaos of rocks, whose rude crests rose above immeasurable abysses, in the bottom of which an invisible stream could be heard indistinctly murmuring.

One false step was mortal; still, Valentine went on with as much assurance as if he were walking in the dazzling sunshine along the finest path of the prairie, turning to the right, then to the left, clambering up a rock, or gliding along an almost perpendicular wall, without once hesitating, or turning to his comrades, to whom he merely said at times in a low voice:

"Courage."

These four men must have been gifted with hearts of bronze, not to display some slight weakness during this rude journey, in regions which the eagle itself does not visit without hesitation. They marched thus for two hours, without exchanging a word; and after a long descent, during which they had twenty times run a risk of rolling to the bottom of a precipice, Valentine made his companions a sign to stop.

They then took an anxious glance around them: they found themselves on a platform of about ten square yards, all around being gloom, and it hung over an abyss of immeasurable depth. The mountain, cut asunder as if by Roland's sword, was separated, into two portions, between which was a yawning gulf about twelve or fifteen yards in width.

"We must pass over this," Valentine said; "you have ten minutes to draw breath and prepare."

"What, across here?" Don Miguel said in amazement: "why, I only see precipices on both sides."

"Well," the hunter replied, "we will cross it."

The hacendero shook his head despondingly, and Valentine smiled.

"Do you know where we are?" he asked.

"No," his comrades replied.

"I will tell you," he continued; "this spot is mournfully celebrated among the redskins and hunters of the prairie; perhaps you have heard its name mentioned, little suspecting that the day would come for you to be so near it: it is called El Mal Paso, owing to that enormous canyon which intersects the mountain, and suddenly intercepts a communication with the opposite side."

"Well?" Don Miguel asked.

"Well," Valentine went on, "some hours back, when from the top of the peak I watched the two travellers we saw at a distance on the Santa Fe road, my eye settled accidentally on the Mal Paso; then I understood that a chance of salvation was left us, and before confessing ourselves beaten, we must try to cross it."

"Then," Don Miguel said, with a shudder, "you are resolved to make this mad attempt?"

"I am."

"It is tempting Heaven."

"No, it is asking for a miracle, that is all. Believe me, my friend, God never abandons those who fully trust in Him. He will come to our help."

"Still," the hacendero began; but Valentine quickly interrupted him.

"Enough," he said; "you have sworn to obey me. I have sworn to save you; keep your oath as I shall mine."

His comrades, awed by Valentine, bowed their heads and made no reply.

"Brothers," the hunter said, solemnly, "let us pray that God will not desert us."

And, giving the example, he fell on his knees on the rock, his comrades imitating him. At the end of a moment, Valentine rose again.

"Have hope," he said.

The hunter then walked to the extremity of the platform and bent over the abyss, and his comrades followed his movements without comprehending them. After remaining motionless for some minutes, the hunter rejoined his friends.

"All goes well," he said.

He then unfastened his lasso from his belt, and coolly began rolling it round his right hand. Curumilla smiled; he had comprehended his meaning, and, according to his wont, without speaking, he unfastened his lasso and imitated his friend.

"Good," Valentine said to him, with a nod of approval; "it's our turn, chief."

The two wood rangers put forward their right legs, threw their bodies back to get a balance, and whirled their lassos round their heads; at an agreed-on signal, the lassos slipped from their hand and whizzed through the air. Valentine and Curumilla had held the end of the rope in their left hand; they pulled at them, but, in spite of all their efforts, the hunters could not unloose them. Valentine uttered a shout of joy, for he had succeeded;

he connected the two lassos, twisted them round a rock; and fastened them securely, then he turned to his comrades.

"Here is a bridge," he said.

"Ah!" the Mexicans exclaimed, "now we are saved."

These men, with their hearts of bronze, who feared no danger, and recognised no obstacle, could speak thus, although the road was most perilous. Valentine and Curumilla had thrown their lassos round a rock that stood on the other side of the canyon, and the running knot had drawn. In this way the communication was established; but the bridge, as Valentine called it, merely consisted of two leathern cords of the thickness of a forefinger, stretched over a precipice of unknown depth, at least fifteen yards in width, and which must be crossed by the strength of the wrists.

Certainly, before crossing this strange bridge, there was matter for reflection, even to the bravest man. To go fifteen yards hanging thus by the arms over an abyss was not tempting this gloomy night, and upon a rope which might break or become unfastened. The hunters hesitated.

"Well;" Valentine said to them, "shall we be off?"

No one answered.

"That is true," the hunter said with a smile; "you wish to know if the bridge be firm. Very good."

Then with that calmness usual to him the hunter advanced to the edge of the barranca. On reaching the lasso, he took it in both hands, and turned to his comrades.

"Look," he said with that carelessness which he never could put off; "the sight costs nothing."

And gently, without hurrying, with the coolness of a professor giving a lesson, he crossed the canyon backwards, in order to show his friends how they were to manage. On reaching the opposite bank, where he left his rifle, he quietly returned to his friends—the latter had anxiously watched him, trembling involuntarily at the danger he had incurred.

"I hope," he said, when he remounted the platform, "that you are now quite sure the lasso is firm, and you will not hesitate."

Without replying, Curumilla crossed.

"There's one," Valentine said with a laugh; "there is no difficulty about it. Whose turn next?"

"Mine," Don Pablo answered.

He crossed.

"Now it is my turn," Don Miguel said.

"Go," Valentine replied.

The hacendero soon found himself on the opposite side; only two men remained, General Ibañez and the hunter.

"Come," Valentine said, "it is your turn, general; I must be the last to pass."

The general shook his head despondingly.

"I cannot," he said.

CHAPTER XXIII
EL RASTREADOR

Valentine fancied he had misunderstood him.

"What!" he said, as he leaned over to the general.

"I can never pass," he answered.

The hunter looked at him in astonishment. He had known the general in too many critical circumstances, to doubt his courage.

"Why so?" he asked him.

The general rose, seized his arm, and almost placing his mouth to his ear, whispered in a low voice as he looked timidly around:

"Because I am afraid."

At this expression, which he was so far from expecting, Valentine gave a start of surprise, and examining his friend with the utmost attention, so monstrous did what he had just heard appear to him from the mouth of such a man, answered—

"You must be joking."

"No," he said, sadly, "I am afraid. Yes, I understand," he added a moment later with a sigh, "it seems strange to you, does it not, that I should say so; I, whom you have seen brave the greatest dangers with a laugh, and whom, up to the present, nothing has surprised. What would you have? My friend, it is so, I am afraid. I know not why, but the idea of crossing that barranca, holding on by my hands to that cord, which may break, causes me a ridiculous, invincible terror for which I cannot account, and which makes me shudder with terror. That death seems to me hideous, and I could not run the risk of it."

While the general spoke, the hunter examined him with the closest attention. He was no longer the same man; his forehead was livid, a cold perspiration inundated his face, a convulsive tremor agitated all his limbs, and his voice was hollow.

"Nonsense!" Valentine said, attempting to smile, "it is nothing; a little resolution, and you will overcome this terror, which is nothing but dizziness."

"I know not what it is, I cannot say; I can only assure you that I have done all it is morally possible to do, in order to conquer this feeling which overpowers me."

"Well."

"All has been useless: even now, I believe that my terror increases with my efforts to overcome it."

"What! You who are so brave!"

"My friend," the general answered with a sad smile, "courage is an affair of the nerves; it is no more possible for a man to be constantly brave than to be continually a coward; there are days when the matter overcomes the intellect, and physical feelings gain the upper hand over the moral. On those days the most intrepid man is afraid; and this is one of those days with me, that is all."

"Come, my friend," Valentine answered, "reflect a little; hang it all; you cannot remain here—returning is impossible; make a virtue of necessity."

"All you say to me," the general interrupted him, "I have said to myself; and I repeat to you, that, sooner than venture by that cord, I would blow out my brains."

"Why, that is madness," the hunter shouted; "there is no common sense in it."

"Call it what you like; I understand as well as you do how ridiculous I am, but it is stronger than I am."

Valentine stamped his foot angrily as he looked across at his comrades, who, collected on the other side of the barranca, knew not to what to attribute this incomprehensible delay.

"Listen, general," he said, after a moment's delay. "I will not desert you thus, whatever may happen; too many reasons connect us for me to leave you to perish of hunger on this rock; you do not live nearly a year with a man in the desert, sharing with him dangers, cold and heat, hunger and thirst, to separate in this way. If it be really impossible for you to cross the canyon as your comrades have done, and will leave me to act, I will find other means."

"Thanks, my friend," the general sadly replied, as he pressed his hand; "but believe me, do not trouble yourself about me, but leave me here: your comrades are growing impatient, so pray be off at once."

"I will not go," the hunter said resolutely; "I swear that you shall come with me."

"No, I tell you, I cannot."

"Try."

"It is useless; I feel that my heart fails me. Good-bye, my friend."

Valentine made no answer—he was thinking. After an instant he raised his head, and his face was radiant.

"By Jove!" he said, gaily, "I was certain I should discover a way before long. Leave me alone, I answer for everything. You shall cross as if in a carriage."

The general smiled.

"Brave heart!" he muttered.

"Wait for me," Valentine went on; "in a few minutes I will return, only grant me the time to prepare what I want."

The hunter seized the rope and passed, but as soon as the general saw him on the other side, he unfastened the lasso and threw it across.

"What are you doing?—Stop!" the hunters shouted in stupor, mingled with horror.

The general bent over the barranca, holding on to a rock with his left hand.

"Red Cedar must not discover your trail," he said; "that is why I unfastened the lasso. Good-bye, brother, and may the Almighty aid you."

An explosion was heard, echoed in the distance by the mountains, and the general's corpse rolled into the abyss, bounding from rock to rock with a dull sound. General Ibañez had blown out his brains.[1]

At this unexpected dénouement the hunters were petrified. They could not understand how, through the fear of killing himself in crossing the canyon, the general had preferred blowing out his brains. Still, the action was logical in itself; it was not death, but only the mode of death that terrified him; and as he fancied it an impossibility to follow his comrades, he had preferred sudden death. Still, in dying, the brave general had rendered them a final and immense service. Thanks to him, their trail had so entirely disappeared, that it would be impossible for Red Cedar to find it again.

The hunters, although they had succeeded in escaping from the fatal circle in which the pirate had thrust them, owing to Valentine's daring resolve, still found themselves in a most critical situation: they must get down into the plain as speedily as possible, in order to find some road, and, as always, happens in the desert under such circumstances, every sympathy must promptly yield to the necessity that held them in its iron arms; the common danger suddenly aroused in them that feeling of self-preservation which never does more than sleep.

Valentine was the first to overcome his grief and regain his self-mastery. Since he had been crossing the desert, the hunter had witnessed so many strange scenes, had been an actor in so many mournful tragedies, that, his tender feelings were considerably blunted, and the most terrible events affected him but slightly.

Still, Valentine felt a deep friendship for the general; in many circumstances he had appreciated all that was really grand and noble in his character, hence the fearful catastrophe which had, without any preparation, broken the ties between them, produced a great impression on him.

"Come, come," he said, shaking his head as if to get rid of painful thoughts, "what can't be cured must be endured. Our friend has left us for a better world,—perhaps it is for the best so. God does everything well; our grief will not restore our dear friend's life, so let us think of ourselves, my friends, for we are not lying on roses, and if we do not make haste, we may run a risk of speedily joining him. Come, let us be men."

Don Miguel Zarate looked at him sadly.

"That is true," he said; "he is happy now; let us attend to ourselves. Speak then, Valentine: what is to be done? We are ready."

"Good," said Valentine; "it is time for our courage to return, for the hardest part of our task is not yet done; it is nothing to have crossed that barranca if our trail can be found here, and that I wish to avoid."

"Hum!" Don Pablo remarked; "that is very difficult, not to say impossible."

"Nothing is impossible with strength, courage, and skill. Listen attentively to what I am about to say to you."

"We will."

"The barranca, on this side of the mountain, is not peaked as it is on the side we have just left."

"That is true," said Don Miguel.

"About twenty yards below us you perceive a platform, close to which begins an inextricable forest, descending to the end of the precipice."

"Yes."

"That is our road."

"What, our road, my friend!" Don Miguel objected; "but how shall we reach the platform to which you allude?"

"In the easiest way: I will let you down with my lasso."

"That is true; it is easy for us, but how will you join us?"

"That need not trouble you."

"Very good," Don Miguel remarked; "but now permit me to make a remark."

"Do so."

"Before us," the hacendero said, stretching out his hand, "is a readily traced road, most convenient to follow, I fancy."

"In truth," Valentine coldly answered, "what you say is most correct; but two reasons prohibit my taking that road, as you call it."

"And those two reasons are?"

"First, that ready traced road is so easy to follow that I am certain Red Cedar's suspicions will be directed to it at once, if the demon allows him to come here."

"And the second?" Don Miguel interrupted.

"Is this," Valentine went on: "in addition to the incontestable advantages the road I propose offers, I do not wish, and I feel sure you are of the same opinion, that the body of my poor comrade, who has rolled to the foot of the precipice, should remain unburied and become the prey of wild beasts. That is my second reason, Don Miguel; what do you think of it?"

The hacendero felt his heart dilate at these noble words; the tears sprung from his eyes and rolled silently down his cheeks. He seized the hunter's hand, and pressed it forcibly.

"Valentine," he said, in a broken, voice, "you are better, than all of us; your noble heart is filled with every great and generous feeling; thanks for your good idea, my friend."

"It is agreed, then," the hunter simply said in response; "we will go."

"Whenever you please."

"Good; but as the night is dark, and the road rather dangerous, Curumilla, who has long been used to the desert, will go first to show you the way. Come, chief, are you ready?"

The Ulmen nodded his assent. Valentine leant his whole weight against a rock, twisted the lasso twice round his body, and let the end fall into the chasm; then, he made the chief, a sign to go down. The latter did not let the invitation be repeated; he seized the rope in both hands; and placing his feet in crevices in the rocks, he gradually descended till he reached the platform.

The hacendero and his son attentively followed the Indian's movements. When they saw him safe on the rock, they gave a sigh of relief, and prepared to follow him, which they did without accident.

Valentine remained alone; consequently, no one could hold the lasso and render him the service he had done his comrades; but he was not embarrassed by so trivial a circumstance. He passed the rope round a rock, so that both ends were even, then slowly descended in his turn, and safely rejoined his comrades, who were startled and frightened at such a daring descent. Then he let go the end of the lasso, drew it to him, rolled it up, and fastened it to his girdle.

"I believe," he said with a smile, "that if we go on thus, Red Cedar will have some difficulty in finding our trail, while we, on the contrary, may find his. Come let us now take a look at our domain, and see a little where we are."

And he at once began walking round the platform. It was much larger than the one they had just left, and at its extremity began the virgin, forest, which descended with a gentle incline to the bottom of the barranca. When Valentine had examined the place, he returned to his comrades, shaking his head.

"What is the matter?" Don Pablo asked; "Have you seen anything suspicious?"

"Hum!" Valentine answered; "I am greatly mistaken, or the lair of a wild beast is somewhere close by."

"A wild beast!" Don Miguel exclaimed; "What, at this elevation?"

"Yes, and it is that very fact which makes me anxious; the traces are wide and deep. Look for yourself, Curumilla," he added, turning to the Indian, and pointing at the spot where he should proceed. Without replying, the Ulmen stooped down, and attentively examined the footprints.

"What animal do you think we have to deal with?" Don Miguel asked.

"A grizzly," Valentine answered.

The grizzly bear is the most terrible and justly feared animal in America. The Mexicans could not repress a start of terror on hearing the name of this terrible adversary pronounced.

"But here's the chief returning," Valentine added. "All our doubts will be cleared up. Well, chief, to what does that sign belong?"

"Grizzly," Curumilla laconically answered.

"I was sure of it," said Valentine; "and what is t more, the animal is large."

"Very large; the footmarks are eight inches wide."

"Oh, oh," Don Miguel said, "we have a rough companion in that case. But in what state is the sign, chief?"

"Quite fresh; the animal passed scarce an hour ago."

"By Jove!" Valentine suddenly shouted, "here is its lair."

And he pointed to a large yawning hole in the mountain side. The hunters gave a start.

"Gentlemen," Valentine went on, "you are no more anxious than myself to measure your strength with a grizzly, I suppose."

"Certainly not," the Mexican exclaimed.

"If you will follow my advice we will not remain any longer here; the animal, I suspect, has gone down to drink, and will speedily return; let us not wait for it, but profit by its absence to be off."

The three men enthusiastically applauded the hunter's proposal; for, although of tried bravery, the contest appeared to them so disproportionate with this redoubtable adversary, that they did not at all desire to come face to face with it.

"Let us be off," they eagerly shouted.

Suddenly the sound of breaking branches was audible in the forest, and a formidable growling troubled the silence of night.

"It is too late," Valentine said; "here is the enemy, the fight will be a tough one."

The hunters leaned against the wall of rock, side by side, and in a few moments the hideous head of the grizzly appeared among the trees on a level with the platform.

"We are lost," Don Miguel muttered as he cocked his rifle; "for any flight from this rock is impossible."

"Who knows?" Valentine answered. "Heaven has done so much for us up to the present, that we should be ungrateful to suppose that we shall be abandoned in this new peril."

[1] This episode, incredible as it may appear, is rigorously true.—G.A.

CHAPTER XXIV
THE CAMP IN THE MOUNTAINS

On leaving the jacal, Red Cedar proceeded towards the mountains. The squatter was one of those old hands to whom all the tracks of the desert are known. From the few words uttered by Father Seraphin, and the haste he had shown in coming to warn him, Red Cedar understood that this time the final contest was about to begin, without truce or pity, in which his enemies would employ all their knowledge and skill to finish with him once for all.

He had been fortunate enough to reach the Sierra de los Comanches soon enough to be able, to efface his trail. During a month he and Valentine had carried on one of those incredible campaigns of skill and boldness in which each employed every scheme his fertile mind suggested to deceive his adversary.

As frequently happens under such circumstances, Red Cedar, who at the outset only accepted unwillingly the struggle into which he was forced, had gradually felt his old wood ranger instincts aroused. His pride had been excited, for he knew he had to deal with Valentine, that is to say, the cleverest hunter on the prairie, and he had consequently displayed a degree of skill that surprised himself, in order to prove to his terrible adversary that he was not unworthy of him.

For a whole month the two had been unsuccessfully manoeuvring within a circle of less than ten leagues, constantly turning round one another, and often only separated by a screen of foliage, or a ravine. But this contest must have an end sooner or later, Red Cedar felt, and being no longer sustained by the same passions which formerly served as the motive of all his actions, despondency was beginning to seize upon him, the more so, because physical pain had been recently joined to his moral sufferings, and threatened to deal him the final blow. Let us see in what condition Red Cedar was at the moment when the exigencies of our story compel us to return to him.

It was about eight o'clock in the evening; three men and a girl, assembled round a scanty fire of *bois de vache*, were warming themselves, and, at times, casting a dull glance at the gloomy gorges of the surrounding mountains. These four persons were Nathan, Sutter, Fray Ambrosio, and Ellen.

The spot where they found themselves was one of those narrow ravines, the bed of dried torrents, so many of which are met with in the Sierra de los Comanches. On the flanks of the ravine was a thick chaparral, the commencement of a gloomy virgin forest, from the mysterious depths of which could be heard at intervals the lengthened howling and roar of wild beasts.

The situation of the fugitives was most critical, and even desperate. Shut up for a month amid these arid mountains, tracked on all sides, they had hitherto only escaped their persecutors through the immense sacrifices and the prodigious craft displayed by Red Cedar. The pursuit had been so active, that, being constantly on the point of being surprised by their enemies, they did not dare kill the few head of game they came across. A shot, by revealing the direction in which they were, would have been sufficient to betray them.

In the meanwhile, the scanty stock of food they had brought with them from the jacal, in spite of their saving, had been consumed, and hunger, but before all, thirst, was beginning to be felt. Of all the scourges that afflict hapless travellers, thirst is indubitably the most terrible. Hunger may be endured during a certain length of time, without excessive suffering, especially at the end of a few days; but thirst occasions atrocious pain, which, after a while, produces a species of furious madness; the palate is parched, the throat is on fire, the eyes are suffused with blood, and the wretched man, a prey to a horrible delirium, which makes him see the desired water everywhere, at length dies in atrocious agony, which nothing can calm.

When their provisions were exhausted, they were compelled to procure others; but in the mountains that was almost impossible, as the fugitives were deprived of their freedom of action. For a few days they continued to support life on roots, and small birds caught in a snare; but unfortunately, the cold became daily sharper, and the birds withdrew to warmer regions; hence they were deprived of this resource.

The little water remaining was by common agreement reserved for Ellen. The maiden declined to accept this sacrifice, but thirst grew upon her with every moment, and, overcome by the entreaties of her companions, she eventually accepted it. The others found no other way of quenching the thirst that devoured them, than slitting the ears of their horses and drinking the blood as it ran. Next, they killed a horse, for the poor brutes found no more food than did their masters. The roasted flesh of this horse enabled them to pass a few days: in short, all four horses were eaten one after the other.

Now, nothing was left the adventurers, and for two days they had nothing to eat. Hence they maintained a mournful silence, exchanging stern glances, and plunging deeper and deeper into sinister reflections.

They felt their senses gradually leaving them and madness seizing on them; they felt the moment approaching when they would be no longer masters of their reason, and become the prey of the fearful calenture, which already pressed their temples as in a vice, and made the most startling images glitter before their fever-dried eyes.

It was a heart-breaking sight to see these three men, round the expiring fire, in this stern desert, lying without strength and almost without courage by the side of the maiden, who, with clasped hands and downcast eyes, prayed in a low voice.

Time passed; the wind howled mournfully in the quebradas; the moon, half veiled by a mass of vapour, only emitted at intervals its pallid rays, which fantastically illumined the scene of desolation, whose sinister silence was only disturbed by a suppressed oath or a groan drawn forth by pain. Ellen raised her head, and looked compassionately at her companions.

"Courage," she murmured in her gentle voice, "courage, brothers! God cannot abandon us thus."

A nervous groan was the only reply she obtained.

"Alas!" she continued, "Instead of, then yielding to despair, why not pray, brothers? It gives strength and restores hope."

"Will it quench the thirst that parches my throat?" the monk asked, brutally, as he rose with an effort on his elbow and gave her a furious glance.

"Silence! You foolish child, if you have no other help than your silly words to give us."

"Silence, villain!" Sutter interrupted him with a groan, "Do not insult my sister; she alone may perchance save us; for if God have pity on us, it will be for her sake."

"Ah!" the monk said, with a hideous grin, "Now you believe in God, my master. You must fancy yourself very near death to be so frightened? God! You poor fool, rejoice that there is none, instead of calling on Him for help; for if He really existed, He would have crushed you long ago."

"Well said, monk," Nathan remarked. "Come, let us have peace. If we are to die here like the dogs we are, let us die, at any rate, pleasantly. That is not asking too much I suppose?"

"Oh, how I suffer!" Sutter muttered, as he rolled wildly on the ground.

Ellen got up, gently approached her; brother, and putting to his lips the mouth of the skin, in which a little water yet remained, she bade him drink. The young man made a movement as if to seize the skin; but at the same instant he repulsed it, shaking his head in refusal.

"No," he replied, mournfully, "keep that, sister; you would give me your life."

"Drink, I insist," she said, authoritatively.

"No," he answered firmly, "that would be cowardly. I am a man, sister; I can suffer."

Ellen understood that her entreaties would be useless, for she knew the superstitious affection her brothers bore her; hence she returned to the fire. She sat down, took three buffalo-horn cups, which she filled with water, and placed before her; then she took a sharp pointed knife, and turning to the three men, who were anxiously watching her, she said—

"Here is water, drink. I swear that if you do not instantly obey me, I will slit the skin in which the little stock of water is left; all will then be lost, and I shall suffer the same pains as you do."

The men made no answer, but looked at each other.

"For the last time, will you drink or not?" she cried, as she placed the point of the knife on the skin.

"Stay," the monk shouted, as he rose and rushed towards her. "Demonios! She would do as she said."

And seizing a cup, he emptied it at a draught, his companions following his example. This mouthful of water—for the cups were very small—sufficed, however to calm their irritation—the fire that burned them was extinguished, they breathed more easily, and gave vent to a grunt of satisfaction, as they fell back on the ground. An angelic smile lit up the maiden's radiant face.

"You see," she said, "all is not lost yet."

"Come, come, Niña," the monk remarked, tranquilly, "why lull us with foolish hopes? The drop of water you have given us can only check our sufferings for a little while; within an hour our thirst will be more ardent and terrible than ever."

"Do you know what Heaven may reserve for you between this and then?" she asked, softly. "A respite, however short it may be, is in your position everything; all depends for you, not on the present moment, but on the coming one."

"Good, good! We'll not dispute after the service you have rendered us, Niña; still, everything seems to prove you wrong."

"How so?"

"Why, Caspita, what I say is very easy to understand; without going further, your father, who pledged his word never to desert us—"

"Well?"

"Where is he? Since daybreak he has left us to go—the deuce alone knows where? Night has long set in, and, and as you see, he has not returned."

"What does that prove?"

"*Canarios!* That he has gone away, that is all."

"Do you believe it, señor?"

"I am sure of it, Niña."

Ellen gave a contemptuous look.

"Señor," she haughtily answered, "you do not know my father if you consider him capable of such cowardice."

"Hum! In our position he would almost have an excuse for doing so."

"He might have done so, perhaps," she went on, quickly, "if he had no other comrade but yourself, caballero; but he would leave his children here, and he is not the man to abandon them when in danger."

"That is true," the monk said, with humility; "I did not think of that, so forgive me. Still, you will permit me to remark that it is an extraordinary thing your father has not yet returned?"

"Well, señor," the maiden said, warmly, "although you are so ready to accuse a friend, who has constantly offered you the most unequivocal proofs of his unknown devotion, how do you know that he is not delayed by his desire to save us?"

"Well spoken, by Heaven!" a rough voice said; "Thank you, my daughter."

The adventurers turned with an involuntary start; at this moment the bushes were parted by a firm hand, a heavy step sounded on the pebbles, and Red Cedar appeared, bearing a doe on his shoulder. On reaching the light of the fire he stopped, threw his burden the ground, and looked sarcastically around him.

"Oh, oh," he said, with a grin, "it seems that I have arrived just in time, señor Padre. *Viva Dios!* you were giving me a fine character in my absence;

is that the way in which you understand Christian charity, gossip? Cristo! I do not compliment you on it, if that be the case."

The monk, startled by the sudden appearance and rough address, found no answer, so Red Cedar went on:

"By Jove! I am a better fellow than yourself, for I bring you food, and it was not without difficulty that I succeeded in killing that confounded animal, I can tell you. But now look sharp and roast a joint."

Sutter and Nathan had not waited for their father's orders, but had already begun skinning the doe.

"Hilloh!" Nathan remarked, "to roast this meat, we must enlarge our fire; and how about our pursuers?"

"It is a risk to run," Red Cedar replied; "settle among ourselves if you will incur it."

"What is your opinion?" the monk asked.

"It is a matter of perfect indifference to me; but I wish you to understand one thing, once for all, as I am intimately convinced that we shall fall into the hands of our pursuers, I care very little whether it happen today or in a week's time."

"Confusion! You are not at all encouraging, gossip," Fray Ambrosio exclaimed. "Have you lost your courage too, or discovered any suspicious trail?"

"My courage never fails me; I know very well the fate reserved for me, and hence my mind is made up. As for suspicious signs, as you say, a man must be blind not to see them."

"Then there is no hope," the three men said, with ill-disguised terror.

"On my honour I do not think there is; but," he added, with a mocking accent, "why do you not roast the meat? You must be almost dead of hunger."

"That is true; but what you tell us has taken away our appetite," Fray Ambrosio remarked, sadly.

Ellen rose, approached the squatter, and laying her hand softly on his shoulder, placed her charming face close to his. Red Cedar smiled.

"What do you want, my girl?" he asked her.

"I wish, father," she said, in a coaxing voice, "that you should save us."

"Save you, poor child," he said, as he shook his head gravely, "I am afraid that is impossible."

"Then," she continued, "you will let us fall into the hands of our enemies?"

The squatter shuddered.

"Oh! Do not say that, Ellen," he replied, hoarsely.

"Still, my father, as you cannot help us to escape—"

Red Cedar passed the back of his hard hand over his dark forehead.

"Listen," he said presently, "there is perhaps one way—"

"What is it?" the three men said, eagerly, as they collected round him.

"It is very precarious, dangerous, and probably will not succeed."

"Tell it us for all that," the monk pressed him.

"Yes, yes—speak father," Ellen urged him.

"You desire it?"

"Yes, yes."

"Very well, then, listen to me attentively, for the means I am about to propose, strange as they may at first appear to you, offer a chance of success, which, in our desperate situation, must not be despised."

"Speak, pray speak!" the monk said impatiently.

Red Cedar looked at him with a grin.

"You are in a precious hurry," he said; "perhaps you will not be so presently."

CHAPTER XXV
A GAME AT HAZARD

"Before explaining my plan to you," Red Cedar went on, "I must tell you what our position really is, so that when I have described the means I wish to employ, you can decide with a full knowledge of the facts."

His hearers gave a nod of assent, but no one made an answer.

The squatter continued—

"We are surrounded on three sides: firstly, by the Comanches, next by Bloodson's rangers, and lastly by the French hunter and his friends. Weakened as we are by the terrible privations we have suffered since we came into the mountains, any contest is impossible; we must, therefore, give up all hope of opening a passage by force."

"What is to be done, then?" the monk asked; "it is plain that we must escape, and each second that slips away renders our prospects worse."

"I am as fully convinced of that as you can be. My absence today had a double object; the first was to obtain provisions, in which, as you see, I succeeded—"

"That is true."

"Secondly, to reconnoitre carefully the positions held by our enemies."

"Well?" they asked anxiously.

"I have succeeded. I advanced unnoticed close to their camps; they keep a good watch, and it would be madness to try and pass through them; they form a wide circle around us, of which we are the centre; this circle is being daily contracted, so that in two or three days, perhaps before, we shall find ourselves so pressed that it will be impossible to hide ourselves, and we must fall into their hands."

"Demonios!" Fray Ambrosio exclaimed, "that is anything but a pleasant prospect; we have no mercy to expect from these villains, who will, on the contrary, find a pleasure in torturing us in every way possible. Hum! the mere thought of falling into their hands makes my flesh creep; I know what the Indians are capable of in torturing, for I have seen them at work often enough."

"Very good; I will not press that point then."

"It would be perfectly useless. You will do better to explain to us the plan you have formed, and which, as you say, can save us."

"Pardon me! I did not offer you any certainty; I merely said that it had some chances of success."

"We are not in a position to quibble about words; let us have your scheme."

"It is this—"

The three men listened with the deepest attention.

"It is evident," Red Cedar went on, "that if we remain together, and try to fly in one direction, we shall be infallibly lost, supposing, as is certain, that our trail is discovered by our pursuers."

"Very well," the monk growled; "go ahead; I do not exactly understand what you want to come at."

"I have, therefore, reflected on this inconvenience, and I have formed the following scheme."

"Out with it."

"It is very simple; we will make a double trail."

"Hum! I suppose you mean, a false and a true one. The plan seems to me defective."

"Why so? Red Cedar asked with a smile.

"Because there must be a point where the false trail runs into the real one, and—"

"You are mistaken, gossip," Red Cedar sharply interrupted him; "both trails will be true, otherwise the idea would be absurd."

"In that case, I do not understand you."

"You soon will, if you will allow me to speak. One of us will devote himself to save the others; while we fly in one direction, he will go on another, trying to draw the enemy on his trail. In this way, he will open us a passage, through which we shall pass, without being discovered. Do you understand me now?"

"Caspita! I should think I did—the idea is magnificent," the monk exclaimed enthusiastically.

"All now wanted is to carry it out."

"Yes, without any delay."

"Very good! Who will sacrifice himself to save his comrades?"

No one answered.

"What," Red Cedar went on, "are you all silent? Come, Fray Ambrosio, you are a priest, so give us an example."

"Thank you, gossip, but I never felt any call to martyrdom. I am not at all ambitious."

"Still, we must get out of this scrape."

"Caramba! I wish for nothing better; still, I am not desirous that it should be at the expense of my scalp."

Red Cedar reflected for an instant. The adventurers looked at him anxiously, waiting till he had found the solution of this difficult problem. All at once the squatter raised his head.

"Hum!" he said, "Any discussion would be useless, for you are not the men to be led by your feelings."

They nodded their assent.

"This is what we will do; we will draw lots who shall devote himself; the one on whom it devolves will obey without a murmur. Does that suit you?"

"As we must bring matters to an end," said Nathan, "why, the sooner the better; that way is as good as another, so I do not object."

"Nor I," Sutter remarked.

"Nonsense!" The monk exclaimed; "I was always lucky at games of chance."

"It is settled then; you swear that the man on whom the lot falls, will obey without hesitation, and accomplish his task honourably?"

"We swear it," they said with one voice; "come, Red Cedar, let us have it over."

"Yes; but in what way shall we consult chance?" Red Cedar observed.

"That need not trouble you, gossip," Fray Ambrosio said with a laugh; "I am a man of caution."

While speaking thus, the monk fumbled in his vaquera boots, and produced a greasy pack of cards.

"These will do the trick," he went on with a triumphant air. "This pretty child," he added, turning to Ellen, "will shuffle the cards; one of us will cut them, and then she will deal the cards one by one, and the man who has the two of spades will have to make the double trail. Does that suit you?"

"Admirably," they replied.

Ellen took the cards from the monk and shuffled them, while a zarapé was laid on the ground by the fire, so that the colour of the cards might be distinguished by the flame.

"Cut," she said, placing the pack on the zarapé.

Fray Ambrosio thrust out his hand; but Red Cedar laughingly caught hold of his arm.

"A moment," he said; "those cards are yours, gossip, and I know your talent: permit me to cut."

"As you please," the monk said with a grimace of disappointment.

The squatter cut, and Ellen began dealing the cards.

There was something most strange about the scene. On a gloomy night, in the heart of this desolate gorge, with the wind moaning through the trees, these four men bending forward, anxiously watching the pale-browed girl, who, by the capricious and changing glare of the fire, seemed performing a cabalistic work, and the sinister looks of these men, staking their lives at this moment on a card—assuredly, a stranger who could have watched the extraordinary spectacle, himself unseen, would have fancied it an hallucination of the brain.

With frowning brows, pale faces, and heaving chests, they followed with a feverish glance each card as it fell, wiping away at intervals the cold perspiration that beaded on their temples. The cards still fell, but the two of spades had not yet appeared; Ellen had not more than ten cards left in her hand.

"Ouf!" the monk said, "It is a long job."

"Bah!" Red Cedar said with a grin; "perhaps you will find it too short."

"It is I," Nathan said in a choking voice. In fact, the two of spades fell to him, and all breathed freely again.

"Well," the monk said, as he tapped him on the shoulder, "I congratulate you, my friend Nathan: you have a glorious mission."

"Will you undertake it in my stead?" the other remarked with a grin.

"I would not deprive you of the honour of saving us," Fray Ambrosio said with magnificent coolness.

Nathan gave him a look of pity, shrugged his shoulders, and turned his back on him. Fray Ambrosio collected the cards, and replaced them in his boot with evident satisfaction.

"Hum!" he muttered, "They may still be of service; we cannot tell in what circumstances chance may place us."

After this philosophic reflection, the monk, cheered up by the certainty of not being obliged to sacrifice himself for his friends, quietly sat down again by the fire. In the meanwhile, Red Cedar, who did not let out of sight the execution of his plan, had placed some lumps of meat on the fire, that his companions might acquire the necessary strength for the fatigues they would have to endure.

As usually happens under similar circumstances, the meal was silent; each, absorbed in his thoughts, ate rapidly without thinking of keeping up idle conversation. It was about five in the morning, and the sky was beginning to assume those opaline tints which summoned daybreak. Red Cedar rose, and the rest imitated him.

"Come, lad," he said to Nathan, "are you ready? The hour has arrived."

"I will start whenever you please, father," the young man answered, resolutely. "I am only awaiting your final instructions, that I may know the directions I have to follow, and at what place I shall find you again, if, as is not very likely, I have the luck to escape safe and sound."

"My instructions will not be lengthy, my lad. You must go north-west, as that is the shortest road to leave these accursed mountains. If you can reach the high road to Independence, you are saved; thence it will be easy for you to reach in a short time the cavern of our old comrades, where you will hide yourself while waiting for us. I recommend you specially to hide your trail as well as you can. We have to deal with the craftiest men on the prairie; an easy trail would arouse their suspicions, and our design would be entirely foiled. You understand me, I think?"

"Perfectly."

"For the rest, I trust to you; you know desert life too well to be humbugged; you have a good rifle, powder, and bullets. I wish you luck, lad! But do not forget that you have to draw our enemies after you."

"Do not be frightened," Nathan replied, roughly, "I am no fool."

"That is true; take a lump of meat, and good-bye."

"Good-bye, and the devil take you but watch over my sister; I care precious little for your old carcass, so long as the girl runs no danger."

"All right," the squatter said, "We will do what is needful to protect your sister, so do not trouble yourself about her; come, be off."

Nathan embraced Ellen, who affectionately pressed his hand, as she wiped away her tears.

"Don't cry, Ellen," he said hoarsely; "a man's life is nothing after all; don't bother yourself about me—the devil will look after his friends."

After uttering the words in a tone which he tried in vain to render careless, the young savage threw his rifle on his back, hung a piece of meat to his girdle, and went off hurriedly, not turning round once. Five minutes later, he disappeared in the chaparral.

"Poor brother!" Ellen murmured, "he is going to a certain death."

"Well," Red Cedar said, with a shrug of his shoulders, "we are all going to death, and each step unconsciously brings us nearer to it: what use is it feeling sorry about the fate that threatens him; do we know what awaits ourselves? We are not lying on a bed of roses. My child, I warn you, that we shall require all, our skill and sagacity to get out of it, for I cannot calculate on a miracle occurring."

"That is far more prudent," Fray, Ambrosio said, cunningly; "besides, it is written somewhere, I forget where, 'Help yourself, and heaven will help you.'"

"Yes," the squatter replied, with a grin, "and there never was a finer opportunity for putting the precept in practice."

"I think so, and am waiting for you to explain to us what we have to do."

Without answering the monk, Red Cedar turned to his daughter.

"Ellen, my child," he asked her, in an affectionate voice, "do you feel strong enough to follow us?"

"Do not trouble yourself about me, father," she replied; "wherever you pass, I will pass: you know that I have been accustomed to the desert from my childhood."

"That is true," Red Cedar remarked doubtfully: "but this is the first time you have tried the mode of travelling we shall be obliged to adopt."

"What do you mean? People travel on foot, horseback, or in a boat. We have moved about in one of those fashions twenty times before."

"You are right; but now we are constrained by circumstances to modify our mode of marching. We have no horses, no river, and our enemies hold the ground."

"In that case," the monk exclaimed with a grin, "we will imitate the birds, and fly through the air."

Red Cedar, looked at him earnestly.

"You have nearly guessed it," he said.

"What?" the monk remarked, "you are making fun of us, Red Cedar. Do you think this the proper moment for jesting?"

"I am not naturally inclined to jesting," the squatter coldly replied, "and at this moment less than ever. We shall not fly like the birds, because we have no wings; but for all that, we will make our journey in the air, in this way. Look around you; on the sides of the mountains extend immense virgin forests, in which our enemies are concealed. They are coming on quietly, carefully picking out every sign of our passing they can discover."

"Well?" the monk asked.

"While they are seeking our trail on the ground, we will slip through their hands like serpents, passing from tree to tree, from branch to branch, thirty yards above their heads, and they not dreaming of looking up, which would, indeed, be useless, for the foliage is too dense, the creepers too close for them to discover us. And then, again, this chance of safety, though very slight, is the only one left us. Have you the courage to try it?"

There was a momentary silence. At length the monk took the squatter's hand, and shook it heartily.

"Canarios! Gossip," he said to him, with a species of respect, "you are a great man. Forgive my suspicions."

"You accept, then?"

"*Caspita!* You need not ask that. Eagerly, and I swear it, that never squirrel leaped as I will do."

CHAPTER XXVI
NATHAN PAINTS HIMSELF

So soon as he had got out of sight of his comrades, Nathan halted. He was neither so careless nor confident as he wished to appear. When he was alone and away from those who might ridicule, he gave way to his ill temper, and cursed the chance that placed him in such a precarious and dangerous position.

Nathan, we think we have already said, was a species of Hercules, gifted with uncommon energy and ferocity. Accustomed from his childhood to a desert life and its sanguinary tragedies, he was not the man to despond and despair easily. Pitiless to himself as to others, he perfectly accepted the consequences of the situation in which he found himself at times placed, and, in case of necessity, was resolved to fight to the death in defence of his scalp.

At this moment, however, it was not his position in itself that rendered him anxious. He had been a hundred times beset by equal danger in crossing the prairie; but hitherto, when he had perilled his life, he had done it with an object he knew perfectly well, with the prospect, near or remote, of some profit; but this time he regarded himself as obeying a will he was ignorant of, for a purpose he did not understand, and for interests that were not his own. Hence, he cursed his father, Fray Ambrosio, and himself for having thus got into a trap, whence he did not know how to escape.

Red Cedar's last recommendation was necessary. Nathan was not at all anxious to have his trail discovered. He employed all the means his intelligence suggested to him to hide it from the keenest glance, only taking a step after convincing himself that the trace of the previous one had disappeared. After ripe reflection, he had arrived at the following conclusion—

"It's all the worse for them, but each for himself! If I lose my scalp they will not give it me back. I will, therefore, defend it as well as I can. They must do what they can, but for my part I must do my best to get out of the scrape."

After these words, uttered in a loud voice, in the way of men accustomed to live alone, Nathan gave that almost imperceptible shrug of his shoulders, which in all countries signifies "let what will happen." And, after carefully examining his rifle, he started afresh.

Europeans, accustomed to the horizons of the old world, to macadamised roads, bordered by pleasant houses and traversed in every direction, cannot form, even approximately, a correct idea of the position of a man alone in that ocean of verdure called the "Far West", who feels himself watched by invisible eyes, and knows he is tracked like a wild beast.

A man, however brave he may be, and accustomed to the adventurous life of the desert, shudders and feels very weak when he turns an enquiring glance around him, and sees himself, so little in the immensity that surrounds him. In the desert, if you wish to go north, you must march to the south; be attentive not to crush the leaves on which you walk, break the branches that bar the way, and, above all, not to make the pebbles on which you step grate against each other.

All the sounds of the desert are known to, explained, and commented on by the redskins. After listening for a few seconds, they can tell you if the animal whose footfall is heard in the distance, is a horse, a bear, a buffalo, an elk, or an antelope. A pebble rolling down the side of a ravine suffices to denounce a prowler. A few drops of water spilt on the edge of a ford, clearly reveal the passing of several travellers. An unusual movement in the tall grass, betrays a watching spy. Everything, in short, from the down-trodden blade of grass to the buffalo that suddenly cocks its ears while browsing, or the asshata bounding in alarm without cause—all in the desert serves as a book, in which the Indian reads the passage of friend or foe, and puts him on his trail, even though they be one hundred miles apart.

The men who live in these countries, where material life is everything, acquire a perfection of certain organs which, seems incredible; sight and hearing especially are enormously developed in them; and this, combined with extreme agility, dauntless courage, and sustained by muscles of remarkable vigour, renders them dangerous adversaries. In addition to this, we have that cunning and treachery which are never apart, and are the two great means which the Indians employ to seize their foes, whom they never attack face to face, but always by surprise. Necessity is the supreme law of the Indian, and he sacrifices everything to it, and, like all incomplete or badly-developed natures, he only admits physical qualities, caring nothing for virtues he does not want, but, on the contrary, would injure him in the life he leads.

Nathan was himself almost a redskin: only at rare intervals had he visited, for a few days at a time, the towns of the American Union. Hence all he knew of life he had learned in the desert; and that education is as good as another when the instincts of the man who receives it are good; because he is able to make a choice, and take what is noble and generous, laying aside what is bad. Unfortunately, Nathan had never any other teacher of morality but his father. From an early age he had been accustomed to regard things in the same way as the squatter did, and that was the worst of all. Hence with years the teaching be received had fructified so fully that he had become the true type of the civilised man who has turned savage; the most hideous transformation of species that can be imagined.

Nathan loved nothing, believed in nothing, and respected nothing. Only one person had any influence over him, and that was Ellen; but at this moment she was no longer by his side.

The young man marched on for a long time without perceiving anything that revealed the approach of danger; still this factitious security did not make him neglect his precautions. While walking on, with rifle thrust out before him, his body bent forward, and eye and ear on the watch, he thought, and the further he went, the more gloomy his thoughts became.

The reason was simple; he knew that he was surrounded by implacable foes, watched by numerous spies, and yet nothing disturbed the quiet of the prairie. All appeared to be in its ordinary state; it was impossible to notice the least suspicious movement in the grass or shrubs. This calmness was too profound to be natural, and Nathan was not deceived by it.

"Humph!" he said to himself, "I shall have a row presently, I feel certain; deuce take those brutes of redskins for not giving a sign of life. I am walking blindly, not knowing where I am going, I am convinced I shall fall into some trap laid for me by these villains, and which it will be impossible for me to get out of."

Nathan went on walking till about ten in the morning. At that hour, as he felt hungry, and his legs were rather stiff, he resolved at all hazards to take a few moments' rest and some mouthfuls of meat. He mechanically looked round him to seek a suitable, spot, but he suddenly gave a start of surprise as he raised his rifle, and hid himself behind an enormous tree. He had noticed, scarce fifty yards from him, an Indian, sitting carelessly on the ground and quietly eating a little pemmican.

After the first emotion had worn off, Nathan attentively examined the Indian. He was a man of thirty at the most; he did not wear the garb of a warrior, and two screech owl feathers fixed in his thick hair, over his right ear, rendered it easy to recognise a Nez-Percé Indian. The adventurer looked at him a long time ere he could make up his mind what to do; at length he threw his rifle on his shoulder, left his hiding place, and walked up to the Indian. The latter probably saw him, though he displayed no alarm, and quietly went on eating. When about two paces from the Nez-Percé the American stopped.

"I salute my brother," he said, raising his voice, and unfolding his zarapé in sign of peace; "may the Wacondah grant him a great hunt."

"I thank my paleface brother," the Indian replied, as he looked up; "he is welcome, I have two handfuls of pemmican left, and there is a place for him at my fire."

Nathan approached, and, without further ceremony, sat down by the side of his new friend, who paternally shared his food with him, but asked him no questions. After feeding, the Nez-Percé lit an Indian pipe, in which his companion at once imitated him.

The two men remained there, silently puffing the smoke in each other's face. When the Nez-Percé had finished his calumet, he shook out the ash on his thumb, placed the pipe in his belt, and and then resting his elbows on his knees, and his face in the palm of his hands, he plunged into that state of ecstatic beatitude which the Italians call the *dolce far niente*, the Turks *keff*, and which has no equivalent in English. Nathan filled his pipe a second time, and then turned to his comrade.

"Is my brother a chief?" he asked him.

The Indian raised his head.

"No," he answered, with a proud smile, "I am one of the masters of the great medicine."

Nathan bowed respectfully.

"I understand," he said, "my brother is one of the wise men, whom the redskins call *allanus*."

"I am also a sorcerer," the Nez-Percé said.

"Oh, oh! What, is my brother one of the Ministers of the Great Turtle?"

"Yes," he answered, "we command the caciques and warriors; they only act on our orders."

"I know it; my father has great learning, his power extends over the whole earth."

The Nez-Percé smiled condescendingly at this praise, and holding up a small staff decorated with gay feathers and bells which he held in his right hand, he said:

"This *mulbache* is a more tremendous weapon than the thunder of the palefaces; everywhere it makes me feared and respected."

A sinister smile for the second time curled the American's lips.

"Is my brother returning to his nation?" he asked.

"No," the Indian said with a shake of the hand; "I am expected at the village of the Buffalo Apaches, who require my counsel and my medicine, in order to undertake, under favourable auspices, a great expedition they are meditating at this moment. My brother will therefore forgive my leaving him, for I must reach the end of my journey this night."

"I will not leave my red brother," Nathan answered; "if he will permit me, I will walk in his moccasins, for my footsteps have the same direction as my brother's."

"I gladly accept my brother's proposition; let us start then."

"I am ready."

After rising and adjusting his dress, the Indian stooped to pick up a small bundle, which probably contained his scanty property. Nathan profited by the movement; swift as thought he drew his knife, and buried it to the hilt between the Indian's shoulders. The unhappy man uttered a stifled cry, stretched out his arms, and fell dead. The American phlegmatically drew his knife from the horrible wound, wiped it in the grass, and returned it to his girdle.

"Hum!" he said, with a grin; "there's a poor devil of a sorcerer, whose skill could not save him: I will try whether I cannot succeed better."

While talking with the redskin, whom he had at first no intention of killing, and whom he only wished to make a protector, a sudden idea crossed his mind. This idea, which at the first blush will seem extraordinary, suited the bandit, owing to the boldness and daring it required to carry it out successfully. He made up his mind to assume the sorcerer's clothes, and pass for him among the redskins. Long conversant with Indian habits and customs, Nathan felt sure he should play this difficult part with all the perfection necessary to deceive even sharper eyes than those of the savages. After assuring himself that his victim gave no sign of life, Nathan began removing his garments, which he put on instead of his own. When this first change was effected, he riffled the sorcerer's bag, took out a mirror, bladders filled with vermilion, and a black pigment, and with small pieces of wood painted on his face the strange figures that were on the sorcerer's. The imitation was perfect; from the face he passed to the body; then he fastened on his hair, and stuck in it the two screech owl feathers. Nathan had frequently disguised himself as an Indian, when going scalp hunting with his father, hence the metamorphosis in a few seconds.

"This carrion must not be found," he said.

Taking the body on his back, he hurled it to the bottom of a precipice.

"Well, that is settled," he continued, with a laugh; "if the Apaches are not satisfied with the great medicine man who is coming to them, they will be difficult to please."

As he did not wish to lose his clothes, he hid them in the Indian's bundle, which he passed over his rifle barrel; he then took the poor sorcerer's staff, and gaily set out, muttering to himself with an impudent smile—

"We shall soon see whether this mulbache really possesses the magic powers that are attributed to it."

CHAPTER XXVII
A TRAIL IN THE AIR

Travellers and tourists who have only seen European forests, cannot imagine the grand, majestic, and sublime view offered by a virgin forest in the New World. There are none of those glades four or five yards wide, stretching out before you, straight and stiff for miles, but everything is abrupt and savage. There is no prospect, for the eye cannot see more than thirty or forty paces at the most in any direction. The primitive soil has disappeared beneath the detritus of trees dead from old age, and which time, rain, and sunshine have reduced to dust.

The trees grow very freely, enveloped by thick lianas, which twine around the stems and branches in the strangest curves, dashing in every direction, plunging into the ground to reappear again a yard further on, and chaining the trees together for enormous distances. The wood varies but slightly in certain districts, and hence, one tree serves the repetition of all. Then again, a grass, close and thick like the straw of a wheat field, grows to a height of five and often six feet.

Suddenly immense pits open beneath the feet of the imprudent traveller, or bogs covered by a crust scarce an inch in thickness, which swallow up in their fetid mud the man who ventures to put a foot on them; further on, a stream runs silent and unvisited, forming rapids, and forcing a path with difficulty through the heaps of earth and dead trees which it collects and deposits on the banks. From this short description it may be understood that it is not so difficult as might be supposed to pass from one tree to another for a long distance.

In order, however, to explain this thoroughly to the reader, we will tell him what he is probably ignorant of: that in certain parts of the prairie this mode of travelling is employed, not, as might be supposed, to escape the obstinate pursuit of an enemy, but simply to get on the more rapidly, not to be obliged to cut a path with the axe, and run no risk of falling down a precipice, the more so as most of the trees are enormous, and their solid branches so intertwined, that they thus form a convenient flooring, at eighty feet above the ground.

Hence Red Cedar's proposition had nothing extraordinary in itself, when made to men who had probably tried this mode of locomotion before. But what would have been an easy and simple thing for the adventurers, became serious and almost impossible for a girl like Ellen, who, though strong and skillful, could not take a step without running a risk of breaking her neck, owing to her dress catching in every branch. A remedy for this must be found, and the three men reflected on it for an hour, but discovered nothing which offered the necessary security. It was Ellen again who came to their help, and relieved them from the trouble.

"Well," she asked her father, "what are we doing here? Why do we not start? Did you not say we had not a moment to lose?"

Red Cedar shook his head.

"I said so, and it is true; each moment we lose robs us of a day of life."

"Let us be off, then."

"It is not possible yet, my child, till I have found what I am seeking."

"What is it, father? Tell, me, perhaps I can help you."

"Bah!" Red Cedar said, suddenly making up his mind, "Why should I make a secret of what concerns you as much as myself?"

"What is it, then, father?"

"Hang it all, your confounded gown, which renders it impossible for you to leap from one branch to another as we shall do."

"Is that all that troubles you?"

"Yes, nothing else."

"Well then, you were wrong not to speak to me sooner, for the evil would have been repaired, and we on the road."

"Is it true?" the squatter exclaimed joyfully.

"You shall see how quickly it will be done."

The girl rose, and disappeared behind a clump. In ten minutes she returned; her gown was so arranged that while allowing her the free use of her limbs, it no longer floated, and consequently ran no risk of being entangled in the trees.

"Here I am," she said, with a laugh; "how do you find me?"

"Admirable."

"Well, then, we will start when you please."

"At once."

Red Cedar made his final preparations; these were not long, for he had but to remove all traces of his encampment. More difficult still, none of the pursuers, if they happened to pass that way, should be able to discover the road taken by the adventurers. In consequence, Red Cedar took his daughter on his muscular shoulders, and heading the party in Indian file he followed for about an hour the road taken by Nathan. Then, he and his comrades returning, marching backwards, gradually effacing the footprints, not so carefully that they could not be discovered, but sufficiently so for those who found them not to suppose they had been left expressly.

After two hours of this fatiguing march, during which the adventurers had not exchanged a syllable, they reached a granite plateau, where they were enabled to rest for a few moments without any fear of leaving a trail, for the rock was too hard to take their footprints.

"Ouf!" Fray Ambrosio muttered, "I am not sorry to take breath, for this is the devil's own work."

"What, are you tired already, señor Padre?" Sutter replied with a grin; "You are beginning early; but wait a while; what you have done is nothing compared with what you have to do."

"I doubt whether the road we shall now follow can present so many difficulties; if so, we had better give it up."

"Well, if you prefer making a present of your scalp to those demons of Comanches, it is the easiest thing in the world; you need only remain quietly, where you are, and you may be certain they will soon pay you a visit. You know that the redskins are like vultures; fresh meat attracts them, and they scent it for a long distance."

"Canarios! I would sooner be roasted at a slow fire than fall into the hands of those accursed pagans."

"Come, come," Red Cedar interposed, "all that talking is of no use— what is written is written—no one can escape his destiny; hence, troubling oneself about what is going to happen is folly, take my word for it."

"Well said, Red Cedar; you have spoken like a man of great good sense, and I am completely of your opinion. Well, what have you to say to us?"

"I believe that, thanks to the manoeuvre we have employed, we have managed to hide our trail so cleverly, that the demon himself could not guess the direction we have taken. The first part of our task has been accomplished without an obstacle; now let us not betray ourselves by imprudence or extreme precipitation. I have brought you here, because, as you see, the virgin forest begins at the end of this platform. The most difficult task is to climb the first tree without leaving a trail; as for the rest, it is merely a question of skill. Leave me to act as I think proper, and I warrant you will have no cause to repent it."

"I know it; so, for my part, I assure you that you are quite at liberty to act as you please."

"Very good; that is what we will do; you see that enormous branch jutting out about thirty feet above our heads?"

"I see it—what next?"

"I will seize its end with my lasso, and we will pull it down till it touches the ground; we will hold it so while daughter mounts and reaches the higher branches; you will pass next, then Sutter, and myself last; in that way we shall leave no sign of our ascent."

"Your idea is very ingenious, I approve of it highly, especially as that way of mounting will be easy for your daughter and myself, while Sutter will not have much trouble. Still one thing bothers me."

"Out with it."

"So long as anyone is here to hold the branch, of course it will remain bent; but when we are up and you remain alone, how will you follow us? That I do not understand, and I confess I should not be sorry to learn it."

Red Cedar burst into a laugh.

"That need not bother you, señor Padre; I am too much used to the desert not to calculate my slightest actions."

"As it is so, we will say no more it. What I said was through the interest I take in you."

The squatter looked him in the face.

"Listen, Fray Ambrosio," he said as he laid his hand lightly on his shoulder, "we have known one another for a long while, so let us have no falsehoods; we shall never manage to divine each other, so let us remain as we are. Is that agreed, eh?"

The monk was upset by this harsh address; he lost countenance, and stammered a few words. Red Cedar had taken his lasso, and row whirled it round his head. He had measured so exactly, that the running knot caught the end of the branch.

"Help, all!" the squatter shouted.

Under their united efforts the branch gradually bent down to the level of the platform, as Red Cedar had foreseen.

"Make haste; Ellen, make haste, my child!" he shouted to the maiden.

The latter did not need any repetition of the invitation; she ran lightly along the branch, and in a twinkling was leaning against the stem. By her father's request she mounted to the upper branches, among which she disappeared.

"It is your turn, Fray Ambrosio," the squatter said.

The monk disappeared in the same way.

"It is yours, lad," the squatter said.

Sutter rejoined the other two. When left alone, Red Cedar put forth all his strength to hold the branch down, while he clung to its lower surface with his hand and feet. So soon as the branch was no longer held down, it rose, with a shrill whistle and a rapidity enough to make him giddy. The tree trembled to its roots. Ellen uttered a cry of terror and closed her eyes. When she opened them again, she saw her father astride on the end of the tree engaged in unfastening the running knot of his lasso, after which the squatter rose with perfect calmness, and while rolling the lasso round his loins, joined his companions.

"Well," he said to them, "you see it is finished; now we must continue our journey; are you ready?"

"Quite," they all said.

We repeat our assertion, that with the exception of the strangeness of the road, this way of travelling had nothing dangerous or even inconvenient about it, owing to the immense network of lianas that twined capriciously round the trees and the interlaced branches. The party proceeded, almost without perceiving it, from one tree to the other, constantly suspended over an abyss of sixty, even eighty, feet in depth.

Beneath them they at times perceived the wild beasts which they troubled in their mysterious lairs, and which, with outstretched necks and flashing eyes, watched them pass in surprise, not understanding what they saw. They marched thus the whole day, stopping for a moment to take breath, and starting again immediately. They had crossed, still on their floating bridge, a rather wide stream, and would soon find themselves in the lowlands.

It was about five in the evening; the beams of the setting sun lengthened the shadows of the trees; the owls, attracted by the startled flight of the beetles, of which they are excessively fond, were already flying about; a dense vapour rose from the ground, and formed a mist, in which the four persons almost disappeared: all, in a word, announced that night would soon set in.

Red Cedar had taken the lead of the little party for fear lest his companions might take a wrong direction in the inextricable labyrinth of the virgin forest; for at the height where they were the outlines of the ground entirely disappeared, and only an immense chaos of tufted branches and interlaced creepers could be seen.

"Hilloa, gossip!" Fray Ambrosio said, who, little accustomed to long walks, and weakened by the lengthened privations he had gone through, had walked for some time with extreme difficulty, "Shall we soon stop? I warn you that I can go no further."

The squatter turned sharply and laid his large hand on the monk's mouth.

"Silence!" he hissed; "Silence, if you value your scalp!"

"Cristo, if I value it!" the other muttered, with a movement of terror; "But what is happening fresh?"

Red Cedar cautiously moved a mass of leaves, and made a sign to his comrades to imitate him.

"Look," he said.

In a second the monk drew himself back with features convulsed with terror.

"Oh," he said, "this time we are lost!"

He tottered, and would have fallen, had not the squatter seized him by the arm.

"What is to be done?" he said.

"Wait," Red Cedar coldly answered: "our position for the present is not so desperate; you see them, but they do not see us."

Fray Ambrosio shook his head sadly,

"You have led us to our ruin," he said, reproachfully.

"You are an ass," Red Cedar answered with contempt; "do I not risk as much as you? Did I not warn you that we were surrounded? Leave me to act, I tell you."

CHAPTER XXVIII
THE FIGHT WITH THE GRIZZLY

The New World has no reason to envy the Old in the matter of ferocious animals of every description and every species. The family of the plantigrades has obtained an enormous development in America, and possesses races of a ferocity before which all the wild beasts of our continent turn pale.

We will speak here of the animal endowed with a prodigious strength, blind courage, and unbounded cruelty, which the learned call *ursus cinereus*, and the Americans the grizzly bear. Most travellers draw a terrific feature of this animal, saying that it combines with the stupidity of the Polar bear the ferocity and courage of the great carnivora. Though a traveller myself, I am forced humbly to confess that the stories of these gentry must be accepted with some reserve, who, often placed in perilous situations, or ill-disposed mentally and bodily, have seen badly, and, in spite of themselves, yielding to the influence of the moment, have unconsciously indulged in exaggerations, which have gradually become articles of faith, and are now accepted as such.

I have no intention to rehabilitate the grizzly bear in the minds of my readers; still, I will ask them not to be more unjust to it than they are to other animals sent into the world by the Creator. Hence, laying aside all exaggerations, and confining ourselves to the strictest truth, we will, in a few words, describe the grizzly bear and its habits. During our long stay in America, we saw enough of these animals, and in sufficient proximity to be accepted as a credible witness.

My readers will see from the portrait of this animal, correct, if not flattering though it be, that it is naturally ugly enough, both morally and physically, not to require to be rendered more hideous and converted into a monster. The grizzly, when it has reached its full growth, is about ten feet in length; its coat is woolly, very thick, and perfectly grey, excepting round the ears, where it is brown. Its face is terrible; it is the most ferocious and dangerous of all the American carnivora. In spite of its clumsy shape and heavy appearance, its agility is extreme. It is the more to be feared, because its indomitable courage emanates from the consciousness of its prodigious strength, and is always akin to fury. The grizzly attacks all animals, but chiefly the larger ruminants, such as buffaloes, oxen, &c. What has probably given rise to the exaggerated stories of travellers, is the fact that the grizzly bear does not hibernate, and as during winter it starves among the snow-covered mountains, it descends to the plains to find food. The redskins carry on a deadly warfare with it, in order to obtain its long sharp claws, of which they form collars, to which they set great value.

It was with one of these formidable animals that Valentine suddenly found himself face to face. The rencontre was most disagreeable; still when the first emotion had passed off, the hunters boldly made up their minds.

"It is a combat to death," Valentine said laconically; "you know the grizzly never draws back."

"What shall we do?" Don Miguel asked.

"See what he does first," the hunter continued. "It is evident that this animal has fed, else it would not return to its lair. You know that bears go out but little; if we are lucky enough to deal with a bear that has had a good dinner, it will be an immense advantage for us."

"Why so?"

"For the simple reason," Valentine said with a laugh, "that, like all people whose meal hours are irregular, when bears sit down to dinner, they eat with extreme gluttony, which renders them heavy, sleepy, and deprives them, in a word, of one half their faculties."

"Hum!" Don Miguel observed; "I fancy what is left them is quite enough."

"And so do I; but, quiet, I fancy the beast has made up his mind."

"That is to say," Don Pablo remarked, "that it is making its arrangements to attack us."

"That is what I meant to say," Valentine replied.

"Well, we will not let it make the first demonstration."

"Oh, don't be frightened, Don Miguel, I am used to bear hunting; this one certainly does not expect what I am preparing for it."

"Providing you do not miss your shot: in that case we should be lost," Don Miguel observed.

"By Jove! I know that: so I shall take my measures in accordance."

Curumilla, stoical as ever, had cut a piece of candlewood, and concealed himself in the shrubs only a few paces from the wild beast. The bear, after a moment's hesitation, during which it looked round with an eye flashing with gloomy fire, as if counting the number of foes it had to fight, uttered a second growl, as it passed a tongue as red as blood over its lips.

"That is it," Valentine said with a laugh; "lick your chops, my fine fellow; still, I warn you that your mouth is watering too soon—you have not got us yet."

The bear seemed to notice the bravado, for it made an effort, and its monstrous head entirely appeared above the level of the platform.

"Did I not tell you it had eaten too much?" the hunter went on. "See what difficulty it finds in moving. Come, sluggard," he said, addressing the terrible animal, "shake yourself up a little."

"Take care," Don Miguel shouted.

"The brute is going to leap on you," Don Pablo said in agony.

In fact, the bear, by a movement swift as lightning, had escaladed the platform with a gigantic bound, and was now scarce twenty yards from the intrepid hunter. Valentine did not move, not one of his muscles shook: he merely clenched his teeth as if going to break them, and a white foam appeared at the corner of his lips. The beast, surprised by the intrepidity of the man, cowed by the electric fluid that flashed from the hunter's haughty eye, fell back a step. For a moment it remained motionless, with hanging head; but it soon began tearing up the ground with its formidable claws, as if encouraging itself to begin the attack.

Suddenly it turned round. Curumilla profited by the movement, of the torch he held in readiness for the purpose, and at a signal from Valentine, made the light flash before the bear. The animal, dazzled by the brilliant glare of the torch, which suddenly dissipated the darkness that surrounded it, savagely rose on its hind legs, and turning toward the Indian, tried to clutch the torch with one of its forepaws, probably in order to put it out.

Valentine cocked his rifle, stood firmly on his legs, aimed carefully, and began whistling softly. So soon as the sound reached the bear's ears, it stopped, and remained thus for some seconds as if trying to account for this unusual noise. The hunter still whistled: the witnesses of the scene held their breath, so interested were they in the strange incidents of this duel between intellect and brute strength. Still they kept their hands on their weapons, ready to hurry to their friend's help, should he be in danger.

Valentine was calm, gently whistling to the bear, which gradually turned its head toward him. Curumilla, with the lighted torch in his hand, attentively watched all the animal's movements. The bear at length faced the hunter; it was only a few paces from him, and Valentine felt its hot and fetid breath. The man and the brute gazed on each other; the bear's bloodshot eye seemed riveted on that of the Frenchman, who looked at it intrepidly while continuing to whistle softly.

There was a moment, an age of supreme anxiety. The bear, as if to escape the strange fascination it suffered under, shook its head twice, and then rushed forward with a fearful growl. At the same instant a shot was fired.

Don Miguel and his son ran up. Valentine, with his rifle butt resting on the ground, was laughing carelessly, while two paces from him the terrible animal was uttering howls of fury, and writhing in its dying convulsions. Curumilla bending forward, was curiously watching the movements of the animal as it rolled at his feet.

"Thank Heaven," Don Miguel eagerly exclaimed. "You are safe, my friend."

"Did you fancy that I ran any danger?" the hunter answered simply.

"I trembled for your life," the hacendero said with surprise and admiration.

"It was not worth the trouble, I assure you," the hunter said carelessly; "grizzly and I are old acquaintances; ask Curumilla how many we have knocked over in this way."

"But," Don Pablo objected, "the grizzly bear is invulnerable; bullets flatten on its skull, and glide off its fur."

"That is perfectly true; still, you forget there is a spot where it can be hit."

"I know it, the eye; but it is almost impossible to hit it at the first shot; to do so a man must be endowed with marvellous skill, not to say admirable courage and coolness."

"Thank you," Valentine replied with, a smile; "now that our enemy is dead, I would ask you to look and tell me where I hit it."

The Mexicans stooped down quickly; the bear was really dead. Its gigantic corpse, which Curumilla was already preparing to strip of its magnificent coat, covered a space of nearly ten feet. The hunter's bullet had entered its right eye; the two gentlemen uttered a cry of admiration.

"Yes," Valentine said, replying to their thought, "it was not a bad shot; but be assured that this animal enjoys an usurped reputation, owing to the habit it has of attacking man, whom, however, it hardly ever conquers."

"But look, my friend, at those sharp claws; why, they are nearly six inches long."

"That is true; I remember a poor Comanche, on whose shoulder a grizzly let his paw fall, and completely smashed it. But, is it an interesting sport? I confess that it possesses an irresistible attraction for me."

"You are quite at liberty, my friend," said Don Miguel, "to find a delight in fighting such monsters, and I can account for it; the life you lead in the desert has so familiarised you with danger, that you no longer believe in it; but we dwellers in towns have, I confess, an invincible respect and terror for this monster."

"Nonsense, Don Miguel, how can you say when I have seen you engaged in a hand-to-hand fight with tigers?"

"That is possible, my friend; I would do so again, if necessary—but a jaguar is not a grizzly."

"Come, come, I will not tease you any longer. While Curumilla prepares our breakfast, I will go down into the ravine. Help my friend to roast a piece of my game, and I am sure when you have tasted it, the exquisite flavour will make you quite alter your opinion about friend Grizzly."

And carelessly throwing his rifle on his shoulder, which he had reloaded, Valentine then entered the chaparral, in which he almost immediately disappeared.

The game, as Valentine called the grizzly, weighed about four hundred weight. After flaying it with that dexterity the Indians possess, Curumilla, aided by the two Mexicans, hung up the body to a branch, that bent beneath its weight; he cut steaks from the loin, and took out the pluck, which regular hunters consider the most delicate part of the beast; and then, while Don Miguel and Don Pablo lit the fire, and laid the steaks on the ashes, the Indian entered the cave.

Don Pablo and his father, long accustomed to the Araucano chief's way of behaving, made no remark, but went on with the preparations for breakfast actively, the more so because the night's fatigues and their long privations had given them an appetite which the smell of the cooking meat only heightened.

Still, the meal had been ready some time, and Valentine had not returned. The two gentlemen were beginning to feel anxious. Nor did Curumilla emerge either from the cavern in which he had now been upwards of an hour. The Mexicans exchanged a glance.

"Can anything have happened?" Don Miguel asked.

"We must go and see," said Don Pablo.

They rose; Don Pablo proceeded toward the cave, while his father went to the end of the platform. At this moment Valentine arrived on one side, Curumilla on the other, holding two young bearskins in his hands.

"What does that mean?" Don Pablo in his surprise could not refrain from asking.

The Indian smiled. "It was a she-bear," he said.

"Are we going to breakfast?" Valentine asked.

"Whenever you like, my friend," Don Miguel answered; "we were only waiting for you."

"I have been gone a long time."

"More than an hour."

"It was not my fault. Just fancy, down there it is as dark as in an oven. I had great difficulty in finding our friend's body; but, thanks to heaven, it is now in the ground, and protected from the teeth of the coyotes and the other vermin of the prairie."

Don Miguel took his hand and pressed it tenderly, while tears of gratitude ran down his cheeks.

"Valentine," he said, with great emotion. "You are better than all of us; you think of everything; no circumstance, however grave it may be, can make you forget what you regard in the light of a duty. Thanks, my friend, thanks, for having placed in the ground the poor general's body; you have made me very happy."

"That will do," Valentine said, as he turned his head away, not to let the emotion he felt in spite of himself, be noticed; "suppose we feed? I am fearfully hungry; the sun is rising, and we have not yet quitted that frightful labyrinth in which we so nearly left our bones."

The hunters set down round the fire, and began sharply attacking the meal that awaited them. When they had finished eating, which did not take long, thanks to Valentine, who continually urged them to take double mouthfuls, they rose and prepared to start again.

"Let us pay great attention, caballeros," the hunter said to them, "and carefully look around us, for I am greatly mistaken if we do not find a trail within an hour."

"What makes you suppose so?"

"Nothing, I have found no sign," Valentine answered, with a smile; "but I feel a foreboding that we shall soon find the man we have been seeking so long."

"May heaven hear you, my friend! Don Miguel exclaimed.

"Forward! Forward!" Valentine said, as he set out.

His comrades followed him. At this moment the sun appeared above the horizon, the forest awoke as if by enchantment, and the birds, concealed beneath the foliage, began their matin hymn, which they sing daily to salute the sun.

CHAPTER XXIX
A MOTHER'S LOVE

As we have said, Madame Guillois was installed by her son at the winter village of the Comanches, and the Indians gladly welcomed the mother of the adopted son of their tribe. The most commodious lodge was immediately placed at her service, and the most delicate attentions were lavished on her.

The redskins are incontestably superior to the whites in all that relates to hospitality. A guest is sacred to them to such an extent, that they become his slaves, so to speak, so anxious are they to satisfy all his desires, and even his slightest caprices.

After Father Seraphin had warned Red Cedar to be on his guard, he returned to Madame Guillois in order to watch more directly over it. The worthy missionary was an old acquaintance and friend of the Comanches, to whom he had been useful on several occasions, and who respected in him not the priest, whose sublime mission they could not understand, but the good and generous man, ever ready to devote himself to his fellow men.

Several weeks passed without producing any great change in the old lady's life. Sunbeam, on her own private authority, had constituted herself her handmaiden, amusing her with her medley of Indian-Spanish and French, attending to her like a mother, and trying, by all the means in her power, to help her to kill time. So long as Father Seraphin remained near her, Madame Guillois endured her son's absence very patiently. The missionary's gentle and paternal exhortations made her—not forget, because a mother never does that—but deceive herself as to the cruelty of this separation.

Unhappily, Father Seraphin had imperious duties to attend to which he could no longer neglect; to her great regret he must recommence his wandering life, and his mission of self-denial and suffering, while carrying to the Indian tribes, the light of the gospel, and the succour of religion. Father Seraphin was in Madame Guillois's sight a link of the chain that attached her to her son; she could speak about him with the missionary, who knew the most secret thoughts of her heart, and could by one word calm her alarm, and restore her courage. But when he left her for the first time since her arrival in America, she really felt alone, and lost her son once again, as it were. Thus the separation was cruel; and she needed all her Christian resignation and long habit of suffering to bear meekly the fresh blow that struck her.

Indian life is very dull and monotonous, especially in winter, in the heart of the forest, in badly built huts, open to all the winds, when the leafless trees are covered with hoar-frost; the villages are half buried beneath the snow, the sky is gloomy, and during the long nights the hurricane may be heard howling, and a deluge of rain falling.

Alone, deprived of a friend in whose bosom she could deposit the overflowing of her heart, Madame Guillois gradually fell into a gloomy melancholy, from which nothing could arouse her. A woman of the age of the hunter's mother does not easily break through all her habits to undertake a journey like that she had made across the American desert. However simple and frugal the life of a certain class of society may be in Europe, they still enjoy a certain relative comfort, far superior to what they may expect to find in Indian villages, where objects of primary necessity are absent, and life is reduced to its simplest expression.

Thus, for instance, a person accustomed to work in the evening in a comfortable chair, in the chimney corner, by the light of a lamp, in a well-closed room, would never grow used to sit on the beaten ground, crouching over a fire, whose smoke blinds her, in a windowless hut, only illumined by the flickering flame of a smoky torch.

When Madame Guillois left Havre, she had only one object, one desire, to see her son again; every other consideration must yield to that: she gladly sacrificed the comfort she enjoyed to find the son whom she believed she had lost, and who filled her heart.

Still, in spite of her powerful constitution and the masculine energy of her character, when she had endured the fatigue of a three months' voyage, and the no less rude toil of several weeks' travelling through forests and over prairies, sleeping in the open air, her health had gradually broken down, her strength was worn out in this daily and hourly struggle, and wounded, both physically and morally, she had been at length forced to confess herself beaten, and to allow that she was too weak to endure such an existence longer.

She grew thin and haggard visibly; her cheeks were sunken, her eyes buried more and more deeply in their orbits, her face was pale, her look languishing—in short, all the symptoms revealed that the nature which had hitherto so valiantly resisted, was rapidly giving way, and was undermined by an illness which had been secretly wasting her for a long time, and now displayed itself in its fell proportions.

Madame Guillois did not deceive herself as to her condition, she calculated coolly and exactly all the probable incidents, followed step by step the different phases of her illness, and when Sunbeam anxiously enquired what was the matter with her, and what she suffered from, she answered her with that calm and heart-breaking smile which the man condemned to death puts on when no hope is left him—a smile more affecting than a sob—

"It is nothing, my child,—I am dying."

These words were uttered with so strange an accent of gentleness and resignation that the young Indian felt her eyes fill with tears, and hid herself to weep.

One morning a bright sun shone on the village, the sky was blue, and the air mild. Madame Guillois, seated in front of her calli, was warming herself in this last smile of autumn, while mechanically watching the yellow leaves, which a light breeze turned round. Not far from her the children were sporting, chasing each other with merry bursts of laughter. Unicorn's squaw presently sat down by the old lady's side, took her hand, and looked at her sympathisingly.

"Does my mother feel better?" she asked her in her voice which was soft as the note of the Mexican nightingale.

"Thanks, my dear little one," the old lady answered, affectionately, "I am better."

"That is well," Sunbeam replied, with a charming smile; "for I have good news to tell my mother."

"Good news?" she said, hurriedly, as she gave her a piercing glance; "has my son arrived?"

"My mother would have seen him before this," the squaw said, with a tinge of gentle reproach in her voice.

"That is true," she muttered; "my poor Valentine!"

She let her head sink sadly on her bosom. Sunbeam looked at her for a moment with an expression of tender pity.

"Does not my mother wish to hear the news I have to tell her?" she went on.

Madame Guillois sighed.

"Speak, my child," she said.

"One of the great warriors of the tribe has just entered the village," the young woman continued; "Spider left the chief two days ago."

"Ah!" the old lady said, carelessly, seeing that Sunbeam stopped; "and where is the chief at this moment?"

"Spider says that Unicorn is in the mountains, with his warriors; he has seen Koutonepi."

"He has seen my son?" Madame Guillois exclaimed.

"He has seen him," Sunbeam repeated; "the hunter is pursuing Red Cedar with his friends."

"And—he is not wounded?" she asked anxiously.

The young Indian pouted her lips.

"Red Cedar is a dog and cowardly old woman," she said; "his arm is not strong enough, or his eye sure enough to wound the great pale hunter. Koutonepi is a terrible warrior, he despises the barkings of the coyote."

Madame Guillois had lived long enough among the Indians to understand their figurative expressions; she gratefully pressed the young squaw's hand.

"Your great warrior has seen my son?" she said eagerly.

"Yes," Sunbeam quickly answered, "Spider saw the pale hunter, and spoke. Koutonepi gave him a necklace for my mother."

"A necklace?" she repeated, in surprise, not understanding what the woman meant; "What am I to do with it?"

Sunbeam's face assumed a serious expression.

"The white men are great sorcerers," she said, "they know how to make powerful medicines; by figures traced on birch bark communicate their thoughts at great distances; space does not exist for them. Will not my mother receive the necklace her son sends her?"

"Give it me, my dear child," she eagerly answered; "everything that comes from him is precious to me."

The young squaw drew from under her striped calico dress a square piece of bark of the size of her hand, and gave it to her. Madame Guillois took it curiously, not knowing what this present meant. She turned it over and over, while Sunbeam watched her attentively. All at once the old lady's features brightened, and she uttered a cry of joy; she had perceived a few words traced on the inside of the bark with the point of a knife.

"Is my mother satisfied?" Sunbeam asked.

"Oh, yes," she answered.

She eagerly perused the note; it was short, contained indeed but a few words, yet they filled the mother with delight; for they gave her certain news of her son. This is what Valentine wrote—

"My dear mother, be of good cheer, my health is excellent, I shall see you soon: your loving son, Valentine."

It was impossible to write a more laconic letter; but on the desert, where communication is so difficult, a son may be thanked for giving news of himself, if only in a word. Madame Guillois was delighted, and when she had read the note again, she turned to the young squaw.

"Is Spider a chief?" she asked.

"Spider is one of the great warriors of the tribe," Sunbeam answered proudly; "Unicorn places great confidence in him."

"Good; I understand. He has come here on a particular mission?"

"Unicorn ordered his friend to choose twenty picked warriors from the tribe, and lead them to him."

A sudden idea crossed Madame Guillois's mind.

"Does Sunbeam love me?" she asked her.

"I love my mother," the squaw replied, feelingly; "her son saved my life."

"Does not my daughter feel grieved at being away from her husband?" the old lady continued.

"Unicorn is a great chief; when he commands, Sunbeam bows and obeys without a murmur; the warrior is the strong and courageous eagle, the squaw is the timid dove."

There was a long silence, which Sunbeam at last broke by saying, with a meaning smile—

"My mother had something to ask of me?"

"What use is it, dear child?" she answered hesitatingly, "As you will not grant my request."

"My mother thinks so, but is not sure," she said, maliciously.

The old lady smiled.

"Have you guessed, then, what I was about to ask of you?" she said.

"Perhaps so; my mother will explain, so that I may see whether I was mistaken."

"No, it is useless; I know that my daughter will refuse."

Sunbeam broke into a fresh and joyous laugh as she clapped her little hands.

"My mother knows the contrary," she said; "why does she not place confidence in me? Has she ever found me unkind?"

"Never; you have always been kind and attentive to me, trying to calm my grief, and dissipate my fears."

"My mother can speak then, as the ears of a friend are open," Sunbeam said to her quietly.

"In truth," the old lady remarked, after some thought, "what I desire is just. Is Sunbeam a mother?" she said, meaningly.

"Yes," she quickly replied.

"Does my daughter love her child?"

The Indian looked at her in surprise.

"Are there mothers in the great island of the whites who do not love their child?" she asked; "My child is myself, is it not my flesh and blood? What is there dearer to a mother than her child?"

"Nothing, that is true." Madame Guillois sighed. "If my daughter were separated from her child, what Would she do?"

"What would I do?" the Indian exclaimed, with a flash in her black eye; "I would go and join him, no matter when, no matter how."

"Good," the old lady remarked, eagerly; "I, too, love my child, and my daughter knows it. Well, I wish to join him, for my heart is lacerated at the thought of remaining any longer away from him."

"I know it, that is natural, it cannot be opposed. The flower fades when separated from the stem, the mother suffers when away from the son she nourished with her milk. What does my mother wish to do?"

"Alas! I wish to start as soon as possible to embrace my son."

"That is right: I will help my mother."

"What shall I do?"

"That is my business. Spider is about to assemble the council in order to explain his mission to the chiefs. Many of our young men are scattered through the forest, setting traps and hunting the elk to support their family. Spider will want two days to collect the warriors he needs, and he will not start till the third day. My mother can be at rest; I will speak to Spider, and in three days we will set out."

She embraced the old lady, who tenderly responded, then rose and went away, after giving her a final sign of encouragement. Madame Guillois returned to her calli, her heart relieved of a heavy weight; for a long time she had not felt so happy. She forgot her sufferings and the sharp pangs of illness that undermined her, in order to think only of the approaching moment when she would embrace her son.

All happened as Sunbeam had foreseen. An hour later, the hachesto convened the chiefs to the great medicine lodge. The council lasted a long time, and was prolonged to the end of the day. Spider's demand was granted, and twenty warriors were selected to go and join the sachem of the tribe. But, as the squaw had foretold, most of the warriors were absent, and their return had to be awaited.

During the two succeeding days Sunbeam held frequent conferences with Spider, but did not exchange a word with Madame Guillois, contenting herself, when the mother's glance became too inquiring, by laying her finger on her lip with a smile. The poor lady sustained by factitious strength, a prey to a burning fever, sadly counted the hours while forming the most ardent vows for the success of her plan. At length, on the evening of the second day, Sunbeam, who had hitherto seemed to avoid the old lady, boldly approached her.

"Well?" the mother asked.

"We are going."

"When?"

"Tomorrow, at daybreak."

"Has Spider pledged his word to my daughter?"

"He has; so my mother will hold herself in readiness to start."

"I am so now."

The Indian woman smiled.

"No, tomorrow."

At daybreak, as was agreed on the previous evening, Madame Guillois and Sunbeam set out under the escort of Spider and his twenty warriors to join Unicorn.

CHAPTER XXX
THE SORCERER

Although Spider was a Comanche warrior in the fullest meaning of the term, that is to say rash, cunning, brutal and cruel, the laws of gallantry were not entirely unknown to him, and he had eagerly accepted Sunbeam's proposition. The Indian, who, like most of his countrymen, was under great obligations to Valentine, was delighted at the opportunity to do him a kindness.

If Spider had only travelled with his warriors the journey would have been accomplished, to use a Comanche expression, between two sunsets; but having with him two women, one of whom was not only old, but a European, that is to say, quite unused to desert life, he understood, without anyone making the remark—for Madame Guillois would have died sooner than complain, and she alone could have spoken—that he must completely modify his mode of travelling, and he did so.

The women, mounted on powerful horses (Madame Guillois being comfortably seated on a cushion made of seven or eight panthers' skins) were, for fear of any accident, placed in the middle of the band, which did not take Indian file, owing to its numerical strength.

They trotted on thus during the whole day, and at sunset Spider gave orders to camp. He was one of the first to dismount, and cut with his knife a number of branches, of which he formed, as if by enchantment, a hut to protect the two females from the dew. The fires were lighted, supper prepared, and immediately after the meal, all prepared to sleep except the sentries.

Madame Guillois alone did not sleep, for fever and impatience kept her awake; she therefore spent the whole night crouched in a corner of the hut, reflecting. At sunrise they started again; as they were approaching the mountains the wind grew cold, and a dense fog covered the prairie. All wrapped themselves up carefully in their furs until the sun gained sufficient strength to render this precaution unnecessary.

In some parts of America the climate has this disagreeable peculiarity, that in the morning the frost is strong enough to split stones, at midday the heat is stifling, and in the evening the thermometer falls again below zero.

The day passed without any incident worth recording. Toward evening, at about an hour before the halt, Spider, who was galloping as scout about one hundred yards ahead of the band, discovered footsteps. They were clear, fresh, regular, deep, and seemed to be made by a young, powerful man accustomed to walking.

Spider rejoined his party without imparting his discovery to anyone; but Sunbeam, by whose side he was riding, suddenly tapped him on the shoulder, to attract his attention.

"Look there, warrior," she said, pointing a little to the left "does that look like a man marching?"

The Indian stopped, put his hand over his eyes as a shade, to concentrate his attention, and examined for a long time the point the chief's squaw pointed out. At length he set out again, shaking his head repeatedly.

"Well, what does my brother think?" Sunbeam asked.

"It is a man," he answered; "from here it appears an Indian, and yet I either saw badly, or am mistaken."

"How so?"

"Listen: you are the wife of the first chief of the tribe, and so I can tell you this, there is something strange about the affair. A few minutes back I discovered footprints; by the direction they follow it is plain they were made by that man—the more so, as they are fresh, as if made a little while ago."

"Well?"

"These are not the footprints of a redskin, but of a white."

"That is really strange," the squaw muttered and became serious; "but are you quite sure of what you assert?"

The Indian smiled contemptuously.

"Spider is a warrior," he said; "a child of eight years could have seen it as well as I; the feet are turned out, while the Indians turn them in; the great toe is close to the others, while ours grow out considerably. With such signs, I ask my sister can a man be deceived?"

"That is true," she said; "I cannot understand it."

"And stay," he continued; "now we are nearer the man, just watch his behaviour, it is plain he is trying to hide himself; he fancies we have not yet remarked him, and is acting in accordance. He is stooping down behind that mastic: now he reappears. See, he stops, he is reflecting; he fears lest we have seen him, and his walking may appear suspicious to us. Now he is sitting down to await us."

"We must be on our guard," said Sunbeam.

"I am watching," Spider replied, with an ill-omened smile.

In the meanwhile all Spider had described had taken place, point by point. The stranger, after trying several times to hide himself behind the bushes or disappear in the mountains, calculated that if he fled the persons he saw could soon catch him up, as he was dismounted. Then, making up his mind to risk it, he sat down with his back against a tamarind tree, and quietly smoked while awaiting the arrival of the horsemen, who were quickly coming up.

The nearer the Comanches came to this man, the more like an Indian he looked. When they were only a few paces from him, all doubts were at an end; he was, or seemed to be, one of those countless vagabond sorcerers who go from tribe to tribe in the Far West to cure the sick and practice their enchantment. In fact, the sorcerer was no other than Nathan, as the reader has doubtless guessed.

After so nobly recompensing the service rendered him by the poor juggler, whose science had not placed him on his guard against such abominable treachery, Nathan went off at full speed, resolved on crossing the enemy's lines, thanks to the disguise he wore with rare perfection.

When he perceived the horsemen, he attempted to fly; but unfortunately for him he was tired, and in a part so open and denuded of chaparral, that he soon saw, if he attempted to bolt, he should inevitably ruin himself by arousing the suspicions of these men, who, on the other hand, as they did not know him, would probably pass him with a bow. He also calculated on the superstitious character of the Indians and his own remarkable stock of impudence and boldness to deceive them.

These reflections Nathan made with that speed and certainty which distinguish men of action; he made up his mind in a moment, and sitting down at the foot of a tree, coolly awaited the arrival of the strangers. Moreover, we may remark, that Nathan was gifted with daring and indomitable spirit; the critical position in which chance suddenly placed him, instead of frightening pleased him, and caused him a feeling which was not without its charm with a man of his stamp. He boldly assumed the borrowed character, and when the Indians stopped in front of him, he was the first to speak.

"My sons are welcome to my bivouac," he said, with that marked guttural accent that belongs to the red race alone, and which the white men have such difficulty in imitating; "as the Wacondah has brought them here, I will strive to fulfil his intentions by receiving them as well as I possibly can."

"Thanks," Spider replied, giving him a scrutinising glance; "we accept our brother's offer as freely as it is made. My young men will camp with him."

He gave his orders, which were immediately carried out. As on the previous evening. Spider built a hut for the females, to which they immediately withdrew. The sorcerer had given them a glance which made them shudder all over.

After supper; Spider lit his pipe and sat down near the sorcerer; he wished to converse with him and clear up, not his suspicions, but the doubts he entertained about him. The Indian, however, felt for this man an invincible repulsion for which he could not account. Nathan, although smoking with all the gravity the redskins display in this operation, and wrapping himself up in a dense cloud of smoke, which issued from his mouth and nostrils, closely watched all the Indian's movements, while not appearing to trouble himself about him.

"My father is travelling?" Spider asked.

"Yes," the pretended sorcerer laconically replied.

"Has he done so long?"

"For eight moons."

"Wah!" the Indian said in surprise; "Where does my father come from, then?"

Nathan took, his pipe from his lips, assumed a mysterious air, and answered gravely and reservedly —

"The Wacondah is omnipotent, those to whom the Master of Life speaks, keep his words in their heart."

"That is just," Spider, who did not understand him, answered, with a bow.

"My son is a warrior of the terrible queen of the prairies?" the sorcerer went on.

"I am indeed, a Comanche warrior."

"Is my son on the hunting path?"

"No, I am at this moment on the war trail."

"Wah! Does my son hope to deceive a great medicine man, that he utters such word before him?"

"My words are true, my blood runs pure as water in my veins, a lie never sullied my lips, my heart only breathes the truth," Spider answered, with a certain haughtiness, internally wounded by the sorcerer's suspicions.

"Good, I am willing to believe him," the latter went on; "but when did the Comanches begin to take their squaws with them on the war path?"

"The Comanches are masters of their actions; no one has a right to control them."

Nathan felt that he was on a wrong track, and that if the conversation went on in this way, he should offend a man whom he had such an interest in conciliating. He therefore altered his tactics.

"I do not claim any right," he said quietly, "to control the acts of warriors for am I not a man of peace?"

Spider smiled contemptuously.

"In truth," he said, in a good-humoured tone, "great medicine men such as my father are like women, they live a long time; the Wacondah protects them."

The sorcerer refrained from noticing the bitter sarcasm the speaker displayed in his remark.

"Is my son returning to his village?" he asked him.

"No," the other answered, "I am going to join the great chief of my tribe, who is on an expedition, with his most celebrated warriors."

"To what tribe does my son belong, then?"

"To that of Unicorn."

Nathan trembled inwardly, though his face remained unmoved.

"Wah!" he said, "Unicorn is a great chief; his renown is spread over the whole earth. What warrior could contend with him on the prairie?"

"Does my father know him?"

"I have not the honour, though I have often desired it; never to this day have I been able to meet the celebrated chief."

"If my father desires it, I will introduce him."

"It would be happiness for me; but the mission the Wacondah has confided to me claims my presence far from here. Time presses; and, in spite of my desire, I cannot leave my road."

"Good! Unicorn is hardly three hours march from the spot where we now are; we shall reach his camp at an early hour tomorrow."

"How is it that my son, who seems to me a prudent warrior, should have halted here, when so near his chief?"

All suspicion had been removed from the Indian's mind, so he answered frankly this time, without trying to disguise the truth, and laying all reticence aside.

"My father is right. I would certainly have continued my journey to the chief's camp, and reached it this evening before the shriek of the owl, but the two squaws with me delayed me and compelled me to act as I have done."

"My son is young," Nathan answered, with an insinuating smile.

"My father is mistaken; the squaws are sacred to me; I love and respect them. The one is Unicorn's own wife, who is returning to her husband; the other is a paleface, her hair is white as the snow that passes over our heads driven by the evening breeze, and her body is bowed beneath the weight of winters; she is the mother of a great hunter of the palefaces, the adopted son of our tribe, whose name has doubtless reached our father's ears."

"How is he called?"

"Koutonepi."

At this name, which he might have expected, however, Nathan involuntarily gave such a start that Spider perceived it.

"Can Koutonepi be an enemy of my father?" he asked, with astonishment.

"On the contrary," Nathan hastened to reply; "the men protected by the Wacondah have no enemies, as my son knows. The joy I felt on hearing his name uttered caused the emotion my son noticed."

"My father must have powerful reasons for displaying such surprise."

"I have, indeed, very powerful," the sorcerer replied with feigned delight; "Koutonepi saved my mother's life."

This falsehood was uttered with such magnificent coolness, and such a well-assumed air of truth, that the Indian was convinced and bowed respectfully to the pretended sorcerer.

"In that case," he said, "I am certain that my father will not mind leaving his road a little to see the man to whom he is attached by such strong ties of gratitude; for it is very probable that we shall meet Koutonepi at Unicorn's camp."

Nathan made a grimace; as usually happens to rogues, who try to prove too much, in dissipating suspicions at all hazards, he had caught himself. Now he understood that, unless he wished to become again suspected, he must undergo the consequences of his falsehood and go with Spider to his destination. The American did not hesitate; he trusted to his star to get him out of the scrape. Chance is, before all, the deity of bandits; they count on it, and we are forced to concede that they are rarely deceived.

"I will accompany my son to Unicorn's camp," he said.

The conversation went on for some time, and when the night had quite set in, Spider took leave of the sorcerer, and following his custom since the beginning of the journey, lay down across the door of the hut in which the two females reposed and speedily fell asleep.

Left alone by the fire, Nathan took a searching glance around; the sentinels, motionless as statues of bronze, were watching as they leant on their long lances. Any flight was impossible. The American gave a sigh of regret, wrapped himself in his buffalo robe, and lay down, muttering—

"Bah! Tomorrow it will be day. Since I have succeeded in deceiving this man, why should I not do the same with the others?"

And he fell asleep.

CHAPTER XXXI
WHITE GAZELLE

The night passed quietly.

As soon as the sun appeared on the horizon, all were in motion in the camp, preparing for departure. The horses were saddled, the ranks formed, the two females left the hut, placed themselves in the middle of the detachment, and only the order to start was awaited. Nathan, then acting in conformity with his sorcerer's character, took a calabash, which he filled with water, and dipping a branch of wormwood in it, he sprinkled the four winds, muttering mysterious words to exorcise the spirit of evil; then he threw the contents of the calabash toward the sun, shouting in a loud voice, three different times—

"Sun, receive this offering; regard us with a favourable eye, for we are thy children."

So soon as this ceremony was ended, the Indians joyously set out. The sorcerers incantation had pleased them, the more so as at the moment of starting, four bald-headed eagles, unfurling their wide wings, had slowly risen on their right, mounting in a straight line to heaven, when they soon disappeared at a prodigious height. The omens were, therefore, most favourable, and the sorcerer suddenly acquired immense importance in the eyes of the superstitious Comanches.

Still, two persons felt a prejudice for this man which they could not overcome: they were Sunbeam and the hunter's mother. Each moment they involuntarily looked at the sorcerer, who, warned by a species of intuition of the scrutiny of which he was the object, kept at a respectful distance, walking at the head of the party by the side of Spider, with whom he conversed in a low voice to keep him by him, and prevent him joining the two females, who might have communicated their suspicions to him.

The party ambled through a grand and striking scenery; here and there they saw, scattered irregularly over the plains, spherically shaped rocks, whose height varied from two to four, and even five hundred feet. On the east rose the spires of the Sierra de los Comanches, among which the travellers now were. The denuded peaks raised their white summits to the skies, extending far north, until they appeared in the horizon only a slight vapour, which an inexperienced eye might have taken for clouds, but the Comanches recognised very plainly as a continuation of the Rocky Mountains. On the left of the travellers, and almost at their feet, extended an immense desert, bordered on the distant horizon by another line of almost imperceptible vapour, marking the site of the Rocky Chain.

The Indians ascended insensibly, by almost impracticable paths, where their horses advanced so boldly, however, that they seemed rooted to the ground, so secure was their foothold. As they got deeper into the mountains the cold grew sharper; at length, about nine o'clock, after crossing a deep gorge let in between two tall mountains, whose masses intercepted the sunbeams, they entered a smiling valley about three miles in extent, in the centre of which the tents rose and the campfires smoked.

So soon as the vedettes signalled the approach of Spider's detachment, some sixty warriors mounted and rode to meet them, firing guns, and uttering shouts of welcome, to which the newcomers responded by blowing their war whistles, from which they produced sharp and prolonged sounds.

They then entered the camp, and proceeded toward Unicorn's hut; the chief, already informed of the arrival of the reinforcement he expected, was standing with folded arms before his calli, between the totem and the great calumet. Unicorn inspected the warriors with a rapid glance, and noticed the two females and the strange sorcerer they brought with them; still he did not appear to see them: his face revealed no sign of emotion: and he waited stoically for Spider to give him a report of his mission.

The Comanche warrior dismounted, threw his bridle to one of his comrades, crossed his hands on his chest, bowed deeply each time he took a step, and on arriving a short distance from the sachem, he bowed a last time as he said—

"Spider has accomplished his mission: he put on gazelle's feet to return more speedily."

"Spider is an experienced warrior, in whom I have entire confidence. Does he bring me the number of young men I asked of the nation?" Unicorn replied.

"The elders assembled round the council fire, they lent an ear to Spider's words. The twenty young warriors are here, boiling with courage, and proud to follow on the war trail so terrible a chief as my father."

Unicorn smiled proudly at this compliment; but assuming almost immediately the rigid expression which was the usual character of his face, he said—

"I have heard the song of the centzontle, my ear was struck by the melodious modulations of its voice. Am I mistaken, or has it really formed its nest beneath the thick foliage of the oaks or pines in this valley?"

"My father is mistaken; he has not heard the song of the nightingale, but the voice of the friend of his heart has reached, him and caused him to start," Sunbeam said softly, as she timidly approached him.

The chief looked at his wife with a mixture of love and sternness.

"Soul of my life," he said, "why have you left the village? Is your place among the warriors? Ought the wife of a chief to join him on the war trail without permission?"

The young squaw let her eyes fall, and two liquid pearls trembled at the end of her long eyelashes.

"Unicorn is severe to his wife," she replied sadly; "winter is coming on apace, the tall trees have been stripped of their leaves, the snow is falling on the mountains, Sunbeam is restless in her solitary lodge; for many moons the chief has left his squaw alone, and gone away; she wished to see once more the man she loves."

"Sunbeam is the wife of a chief, her heart is strong; she has often been separated from Unicorn, and ever awaited his return without complaining; why is her conduct different today?"

The young woman took Madame Guillois's hand.

"Koutonepi's mother wishes to see her son again," she simply answered.

Unicorn's face grew brighter, and his voice softened.

"My brother's mother is welcome in Unicorn's camp," he said, as he courteously bowed to the old lady.

"Is not my son with you, chief?" she anxiously asked.

"No, but my mother can be at rest; if she desire it, she shall see him before the second sun."

"Thanks, chief."

"I will send a warrior to tell Koutonepi of his mother's presence among us."

"I will go myself," Spider said.

"Good! That is settled. My mother will enter my lodge to take the rest she needs."

The two females withdrew, and only one person now remained before Unicorn, and that was the feigned sorcerer. The two men examined each other attentively.

"Oh," the chief said, "what fortunate accident brings my father to my camp?"

"The messengers of Wacondah go whither he orders them without discussing his will," Nathan answered drily.

"That is true," the chief went on; "what does my father desire?"

"Hospitality for the night."

"Hospitality is granted even to an enemy in the desert; is my father ignorant of the customs of the prairie, that he asks it of me?" the chief said, giving him a suspicious look.

Nathan bit his lips.

"My father did not quite understand my words," he said.

"No matter," Unicorn interrupted him authoritatively; "the Great Medicine man will pass the night in the camp; a guest is sacred to the Comanches; only traitors, when they are unmasked, are punished as they deserve. My father can retire."

Nathan shuddered inwardly at these words, which apparently indicated that the sachem had his suspicions. Still, he shut up his fears in his heart, and continued to keep a good countenance.

"Thanks," he said with a bow.

Unicorn returned his salute, and walked away.

"Hum!" the American muttered to himself; "I fancy I did wrong to venture among these demons; the eyes of that accursed chief seemed to read me through. I must be on my guard."

While making these reflections, Nathan walked slowly on, with head erect, apparently delighted at the result of his interview with Unicorn. At this moment, a rider entered the valley at full speed, and passed two paces from the sorcerer, exchanging a glance with him. Nathan started.

"If she recognised me, I am a gone 'coon," he said.

It was White Gazelle, whom the Comanches saluted as she passed, and she proceeded to Unicorn's lodge.

"I am in the wolf's throat," Nathan went on; "my presumption will cause my ruin. There is one thing a man cannot disguise, and that is his eye;

the Gazelle knows me too well to be deceived; I must try to get away while there is still time."

Nathan was too resolute a man to despair uselessly; he did not lose a moment in idle lamentations; on the contrary, with that clearness of perception which danger gives to courageous people, he calculated in a few moments the chances of success left him, and prepared for a desperate struggle. He knew too well the horrible punishment that menaced him, not to defend his life to the last extremity.

Without stopping, or altering his pace, he walked on in the previous direction, returning the salutes the warriors gave him. Thus he reached, undisturbed, the end of the camp. He did not dare turn his head to see what was going on behind, him; but his practised ear listened for every suspicious sound; nothing apparently confirmed his apprehensions, and the camp was still plunged in the same repose.

"I was mistaken," he, muttered; "she did not recognise me. My disguise is good, I was too easily frightened. It would, perhaps, be better to remain. Oh no, it is not," he added almost directly; "I feel convinced I am not safe there."

He took a step to enter the forest; but at this moment a heavy hand fell on his shoulder. He stopped and turned; Spider was by his side.

"Where is my father going?" the warrior asked, in a slightly sarcastic voice, well adapted to increase the American's alarm; "I think he must be mistaken."

"Why so?" Nathan asked, striving to regain his coolness.

"In the way my father is going, he is leaving the camp."

"Well, what then?"

"Did not my father ask hospitality of the sachem?"

"Yes, I did."

"Then, why is he going away?"

"Who told you I was going, warrior?"

"Why, I fancy the direction you have taken leads to the forest."

"I am well aware of that, for I was going there to pluck some magic plants, in order to compose a great medicine, which I wish to offer the chief to render him invulnerable."

"Wah!" the Indian said, with sparkling eyes; "when you tell him that, I do not doubt he will let you go wherever you please."

"What, am I a prisoner, then?"

"Not at all; but the order has been given that no one should leave the camp without permission; and as you did not ask for it, I am forced, to my great regret, to stop you."

"Very well; I remain, but I will remember the way in which the Comanches offer hospitality."

"My father does wrong to speak thus; the honour of the nation demands that this matter should be settled without delay. My father will follow me to the chief; I am certain that, after a short explanation, all misunderstanding will cease."

Nathan scented a trap. Spider, while speaking to him, had a soothing way, which only slightly reassured him. The proposal made him was not at all to his taste; but as he was not the stronger, and had no chance of evasion, he consented, much against the grain, to follow Spider and return to Unicorn's lodge.

"Let us go," he said to the Indian.

Nathan silently followed Spider. Unicorn was seated before his lodge, surrounded by his principal chiefs; near him stood White Gazelle, leaning on her rifle barrel. When the pretended sorcerer arrived, the Indians did not give the slightest intimation that they knew who he was. The American took a sharp look round.

"I am done," he muttered to himself, "they are too quiet."

Still, he placed himself before them, crossed his arms on his chest, and waited. Then White Gazelle fixed on him an implacable glance, and said, in a voice which made his blood run cold:—

"Nathan, the chiefs wish you to perform one of those miracles of which the sorcerers of their tribes possess the secret, and of which they are so liberal."

All eyes were curiously turned to the American; all awaited his reply to judge whether he was a brave man or coward. He understood this, for he shrugged his shoulders with, disdain, and answered, with a haughty smile:

"The Comanches are dogs and old women—the men of my nation drive them back with whips. They pretend to be so clever, and yet a white man has deceived them, and had it not been for you, Niña, deuce take me if they would have detected me."

"Then you confess you are not an Indian sorcerer?"

"Of course I do. This Indian skin I have put on smells unpleasantly, and oppresses me; I throw it off to resume my proper character, which I ought never to have left."

White Gazelle turned with a smile to Unicorn.

"The chief sees," she said.

"I do see," he replied, and addressing the American, he asked—"Is my brother a warrior in his nation?"

The other grinned. "I am," he answered, dauntlessly, "the son of Red Cedar, the implacable foe of your accursed race; my name is Nathan. Do with me what you like, dogs, but you will not draw a complaint from my lips, a tear from my eyes, or a sigh from my lips."

At these haughty words a murmur of satisfaction ran round the audience.

"Ah!" Unicorn said, to whom White Gazelle had whispered, "What was Red Cedar's son doing in the camp of the Comanches?"

"I should be greatly embarrassed to tell you, chief," the young man answered, frankly; "I was not looking for you, but only wished to cross your lines and escape. That was all."

An incredulous smile played round White Gazelle's lips.

"Does Nathan take us for children," she said, "that he tries so clumsily to deceive us?"

"Believe me what you please, I do not care; I have answered you the truth."

"You will not persuade us that you fell unwittingly among your enemies while thus disguised."

"You have done so too, Niña; one is not more extraordinary than the other, I presume. However, I repeat accident did it all."

"Hum! that is not very probable; your father and brother are in the vicinity through the same accident, I suppose?"

"As for them, may the devil twist my neck if I know where they are at this moment."

"I expected that answer from you; unluckily warriors have scattered in every direction, and will soon find them."

"I do not believe it; however, what do I care? All the better for them if they escape; all the worse if they fall into your hands."

"I need not tell you, I fancy, the fate that awaits you?"

"I have known it a long time; the worthy redskins will probably amuse themselves with flaying me alive, roasting me at a slow fire, or some other politeness of that sort. Much good may it do them."

"Suppose they spared your life, would you not reveal where your father, brother, and that excellent Fray Ambrosio are?"

"I would not. Look you, I am a bandit, I allow it, but, Niña, I am neither a traitor nor an informer. Regulate your conduct by that, and if you are curious to see a man die well, I invite you to be present at my punishment."

"Well?" Unicorn asked the girl.

"He will not speak," she replied; "although he displays great resolution, perhaps the torture you will make him undergo may overcome his courage, and he consent to speak."

"Hum!" the chief went on, "my sister's advice is—"

"My advice," she quickly interrupted, "is to be as pitiless to him as he has been to others."

"Good!"

The chief pointed to the American.

"Take him away," he said, "and let all the preparations be made for torture."

"Thanks," Nathan replied; "at any rate you will not make me languish, that is a consolation."

"Wait before you rejoice, till you have undergone the first trial," White Gazelle said ironically.

Nathan made no answer, but went away whistling with two warriors. They fastened him securely to the trunk of a tree, and left him alone, after assuring themselves that he could not move, and consequently flight was impossible. The young man watched them go off, and then fell on the ground, carelessly muttering—

"The disguise was good for all that; had it not been for that she-devil, I must have escaped."

CHAPTER XXXII
THE ESCAPE

Red Cedar had seen his son tied up, from the tree where he was concealed. This sight suddenly stopped him; he found himself just over the Comanche camp, in a most perilous situation, as the slightest false movement, by revealing his presence, would be sufficient to destroy him. Sutter and Fray Ambrosio in turn parted the branches and looked down at Nathan, who certainly was far from suspecting that the persons he had left on the previous day were so near him.

In the meanwhile the shadows gradually invaded the clearing, and soon all objects were confounded in the gloom, which was rendered denser by the gleam of the fires lighted from distance to distance, and which shed an uncertain light around. The squatter did not love his son; for he was incapable of feeling affection for more than one person, and it was concentrated on Ellen. Nathan's life or death, regarded in the light of paternal love, was of very slight consequence to him; but in the situation where his unlucky star placed him, he regretted his son, as one regrets a jolly comrade, a bold man and clever marksman—an individual, in short, who can be relied on in a fight.

We need not here describe Red Cedar's resolute character, for the reader is acquainted with it. Under these circumstances, a strange idea crossed his brain; and as, whenever he had formed a resolution, nothing could stop it, and he would beard all dangers in carrying it out, Red Cedar had resolved on delivering his son, not, we repeat through any paternal love, but to have a good rifle more, in the very probable event that he should have to fight.

But it was not an easy matter to liberate Nathan. The young man was far from suspecting that at the moment he was awaiting worse than death, his father was only a few paces from him, preparing everything for his flight. This ignorance might compromise the success of the daring stroke the squatter intended to attempt.

The latter, before undertaking anything, called his two companions to him and imparted his plan to them. Sutter, adventurous and rash as his father, applauded the resolve. He only saw in the bold enterprise a trick to be played on his enemies, the redskins, and rejoiced, not at carrying off his brother from among them, but at the faces they would cut when they came to fetch their prisoner to fasten him to the stake and no longer found him.

Fray Ambrosio regarded the question from a diametrically opposite point of view: their position, he said, was already critical enough, and they ought not to render it more perilous by trying to save a man whom they could not succeed in enabling to escape, and which would hopelessly ruin them, by informing the redskins of their presence.

The discussion between the three adventurers was long and animated, for each obstinately held to his opinion. They could not come to an agreement; seeing which, Red Cedar peremptorily cut short all remarks by declaring that he was resolved to save his son, and would do so, even if all the Indians of the Far West tried to oppose it. Before a resolution so clearly intimated, the others could only be silent and bow their heads, which the monk did. The trapper then prepared to carry out his design.

By this time, the shades of night had enveloped the prairie in a black winding sheet; the moon, which was in her last quarter, would not appear before two in the morning; it was now about eight in the evening, and Red Cedar had six hours' respite before him, by which he intended to profit. Under circumstances so critical as the adventurers were now placed, time is measured with the parsimony of the miser parting with his treasure, for five minutes wasted may ruin everything.

The night became more and more gloomy; heavy black clouds, charged with electricity, dashed against each other and intercepted the light of the stars; the evening breeze had risen at sunset, and whistled mournfully through the branches of the primæval forest. With the exception of the sentries placed round the camp, the Indians were lying round the decaying fires, and, wrapped in their buffalo robes, were soundly asleep. Nathan, securely tied, slept or feigned to sleep. Two warriors, lying not far from him, and ordered to watch him, seeing their prisoner apparently so resigned to his fate, at length yielded to slumber.

Suddenly, a slight hiss, like that of the whip snake, was audible from the top of the tree to which the young man was fastened. He opened his eyes with a start, and looked searchingly round him, though not making the slightest movement, for fear of arousing his guardians. A second hiss, more lengthened than the first, was heard, immediately followed by a third.

Nathan raised his head cautiously, and looked up; but the night was so dark that he could distinguish nothing. At this moment, some object, whose shape it was impossible for him to guess, touched his forehead and struck it several times, as it oscillated. This object gradually descended, and at length fell on the young man's knees.

He stooped down and examined it.

It was a knife!

Nathan with difficulty repressed a shout of joy. He was not entirely abandoned, then! Unknown friends took an interest in his fate, and were trying to give him the means of escape. Hope returned to his heart; and like a boxer, stunned for a moment by the blow he had received, he collected all his strength to recommence the contest.

However intrepid a man may be, although if conquered by an impossibility he has bravely sacrificed his life, still, if at the moment of marching to the place of punishment a gleam of hope seems to dazzle his astonished eyes, he suddenly draws himself up—the image of death is effaced from his mind, and he fights desperately to regain that life which he had so valiantly surrendered. This is what happened to Nathan; he gradually sat up, with his eyes eagerly fixed on his still motionless guards.

My readers must pardon the following trifling detail, but it is too true to be passed over. When the first hiss was heard, the young man was snoring, though wide awake; he now continued the monotonous melody which lulled his keepers to sleep. There was something most striking in the appearance of this man, who, with eyes widely open, frowning brow, features painfully contracted by hope and fear, was cutting through the cords that fastened his elbows to the tree, while snoring as quietly as if he were enjoying the quietest sleep.

After considerable efforts, Nathan managed to cut through the ligatures; the rest was nothing, as his hands were at liberty. In a few seconds he was completely freed from his bonds, and seized the knife, which he thrust into his girdle. The cord that let it down was then drawn up again.

Nathan waited in a state of indescribable agony. He had returned to his old position, and was snoring. All at once one of his guardians turned towards him, moved his limbs, stiffened with cold, rose and bent over him with a yawn. Nathan, with half-closed, eyes, carefully watched his movements. When he saw the redskin's face only two inches from his own, with a gesture swift as thought, he threw his hands round his neck, and that so suddenly that the Comanche, taken unawares, had not the time to utter a cry.

The American was endowed with Herculean strength, which the hope of deliverance doubled at this moment. He squeezed the warrior's neck as in a vice; and the latter struggled in vain to free himself from this deadly pressure. The bandit's iron hands drew tighter and tighter with a slow, deliberate, but irresistible pressure. The Indian, his eyes suffused with blood, his features horribly contracted, beat the air two or three times mechanically, made one convulsive effort, and then remained motionless. He was dead.

Nathan held him for two or three minutes, to be quite certain that all was over, and then laid the warrior by his side, in a position that admirably resembled sleep. He then passed his hand over his forehead to wipe away the icy perspiration, and raised his eyes to the tree, but nothing appeared there. A frightful thought then occupied the young man; suppose his friends, despairing of saving him, had abandoned him? A horrible agony contracted his chest.

Still, he had recognised his father's signal: the hiss of the whip snake had been long employed by them to communicate under perilous circumstances. His father was not the man to leave any work he had begun undone, whatever the consequences might be. And yet the moments slipped away one after the other, and nothing told the wretch that men were at work for his deliverance; all was calm and gloomy.

Nearly half an hour passed thus. Nathan was a prey to feverish impatience and a terror impossible to describe. Up to the present, it was true, no one in camp had perceived the unusual movement he had been obliged to make, but an unlucky chance might reveal his plans for flight at any moment; to effect this, an Indian aroused by the sharp cold need only pass by him while trying to restore the circulation of his blood by a walk.

As his friends forgot him, the young man resolved to get out of the affair by himself. In the first place, he must get rid of his second watcher, and then he would settle what next to do. Hence, still remaining on the ground, he slowly crawled toward the second warrior. He approached him inch by inch, so insensible and deliberate were his movements! At length he arrived scarce two paces from the warrior, whose tranquil sleep told him that he could act without fear. Nathan drew himself up, and bounding like a jaguar, placed his knee on the Indian's chest, while with his left hand he powerfully clutched his throat.

The Comanche, suddenly awakened, made a hurried movement to free himself from this fatal pressure, and opened his eyes wildly, as he looked round in terror. Nathan, without uttering a word, drew his knife and buried it in the Indian's heart, while still holding him by the throat. The warrior fell back as if struck by lightning, and expired without uttering a cry or giving a sigh.

"I don't care," the bandit muttered, as he wiped the knife, "it is a famous weapon. Now, whatever may happen, I feel sure of not dying unavenged."

Nathan, when he found his disguise useless, had asked leave to put on his old clothes, which was granted. By a singular chance, the Indian he stabbed had secured his game bag and rifle, which the young man at once took back. He gave a sigh of satisfaction at finding himself again in possession of objects so valuable to him, and clothed once more in his wood ranger's garb.

Time pressed; he must be off at all risks, try to foil the sentries, and quit the camp. What had he to fear in being killed? If he remained, he knew perfectly well the fate that awaited him; hence the alternative was not doubtful; it was a thousandfold better to stake his life bravely in a final contest, than wait for the hour of punishment.

Nathan looked ferociously around, bent forward, listened, and silently cocked his rifle. The deepest calm continued to prevail around.

"Come," the young man said, "there can be no hesitation; I must be off."

At this moment the hiss of the whip snake was again audible.

Nathan started.

"Oh, oh!" he said, "It seems that I am not abandoned as I fancied."

He lay down on the ground again and crawled back to the tree to which he had been fastened. A lasso hung down to the ground, terminating in one of those double knots which sailors call "chairs," one half of which passes under the thighs, while the other supports the chest.

"By jingo!" Nathan muttered joyfully, "Only the old man can have such ideas. What a famous trick we are going to play those dogs of redskins! They will really believe me a sorcerer; for I defy them to find my trail."

While talking thus to himself, the American had seated himself in the chair. The lasso drawn by a vigorous hand, rapidly ascended, and Nathan soon disappeared among the thick foliage of the larch tree. When he reached the first branches, which were about thirty feet from the ground, the young man removed the lasso, and in a few seconds rejoined his comrades.

"Ouf!" he muttered, as he drew two or three deep breaths, while wiping the perspiration from his face; "I can now say I have had a lucky escape, thanks to you; for, deuce take me, without you, I had been dead."

"Enough of compliments," the squatter sharply answered; "we have no time to waste in that nonsense. I suppose you are anxious to be off?"

"I should think so; in which direction are we going?"

"Over there," Red Cedar answered, holding his arm out in the direction of the camp.

"The devil!" Nathan sharply objected, "Are you mad, or did you pretend to save my life, merely to deliver me to our enemies with your own hands?"

"What do you mean?"

"Something you would see as well as I, if it were day; the forest suddenly terminates a few yards from here on the edge of an immense quebrada."

"Oh, oh," Red Cedar said, with a frown; "what is to be done in that case?"

"Return by the road you came for about half a league, and then go to the left. I have seen enough of the country since I left you to have a confused resemblance of the shape of the mountain, but, as you say, the main point at this moment is to be off from here?"

"The more so, as the moon will soon rise," Sutter observed, "and if the redskins perceived Nathan's escape, they would soon find our trail."

"Well said," Nathan replied, "let us be off."

Red Cedar placed himself once more at the head of the small party, and they turned back. Progress was extremely difficult in this black night; they were obliged to grope, and not put down their foot till they were certain the support was solid. If they did not, they ran a risk of falling and being dashed on the ground, at a depth of seventy or eighty feet.

They had scarcely gone three hundred yards in this way, when a frightful clamour was heard behind them: a great light illumined the forest, and between the leaves the fugitives perceived the black outlines of the Indians running in every direction, gesticulating and yelling ferociously.

"Hilloh," Red Cedar said, "I fancy the Comanches have found out your desertion."

"I think so, too," Nathan replied, with a grin; "poor fellows! They are inconsolable at my loss."

"The more so, because you probably did not quit them without leaving your card."

"Quite true, father," the other said, as he raised his hunting shirt and displayed two bloody scalps suspended to his girdle; "I did not neglect business."

The wretch, before fastening the lasso round him, had, with horrible coolness, scalped his two victims.

"In that case," Fray Ambrosio said, "they must be furious; you know that the Comanches never forgive. How could you commit so unworthy an action?"

"Trouble yourself about your own affairs, señor Padre," Nathan said, brutally, "and let me act as I think proper, unless you wish me to send you to take my place with the butt end of my rifle."

The monk bit his lips.

"Brute beast!" he muttered.

"Come, peace, in the devil's name!" Red Cedar said; "let us think about not being caught."

"Yes," Sutter supported him, "when you are in safety, you can have an explanation with knives, like true caballeros. But, at this moment, we have other things to do than quarrel like old women."

The two men exchanged a glance full of hatred, but remained silent. The little party, guided by Red Cedar, gradually retired, pursued by the yells of the Comanches, who constantly drew nearer.

"Can they have discovered our track?" Red Cedar said, shaking his head sadly.

CHAPTER XXXIII
PLOT AND COUNTERPLOT

We will now return to Valentine and his friends, whom we left preparing to pursue Red Cedar once more.

Valentine had began to take a real interest in this protracted manhunt; it was the first time since he had been in the desert that he had to deal with a foeman so worthy of his steel as was Red Cedar.

Like him, the squatter possessed a thorough knowledge of life in the Far West—all the sounds of the prairie were known to him, all tracks familiar; like him, he had made Indian trickery and cunning his special study; in a word, Valentine had found his equal, if not his master. His powerfully excited self-love urged him to bring this game of chess to a conclusion; hence he was resolved to press matters so vigorously that, in spite of his cleverness, Red Cedar must soon fall into his hands.

After leaving, as we have seen, the upper regions of the Sierra, the hunters advanced in the shape of a fan, in order to find some sign which would enable them to find the long lost trail, for, according to the axiom well known to the wood rangers, any rastreador, who holds one end of a trail, must infallibly reach the other within a given time. Unfortunately, no trace or sign was visible; Red Cedar had disappeared, and it was impossible to find the slightest trace of the way he had gone.

Still, Valentine did not give in; he studied the ground, examined every blade of grass, and cross-questioned the shrubs with a patience nothing could weary. His friends, less accustomed than himself to the frequent disappointments in a hunter's life, in vain gave him despairing glances; he walked on, with his head bent down, neither seeing their signals nor hearing their remarks.

At length, about midday, after going nearly four leagues in this fashion—a most wearying task—the hunters found themselves on a perfectly naked rock. At this spot it would have been madness to look for footprints, as the granite would not take them. Don Miguel and his son fell to the ground, more through despondency than fatigue.

Curumilla began collecting the scattered leaves to light the breakfast fire, while Valentine, leaning on his rifle, with his forehead furrowed by deep wrinkles, looked scrutinisingly round. At the spot where the hunters had established their temporary bivouac, no vegetation grew on the barren rocks; while an immense larch tree over-shadowed it with its well-covered branches.

The hunter incessantly turned his intelligent eye from earth to sky, as if he had a foreboding that at this spot he must find the trail he had so long been seeking. All at once he uttered a sonorous "hum!" At this sound, a signal agreed on between the Indian and him, Curumilla left off collecting the leaves, raised his head, and looked at him. Valentine walked towards him with a hasty step; the two Mexicans eagerly rose and joined him.

"Have you discovered anything?" Don Miguel asked, curiously.

"No," Valentine replied, "but in all probability I soon shall."

"Here?"

"Yes, at this very spot," he said, with a knowing smile; "believe me, you shall soon see."

While saying this, the hunter stooped, picked up a handful of leaves, and began examining them attentively, one by one.

"What can those leaves teach you?" Don Miguel asked with a shrug of his shoulders.

"Everything," Valentine firmly replied, as he continued his examination.

Curumilla was surveying the ground, and questioning the rock.

"Wah!" he said.

All stopped; the chief pointed to a line about half an inch, of the thickness of a hair, recently made on the rock.

"They have passed this way," Valentine went on, "that is as certain to me as that two and two make four; everything proves it to me; the steps we discovered going away from the spot where we now are—are a sure proof."

"How so?" Don Miguel asked in amazement.

"Nothing is more simple; the traces that deceived you could not humbug an old wood ranger like myself; they pressed too heavily on the heel, and were not regular, proves them false."

"Why false?"

"Of course. This is what Red Cedar did to hide the direction he took; he walked for nearly two leagues backwards."

"You think so?"

"I am sure of it. Red Cedar, though aged, is still possessed of all the vigour of youth; his steps are firm and perfectly regular; like all men accustomed to forest life, he walks cautiously, that is to say, first putting down the point of his foot, like every man who is not certain that he may not have to go back. In the footsteps we saw, as I told you, the heel was put down first, and is much deeper buried than the rest of the foot; that is quite impossible, unless a person has walked backwards, especially for some time."

"That is true," Don Miguel answered; "what you say could not be more logical."

Valentine smiled.

"We have not got to the end yet," he said; "let me go on."

"But," Don Pablo remarked, "supposing that Red Cedar did come here, which I now believe as fully as you do, how is it that we do not find his traces on the other side of the rock? However carefully he may have hidden them, we should discover them, if they existed."

"Of course; but they are not here, and it is useless to lose time in looking for them. Red Cedar has come here, as this mark proves; but you will ask me why he did so? For a reason very easy to comprehend; on this granite soil, footsteps are effaced; the squatter wished to throw us out by bringing us to a spot where we must completely lose his direction, if we succeeded in finding his track. He succeeded up to a certain point; but he wished to be too clever, and went beyond his object; before ten minutes, I will show you the trail as clear as if we had been present when he went off."

"I confess, my friend, that all you say greatly astonishes me," Don Miguel replied. "I never could understand this species of sublime instinct which helps you to find your way in the desert, although you have already given me the most astonishing proofs; still, I confess that what is taking place at this moment surpasses everything I have hitherto seen you do."

"Good gracious!" Valentine answered; "you pay me compliments I am far from deserving; all this is an affair of reasoning, and especially of habit. Thus, it is as plain to you as it is to me, that Red Cedar came here?"

"Yes."

"Very good; as he came, he must have gone away again," the hunter said with a laugh; "for the reason that he is no longer here, or we should have him."

"That is certain."

"Good; now look how he can have gone."

"That is exactly what I do not see."

"Because you are blind, or because you will not take the trouble."

"Oh, my friend, I swear—"

"Pardon, I am in error: it is because you cannot explain what you see."

"What?" Don Miguel said, slightly piqued by this remark.

"Certainly," Valentine went on phlegmatically; "and you shall confess I am in the right."

"I shall be delighted to do so."

In spite of his good sense, and the other great qualities with which he was gifted, Valentine had the weakness, common to many men, of liking, under certain circumstances, to, make a parade of his knowledge of desert life. This defect, which is very frequently found on the prairies, in no way injured his character, and was pardonable after all.

"You shall see," he said with that sort of condescension which persons who know a thing thoroughly, assume on explaining it to the ignorant: "Red Cedar has been here and has disappeared: I arrive and look: he cannot have flown away, or buried himself in the ground: hence he must absolutely have gone by some road a man can use; look at these leaves scattered over the rock, they are sign No. 1."

"How so?"

"Hang it! That is clear enough, we are not at the season when trees lose their leaves: hence they did not fall."

"Why so?"

"Because, if they had, they would be yellow and dry, and instead they are green, crumpled, and some are even torn; hence it is positive, I think, that they have been removed from the tree by violence."

"That is true," Don Miguel muttered, his surprise at its height.

"Now, let us seek what unknown force tore them from the tree."

While saying this, Valentine had begun walking on, with his body bent to the ground, in the direction where he had seen the black line. His friends imitated his movements and followed him, also looking carefully on the ground. All at once Valentine stooped, picked up a piece of bark about the size of half his hand, and showed it to Don Miguel.

"All is explained to me now," he said: "look at that piece of bark: it is pressed and broken as if a rope had been round it, I think?"

"It is."

"Well, do you not understand?"

"On my word, no more than I did just now."

Valentine shrugged his shoulders.

"Listen to me then," he said; "Red Cedar came thus far: with his lasso he caught the end of that heavy branch just above our heads; and with the help of his companions, pulled it down to the ground. The black mark we saw proves what an effort they made. Once the bough was bent, the squatter's comrades mounted on it one after the other: Red Cedar, the last, went up with it, and all found themselves some seventy feet above ground. You must allow this is all very ingenious; but, unluckily, the squatter's boots left on this rock a graze about the width of a hair, and leaves fell from the tree; on unfastening his lasso, a piece of bark broke off, and as he was in a hurry, and could not come down again to remove all these ruinous proofs, I have seen them, and now I know as well all that happened here, as if I had been present."

The hunters did not merely display surprise at this clear and lucid explanation, but seemed struck speechless by such an incredible proof of sagacity.

"It is miraculous," Don Miguel at length exclaimed; "then you believe Red Cedar went off by that tree?"

"I would bet anything on it. However, you shall soon be convinced of it, for we shall follow the same road."

"But we cannot go far on that way."

"You are mistaken. In the virgin forests like the one that stretches out before us, the road we are about to follow is often the only one practicable. And now that we have found the bandits' trail, not to lose it again, I hope, let us breakfast quickly, so as to start the sooner in pursuit."

The hunters sat down gaily round the fire, and ate some grizzly bear meat. But their impatience made them take double mouthfuls, so that the meal was over in a twinkling, and they were soon ready to commence their researches. Valentine, in order to prove to his friends the exactness of the information he had given them, employed the same means Red Cedar had done to mount the tree, and when the hunters had assembled there, they allowed the truth of Valentine's statements: Red Cedar's trail was plainly visible.

They went on thus for a long time following the bandit's trail; but the further they went, the less distinct it became, and it was soon lost for the second time.

Valentine stopped and collected his friends.

"Let us hold a council," he said.

"I think," Don Miguel observed, "that Red Cedar fancied he had been long enough up a tree, and so went back to the ground."

Valentine shook his head.

"You have not got it," he said, "what you assert, my friend, is materially impossible."

"Why so?"

"Because the trail, as you see, suddenly ceases over a lake."

"That is true."

"Hum! It is plain that Red Cedar did not swim across it. Let us go on at all hazards, I feel certain that we shall speedily recover the trail; that direction is the only one Red Cedar could have followed. His object is to cross the line of foes who surround him on all sides; if he buried himself in the mountains, we know by experience, and he knows as well as we do, he would infallibly perish; hence he can only escape in this way, and we must pursue him."

"Still remaining on the trees?" Don Miguel asked.

"By Jove! Do not forget, my friends, that the bandits have a girl with them. The poor child is not accustomed like them to these fearful desert journeys; she could not endure them for an hour if her father and brothers were not careful to lead her by comparatively easy roads. Look beneath you, and you will feel convinced that it is impossible for a girl to have passed that way. This is our road," he added peremptorily, "and it is the only one by which we shall discover our enemy."

"Let us go, then," the Mexicans exclaimed.

Curumilla, according to his habit, said nothing; he had not even stopped to listen to the discussion, but walked on.

"Wah!" he suddenly said.

His friends eagerly hurried up. The chief held in his hand a piece of striped calico, no larger than a shilling.

"You see," Valentine said, "we are in a good direction, so we will not leave it."

This discovery stopped all discussion. The day gradually passed away, the red globe of the sun appeared in the distance between the stems of the trees, and after marching two hours longer, the darkness was complete.

"What is to be done?" Don Miguel asked; "We cannot spend the night perched up here, like parakeet. Let us choose a convenient spot to camp; tomorrow, at daybreak, we will ascend again and continue the chase."

"Yes," Valentine said, with a laugh, "and during the night, while we are quietly asleep down there, if any incident occurs that compels Red Cedar to turn back, he will slip through our fingers like a snake, and we know nothing about it. No, no, my friend, you must make up your mind to perch here for the night like a parroquet, as you say, if you do not wish to lose the fruit of all your trouble and fatigue."

"Oh, oh, if it is so," Don Miguel exclaimed, "I consent. I would sooner sleep a week in a tree than let that villain escape."

"Do not be alarmed; he will not keep us at work all that time; the boar is at bay, and will soon be found. However large the desert may be, it possesses no unexplored refuge to men who are accustomed to traverse it in every direction. Red Cedar has done more than a common man to escape us. Now all is over with him, and he understands that it is only a question of time."

"May Heaven grant it, my friend. I would give my life to avenge myself on that monster."

"He will soon be in your power, I assure you."

At this moment Curumilla laid his hand on Valentine's arm.

"Well, chief, what is it?" the latter asked.

"Listen!"

The hunters did so. They soon heard, at a considerable distance, confused cries, which momentarily became more distinct, and soon merged into a fearful clamour.

"What is happening now?" Valentine asked, thoughtfully.

The shouts increased fearfully, strange lights illumined the forest, whose guests, disturbed in their sleep, flew heavily here and there, uttering plaintive cries.

"Attention!" the hunter said, "Let us try and discover what all this means."

But their uncertainty did not last long. Valentine all at once left the branch behind which he was concealed, and uttered a long, shrill cry, which was replied to with fearful yells.

"What is it?" Don Miguel asked.

"Unicorn!" Valentine answered.

CHAPTER XXXIV
COUSIN BRUIN

Nathan's flight was discovered by a singular accident. The Comanches are no more accustomed than other Indians to have grand rounds and night patrols during the night, which are inventions of civilised nations quite unknown on the prairie. In all probability, the Indians would not have perceived their prisoner's disappearance till daybreak.

Nathan fully built on this. He was too well acquainted with Indian habits not to know what he had to depend on in this respect. But he had not taken hatred into calculation, that vigilant sentry which nothing can send to sleep.

About an hour after Nathan's successful ascent, White Gazelle, aroused by the cold, and more probably by the desire of assuring herself that the prisoner could not escape, rose, and crossed the camp alone, striding over the sleeping warriors, and feeling her way as well as she could in the dark; for most of the fires had gone out, and those which still burned spread only an uncertain light. Impelled by that feeling, of hatred which so rarely deceives those who feel its sharpened sting, she at length found her way through this inextricable labyrinth, and reached the tree to which the prisoner had been fastened. The tree was deserted. The cords which had bound Nathan lay cut a few paces off, while Gazelle was stupefied for a moment at this sight, which she was so far from expecting.

"Oh!" she muttered savagely, "it is a family of demons! But how has he escaped? Where can he have fled?"

"Those villains are quietly asleep," she said, seeing the warriors reposing, "while the man they were ordered to watch is laughing at them far away."

She spurned them with her foot.

"Accursed dogs!" she yelled, "wake up! The prisoner has escaped!"

The men did not stir.

"Oh, oh!" she said, "What means this?"

She stooped down and carefully examined them: all was revealed to her at once.

"Dead!" she said; "he has assassinated them. What diabolical power must this race of reprobates possess!"

After a moment of terror, she sprang up furiously and rushed through the camp, shouting in a shrill voice:

"Up, up! Warriors, the prisoner has fled!"

All were on their feet in a moment. Unicorn was one of the first to seize his weapons, and hurried towards her, asking the meaning of those unusual sounds. In a few words White Gazelle informed him, and Unicorn, more furious than herself, aroused his warriors, and sent them in all directions in pursuit of Nathan.

But we know that, temporarily at least, the squatter's son had nothing to fear from this vain search. The miraculous flight of a man from the middle of a camp of warriors, unperceived by the sentries, had something so extraordinary about it, that the Comanches, superstitious as all Indians, were disposed to believe in the intervention of the Genius of Evil. The whole camp was in confusion: every one ran in a different direction, brandishing torches. The circle widened more and more. The warriors, carried away by their ardour, left the clearing and entered the forest.

All at once a shrill cry broke through the air, and everybody stopped as if by enchantment.

"Oh," White Gazelle asked, "what is that?"

"Koutonepi, my brother," Unicorn replied briefly, as he repeated the signal.

"Let us run to meet him," the girl said.

They hurried forward, closely followed by a dozen warriors, and soon stood under the tree where Valentine and his companions were standing. The hunter saw them coming, and hence called to them.

"Where are you?" Unicorn asked.

"Up this larch tree," Valentine shouted; "stop and look."

The Indians looked up.

"Wah!" Unicorn said with astonishment, "What is my brother doing there?"

"I will tell you, but first help me to come down; we are not comfortably situated for conversing, especially for what I have to tell you, chief."

"Good; I await my brother."

Valentine fastened his lasso to a branch and prepared to slide down, but Curumilla laid a hand on his shoulder.

"What do you want, chief?"

"Is my brother going down?"

"You see," Valentine said, pointing to the lasso.

Curumilla shook his head with an air of dissatisfaction.

"Red Cedar!" he said.

"Ah, *Canarios!*" the hunter exclaimed, as he struck his forehead, "I did not think about him. Why, I must be going mad. By Jove, chief! You are a precious man, nothing escapes your notice—wait."

Valentine stooped, and forming his hands into a speaking-trumpet, shouted—

"Chief, come up."

"Good."

The sachem seized the lasso, and by the strength of his wrists raised himself to the branch, where Valentine and Curumilla received him.

"Here I am," he said.

"By what chance are you hunting in the forest at this time of night?" the hunter asked him.

Unicorn told him in a few words what had occurred. At this narration Valentine frowned, and in his turn informed the chief of what he had done.

"It is serious," Unicorn said, with a shake of his head.

"It is," Valentine answered; "it is plain the men we seek are not far from here. Perhaps they are listening to us."

"It is possible," Unicorn muttered; "but what is to be done in the darkness?"

"Good! Let us be as clever as they. How many warriors have you down there?"

"Ten, I believe."

"Good. Have you among them any in whom you can trust?"

"All," the sachem answered, proudly.

"I do not allude to courage, but to experience."

"Wah! I have Spider."

"That's the man. He will take our place here with his warriors; he will cut off the communication aloft, while my comrades and I follow you. I should like to inspect the spot where your prisoner was tied up."

All was arranged as Valentine proposed. Spider established himself on the trees with his warriors, with orders to keep a good look-out; and Valentine, now sure of having raised an impassible barrier before Red Cedar, prepared to go to the camp, accompanied by Unicorn. Curumilla again interposed.

"Why go down?" he said.

Valentine was so well acquainted with his comrade's way of speaking, that he understood him at half a word.

"True," he said to Unicorn; "let us go to the camp, proceeding from branch to branch. Curumilla is right; in that way, if Red Cedar is concealed in the neighbourhood, we shall discover him."

The Comanche Sachem nodded his head in assent, and they set out. They had been walking for about half an hour, when Curumilla, who was in front, stopped and uttered a suppressed cry. The hunters raised their heads, and perceived, a few yards above them, an enormous black mass, carelessly swaying about.

"Well," Valentine said, "what is that?"

"A bear," Curumilla replied.

"Indeed!" said Don Pablo; "it is a splendid black bear."

"Let us give him a bullet," Don Miguel remarked.

"Do not fire, for Heaven's sake!" Don Pablo exclaimed eagerly, "it would give an alarm and warn the fellows we are looking for of the spot where we are."

"Still, I should like to collar it," Valentine observed, "were it only for its fur."

"No," Unicorn peremptorily said, who had hitherto been silent, "bears are the cousins of my family."

"In that case it is different," said the hunter, concealing with difficulty an ironical smile.

The prairie Indians, as we think we have said before, are excessively superstitious. Among other articles of faith, they believe they spring from certain animals, which they treat as relatives, and for which they profess a profound respect, which does not prevent them, however, from killing them occasionally, as, for instance, when they are pressed by hunger, as frequently happens; but we must do the Indians the justice of saying, that they never proceed to such extremities with their relatives without asking their pardon a thousand times, and first explaining to them that hunger alone compelled them to have recourse to this extreme measure to support life.

Unicorn had no need of provisions at this moment, for his camp was choked with them, hence he displayed a praiseworthy politeness and gallantry to his cousin Bruin. He bowed to him, and spoke to him for some minutes in the most affectionate way, while the bear continued to sway about, apparently not attaching great importance to the chief's remarks, and rather annoyed than flattered by the compliments his cousin paid him. The chief, internally piqued by this indifference in such bad taste, gave a parting bow to the bear, and went on. The little party advanced for some time in silence.

"I do not care," Valentine suddenly said; "I do not know why, but I should have liked to have your cousin's hide, chief."

"Wah!" Unicorn answered, "there are buffaloes in camp."

"I know that very well," Valentine said, "so that is not my reason."

"What is it, then?"

"I don't know, but that bear did not seem to me all right, and had a suspicious look about it."

"My brother is jesting."

"No; on my word, chief, that animal did not seem to me true. For a trifle, I would return and have it out."

"Does my brother think, then, that Unicorn is a child, who cannot recognise an animal?" the sachem asked, haughtily.

"Heaven forbid my having such a thought, chief; I know you are an experienced warrior, but the cleverest men may be taken in."

"Oh! Oh! what does my brother suppose, then?"

"Will you have my honest opinion?"

"Yes, my brother will speak; he is a great hunter, his knowledge is immense."

"No, I am only an ignorant fellow, but I have carefully studied the habits of wild beasts."

"Well," Don Miguel asked, "your opinion is that the bear—?"

"Is Red Cedar, or one of his sons," Valentine quickly interrupted.

"What makes you think so?"

"Just this: at this hour wild beasts have gone down to drink; but even supposing that bear had returned already, do you not know that all animals fly from man? This one, dazzled by the light, startled by the cries it heard in the usually quiet forest, ought to have tried to escape if it obeyed its instincts, which would have been easy to do, instead of impudently dancing before us at a height of one hundred feet from the ground; the more so, because the bear is too prudent and selfish an animal to confide its precious carcase so thoughtlessly to such slender branches as those on which it was balancing. Hum! The more I reflect, the more persuaded I am that this animal is a man."

The hunters, and Unicorn himself, who listened with the utmost attention to Valentine's words, were struck with the truth of his remarks; numerous details which had escaped them now returned to their minds, and corroborated the Trail-hunter's suspicions.

"It is possible," Don Miguel said, "and for my part I am not indisposed to believe it."

"Good gracious!" Valentine went on, "You can understand that on so dark a night as this it was easy for the chief, in spite of all his experience, to be deceived—especially at such a distance as we were from the animal, which we only glimpsed; still, we committed a grave fault, and I first of all, in not trying to acquire a certainty."

"Ah!" the Indian said, "my brother is right; wisdom resides in him."

"Now it is too late to go back—the fellow will have decamped," Valentine remarked, thoughtfully; "but," he added a moment after, as he looked round, "where on earth is Curumilla?"

At the same instant a loud noise of breaking branches, followed by a suppressed cry, was heard a little distance off.

"Oh, oh!" Valentine said, "Can the bear be at any tricks?"

The cry of the jay was heard.

"That is Curumilla's signal," said Valentine; "what the deuce can he be up to?"

"Let us go back and see," Don Miguel remarked.

"By Jove! Do you fancy I should desert my old companion so?" Valentine exclaimed, as he replied to his friend by a similar cry to the one he had given.

The hunters hurried back as quickly as the narrow and dangerous path they were following allowed. Curumilla, comfortably seated on a branch whose foliage completely hid him from anyone who might be spying overhead, was laughing to himself. It was so extraordinary to see the Ulmen laugh, and the hour seemed so unsuited for it, that Valentine was alarmed, and at the first moment was not far from believing that his worthy friend had suddenly gone mad.

"Halloh, chief," he said, as he looked round, "tell me why you are laughing so. Were it only to follow your example, I should be glad to know the cause of this extreme gaiety."

Curumilla fixed his intelligent eye on him, and replied, with a smile full of good humour—

"The Ulmen is pleased."

"I can see that," Valentine replied, "but I do not know why, and want to do so."

"Curumilla has killed the bear," the Aucas said, sententiously.

"Nonsense!" Valentine remarked, in surprise.

"My brother can look, there is the chief's cousin."

Unicorn looked savage, but Valentine and his friends peered in the direction indicated by the Araucano. Curumilla's lasso, securely fastened to the branch on which the hunters were standing, hung downwards, with a black and clumsy mass swaying from its extremity. It was the bear's carcass.

Curumilla, during the conversation between Unicorn and his relative, carefully watched the animal's movement; like Valentine, its motions did not seem to him natural enough, and he wished to know the truth. Consequently, he waited the departure of his friends, fastened his lasso to a branch, and while the bear was carelessly descending from its perch, fancying it had got rid of its visitors, Curumilla lassoed it. At this unexpected attack the animal tottered and lost its balance—in short, it fell, and remaining suspended in the air; thanks to the slip knot, which pressed its throat and saved it from broken bones; as a recompense, however, it was strangled.

The hunters began drawing up the lasso, for all burned to know were they deceived. After some efforts the animal's corpse was stretched out on a branch. Valentine bent over it, but rose again almost immediately.

"I was sure of it," he said, contemptuously.

He kicked off the head, which fell, displaying in its stead Nathan's face, whose features were frightfully convulsed.

"Oh!" they exclaimed, "Nathan."

"Yes," Valentine remarked. "Red Cedar's eldest son."

"*One!*" Don Miguel said, in a hollow voice.

Poor Nathan was not lucky in his disguises; in the first he was all but burnt alive, in the second he was hanged.

CHAPTER XXXV
THE HUNT CONTINUED

The hunters stood for a moment silent, with their eyes fixed on their enemy. Unicorn, who doubtless owed Nathan a grudge for the way in which he had deceived him by passing for one of his relatives, broke the sort of charm that enthralled them, by drawing his scalping knife and raising the poor fellow's hair with uncommon dexterity.

"It is the scalp of a dog of the Long-knives," he said, contemptuously as he placed his bleeding trophy in his girdle: "his lying tongue will never again deceive anybody."

Valentine was deep in thought.

"What are we to do now?" Don Miguel asked.

"*Canelo!*" Don Pablo exclaimed, "That is not difficult to guess, father—start at once in pursuit of Red Cedar."

"What does my brother say?" Unicorn asked, as he turned deferentially to Valentine.

The latter raised his head.

"All is over for this night," he replied; "that man was ordered to amuse us while his friends fled. Trying to pursue them at this moment would be signal folly; they have too great a start for us possibly to catch them up, and the night is so black that we should want a sentry on every branch. We will content ourselves for the present by keeping our line of scouts as we placed them. At daybreak the council of the tribe will assemble, and decide on the further measures to be taken."

All followed the hunter's advice, and they returned towards the camp, which they reached an hour later. On entering the clearing, Unicorn tapped Valentine on the shoulder.

"I have to speak with my brother," he said.

"I am listening to my brother," the hunter replied; "his voice is a music that always rejoices my heart."

"My brother will be much more rejoiced," the chief answered, smiling, "when he hears what I have to tell him."

"The sachem can only be the bearer of good news to me; what has he to tell me?"

"Sunbeam reached the camp today."

Valentine started.

"Was she alone?" he asked, eagerly.

"Alone! She would not have dared to come," the chief remarked, with some haughtiness.

"That is true," Valentine said, anxiously; "then my mother—"

"The hunter's mother is here; I have given her my calli."

"Thanks, chief," he exclaimed, warmly; "oh! You are truly a brother to me."

"The great pale hunter is a son of the tribe; he is the brother of all of us."

"Oh, my mother, my good mother! How did she come hither? Oh, I must run to see her."

"Here she is," said Curumilla.

The Araucano, at the first word uttered by Unicorn, guessing the pleasure he should cause his friend, had gone, without saying a word, to seek Madame Guillois, whom anxiety kept awake, though she was far from suspecting that her son was near her.

"My child!" the worthy woman said, as she pressed him to her heart.

After the first emotion had passed over, Valentine took his mother's arm in his, and led her gently back to the calli.

"You are not wise, mother," he said, with an accent of reproach. "Why did you leave the village? The season is advanced, it is cold, and you do not know the deadly climate of the prairies; your health is far from strong, and I wish you to nurse yourself. I ask you to do so, not for yourself but for me. Alas! What would become of me, were I to lose you!"

"My dear child," the old lady replied, tenderly. "Oh! How happy I am to be thus loved. What I experience at present amply repays all the suffering your absence occasioned me. I implore you to let me act as I like; at my age, a woman should not calculate on a morrow. I will not separate far from you again; let me, at any rate, have the happiness of dying in your arms, if I am not permitted to live."

Valentine regarded his mother attentively. These ill-omened words struck him to the heart. He was frightened by the expression of her face, whose pallor and extreme tenuity had something fatal about it. Madame Guillois perceived her son's emotion, and smiled sadly.

"You see," she said, gently, "I shall not be a burden to you long; the Lord will soon recall me to him."

"Oh, speak not so, mother. Dismiss those gloomy thoughts. You have, I hope many a long day to pass by my side."

The old lady shook her head, as aged persons do when they fancy themselves certain of a thing.

"No weak illusions, my son," she said, in a firm voice; "be a man— prepare yourself for a speedy and inevitable separation. But promise me one thing."

"Speak, mother."

"Whatever may happen, swear not to send me away from you again."

"Why, mother, you order me to commit a murder. In your present state you could not lead my mode of life for two days."

"No matter, my son, I will not leave you again: take the oath I demand of you."

"Mother!" he said, hesitating.

"You refuse me, my son!" she exclaimed, in pain.

Valentine felt almost heart-broken; he had not the courage to resist longer.

"Well," he murmured, sorrowfully, "since you insist, mother, be it so; I swear that we shall never be separated again."

A flush of pleasure lit up the poor old lady's face, and for a moment she looked happy.

"Bless you, my son," she said. "You render me very happy by granting what I ask."

"Well," he said, with a stifled sigh, "it is you who wish it, mother: your will be done, and may Heaven not punish me for having obeyed you. Now it is my turn to ask; as henceforth the care of your health concerns me alone."

"What do you want?" she said, with an ineffable smile.

"I wish you to take a few hours' indispensable rest, after your fatigues of the day."

"And you, dear child?"

"I shall sleep too, mother; for if today has been fatiguing, tomorrow will be equally so; so rest in peace, and feel no anxiety on my account."

Madame Guillois tenderly embraced her son, and threw herself on the bed prepared for her by Sunbeam's care. Valentine then left the calli, and rejoined his friends, who were reposing round a fire lit by Curumilla. Carefully wrapping himself in his buffalo robe he laid on the ground, closed his eyes, and sought sleep—that great consoler of the afflicted, who often call it in vain for a long time ere it deigns to come for a few hours, and enable them to forget their sorrows. He was aroused, towards daybreak, by a hand being softly laid on his shoulder, and a voice timidly murmuring his name. The hunter opened his eyes, and sat up quickly.

"Who goes there?" he said.

"I! White Gazelle."

Valentine, now completely awake, threw off his buffalo robe, got up and shook himself several times.

"I am at your orders," he said. "What do you desire?"

"To ask your advice," she replied.

"Speak: I am listening."

"Last night, while Unicorn and yourself were looking for Red Cedar on one side, Black Cat and I were looking on the other."

"Do you know where he is?" he quickly interrupted her.

"No; but I suspect it."

He gave her a scrutinising glance, which she endured without letting her eyes sink.

"You know that I am now entirely devoted to you," she said, candidly.

"Pardon me—I am wrong: go on, I beg you."

"When I said I wished to ask your advice, I was wrong; I should have said I had a prayer to address to you."

"Be assured that if it be possible for me to grant it, I will do so without hesitation."

White Gazelle stopped for a moment; then, making an effort over herself, she seemed to form a resolution, and went on:

"You have no personal hatred to Red Cedar?"

"Pardon me. Red Cedar is a villain, who plunged a family I love into mourning and woe: he caused the death of a maiden who was very dear to me, and of a man to whom I was attached by ties of friendship."

White Gazelle gave a start of impatience, which she at once repressed. "Then?" she said.

"If he fall into my hands, I will remorselessly kill him."

"Still, there is another person who has had, for many years, terrible insults to avenge on him."

"Whom do you allude to?"

"Bloodson."

"That is true; he told me he had a fearful account to settle with this bandit."

"Well," she said quickly, "be kind enough to let my uncle, I mean Bloodson, capture Red Cedar."

"Why do you ask this of me?"

"Because the hour has arrived to do so, Don Valentine."

"Explain yourself."

"Ever since the bandit has been confined in the mountains with no hope of escape; I was ordered by my uncle to ask you to yield this capture to him, when the moment came for it."

"But suppose he let him escape!" said Valentine.

She smiled with an indefinable expression.

"That is impossible," she answered, "you do not know what a twenty years' hatred is."

She uttered these words with an accent that made the hunter, brave as he was, tremble.

Valentine, as he said, would have killed Red Cedar without hesitation, like a dog, if chance brought them face to face in a fair fight; but it was repulsive to his feelings and honour to strike a disarmed foe, however vile and unworthy he might be. While inwardly recognising the necessity of finishing once for all with that human-faced tiger called Red Cedar, he was not sorry that another assumed the responsibility of such an act, and constituted himself executioner. White Gazelle carefully watched him, and anxiously followed in his face the various feelings that agitated him, trying to guess his resolution.

"Well?" she asked at the end of a moment.

"What is to be done?" he said.

"Leave me to act; draw in the blockading force, so that it would be impossible for our foe to pass, even if he assumed the shape of a prairie dog, and wait without stirring."

"For long?"

"No; for two days, three at the most; is that too long?"

"Not if you keep your promise."

"I will keep it, or, to speak more correctly, my uncle shall keep it for me."

"That is the same thing."

"No, it is better."

"That is what I meant."

"It is settled, then!"

"One word more. You know how my friend Don Miguel Zarate suffered through Red Cedar, I think?"

"I do."

"You know the villain killed his daughter?"

"Yes," she said, with a tremor in her voice, "I know it; but trust to me; Don Valentine; I swear to you that Don Miguel shall be more fully avenged than ever he hoped to be."

"Good; if at the end of three days I grant you, justice is not done on that villain, I will undertake it, and I swear in my turn that it will be terrible."

"Thanks, Don Valentine, now I will go."

"Where to?"

"To join Bloodson, and carry him your answer."

White Gazelle leaped lightly on her horse, which was fastened ready saddled to a tree, and set off at a gallop, waving her hand to the hunter for the last time in thanks.

"What a singular creature!" Valentine muttered.

As day had dawned during this conversation, the Trail-hunter proceeded toward Unicorn's calli, to assemble the great chiefs in council. So soon as the hunter entered the lodge, Don Pablo, who had hitherto remained motionless, pretending to sleep, suddenly rose.

"Good Heavens!" he exclaimed as he clasped his hands fervently. "How to save poor Ellen? If she falls into the hands of that fury, she is lost."

Then, after a moment's reflection, he ran toward Unicorn's calli: Valentine came out of it at the moment the young man reached the door.

"Where are you going to at that rate, my friend?" he asked him.

"I want a horse."

"A horse?" Valentine said in surprise; "What to do?"

The Mexican gave him a glance of strange meaning.

"To go to Bloodson's camp," he said resolutely.

A sad smile played round the Trail-hunter's lips. He pressed the young man's hand, saying in a sympathising voice—"Poor lad!"

"Let me go, Valentine, I implore you," he said earnestly.

The hunter unfastened a horse that was nibbling the young tree shoots in front of the lodge. "Go," he said, sadly, "go where your destiny drags you."

The young man thanked him warmly, leaped on the horse, and started off at full speed. Valentine looked after him for some time, and when the rider had disappeared, he gave vent to a profound sigh, as he murmured:

"He, too, loves—unhappy man!"

And he entered his mother's calli, to give her the morning kiss.

CHAPTER XXXVI
THE LAST REFUGE

We must now return to Red Cedar. When the squatter heard the yells of the redskins, and saw their torches flashing through the trees in the distance, he at the first start of terror thought himself lost, and burying his head in his hands, he would have fallen to the ground, had not Fray Ambrosio caught hold of him just in time.

"Demonios!" the monk exclaimed, "take care, gossip, gestures are dangerous here."

But the bandit's despondency lasted no longer than a flash of lightning; he drew himself up again, almost as haughty as he had been previously, saying in a firm voice—"I will escape."

"Bravely spoken, gossip," the monk said; "but we must act."

"Forward!" the squatter howled.

"What do you mean?" the monk cried, with a start of terror; "why, that leads to the redskins' camp."

"Forward, I tell you."

"Very good, and may the devil protect us!" Fray Ambrosio muttered.

The squatter, as he said, marched boldly toward the camp; they soon reached the spot where they let down a lasso for Nathan, and which they had beaten a retreat from in their first movement of terror. On reaching it, the squatter parted the branches, and looked down. All the camp was aroused; Indians could be seen running about in all directions.

"Oh," Red Cedar muttered, "I hoped all these demons would start in pursuit of us; it is impossible to cross there."

"We cannot think of it," said Nathan, "we should be hopelessly lost."

"Let us do something," said the monk.

Ellen, exhausted with fatigue, seated herself on a branch, and her father gazed at her in despair.

"Poor child," he said, in a low voice, "how she suffers!"

"Do not think about me, father," she said; "save yourself, and leave me here."

"Leave you!" he cried, savagely; "never! Not if I died; no, no, I will save you."

"What have I to fear from these men, to whom I never did any harm?" she continued; "they will have pity on my weakness."

Red Cedar burst into an ironical laugh. "Ask the jaguars if they pity the antelopes," he said. "You do not know the savages, poor child. They would torture you to death with ferocious joy."

Ellen sighed, and let her head droop.

"Time is slipping away; let us decide on something," the monk repeated.

"Go to the demon!" the squatter said brutally; "You are my evil genius."

"How ungrateful men are!" the monk said, ironically, as he raised his hypocritical eyes to Heaven; "I, who am his dearest friend."

"Enough," Red Cedar said, furiously; "we cannot remain here, so let us go back."

"What, again?"

"Do you know any other road, demon?"

"Where is Nathan?" the squatter suddenly asked; "has he fallen off?"

"Not such a fool," the young man said, with a laugh; "but I have changed my dress."

He parted the leaves that hid him, and his comrades gave a cry of surprise. Nathan was clothed in a bearskin, and carried the head in his hand.

"Oh, oh!" said Red Cedar, "That is a lucky find; where did you steal that, lad?"

"I only had the trouble to take it off the branch where it was hung to dry."

"Take care of it, for it may be of use ere long."

"That is what I thought."

After taking a few steps, Red Cedar stopped, stretched out his arm to warn his comrades, and listened. After two or three minutes, he turned to his comrades and whispered—"Our retreat is cut off; people are walking on the trees, I heard branches creaking and leaves rustling."

They gazed at each other in terror.

"We will not despair," he went on, quickly, "all is not yet lost; let us go higher, and on one side, till they have passed; during that time, Nathan will amuse them; the Comanches rarely do an injury to a bear."

No one made any objection, so Sutter started first, and the monk followed. Ellen looked at her father sorrowfully. "I care not," she said.

"I say again, I will save you, child," he replied with great tenderness.

He took the maiden in his powerful arms, and laid her softly on his shoulder.

"Hold on," he muttered, "and fear nothing."

Then, with a dexterity and strength doubled by a father's love, the bandit seized the bough over his head with one hand, and disappeared in the foliage, after saying to his son: "Look out, Nathan, play your part cleverly, lad, our safety depends on you."

"Don't be frightened, old one," the young man replied, as he put on the bear's head; "I am not more stupid than an Indian; they will take me for their cousin."

We know what happened, and how this trick, at first so successful, was foiled by Curumilla. On seeing his son fall, the squatter was momentarily affected by a blind rage, and pointed his rifle at the Indian. Fortunately the monk saw the imprudent gesture soon enough to check him. "What are you about?" he hoarsely whispered, as he struck up the barrel; "you will destroy your daughter."

"That is true," the squatter muttered.

Ellen, by an extraordinary hazard, had seen nothing; had she done so, it is probable that her brother's death would have drawn from her a cry of agony, which must have denounced her companions.

"Oh," Red Cedar said, "still that accursed Trail-hunter and his devil of an Indian. They alone can conquer me."

The fugitives remained for an hour in a state of terrible alarm, not daring to stir, through fear of being discovered. They were so close to their pursuers that they distinctly heard what they said, but at length the speakers retired, the torches were put out, and all became silent again.

"Ouf!" said the monk, "they have gone.

"Not all," the squatter answered; "did you not hear that accursed Valentine?"

"That is true; our retreat is still cut off."

"We must not despair yet; for the present we have nothing to fear here; rest a little while, while I go on the search."

"Hum!" Fray Ambrosio muttered; "why not go all together? That would be more prudent, I think."

Red Cedar laughed bitterly. "Listen, gossip," he said to the monk, as he seized his arm, which he pressed like a vice: "you distrust me, and you are wrong. I wished once to leave you, I allow, but I no longer wish it. We will perish or escape together."

"Oh, oh! Are you speaking seriously, gossip?"

"Yes; for, trusting to the foolish promises of a priest, I resolved to reform; I altered my life, and led a painful existence; not injuring anybody, and toiling honestly. The men I wished to forget remembered me in their thirst for revenge. Paying no heed to my wish to repent, they fired my wretched jacal and killed my son. Now they track me like a wild beast, the old instincts are aroused in me, and the evil leaven that slept in my heart is fermenting afresh. They have declared a war to the death. Well, by heaven, I accept it, and will wage it without pity, truce, or mercy, not asking of them, if they captured me, less than I would give them if they fell into my hands. Let them take care, for I am Red Cedar! He whom the Indians call the *Maneater* (Witchasta Joute) and I will devour their hearts. So, at present, be at your ease, monk, we shall not part again: you are my conscience—we are inseparable."

The squatter uttered those atrocious words with such an accent of rage and hatred, that the monk saw he really spoke the truth, and his evil instincts had definitively gained the upper hand. A hideous smile of joy curled his lips. "Well, gossip," he said, "go and look out, we will await you here."

During the squatter's absence not a word was uttered. Sutter was asleep, the monk thinking, and Ellen weeping. The poor girl had heard with sorrow mingled with horror her father's atrocious sentiments. She then measured the fearful depth of the abyss into which she was suddenly hurled, for Red Cedar's determination cut her off eternally from society, and condemned her to a life of grief and tears. After about an hour's absence Red Cedar reappeared, and the expression of his face was joyous.

"Well?" the monk anxiously asked him.

"Good news," he replied; "I have discovered a refuge where I defy the cleverest bloodhounds of the prairies to track me."

"Is it far from here?"

"A very little distance; but that will prove our security. Our enemies will never suppose we had the impudence to hide so close to them."

"That is true; we will go there, then."

"When you please."

"At once."

Red Cedar told the truth. He had really discovered a refuge, which offered a very desirable guarantee of security. Had we not ourselves witnessed a similar thing in the Far West, we should not put faith in the possibility of such a hiding place. After going about one hundred and fifty yards, the squatter stopped before an enormous oak that had died of old age, and whose interior was hollow.

"It is here," he said, cautiously parting the mass of leaves, branches, and creepers that completely concealed the cavity.

"Hum!" the monk said, as he peered down into the hole, which was dark as pitch; "Have we got to go down there?"

"Yes," Red Cedar replied; "but reassure yourself, it is not very deep."

In spite of this assurance the monk still hesitated.

"Take it or leave it," the squatter went on; "do you prefer being captured?"

"But we shall not be able to stir down there?"

"Look around you."

"I am looking."

"Do you perceive that the mountain is perpendicular here?"

"Yes, I do."

"Good; we are on the edge of the precipice which poor Nathan told us of."

"Ah!"

"Yes; you see that this dead tree seems, as it were, welded to the mountain?"

"That is true. I did not notice it at first."

"Well; going down that cavity, for fifteen feet at the most, you will find another which passes the back of the tree, and communicates with a cavern."

"Oh!" the monk exclaimed gleefully, "How did you discover this hiding place?"

The squatter sighed. "It was long ago," he said.

"Stay," Fray Ambrosio objected; "others may know it beside yourself."

"No," he answered, shaking his head; "only one man knows it beside myself, and his discovery cost him his life."

"That is reassuring."

"No hunter or trapper ever comes this way, for it is a precipice; if we were to take a few steps further in that direction, we should find ourselves suspended over an abyss of unknown depth, one of the sides of which this mountain forms. However, to quiet your fears, I will go down first."

Red Cedar threw into the gaping hollow a few pieces of candlewood he had procured; he put his rifle on his back, and, hanging by his hands, let himself down to the bottom of the tree, Sutter and the monk curiously watching him. The squatter struck a light, lit one of the torches, and waved it about his head; the monk then perceived that the old scalp hunter had spoken the truth. Red Cedar entered the cavern, in the floor of which he stuck his torch, so that the hollow was illumined, then came out and rejoined his friends by the aid of his lasso.

"Well," he said to them, "what do you think of that?"

"We shall be famous there," the monk answered.

Without further hesitation he slipped into the tree and disappeared in the grotto. Sutter followed his example, but remained at the bottom of the tree to help his sister down. The maiden appeared no longer conscious of what was going on around her. Kind and docile as ever, she acted with automatic precision, not trying to understand why she did one thing more than another; her father's words had struck her heart, and broken every spring of her will. When her father let her down the tree, she mechanically followed her brother into the cave.

When left alone, the squatter removed with minute care any traces which might have revealed to his enemies' sharp eyes the direction in which he had gone; and when he felt certain that nothing would denounce him, he entered the cave in his turn.

The bandits' first care was to inspect their domain, and they found it was immense. The cavern ran for a considerable distance under the mountain; it was divided into several branches and floors, some of which ran up to the top of the mountain, while others buried themselves in the ground; a subterranean lake, the reservoir of some nameless river, extended for an immense distance under a low arch, all black with bats.

The cavern had several issues in diametrically opposite directions; and they were so well hidden, that it was impossible to notice them outside. Only one thing alarmed the adventurers, and that was the chances of procuring food; but to that Red Cedar replied that nothing was easier than to set traps, or even hunt on the mountain.

Ellen had fallen into a broken sleep on a bed of furs her father had hastily prepared for her. The wretched girl had so suffered and endured such fatigue during the last few days, that she literally could not stand on her feet. When the three men had inspected the cave, they returned and sat down by her side; Red Cedar looked at her sleeping with an expression of infinite tenderness; he was too fond of his daughter not to pity her, and think with grief of the fearful destiny that awaited her by his side; unhappily, any remedy was impossible. Fray Ambrosio, whose mind was always busy, drew the squatter from his reverie.

"Well, gossip," he said, "I suppose we are condemned to spend some time here?"

"Until our pursuers, tired of seeking us in vain, at length determine to go off."

"They may be long; hence, for the greater secrecy, I propose one thing."

"What is it?"

"There are blocks of stone here which time has detached from the roof; before we go to sleep, I propose that we roll three or four of the largest into the hole by which we entered."

"Why so?" the squatter asked abruptly.

"In our present position two precautions are better than one; the Indians are such cunning demons, that they are capable of coming down the tree."

"The padre is right, old one," Sutter, who was half asleep, said; "it is no great task to roll the stones; but in that way we shall be easy in our minds."

"Do what you like," the squatter answered, still continuing to gaze on his daughter.

The two men, with their chief's approval, rose to carry out their plan, and half an hour later the hole was so artistically closed up, that no one would have suspected it had he not known it before.

"Now we can sleep, at any rate," said Fray Ambrosio.

CHAPTER XXXVII
THE CASKET

In spite of the start White Gazelle had, Don Pablo caught up to her before she had gone two leagues from camp. On hearing a horse galloping behind her, the girl turned, and one glance was sufficient for her to recognise the Mexican. At the sight of him a feverish flush suffused her face, a convulsive tremor fell upon her, and, in short, the emotion she felt was so powerful, that she was compelled to stop. Still, ashamed of letting the man she hopelessly loved see the impression the sight of him produced on her, she made a supreme effort, and managed to assume a look of indifference, while thoughts crowded her brain.

"What is he going to do here? Where is he going? We shall see," she added to herself.

She waited, and Don Pablo soon found her. The young man, suffering from extreme nervous excitement, was in the worst possible mood to act diplomatically. On reaching the White Gazelle he bowed, and continued his journey without speaking to her. White Gazelle shook her head.

"I know how to make him speak," she said.

Hitting her horse sharply with her *chicote*, she started at a gallop, and kept by Don Pablo's side. The two riders went on thus for some time without exchanging a syllable. Each of them seemed afraid of opening the conversation, feeling in what direction it must turn. Still galloping side by side, they at length reached a spot where two paths forked. White Gazelle checked her horse, and stretched out her arm in a northerly direction. "I am going there," she said.

"So am I," Don Pablo remarked, without hesitation.

The young woman looked at him with a surprise too natural not to be feigned.

"Where are you going, then?" she went on.

"Where you are," he said again.

"But I am going to Bloodson's camp."

"Well, so am I; what is there so amazing in that?"

"Nothing; how does it concern me?" she said with a significant pout.

"You will, therefore, permit me, Niña, to accompany you to your destination."

"I cannot and will not prevent you from following me; the road is free, caballero," she drily replied.

They were silent as if by common agreement, and were absorbed in thought. White Gazelle gave her companion one of those bright womanly glances that read to the bottom of the heart; a smile played round her cherry lips, and she shook her head maliciously. Singular thoughts doubtless fermented in her head.

At about two of the *tarde*, as they say in Spanish countries, they reached a ford on a small river, on the other side of which the huts of Bloodson's camp could be seen at a distance of about two leagues. White Gazelle halted, and at the moment her companion was about to take to the water, she laid her little hand on his bridle, and checked him, saying, in a soft but firm voice: "Before we go further, a word if you please, caballero."

Don Pablo looked at her in surprise, but made no attempt to remove the obstacle.

"I am listening to you, señorita," he said, with a bow.

"I know why you are going to Bloodson's camp," she continued.

"I doubt it," he said, with a shake of the head.

"Boy! This morning, when I was talking with Don Valentine, you were lying at our feet."

"I was."

"If your eyes were shut, your ears were open."

"What do you mean?"

"That you heard our conversation."

"Suppose I did, what do you conclude from that?"

"You are going to the camp to counteract my plans, and make them fail, if possible."

The young man started and looked disappointed at being so truly judged.

"Señorita," he said, with embarrassment.

"Do not deny it," she said kindly; "it would be useless, for I know all."

"All!"

"Yes, and a great deal more than you know yourself."

The Mexican was amazed.

"Let us play fairly," she continued.

"I ask nothing better," he replied, not knowing what he said.

"You love the squatter's daughter?" she said distinctly.

"Yes."

"You wish to save her?"

"Yes."

"I will help you."

There was a silence; these few words had been interchanged by the speakers with feverish rapidity.

"You are not deceiving me?" Don Pablo asked, timidly.

"No," she answered, frankly, "what good would it do me? You have given her your heart, and a man cannot love really twice; I will help you, I say."

The young man gazed at her with surprise mingled with terror. He remembered what an implacable foe White Gazelle had been to poor Ellen only a few months back, and suspected a snare. She guessed it, and a sorrowful smile played round her lips.

"Love is no longer permitted me," she said; "my heart is not even capacious enough for the hatred that devours it. I live only for vengeance. Believe me, Don Pablo, I will treat you honourably. When you are at length happy, and indebted to me for a small portion of the happiness you enjoy, perhaps you will feel a little friendship and gratitude for me. Alas! It is the only feeling I desire now; I am one of those wretched, condemned creatures, who hurled involuntarily into an abyss, cannot check their downward progress. Pity me, Don Pablo, but dismiss all fear; for, I repeat to you, you have not and never will have a more devoted friend than myself."

The girl pronounced these words with such an accent of sincerity, it was so plain that the heart alone spoke, and that the sacrifice was consummated without any after-thought, that Don Pablo felt affected by such abnegation. By an irresistible impulse, he offered her his hand; she pressed it warmly, wiped away a tear, and then banished every trace of emotion.

"Now," she said, "not a word more: we understand one another, I think?"

"Oh, yes," he answered, gladly.

"Let us cross the stream," she said, with a smile; "in half an hour we shall reach the camp; no one must know what has passed between us."

They soon reached Bloodson's camp, where they were received with shouts of pleasure and welcome; they galloped through it and stopped before the ranger's hut, who had come out, aroused by the shouts, and was awaiting. The reception was cordial, and after the first compliments, White Gazelle explained to her uncle the result of her mission and what had occurred in Unicorn's camp while she was there.

"That Red Cedar is a perfect demon," he answered; "I alone have the means in my hands to capture him."

"In what way?" Don Pablo asked.

"You shall see," he said.

Without further explanation, he raised a silver whistle to his lips, and blew a clear and long note. At this summons, the buffalo-hide curtain of the hut was raised from without, and a man appeared, in whom Don Pablo recognised Andrés Garote. The gambusino bowed with that politeness peculiar to Mexicans, and fixed his small grey and intelligent eyes on Bloodson.

"Master Garote," the latter said, turning to him, "I have called you, because I want to speak seriously with you."

"I am at your Excellency's orders," he answered.

"You doubtless remember," Bloodson went on, "the compact you made when I admitted you into my cuadrilla?"

Andrés bowed his affirmative.

"I remember it," he said.

"Very good. Are you still angry with Red Cedar?"

"Not exactly with Red Cedar, Excellency; personally he never did me much harm."

"That is true; but you still have, I suppose, the desire to avenge yourself on Fray Ambrosio?"

A flash of hatred shot from the gambusino's eye.

"I would give my life to have his."

"Good! I like to find you feel in that way; your desire will soon be satisfied, if you are willing."

"If I am willing, Excellency!" the ranchero exclaimed, hotly. "Canarios, tell me what I must do for that, and, on my soul, I will do it. I assure you I will not hesitate."

Bloodson concealed a smile of satisfaction. "Red Cedar, Fray Ambrosio, and their comrades," he said, "are hidden a few miles from here in the mountains; you will go there."

"I will."

"Wait a minute. You will join them in some way, gain their confidences, and when you have obtained this necessary information, you will return here, so that we may crush this brood of vipers."

The gambusino reflected for a moment: Bloodson fancied he was unwilling.

"What, you hesitate!" he said.

"I hesitate!" the ranchero exclaimed, shaking his head with a peculiar smile. "No, no, Excellency, I was merely reflecting."

"What about?"

"I will tell you: the mission you give me is one of life and death. If I fail, I know what I have to expect: Red Cedar will kill me like a dog."

"Very probably."

"He will be right in doing so, and I shall be unable to reproach him; but, when I am dead, I do not wish that villain to escape."

"Trust to my word."

The gambusino's foxy face assumed an extraordinary expression of cunning. "I do trust to it, Excellency," he said; "but you have very serious business that occupies nearly all your time, and perhaps, without desiring it, you might forget me."

"You need not fear that."

"We can answer for nothing, Excellency; there are very strange circumstances in life."

"What do you want to arrive at? Come, explain yourself frankly."

Andrés Garote lifted his zarapé, and took from under it a little steel box, which he placed on the table near which Bloodson was sitting. "Here, Excellency," he said, in that soft voice which never left him; "take that casket; so soon as I am gone break open the lock, I am certain you will find it contains papers that will interest you."

"What do these words mean?" Bloodson asked anxiously.

"You will see," the gambusino replied, quite unmoved; "in that way, if you forget me, you will not forget yourself, and I shall profit by your vengeance."

"Do you know the contents of these papers, then?"

"Do you suppose, Excellency, that I have had that coffer in my possession for six months, without discovering its contents? No, no, I like to know what I have got. You will find it interesting, Excellency."

"But if that be the case, why did you not give me the papers sooner?"

"Because the hour had not arrived to do so, Excellency; I awaited the opportunity that offers today. The man who wishes to avenge himself must be patient. You know the proverb: 'Vengeance is a fruit that must be eaten ripe.'"

While the gambusino was saying this, Bloodson kept his eyes fixed on the casket. "Are you going?" he asked him, when he ceased speaking.

"Directly, Excellency; but if you permit it, we will make a slight alteration in the instruction you have given me."

"Speak."

"It strikes me that, if I am obliged to return here, we shall lose precious time in coming and going: which time Red Cedar, whose suspicions will be aroused, may profit by to decamp."

"That is true; but what is to be done?"

"Oh, it is very simple. When the moment arrives to spread our nets, I will light a fire on the mountain; which will serve as a signal to you to start at once; still, there would be no harm if someone accompanied me, and remained hidden near the spot where I am going."

"It shall be done as you wish," White Gazelle answered: "two persons will accompany you in lieu of one."

"How so?"

"Don Pablo de Zarate and myself intend to go with you," she continued, giving the young man a glance he understood.

"Then all is for the best," the gambusino said, "and we will start when you like."

"At once, at once," the two young people exclaimed.

"Our horses are not tired, and can easily cover that distance," Don Pablo remarked.

"Make haste, then, for moments are precious," said Bloodson, who burned to be alone.

"I only crave a few moments to saddle my horse."

"Go, we will wait for you here."

The gambusino went out. The three persons remained in silence, all equally perplexed about the casket, on which Bloodson had laid his hand as if afraid of having it torn from him again. Very shortly, a horse was heard galloping outside, and Garote put his head in at the door. "I am ready," he said.

White Gazelle and Don Pablo rose. "Let us go!" they shouted as they ran to the door.

"I wish you luck!" Bloodson said to them.

"Excellency, do not forget the coffer," the gambusino said with a grin; "you will find the contents most interesting to you."

So soon as the ranger was alone, he rose, carefully fastened the door, not to be disturbed in the examination he was about to make, and then sat down again, after selecting from a small deerskin pouch some hooks of different size. He then took the coffer, and carefully examined it all over. There was nothing remarkable about it: it was, as we have said elsewhere, a light casket of carved steel, made with the most exquisite taste—a pretty toy, in a word.

In spite of his desire to know its contents, the ranger hesitated to open it; this pretty little toy caused him an emotion for which he could not account: he fancied he had seen it before, but he racked his brains in vain to try and remember where. "Oh!" he said, speaking to himself in a low hoarse voice; "Can I be approaching the consummation of the object to which I have devoted my life?"

He fell into a profound reverie, and remained for a lengthened period absorbed in a flood of bitter memories, that oppressed his breast. At length he raised his head, shook back his thick hair, and passed his hand over his forehead.

"No more hesitation," he said, hoarsely, "let me know what I have to depend on. Something tells me that my researches will this time be crowned with success."

He then seized one of the hooks with a trembling hand, and put it in the lock; but his emotion was so great that he could not make the instrument act, and he threw it angrily from him. "Am I a child, then?" he said; "I will be calm."

He took the hook up again with a firm hand, and the casket opened. Bloodson looked eagerly into the interior; it only contained two letters, which time had turned yellow. At the sight of them, a livid pallor covered the ranger's face. He evidently recognised the handwriting at the first glance. He uttered a howl of joy, and seized the letters, saying, in a voice that had nothing human about it:— "Here, then, are the proofs I believed to be destroyed!" He unfolded the paper with the most minute precautions, for fear of tearing the creases, and began reading. Ere long, a sigh of relief burst from his overladen bosom.

"Ah!" he uttered, "Heaven has at length delivered you to me, my masters; we will settle our accounts."

He replaced the letters in the casket, closed it again, and carefully hid it in his bosom.

CHAPTER XXXVIII
SMOKE IN THE MOUNTAIN

The three adventurers rapidly left Bloodson's camp, and proceeded in the direction of the mountains, galloping silently side by side. They had a foreboding that the finale of this terrible drama was approaching, and involuntarily their thoughts were sad.

Man is so constituted that the feeling which has most power over him is sadness; human organisation is formed for struggling, and joy is only an anomaly; built to resist the hardest trials, the strongest man is frequently the one who yields most easily to great joy; hence, strange to say nothing more resembles happiness than sorrow; the symptoms are so completely the same, that a great joy annihilates the faculties almost as much as a great sorrow does.

At this moment, the three persons we are following were under the weight of an emotion such as we have described. At the instant when they expected the hopes they had so long entertained would be fulfilled, they felt an emotion which completely mastered them, and for which they could not account. They were about to play for a decisive stake. Ever since they had been contending with this rude adversary, they had ever found him standing in the track, returning them trick for trick, and although cruelly wounded, constantly retaining the victory. This time luck had turned; Heaven itself seemed to have interposed to make justice triumph, and the bandit, driven to his last entrenchments, was expecting them to be forced at any moment.

Still they did not conceal from themselves the difficulties of this final struggle, in which the squatter would escape the fate reserved him by death, unless they managed to deceive him by trickery. In such a state of mind, we may easily suppose that they said nothing, and reached the foot of the mountain without exchanging a syllable. Here they stopped.

"Caballeros," the gambusino said, "before going further, we shall not do badly, I fancy, by making some indispensable arrangements."

"What do you mean, my friend?" Don Pablo asked.

"We are going to enter regions," Andrés replied, "where our horses will become more injurious than useful; in the mountains a footman passes anywhere, a horseman nowhere."

"That is true; let us leave our horses here, then; the noble brutes will not stray beyond the spot where they can find provender. When we require them; we shall be sure to find them again, with a little search."

"Is that the señorita's opinion also?" the gambusino asked respectfully.

"Quite," she answered.

"Then let us dismount, remove saddle and bridle, and leave them to their instinct."

They removed everything that could trouble the horses, and then drove them away. The intelligent animals, accustomed to this, only went a few yards, and began quietly nibbling the thick prairie grass.

"That is all right," the gambusino said; "now let us think of ourselves."

"But the harness," White Gazelle remarked; "the moment will come when we shall be glad to have it ready to hand."

"Perfectly true," said Andrés; "so we will put it in a safe place; for instance, this hollow tree will form a famous storeroom."

"Caramba! that is an original idea," Don Pablo said, "and deserves being followed."

The three saddles were placed in the tree, and so covered with dead leaves, that it would be impossible to suspect their presence.

"Now," said White Gazelle, "let us look after a place to bivouac: the nights are cold at this season, especially in the mountains; day is rapidly departing, and we shall soon be in darkness."

Our three scouts had left the camp at a rather late hour: hence, while they were unsaddling their horses, and hiding the harness, the sun had gradually sunk down beneath the horizon: the short period of twilight had begun, during which day finishes, and night begins, in which darkness and light, struggling desperately together, spread over the landscape a mixed haze, through which objects are regarded as through a prism.

They must profit by this moment to look about them, so that they might run no risk of losing themselves so soon as darkness had gained the victory. They did so, therefore: after carefully noting the position of the different peaks, they boldly set out. They walked for nearly an hour up an ascent constantly becoming steeper, and then reached a species of narrow platform, where they halted for a moment; in the first place to take breath, and then to consult about their further operations.

"Suppose we sleep here?" White Gazelle said. "The perpendicular rock behind us offers a famous shelter, from the wind, and, wrapped up in our zarapés and buffalo robes, I feel convinced we should be quite comfortable."

"Patience, Niña," the gambusino said, sententiously, "we must not talk about sleeping at present."

"Why not?" she said, sharply; "for my part, I may tell you I can sleep famously here."

"Possibly so, Niña," Andrés continued; "but we have something else to do at present."

"What then?"

"Look about us."

"Why, you must be mad, my friend. It is as black as in an oven. The demon himself, though so used to darkness, would tread on his tail."

"That is the very reason; let us take advantage of the moon not having yet risen, to explore the neighbourhood."

"I do not understand you."

"See how transparent the atmosphere is; the vacillating and dubious light of the stars is sufficient to let objects be distinguished at an enormous distance. If the men we are pursuing, eat, which is probable, this is just the hour they would select to cook their food."

"Well?" Don Pablo asked, curiously.

"Follow my argument closely; Red Cedar can only expect enemies from the side of the plain."

"That is true."

"Hence his precautions are taken on that side, and not here; he does not suspect us so near him, and, persuaded that no one is spying him, he will let the smoke of his fire rise peacefully to the sky in the shade of night, convinced that nobody will perceive it, which would be perfectly true, if, unfortunately for him, we were not here. Such is the reason why I urged you to enter the mountains, in spite of the advanced hour."

White Gazelle and Don Pablo were struck by the correctness of this reasoning. They began, in consequence, to form a better opinion of their guide, and tacitly recognise in him that superiority which a man who is thoroughly acquainted with a thing, always acquires at a given moment.

"Do as you think proper," Don Pablo said to him.

"We are quite of your opinion," the girl added.

The gambusino displayed no pride or fatuity at this acknowledgement of the justice of his argument; he contented himself with recommending his companions not to leave the spot where they were till his return, and then went off.

When he was alone, instead of walking as he had hitherto done, the gambusino lay down and began crawling slowly along the rocks, stopping every now and then to raise his head, look around him and listen to the thousand sounds of the desert. At the expiration of about two hours he returned.

"Well?" Don Pablo asked him.

"Come!" the gambusino laconically answered.

They followed, and he led them by a most abrupt path, where they were forced to crawl on their hands and knees, to escape falling over the precipices. After a lengthened ascent, made with extraordinary difficulty, the gambusino stood up, making his companions a sign to follow his example. They did not let the invitation be repeated, for they were completely worn out.

They found themselves on a platform like the one they had previously left; this platform, like the other, was commanded by an immense rock, but this rock had an enormous orifice like the entrance of an oven, and, strange enough, at the end of this orifice glittered a light about the size of a star.

"Look!" said the gambusino.

"Oh, oh! What is that?" Don Pablo asked in surprise.

"Can we have found what we are looking for?" White Gazelle exclaimed, as she clasped her hands.

"Silence," Andrés Garote whispered, as he placed his hand on her mouth; "we are at the entrance of a cavern, and these subterraneous passages are excellent sound conductors; Red Cedar has a fine ear, and though he is so far from you at this moment, you must fear his overhearing you."

They gazed for a long time at this flickering light; at times a shadow passed before this star, and its brilliancy was eclipsed for some minutes. The gambusino, when he judged that their curiosity was satisfied, touched them on the arm, and led them gently away.

"Come," he said to them.

They began ascending again. At the end of about half an hour he made them stop a second time, and stretched out his arm. "Look attentively," he said to them.

"Oh," Don Pablo said, at the end of a minute, "smoke."

In fact a slight jet of white smoke seemed to issue from the ground, and rose in a thin and transparent spiral to the sky.

"There is no smoke without fire," the gambusino said, with a grin; "I showed you the fire first, now there is the smoke. Are you convinced? Have we found the tiger's lair?"

"Yes," they said together.

"That is better than sleeping, eh?" he went on, with a slightly triumphant accent.

"What are we to do now?" White Gazelle quickly interrupted him.

"Oh, good gracious! A very simple thing," Andrés replied; "one of you two will immediately return to the camp to announce our discovery, and the master will act as he thinks proper."

"Good!" said the girl; "I will go."

"And you?" the gambusino asked Don Pablo.

"I stay here."

Garote made no objection, and White Gazelle darted down the mountain side with feverish ardour. The gambusino laid his buffalo robe carefully on the ground, wrapped himself in his zarapé, and lay down.

"What are you about?" Don Pablo asked him.

"You see," he replied, "I am preparing to sleep; we have nothing more to do at present, and must wait till tomorrow to act; I advise you to follow my example."

"That is true," the young man said; "you are right."

And, rolling himself in his zarapé, he threw himself on the ground. An hour passed away thus, and the two men slept, or pretended to sleep.

Then Don Pablo rose softly on his elbow, and bent over Andrés Garote, whom he attentively observed; he was sleeping the calmest possible sleep. The young man, reassured by this, rose, examined his weapons, and after giving the sleeper a last glance, descended the mountain.

The moon had risen and cast a light over the landscape scarce sufficient for him to proceed without fear of falling over a precipice. The young man, on reaching the lower platform, on to which the entrance of the cavern opened, stopped for a moment, muttered a fervent prayer, as he raised his eyes to the star-studded sky, and after once more examining his weapons to feel sure they were in good condition, he crossed himself and boldly entered the cavern.

Of a truth, he must have been gifted with ample stock of courage thus to brave a danger which was the more terrible, because it was unknown. With his eye fixed on the fire, which served as his polar star, Don Pablo advanced cautiously with outstretched arms, stopping at intervals to account for the nameless noises which constantly growl in caverns, and ready to defend himself against the invisible foes he suspected in the shadow.

He went on thus for a long time, the fire not appearing to grow larger, when the granite on which he rested his left hand to guide himself suddenly left off, and at the end of a narrow passage, dimly lighted by an expiring torch of candlewood, he perceived Ellen kneeling on the bare ground, and praying fervently.

The young man stopped, struck with admiration at this unexpected sight. The maiden, with her hair untied and floating in long tresses on her shoulders, with pallid face bathed in tears, seemed to be suffering the greatest sorrow. Sobs and heavy sighs were escaping from her burdened bosom.

Don Pablo could not resist the emotion that seized upon him. At this crushing sight, forgetting all prudence, he rushed toward the maiden with open arms, exclaiming, with an accent of supreme love: "Ellen, Ellen, what is the matter?"

At this voice, which smote her ear so unexpectedly, the girl rose, and said, with gestures of great majesty:

"Fly, unhappy man, fly, or you are lost!"

"Ellen," he repeated, as he fell on his knees, and clasped his hands in entreaty, "for mercy's sake hear me!"

"What do you want here?" she continued.

"I have come to save you, or perish in the attempt."

"Save me," she cried, sadly; "no, Don Pablo, my destiny is fixed forever. Leave me—fly—I implore you."

"No. I tell you a terrible danger impends over your father. He is hopelessly lost. Come, fly; there is yet time. Oh, Ellen, I implore you, in the name of our love—so chaste and pure, follow me!"

The maiden shook her head with a movement that set her long, fair tresses waving.

"I am condemned, I tell you, Don Pablo; remaining longer here will be your destruction. You say you love me—well, in the name of your love, or, if you insist, of mine, I implore you to leave me, to shun me forever. Oh, believe me, Don Pablo, my touch brings death. I am an accursed creature."

The young man folded his arms on his chest, and raised his head proudly.

"No," he said resolutely, "I will not go, I do not wish for the devotion to be yours solely. What do I care for life if I may never see you again? Ellen, we will die together."

"Oh, Heavens, how he loves me!" she exclaimed, in despair. "Oh, Lord! Lord! Have I suffered enough? Is the measure now full? Oh, Lord! Give me the strength to accomplish my sacrifice to the end. Listen, Don Pablo," she said to him, as she caught hold of his arm fiercely, "my father is an outlaw, the whole world rejects him; he has only one joy, one happiness in his immense suffering—his daughter. I cannot, I will not abandon him. Whatever love I may feel for you in my heart, Don Pablo, I will never leave my father. No, all is said between us, my love; remaining here longer would be uselessly braving a terrible and inevitable danger. Go, Don Pablo, go—it must be so."

"Remember," the young man said with a groan, "remember, Ellen, that this interview will be the last."

"I know it."

"You still wish me to go?"

"I insist on it."

"Yes, but I do not wish it," a rough voice suddenly said.

They turned in terror, and perceived Red Cedar looking at them with a grin, as he leant on his rifle. Ellen gave her father such a flashing glance, that the old squatter involuntarily looked down without replying. She turned to Don Pablo, and took his hand. "Come," she said to him. She walked resolutely toward her father, who did not stir. "Make way," she said boldly.

"No," the trapper answered.

"Pay attention to me, father," she continued; "I have sacrificed for you my life, my happiness, all my hopes on this earth, but on one condition that his life shall be sacred. Let him go, then; I insist on it."

"No," he said again, "he must die."

Ellen burst into a wild laugh, whose shrill notes made the two men shudder. With a movement swift as thought, she tore a pistol from the squatter's belt, cocked it, and put the muzzle to her forehead. "Make way!" she repeated.

Red Cedar uttered a yell of terror. "Stop!" he shouted, as he rushed toward her.

"For the last time, make way, or I kill myself!"

"Oh!" he said with an expression of rage impossible to endure, "Go, demon, but I shall find you again."

"Farewell, my beloved!" Ellen cried passionately; "farewell for the last time!"

"Ellen," the young man answered, "we shall meet again; I will save you in spite of yourself."

And rushing down the passage, he disappeared.

"And now, father," the maiden said, throwing the pistol far from her, when the sound of her lover's footsteps died away in the distance, "do with me what you please."

"I pardon you, child," Red Cedar replied gnashing his teeth, "but I will kill him."

CHAPTER XXXIX
THE BOAR AT BAY

Don Pablo ran out of the cavern and joined Andrés Garote hastily, who still slept. The young man had some difficulty in waking him, but at length he opened his eyes, sat up, and yawned; but perceiving the stars still shining, he said ill-humouredly: "What fly has stung you? Let me sleep—day is still far off."

"I know that better than you, for I have not lain down."

"Then, you were wrong," the other said, yawning fit to dislocate his jaw; "I am going to sleep, so good night."

And he tried to lie down again, but the young man prevented him. "A pretty time for sleeping," he said as he dragged away the other's zarapé; in which he tried in vain to wrap himself.

"Why, you must be mad to annoy me so," he said furiously; "has anything fresh happened?"

Don Pablo told him what he had done; the gambusino listened with the most profound attention, and when he had finished scratched his head with embarrassment as he said, "*Demonios!* that is serious—excessively serious; all lovers are madmen. You have spoiled our expedition."

"Do you think so?"

"Canelo! I am sure of it; Red Cedar is an old scoundrel, as cunning as an opossum. Now that he is put on his guard, it will take a clever fellow to catch him."

Don Pablo looked at him in consternation.

"What is to be done?" he said.

"Be off, that is the safest; you can understand that the squatter is now on his guard?"

There was rather a lengthened silence between the two speakers.

"Well!" the gambusino said, suddenly, "I will not be beat. I will play the old demon a trick after my fashion."

"What is your plan?"

"That is my business. If you had placed greater confidence in me, all this would not have happened, and we should have settled matters, to the general satisfaction. Well, what is done cannot be undone, and I will try to repair your fault, so now be off."

"Off—where to?"

"To the foot of the mountain; but do not come up again unless your comrades are with you. You will act as their guide to this spot."

"But you?"

"Don't trouble yourself about me. Good-bye."

"Well," the young man said, "I leave you at liberty to act as you think proper."

"You ought to have formed that resolution sooner. Ah, by the way, just leave me your hat."

"With great pleasure; but you have one."

"Perhaps I want another. Ah! one word more."

"Speak."

"If by any chance you should hear a noise—shots fired, say—as you are going down the mountain, do not alarm yourself, or come up again."

"Good—that is agreed; so good-bye."

After tossing his hat to the gambusino, the young man put his rifle on his shoulder, and began descending the mountain: he speedily disappeared in the countless windings of the path. So soon as Andrés Garote was alone, he picked up Don Pablo's hat and threw it over the precipice, eagerly watching its descent. After turning over and over, the hat touched a peak, rebounded, and at length rested on the mountainside a great distance beneath.

"Good," the gambusino said with satisfaction, "that is all right; now for the rest."

Andrés Garote then sat down on the ground, took his rifle, and discharged it in the air; immediately, drawing one of his pistols from his belt, he stretched out his left arm and pulled the trigger; the ball went right through the fleshy part. "Caramba!" he said, as he fell all his length on the ground, "that pains more than I fancied; but no matter; the great point is to succeed, so now to await the result."

Nearly a quarter of an hour elapsed and nothing disturbed the silence of the desert. Andrés, still stretched at full length, was groaning in a way that would move the heart of the rocks. At length a slight noise was heard a short distance off.

"Halloh!" the gambusino muttered, cunningly watching what had happened, "I fancy there's a bite."

"Who the deuce have we here?" a rough voice said; "Go and see, Sutter."

Andrés Garote opened his eyes and recognised Red Cedar, and his son. "Ah!" he said in a hollow voice, "Is that you, old squatter? Where the deuce do you come from? If I expected anybody, it was certainly not you, though I am delighted with you."

"I know that voice," exclaimed Red Cedar.

"It is Andrés Garote, the gambusino," Sutter replied.

"Yes, it is I, my good Sutter," the Mexican said. "Oh! oh! How I suffer!"

"What's the matter with you, and how did you come here?"

"You're all right, I see," the other replied savagely. "Cuerpo de Cristo! Things have gone with me from bad to worse since I left my rancho to come in this accursed prairie."

"Will you answer yes or no?" Red Cedar said angrily, dashing his rifle butt on the ground, and giving him a suspicious glance.

"Well, I am wounded, that, is easy to see; I have a bullet in my arm, and am all over bruises. Santa Maria, how I suffer! But no matter, the brigand who attacked me will never injure anybody again."

"Have you killed him?" the squatter asked eagerly.

"I did my best; look over the precipice—you will see his body."

Sutter bent over. "I see a hat," he said directly after; "the body cannot be far."

"Unless it has rolled to the bottom of the barranca."

"That is probable," Sutter remarked, "for the rock is almost perpendicular."

"Oh, demonios! Nuestra Señora! How I suffer!" the gambusino groaned.

The squatter had in his turn leant over the precipice; he recognised Don Pablo's hat; he gave a sign of satisfaction, and returned to Andrés.

"Come," he said in a gentle tone, "we cannot stop here all night; can you walk?"

"I do not know, but I will try."

"Try, then, in the demon's name."

The gambusino rose with infinite difficulty and tried to walk a little way, but fell back. "I cannot," he said despondingly.

"Nonsense!" said Sutter; "I will take him on my back, he is not very heavy."

"Look sharp, then."

The young man stooped, took the gambusino in his arms, and laid him across his shoulders as easily as if he had been a child. Ten minutes later Andrés Garote was in the cavern lying before the fire, and Fray Ambrosio was bandaging up his arm.

"Well, gossip," the monk said, "you have been very cleverly wounded."

"Why so?" the Mexican asked in alarm.

"Why, a wound in the left arm will not prevent your firing a shot with us in case of an alarm."

"I will do so, you may be sure," he replied, with a singular accent.

"With all that, you have not told me by what chance you were on the mountain," Red Cedar remarked.

"It was simple; since the destruction and dispersion of our poor cuadrilla, I have been wandering about in every direction like a masterless dog; hunted by the Indians to take my scalp, pursued by the whites to be hanged, as forming part of Red Cedar's band, I did not know where to find shelter. About three days back chance brought me to this sierra; tonight, at the moment I was going to sleep, after eating a mouthful, a fellow whom the darkness prevented me recognising, suddenly threw himself on me; you know the rest—but no matter, I settled his little score."

"Good, good," Red Cedar quickly interrupted him, "keep that to yourself; now, good night, you must need rest; so sleep, if you can."

The gambusino's stratagem was too simple and at the same time too cleverly carried out, not to succeed. No one can suppose that an individual would voluntarily, give himself a serious wound, and any suspicions on Red Cedar's part were entirely dissipated by the sight of Don Pablo's hat. How could he suppose that two men of such different character and position should be working together? Anything was credible but that. Hence the bandits, who recognised in Garote one of themselves, did not at all distrust him.

The worthy ranchero, delighted at having got into the lion's den, almost certain of the success of his scheme, and too accustomed to wounds to care much about the one he had given himself with such praiseworthy dexterity, began again the slumber Don Pablo had so roughly interrupted and slept till daybreak. When he awoke, Fray Ambrosio was by his side, preparing the morning meal.

"Well," the monk asked him, "how do you feel now?"

"Much better than I should have fancied," he answered; "sleep has done me good."

"Let me look at your wound, gossip."

Andrés held out his arm, which the monk bandaged afresh, and the two men went on talking like friends delighted at meeting again after a lengthened separation. All at once Red Cedar hurried up, rifle in hand.

"Look out!" he shouted, "Here is the enemy."

"The enemy!" the gambusino said, "Canelo, where is my rifle? If I cannot stand, I will fire sitting down: it shall not be said that I did not help my friends in their trouble."

Sutter now ran up from the other side, shouting:

"Look out!"

This strange coincidence of two attacks made from opposite sides rendered Red Cedar thoughtful. "We are betrayed," he shouted.

"By whom?" the gambusino impudently asked.

"By you, perhaps," the squatter answered furiously.

Andrés began laughing.

"You are mad, Red Cedar," he said: "danger has made you lose your head. You know very well that I have not stirred from here."

The reasoning was unanswerable.

"And yet, I would swear that one of us has been the traitor," the squatter continued passionately.

"Instead of recriminating as you are doing," Andrés said, with an accent of wounded dignity, perfectly played, "you would do better to fly. You are too old a fox to have only one hole to your earth—all the issues cannot be occupied, hang it all: while you are escaping, I, who cannot walk, will cover the retreat, and you will thus see whether I was the traitor."

"You will do that?"

"I will."

"Then you are a man, and I restore you my friendship."

At this moment the war yell of the Comanches burst forth at one of the entrances, while at the opposite could be heard: "Bloodson! Bloodson!"

"Make haste, make haste!" the gambusino shouted, as he boldly seized the rifle lying at his side.

"Oh, they have not got me yet," Red Cedar replied, as he seized his daughter in his powerful arms, who had run up at the first alarm, and was now pressing timorously to his side. The three bandits then disappeared in the depths of the cave. Andrés leaped up as if worked by a spring, and rushed in pursuit of them, followed by twenty Comanche and Apache warriors who had joined him, at whose head were Unicorn, Black Cat, and Spider.

They soon heard the sound of firing re-echoed by the walls of the cavern: the fight had begun.

Red Cedar had found himself face to face with Valentine and his comrades, while trying to fly by an outlet he did not suppose guarded. He fell back hurriedly, but he had been seen, and the firing immediately begun. A terrible combat was about to take place beneath the gloomy avenues of this vast cavern. These implacable enemies, at last face to face, had no mercy to expect from each other. Still Red Cedar did not despond; while replying vigorously to the shots of their adversaries, he incessantly looked round him to discover a fresh outlet.

The perfect darkness that reigned in the cavern aided the bandits, who, owing to their small numbers, sheltered themselves behind rocks, and thus avoided the bullets, while their shots, fired into the compact mass of enemies pressing round them, scarcely ever missed their mark.

All once the squatter uttered a triumphant yell, and, followed by his comrades, disappeared as if by enchantment. The Indians and rangers then dispersed in pursuit of the bandits, but they had vanished and left no sign.

"We shall never find them in this way," Valentine shouted, "and we run a risk of hitting friends; some of the warriors will be detached to cut us torches, while we guard all the outlets."

"It is unnecessary," Curumilla said, coming up, loaded with candlewood.

In a second, the cavern was brilliantly lit up, and then the side passage by which Red Cedar had escaped became visible to the astonished Comanches, who had passed it twenty times without seeing it. They rushed in with a yell but there came a discharge, and three of them fell mortally wounded. The passage was low, narrow, and ascending; it formed a species of staircase. It was, in truth, a formidable position, for four men could with difficulty advance together.

Ten times the Comanches returned to the charge, ten times they were forced to fall back; the dead and wounded were heaped up in the cave, and the position was becoming critical.

"Halt!" Valentine shouted.

All were motionless, and then the white men and principal chiefs held a council; Curumilla had left the cave with a dozen warriors whom he had made a sign to follow him. As happens unfortunately only too often in precarious circumstances, everybody gave a different opinion, and it was impossible to come to an understanding; at this moment Curumilla appeared, followed by the warriors loaded like himself with leaves and dry wood.

"Wait a moment," Valentine said, pointing to the chief; "Curumilla has had the only sensible idea."

The others did not understand yet.

"Come, my lads," the hunter cried, "a final attack."

The Comanches rushed furiously into the passage, but a fresh discharge compelled them again to retire.

"Enough!" the Trail-hunter commanded, "that is what I wanted to know."

They obeyed, and Valentine then turned to the chief who accompanied him.

"It is plain," he said, "that this passage has no outlet; in the first moment of precipitation Red Cedar did not perceive this, else he would not have entered it; had it an outlet, the bandits, instead of remaining, would have profited by the momentary respite we granted them to escape."

"That is true," the chiefs answered.

"What I tell you at this moment, Curumilla guessed long ago; the proof is that he has discovered the only way to make the demons surrender, smoking them out." Enthusiastic shouts greeted these words.

"Warriors," Valentine went on, "throw into that cave all the wood and leaves you can; when there is a large pile, we will set light to it."

Red Cedar and his comrades probably guessing their enemy's intention, tried to prevent it by keeping up an incessant fire, but the Indians, rendered prudent by experience, placed themselves so as to escape the bullets, which hit nobody. The entrance of the passage was soon almost blocked up with inflammable matter of every description. Valentine seized a lighted torch, but before setting fire to the pile he made a sign to command silence, and addressed the besieged:

"Red Cedar," he shouted, "we are going to smoke you out, will you surrender"?

"Go to the devil, accursed Frenchman," the squatter replied.

And three shots served as peroration to this energetic answer.

"Attention now! For when these demons feel themselves broiling, they will make a desperate effort," Valentine said.

He threw the torch into the pile, the fire at once began crackling, and a dense cloud of smoke and flame formed a curtain before the passage. In the meanwhile, all held in readiness to repulse the sortie of the besieged, for the Indians knew that the collision would be rude. They had not to wait long, ere they saw three devils burst through the flames and rushed headlong upon them.

A frightful medley took place in the narrow corridor, which lasted some minutes. Don Pablo, on perceiving Red Cedar, rushed upon him, and in spite of the bandit's resistance, seized Ellen, and bore her away in his arms. The squatter roared like a tiger, felling all who came within his reach. For their part, Sutter and Fray Ambrosio, fought with the courage and resolution of men who knew that they were about to die.

But this desperate struggle of three against several hundred could not last long; in spite of all their efforts they were at length lassoed, and securely bound.

"Kill me, villains," Red Cedar howled in despair.

Bloodson walked up to him, and touched his shoulder.

"You will be tried by Lynch Law, Red Cedar," he said to him.

At the sight of the ranger the squatter made a terrible effort to burst his bonds, and rush upon him; but he did not succeed, and fell back on the ground, which he bit at wildly, and foaming with rage. When the fight was over, Valentine hurried from the cavern to breathe a little fresh air. Sunbeam was waiting for him. "Koutonepi," she said to him, "Seraphin, the Father of Prayer, has sent me to you—your mother is dying."

"My mother!" the hunter exclaimed in despair. "Oh, God! What shall I do to reach her?"

"Curumilla is warned," she answered; "he is waiting for you at the foot of the mountains, with two horses."

The hunter rushed down the path like a madman.

CHAPTER XL
LYNCH LAW

Before going further, we will explain in a few words what Lynch Law is to which we have several times referred in the course of this narrative, and which plays so great a part, not only in the prairies of North America, but also in certain districts of the United States.

Although we Europeans are rightly surprised that such a monstrosity as Lynch Law can exist in a general society, to be just to the Americans, and although we are bound to disapprove their present system derived from the original, this law was the result of imperious circumstances. When the Pilgrim Fathers landed at Plymouth, Lynch Law was the chastisement imposed by a community deprived of all law, who could only have recourse to their own justice to punish crime.

Now-a-days, in the great centres of the Union, this law, on the contrary, is only the illegal exercise of power by a majority acting in opposition to the laws of the country, as well as the punishments, where the population is sparse, and which, according to the Constitution, must have a certain number of inhabitants to be recognised as districts; up to that recognition, those who have come to seek an existence at these settlements among bandits of every description, against whose attacks they cannot appeal to any legal protection, are obliged to protect themselves, and have recourse to Lynch Law. In the prairies of the Far West, this law is exactly the same as the ancient *lex talionis* of the Hebrews.

We will not go deeper into the subject of this law, which is so obscure in its origin, that its very name is an unsolved riddle, although some persons assert wrongly, as we think, that Lynch was a governor who first applied this law. The only difficulty there is against the truth of this derivation is that Lynch Law existed, as we have said, in America, from the first day that Europeans landed there. Without attempting to guarantee the authenticity of our assertion, it is evident that Lynch Law did not really begin to be applied in the civilised provinces of the Union till the last years of the eighteenth century; at that period it was much more summary, for a lamp was taken down, and the victim hoisted in its place; hence we believe that the word Lynch is only a corruption of derivation of light. We will now return to our narrative.

Four days after the events we describe in our last chapter, Unicorn's camp afforded a strange sight; not only did it contain Indian warriors belonging to all the allied nations of the Comanches, but also many hunters, trappers, and half-breeds had hurried in from all parts of the prairies to try the prisoners, and punish them by Lynch Law as understood in the Far West.

Father Seraphin, who was at this moment in camp, busied in offering help and consolation to Madame Guillois, whose illness had reached its last and fatal stage, tried to oppose the trial of the prisoners with all his power. In vain did he present to the Indians and white men that there were upright judges in the United states, who would apply the laws and punish the criminals; his efforts had obtained no result, and he had been obliged to withdraw, heart-broken.

Not being able to save the prisoners, he wished to prepare them for death; but here again the missionary failed: he had found scoundrels with hearts bronzed by crime, who would not listen, but derided him. Singularly enough, since these men had fallen into the hands of their enemies, they had not exchanged a word, crouched in a corner of the hut that served as a prison, sullen as wild beasts, they avoided each other as much as the bonds that attached them permitted them to do.

Ellen alone appeared among them like the angel of consolation, lavishing soft words on them, and trying before all to soothe her father's last hours. Red Cedar only lived in and through his daughter—each smile of the poor girl which hid her tears, brought a smile on his face branded and ravaged by passion: if he could have reformed, his paternal love would surely have affected this prodigy; but it was too late, all was dead in this heart, which now only contained one feeling, a paternal affection like that of tigers and panthers.

"Is it for today, my child?" he asked.

"I do not know, father," she timidly replied.

"I understand you, poor darling, you are afraid of grieving me by letting me know the truth; but undeceive yourself, when a man like me has fallen so low as I have done, the only blessing he craves is death, and, stay, I have my answer then," he added with a grin; "Judge Lynch is about to begin his duty."

A great noise was audible at this moment in the camp; three stakes had been put up in the morning, and round them the population were tumultuously electing the judges ordered to avenge public justice.

The judges were seven in number: Valentine, Curumilla, Unicorn, Black Cat, Spider, and two other Comanche chiefs. Care had been taken not to elect any who had accusations to bring against the prisoners.

At midday precisely, a silence of lead fell on the assembly, a band of warriors and trappers had gone to the prison to fetch the prisoners and lead them before the judges.

Although Father Seraphin's attempts to arouse better feelings in the heart of the bandits had failed, he determined to accompany and exhort them to the last moment; he walked on the right of Red Cedar, and Ellen on his left.

When the prisoners were brought before the tribunal, Valentine, who had been nominated president against his will, summoned the accusers, who at once appeared. They were five in number: Don Miguel, Don Pablo Zarate, Andrés Garote, White Gazelle, and Bloodson. Valentine took the word in a loud and firm voice.

"Red Cedar," he said, "you are about to be tried by Lynch Law: you will hear the crimes of which you are accused, and have entire liberty to defend yourself."

The squatter shrugged his shoulders.

"Your Lynch Law is foolish," he said disdainfully; "it can only kill, and the victim has not even time to feel the pain: instead of taking that absurd vengeance, fasten me to the stake of torture for a day, and then you will have some fun, for you shall see how a warrior can look death in the face, and endure pain."

"You are mistaken as to our intentions: we are not avenging ourselves, but punishing you; the stake is reserved for brave and honourable warriors, but criminals are only worthy of the gallows."

"As you please," he replied carelessly; "what I said was through a wish to afford you pleasure."

"Who are the persons who have charges against Red Cedar?" Valentine went on.

"I, Don Miguel de Zarate."

"I, Don Pablo de Zarate."

"I, who am called Bloodson, but who will reveal my real name if Red Cedar desires it."

"It is unnecessary," he said in a hollow voice.

"I, White Gazelle."

"Bring your charges forward."

"I accuse this man of having carried off my daughter, whom he basely assassinated," Don Miguel said; "I also accuse him of having caused the death of my friend, General Ibañez."

"What reply have you to this?"

"None."

"What does the people say?"

"We attest," the audience replied in one voice.

"I accuse this man of the same crimes," Don Pablo said.

"I accuse this man of having burnt the house of my father and mother, assassinated my parents, and handed me over to bandits to be brought up in crime," White Gazelle said.

"I," Bloodson added, "accuse him of the same crimes: this girl's father was my brother."

There was a start of horror on the audience. Valentine consulted with the judges in a low voice, then said—

"Red Cedar, you are unanimously found guilty and condemned to be scalped, and then hung."

Sutter was condemned to be hanged only; the judges had regard for his youth, and the evil examples he had constantly before him. The monk's turn had now arrived.

"One moment," Bloodson said, as he stepped forward; "this man is a wretched adventurer, who has no right to wear the gown he has so long dishonoured. I ask that it be stripped off him, before he is tried."

"Why waste time in accusing me, and making this mockery of justice?" Fray Ambrosio ironically replied. "All you who try us are as criminal as we are. You are assassins; for you usurp, without any right, functions that do not belong to you. This time you act justly, by chance: a thousand other times, awed by the populace that surrounds you, you condemn innocent men. If you wish to know my crimes, I will tell you them. That man is right. I am no monk—never was one. I began by debauchery; I finished in crime. As an accomplice of Red Cedar, I fired farms, whose inhabitants I burned or assassinated, in order to plunder them afterwards. I have been, still with Red Cedar, a scalp hunter. I helped to carry off that girl. What more? I killed that gambusino's brother in order to obtain the secret of a placer. Do you want any more? Imagine the most atrocious and hideous crimes, and I have committed them all. Now pronounce and carry out your sentence, for you will not succeed in making me utter another word. I despise you. You are cowards."

After uttering these odious words with revolting cynicism, the wretch looked impudently round the audience.

"You are sentenced," Valentine said, after a consultation, "to be scalped, hung up by the arms, seasoned with honey, and remain hanging till the flies and birds have devoured you."

On hearing this terrible sentence, the bandit could not repress a start of terror, while the people frenziedly applauded this severe sentence.

"Now the sentence will be carried out," Valentine said.

"One moment," Unicorn exclaimed, as he sprang up, and stood before the judges; "as regards Red Cedar, the law has not been followed: does it not say, 'eye for eye, and tooth for tooth?'"

"Yes, yes!" the Indians and trappers shouted. Struck by an ominous presentiment, Red Cedar trembled.

"Yes," Bloodson said, in a hollow voice, "Red Cedar killed Doña Clara, Don Miguel's daughter—his daughter Ellen must die."

The judges themselves recoiled in horror, and Red Cedar uttered a terrible howl. Ellen alone did not tremble.

"I am ready to die," she said, in a gentle and resigned voice. "Poor girl! Heaven knows how gladly I would have given my life to save hers."

"My daughter!" Red Cedar exclaimed, in despair.

"Don Miguel felt the same when you were assassinating his daughter," Bloodson retorted, cruelly. "Eye for eye, tooth for tooth."

"Oh! What you are doing there, my brothers, is horrible," Father Seraphin exclaimed. "You are shedding innocent blood, and it will fall on your heads. God will punish you. For pity's sake, brothers, do not kill that innocent maiden!"

At a signal from Unicorn, four warriors seized the missionary, and, despite his efforts, while treating him most kindly, carried him to the chiefs lodge, where they guarded him. Valentine and Curumilla tried in vain to oppose this barbarous and blood-thirsty deed, but the Indians and trappers, worked on by Bloodson, loudly claimed the execution of the law, and threatened to take justice into their own hands.

In vain did Don Miguel and his son implore Unicorn and Bloodson; they could obtain nothing. At length, Unicorn, wearied by the young man's prayers, seized Ellen by the hair, plunged his knife into her heart, and threw her into his arms, shouting:

"Her father killed your sister, and you pray for her. You are a coward."

Valentine, at this unjustifiable deed, hid his face in his hands, and fled. Red Cedar writhed in the bonds that held him. On seeing Ellen fall, a revolution took place in him. Henceforth he only uttered one word, in a heart-rending voice:

"My daughter! My daughter!"

Bloodson and White Gazelle were implacable, and sternly watched the execution of the sentence passed upon the prisoners. Red Cedar and his son did not suffer long, although the former was scalped; the madness that had seized on him rendered him insensible to everything.

The man who suffered the most fearful punishment was Fray Ambrosio; the wretch writhed for two-and-twenty hours in unimaginable suffering, ere death put an end to his fearful tortures.

So soon as the culprits had been executed, Bloodson and White Gazelle mounted their horses and galloped away.

They have never been heard of since, and no one knows what has become of them.

It was the eighth day after the fearful application of Lynch Law we have just described, a little before sunset.

All traces of the execution had disappeared. Unicorn's camp was still established at the same spot, for he insisted on his men remaining there, on account of Madame Guillois's illness rendering the most absolute rest necessary for her. The poor old lady felt herself dying by degrees; day by day she grew weaker, and, gifted with that lucidity which Heaven at times grants to the dying, she saw death approach with a smile, while striving to console her son for her loss.

But Valentine, who after so many years only saw his mother again to separate from her for ever, was inconsolable. Deprived of Don Miguel and Don Pablo, who had returned to the Paso del Norte, bearing with them the body of the hapless Trapper's Daughter, the Trail-hunter wept on the bosom of Curumilla, who, to console him, could only weep with him, and say—

"The Great Spirit recalls my brother's mother; it is because tha
her."

A very long sentence for the worthy chief, and which pro
intensity of his grief.

On the day when we resume our narrative, Madame Guillo
reclining in a hammock in front of her hut, with her face turned to the s
sun. Valentine was standing on her right, Father Seraphin on her lef
Curumilla by his friend's side.

The patient's face had a radiant expression, her eyes sparkled vivi
and a light pink flush gilded her cheeks; she seemed supremely hap
The warriors, sharing in the grief of their adopted brother, were crouchi
silently near the hut.

It was a magnificent evening; the breeze that was beginning to rise gentl
agitated the leaves; the sun was setting in a flood of vapour, iridescent with
a thousand changing tints.

The sick woman uttered at times broken words, which her son
religiously repeated.

At the moment when the sun disappeared behind the snowy peaks of
the mountains, the dying woman rose, as if impelled by an irresistible force,
she took a calm and limpid glance around, laid her hands on the hunter's
head, and uttered one word, with an accent full of strange melody —

"Farewell!"

Then she fell back — she was dead.

Instinctively all present knelt. Valentine bent over his mother's body,
whose face retained that halo of heavenly beauty which is the last adornment
of death; he closed her eyes, kissed her several times, and pressing her right
hand which hung out of the hammock in his, he prayed fervently.

The whole night was spent in this way, and no one left the spot. At
daybreak Father Seraphin, aided by Curumilla, who acted as sacristan, read
the service for the dead. The body was then buried, all the Indian warriors
being present at the ceremony.

When all had retired, Valentine knelt down by the grave, and though
the missionary and the chief urged on him to leave it he insisted on spending
this night also in watching over his dead mother. At daybreak his two
friends returned; they found him still kneeling and praying; he was pale,
and his features were worn; his hair, so black on the eve, had white hairs
now mingling with it.

Father Seraphin tried to restore his courage, but the hunter shook his head sadly at all the priest's pious exhortations.

"What good is it?" he said.

"Oh!" the missionary at length said to him, "Valentine, you, who are so strong, are now weak as a child; grief lays you low without your striking a blow in self-defence. You forget, though, that you do not belong to yourself."

"Alas!" he exclaimed, "What is left me now?"

"God!" the priest said sternly, as he pointed to the sky.

"And the desert!" Curumilla exclaimed, extending his arm toward the rising sun.

A flame flashed from the hunter's black eye; he shook his head several times, bent a glance full of tenderness on the tomb, and said, in a broken voice —

"Mother, we shall meet again."

Then he turned to the Indian chief.

"Let us go," he said, resolutely.

Valentine was about to commence a new existence. His further adventures will be described in a new series of stories, each complete in itself, commencing with the "The Tiger Slayer," and the characters running through the "Gold Seekers," the "Indian Chief," and the "Red Track."